ALTE]]

LI(V)ES

Arnie Arnstein

First published in 2018

© 2018 Arnie Arnstein

About the author

Dr Arnie Arnstein had a varied medical career, working as an anaesthetist at home and abroad. Civilian contact with the UK defence services inspired this story.

Look out for his next book…

Author's note: This is a work of fiction. Any resemblance of any characters to anyone living or dead is purely coincidental. Please accept my apologies.

Cover illustration by Tom Arnstein

For J,T,O,T

And for those who know who look after those who don't.

Prologue

'A lie that is half-truth is the darkest of all lies.'

Alfred Tennyson

'Accident or...?' The police inspector glanced up from his notebook and interrupted the tall middle-aged man standing in front of him. 'I'm sorry sir; I didn't catch your name. Your ID please.'

Mater withdrew a card from his wallet and held it up.

The officer raised his eyebrows, noting the service shown. 'Did she work for you?' enquired the policeman.

Mater ignored the inappropriate question. 'If you don't mind, inspector, there is little time. I need to see the body.'

'Of course, sir, but I warn you the vehicle that hit her must have been travelling very fast.' He pointed to a small table beside a large blue and white tent emblazoned with 'Police'. 'Your PPE. Please wear the full kit. Forensics have yet to complete their work.'

Mater donned a barrier suit, facemask and a pair of nitrile gloves. For an early spring day in Essex, it was surprisingly warm and immediately sweat started to pool inside the impervious material. He stepped over the boundary tape and into the tent that protected the incident scene, preparing himself for the sight within. He was used to grim viewing but despite this, the task he faced was never easy and had grown more challenging as he aged.

Her head had been squashed against the kerb like a mashed rotten pumpkin. Bloody brains, flesh and matted hair; face distorted as the image created by a comic mirror. The mouth, lipstick smeared, lay open with a bloody hole where there were once perfect teeth. One leg, bent in the wrong direction with a fractured bone protruding through ripped jeans, revealed an obvious tyre mark rising up the thigh, at the top of which was a tattoo; unusual in design and location, disrupted by a red wound, almost a scar, but it told Mater what he needed to know. Although surprised that her mangled body failed to shock him, he felt an overwhelming sense of despair and depression. Unlike many, he never thought her attractive but now her basic humanity was gone and, more importantly to him, as an asset she was no longer effective. Intellect and experience spread on the cold tarmac of a minor road in the English Home Counties. His work taught him to be hard; there could be no other way. He turned and stepped from the tent with the picture of her exposed brain burning into his memory. Normally, he would have visited her grieving relatives straightaway to explain, but the current crisis prevented him from doing this or even attending her funeral. At some point, however, he would need to meet her family. Then, he wanted to be sure that what was said, what he added to their understanding, would be, for once, accurate and truthful. Everything else about him or his organisation could be a lie, one big white lie but in death others had to be told the truth; recognising their loss had not been in vain.

As Mater removed his protective clothing, the policeman approached.

'Seen all you need to see, sir?' he enquired, wondering if the man undressing in front of him might divulge the body's identity or why he was interested in her.

He tried to be courteous. 'Thank you, Inspector, plenty. Please ask the investigating officer to send me a copy of their report as soon as possible.' He handed a card to the policeman with a name and London address. 'And you're right; the vehicle must have been travelling fast.'

Mater strode back to his car, resisting the urge to make the necessary call with his mobile. Instead, he would stop at the first public phone he saw. Even if he had an urgent message, it would be safer to follow the protocol.

Call answered, he spoke clearly and briefly, suppressing all emotion.

'Your conclusion or at least supposition M please,' requested the voice.

Mater knew better than to conclude but had little doubt. 'I think targeted likely, an unfortunate accident most improbable, sir. We'll see what the CID come up with, but it was a sunny, dry day, a straight road and the speed limit low. She didn't have a chance. You should receive the formal Police report within days. I'll travel back north straightaway.'

Call over. Another life ended. Time to act. He couldn't afford to delay much longer. The score didn't look good.

Chapter 1

13 weeks earlier.

Even off duty, Mater rose at dawn. His early career required him to be alert just when the enemy was at its lowest ebb and demanded he was strong and supremely fit. The structure and bonds of military service were long gone, but he was marked by the lifestyle and habits of those years. And so each morning he pulled on his tracksuit and trainers, opting for the luxury of a beanie and gloves on days, such as this, when horizontal sleet waited to greet him. The run was predictable, with Burham Hill rising behind the cottage, the trail leading to its invariably muddy summit. His time lengthened year on year but dogged determination flowed through his veins, helping him survive, so he always ran. From the top though, on a clear day, his reward was the sunrise, energising him for Control's next challenge or inhibiting the black dog when work was lean and he might dwell on missed opportunities. Despite being a freelancer he didn't consider himself a free agent. When job offers came, he grabbed them – the cash and sense of purpose welcome but he craved the adventure more.

As he turned from the lane to the hill track, the wind was stronger than expected. This morning the climb to the summit looked formidable and the hot shower waiting for him more inviting than usual. For the first time in years, the comfort of the cottage tempted him to return; warm clothes and breakfast. He slowed as his mobile vibrated in his trouser pocket. Dawn message. Unusual these days. He was adept at running and pulling out his phone just as if it was a weapon. A brief text to contact the Office urgently. Sleet penetrated his clothes. Perhaps he should turn back. No, he would complete his route, wash and then, after porridge, find out what had caused all the fuss.

Stove lit and coffee steaming, Mater felt warm, safe and secure and wondered if most people yearned for their childhood with few worries, always cared for. His early life had not been easy but despite a challenging childhood, he considered he had been fortunate, as his younger years resulted in a stirring within, pushing him to his limits; to explore, discover danger. He doubted he could have suppressed those feelings even if he had wanted to. Instead he had embraced a life of uncertainty, measuring and balancing but then ultimately ignoring any attendant hazards. This mindset had provided him with his unusual line of work but could, at any juncture, result in his demise. He glanced up from the fire to the window. The sleet had turned to snow. Time to return the call.

Laptop on, he made a few practised keystrokes and waited for the Office to open the video link, expecting to speak directly to his superior. Instead, a coded message appeared at the bottom of an otherwise blank screen. Although he hadn't seen it before, he understood immediately: computer hack – revert to basic tradecraft. For Mater, this meant a fast drive to London and a rendezvous. It was 8.15, and he needed to be sitting on a bench in Green Park by 11.30. He wolfed down a stale croissant, drained a second cup of coffee before collecting his keys. He put on a warm brown coat, stuffed a pocket with fleece hat and gloves, grabbed the holdall that always rested by the front door and headed out. Despite the weather, the car started with the first turn of the ignition key. Unobtrusive and tatty but mechanically pristine. He should make London in good time, not least because the service vehicle had much more under the bonnet than the average family saloon it pertained to be. Always a careful driver but with his training he could, if necessary, speed even on a snowy wintry day. If speed limits were broken, cameras using number plate recognition technology would automatically identify his motor as an unmarked security asset to be ignored.

As he headed towards the M2, he switched on the radio hoping to catch the news. Sometimes events overtook the capacity of the Office to contain them. He was bemused by the power of social and traditional media to often gather intelligence faster and with greater accuracy than the professionals. But the media blagged, not realising the damage that might result. When this happened, the Office employed a whole department to spin an alternative view; creating alternative facts. The bulletin came and went: unremarkable, bland. He sensed a tiny transient nip of anxiety. No terrorist event, no new war, no murder of a senior politician, civil servant or member of royalty. What was going on? Perhaps, just perhaps, he hoped, it was all a drill. As he joined the motorway, he pressed the accelerator and watched the speedo climb. Ice and snow. He chose not to breach the ton: extra attention or worse, an accident, best avoided.

Central London was busy with late commuters and enthusiastic sales shoppers but Mater knew the roads better than most cabbies.

Weaving along minor routes, he arrived at Carrington Street and entered the secure underground car-park with thirty minutes to spare. Enough time to pick up coffee and a newspaper on his way to the park. He congratulated himself on his driving ability. With the vehicle's security system activated, he grabbed his coat and climbed out, glancing around to check whether his arrival had been observed. Clear. He ascended the service stairway and stepped out into a grey London. It wasn't snowing in the city but the wind was brisk so he pulled up his collar and headed towards the coffee shop. Inside the waitress smiled even though it was Monday morning. Mater returned the gesture, paid for his drink, adding a generous tip. Her smile cheered him. Back on the street he felt the chill, grateful for the cup warming his hands through his gloves. Fifteen minutes to rendezvous. Better get a move on.

The park-bench, located less than one hundred metres from Green Park tube station, faced south towards Constitution Hill. If the sun deigned to show, the bench's occupants would reap the benefit. There was a small brass plaque attached. Mater wondered who the couple, remembered in the engraving, were. On an earlier visit he determined to find out, but events always overtook the mundane. The proximity of the underground offered a route to obscurity if any difficulties arose and the morning pedestrian traffic provided natural human cover. At Mater's age the nearby public convenience was a bonus, especially after the infusion of caffeine. He looked at his watch. Time to get ready. He folded the paper and tucked it under his left arm, held the coffee cup in his right hand and balanced it on his knee then pretended to doze.

Someone joined him on the bench and a voice called softly. 'Careful, you will spill your drink.'

Mater appeared to waken. 'Thanks. What's the time, please?'

The old man, wrapped up against the cold, wore a grey overcoat and black gloves; his dull appearance brightened up by a vivid yellow scarf. '1.32.'

Precisely two hours and two minutes later than the true time. Mater smiled to himself wondering why, having met Control so many times, that this little traditional piece of tradecraft remained necessary. *Tradition dies hard*, he thought, *even in the more obscure branches of the civil service.* He turned to his boss, whose kindly handsome face usually bore a gentle smile, emanating a warmth that encouraged those he conversed with to engage but today was different. He looked drawn, forehead furrowed and the shadow from days not shaving darkened his neck and cheeks.

Control came straight to the point. 'M, we have a problem. Unexpected. Docherty is dead.'

Mater swallowed hard. Years of dealing with service challenges didn't prevent the three words from boring into the pit of his stomach. Nausea swept over him. Mick Docherty, Mater's right-hand man on many missions. A burly Northern Irishman with a sense of humour that lightened any task. So strong, that Mater was not alone in believing in Mick's invincibility. Surviving undercover work during the troubles, operations in Middle Eastern countries ruled by unsavoury dictators where any slip was likely to mean death. And now Control was saying Mick had died. But one word made Mater even more concerned - 'Unexpected.' 'Explain C,' he requested, concealing his anxiety.

8

But no explanation came. The only words offered by his boss; precise and lacking emotion. 'An excellent operative, a terrible way to go.' Control reached into his coat and pulled out a small Manilla envelope. He turned to Mater and discreetly slipped it inside the newspaper still tucked under Mater's left arm. 'Find out what you can and fast. See if there is another reason. Check that no-one else was involved. I'll leave it to you to inform his ex. Report back ASAP.'

Control rose and, without looking back, joined the steady stream heading to the underground station. Mater brought the coffee cup to his lips. It was cold, but he needed the stimulant. Mick dead: impossible to believe, incomprehensible. How would Mick's ex cope? He recognised their separation had been out of necessity, not from lack of affection or love. There were children too who could never know why their father so often missed their birthdays and rarely spent Christmas with them. Those special events most families enjoy, cementing their memories. How would the other team members take it? Mick had been popular with everyone. The robust bond between them, made ever stronger by each successful mission, now broken. Mater assumed Control would inform them in person.

He resisted a strong urge to open the envelope there and then because despite taking precautions, camera technology might catch him out in the open. He remembered how sometimes civil servants and occasionally even ministers apparently unwittingly released information to journalists by walking along Downing Street with documents held in full view: the media failing to realise this was part of the game. Passing a bin, Mater crushed the coffee cup, tossed it in, then took the envelope from the newspaper and stowed it in a zipped pocket in his coat. Needing to gather his thoughts, he walked the long way back to the car. But as he strode through Green Park's avenues towards the Bomber Command Memorial, Mick's grinning face wouldn't leave him, not even for a moment. At the monument, he paused, stood in front of the bronze figures and read the epitaph to so many brave men. He thought of his own team. Now Mick, who had served his country so quietly, so bravely, gone. Mater knew there would be no lasting memorial for his kind: it could never be sanctioned. Why and how did he die? The desire to examine the report returned, and he reached into his coat. Stopping himself, he turned and hurried on.

Before entering Carrington Road, Mater checked and double checked no-one followed. There really was no need but something made him uneasy and the training kicked in. He breathed a sigh of relief. All quiet. He entered the car-park, returned to his vehicle, slipped into the driver's seat and disabled the car's security system. He surveyed his surroundings with the vehicle's mirrors. Nothing. No-one. After switching on the interior light, he took out the envelope. Printed at the top of the document, the usual filing codes but nothing that linked the papers to anybody or any organisation. He scanned the introductory information and then focussed on the detailed report. Alarm bells had rung when Mick failed to appear for refresher comms training. Someone visited his home in Sheffield but the property was empty. A call to his ex. drew a blank and the regulars in his local watering hole denied having seen him for weeks. The Office staff had become increasingly concerned. They activated their link to the regional and national Police computers; searching missing persons files for bodies described but not identified. Mick's size and build helped narrow the search. The corpse's identity, found in a squalid Brighton flat, suggested first by dental records and then confirmed by formal DNA analysis. In fact, Mick's body had been discovered by the owner of the bedsit during a routine visit to check the building's services. Initially the landlord believed the smell was caused by yet another rat infestation but it was strong and sickly sweet and on reaching the second-floor landing the odour overpowering. When he opened the door to bedsit no.3 the warm stench made him retch. Someone sat in an armchair facing the electric fire but the head that poked above the chair's back was sealed in a plastic bag. He had seen enough and called the Police who attended within minutes. They noted the body had started to decompose and recorded details of the plastic bag, the soiled trousers and underpants dropped to the ankles. The CID team took many photographs and carried out a careful examination of the room to see if they could identify the body and rule out foul play. The local Police concluded that this was purely a case of auto-erotic asphyxia. A middle-aged man messing up during a session of self-pleasure made for a thin file and saved resources for those cases the officers deemed worthier.

Mater read the report twice. *Why was Mick there?* From the Police's investigation, the bedsit was booked through an on-line agency but when they tried to trace the booking's origins, the trail died. Mick, Mater knew, was skilled in covering his tracks but he did not believe his friend would have participated in the sexual perversion detailed. He may have procured the services of prostitutes when single but his tastes always seemed mainstream. Mater turned to the photos. The images of his colleague's body should have appalled him but decades seeing of the grim results of war and acts of terrorism taught him to detach himself from reality. It was never easy but the work ethic took over and he forced himself to scrutinise each picture. He worked by examining the background first. Mick's corpse he would look at last. Initially, nothing appeared unexpected or untoward. Then in the third photo taken from the side of the armchair something lying almost under it caught his eye. A Coca-Cola can. It niggled. Mater knew his team well. You don't spend years at close quarters without learning many mundane and often intimate facts about the men and women with whom you share every waking hour. Even in Mater's line of work where deception was paramount, a subconscious exchange of information detailing personality and lifestyle choices was inevitable. Mick disliked soft drinks and held a particular distaste for cola. 'Would prefer to drink my own piss' always his response when offered one. Mater needed to see the original electronic image. It might reveal more, something that passed the CID by. Maybe, by chance, they had kept objects from the scene; just in case the coroner asked awkward questions. A final element baffled him. The report noted soiled underwear but did not mention semen. He considered the Police's conclusion. Didn't sound like an activity involving human pleasure to him; Mick scared shitless more likely. *We're allowed to be terrified when death comes,* he concluded, *Especially if the end is unpleasant and painful.*

In the envelope, Mater found an identity card for a DCI Robert Somerville from the Metropolitan Police but with Mater's photo attached. He knew it to be a fake but nobody else would. He emptied his usual personal effects into the glove-box and slipped the new ID into his coat pocket. Nearly one o'clock. There was enough time to get ahead of the early rush hour traffic and reach Brighton during office hours. During the drive down, he needed to create a workable cover story to persuade the local force to open their records for him. Normally a routine task he enjoyed but today lacked any pleasure.

Chapter 2

To Mater, the duty desk officer appeared as if he wouldn't receive his pension. *Too many cakes*, he thought, as he noted the bulging uniform that had seen better days.

The bored sergeant was typically unhelpful. He looked Mater up and down. 'Normally sir, we would have received a message informing us of your visit,' his flippant response when Mater showed his ID and requested access to the case file.

Mater was prepared. 'The problem is we believe the body that I have been tasked to investigate may have been one of our Unit 19 team. We need to be discreet but absolutely certain that foul play was not involved.'

'Unit 19, Sir?'

Mater had learnt that the most effective lies lay very near to the truth. 'Yes, that's correct. You may not have heard of this organisation within the force. Major anti-terrorist role. Not widely advertised but very successful during the 2012 Olympic Games: many attacks prevented. Not more am I allowed to say but keep it under your hat.'

The sergeant felt a little more important. 'So, no bomb in the bag you're carrying then, sir?' he joked. 'I will call for the file. You can use Interview Room 3.' He opened a door that led away from the station's reception and pointed along the corridor. 'And you'll find a coffee machine outside. Feel free to help yourself.'

Mater chuckled, showing his appreciation of the sergeant's attempt at humour. 'Thanks sergeant, most helpful. If there's a box of associated artefacts, could I please check those as well?'

He poured himself an espresso and pinched two biscuits from the packet lying alongside. Stealing inside a Police station, even petty theft, amused him briefly, detaching him mentally from the task in hand. He entered the interview room and discreetly checked. The standard interview recording machine was switched off and unplugged. In one corner, high up, was a CCTV camera. He knew there may be hidden microphones, so climbed on a chair, covered the lens with his handkerchief and explained what he was doing to anyone listening but unseen. He couldn't rely on the sergeant's discretion but needn't have worried. The local boys accepted the London officers were a law unto themselves and previous experience had taught them to turn a blind eye. As he stepped from the chair, someone called from behind. A pretty young woman was standing at the door holding two boxes to her chest. She looked surprised by Mater's antics.

'The file and artefacts you requested, sir.'

Mater thought she was probably a civilian assistant to the local force. He decided not to offer an explanation but a compliment. 'That's very kind, such efficient service, thank you,' he said smoothly, as he took the burden from her. 'Had I time, to share a coffee would be great but unfortunately urgent Police work...'

The girl giggled, blushed, turned quickly and left, closing the door firmly behind her. Mater knew that at his age even such an innocent offer would be rejected but it might usefully distract her.

He dragged the chair to the desk, sat down and opened the file first. Most of the information was already familiar. There were some statements from other bedsit residents and neighbours. No-one seemed to have seen the deceased before nor offered any titbit that hinted the event had been anything but an unfortunate accident. There was a poly-wallet containing a USB memory stick. He took his phone out and connected the stick to it. The phone's software would cope with almost all data storage devices and he was confident he would be able to view the contents of this one.

Opening the photo folder, he searched for the copy of the picture he was most interested to see but he couldn't find it. It was puzzling. Some photos were missing or different to the hard copies Control had provided. Mater could not be certain which represented the truth. Concerned, he turned to the cardboard boxes. Each contained small items and samples taken from the bedsit by the scene of crime officers. They were sealed separately in transparent plastic bags, carefully labelled and each carried a warning not to be tampered with. In the second box, Mater found the empty Coca Cola can. He returned to his phone and checked the individual reports associated with each item. The report about the can succinct: 'Aluminium soft drinks container. No residues – specifically no drugs or alcohol. No fingerprints on exterior or DNA detectable from lip.' He wondered why they had kept it. He turned the can over and over in his hands reading the list of contents, the expiry date and manufacturing reference number. Something wasn't right. Nothing in or on it of note, but it was heavier than he expected. He used his phone to access the Office's investigatory databases. The manufacturer data was incomplete. Mater felt a mixture of elation and anxiety. He knew that the Office had become aware of offensive systems being developed by other services that involved potent rapidly acting gaseous agents. These could be delivered into an enclosed or semi-sealed environment, incapacitating the target within seconds. In 2002, the Russians had employed this approach to break the Nord-Ost Moscow theatre siege with devastating consequences. Faced with terrorists holding dozens of theatregoers hostage, they took the fateful decision to pump an anaesthetising gas into the building before assaulting it. Many died when the drug suppressed their breathing whilst others were shot by those sent to rescue them or by the terrorists before they themselves succumbed. Failing to take anyone alive meant the Russians lost the opportunity to glean intelligence. Secret services around the World watched events unfold in disbelief but also with self-satisfaction. Mater remembered the scenario had been used as a training aid to demonstrate how not to do something. *Could Mick have been a victim of such an attack,* he pondered. *The scene where his body was found purely a ruse?* He took photos of the can, checking the pictures showed the printed information on the label and then repacked the cardboard boxes. He returned the USB stick to the poly-wallet and neatly stacked all items on the table. He pushed the chair to the corner of the room, stood on its seat and removed the handkerchief from the camera. On leaving, he stopped briefly to raid the packet of biscuits again, thanking the Police service for its hospitality as he did so. He signed out at the front desk, informing the sergeant that his assistance had been most valuable, but unfortunately the file on the deceased had been unremarkable. It looked like there had simply been an accident.

'Still, must be most upsetting, sir,' commented the sergeant.

Mater turned to go. 'Yes,' he said, 'It's awful losing one of our own; totally appalling.'

16

And as he walked back to his car, *most unsettling too*, he thought. He would drive to the London safe house, contact Control to arrange another meeting, ideally along with someone from the special services department. Their expertise might reveal whether his hypothesis was correct or at least possible. Despite the biscuits, Mater felt tired and hungry. Once in town he would make the necessary calls, treat himself to a long hot shower and head out for dinner and something to drink. He knew a lovely quiet small Italian Bistro in Islington near to the Regents Canal where the owner, whom Mater believed had connections in the underworld, understood discretion. He didn't hold his knowledge of the owner's background against him. 'We all have to make a living,' he had once hinted to Signor Bellita, an atypically thin and wiry man for a restauranteur. The mutual understanding between them meant that Mater routinely left a generous tip in return for excellent service: free wine and privacy. Undisturbed in his favourite alcove whenever he visited alone or with others, he was always welcomed and comfortable in the Taverna. To Bellita, discretion equalled contented customers, which was naturally good for business.

Mater travelled back up the M23, at the speed limit and against the flow of rush hour traffic pouring out of the Metropolis. Despite his mind continually returning to the day's events, he drove with care. He didn't want any more surprises today. Dusk fell as he traversed the South London suburbs but the streets remained busy, lit by a mixture of sodium street lights, neon signs and xenon vehicle headlamps. Mater preferred darkness. At night, in the dark, you could hide and relax. London to him was chaotic and frantic in equal measure. He longed to return to his cottage but could not rest until he had answers and the powers that be in the Office were satisfied that their work could continue as normal.

He crossed the Thames by Blackfriars Bridge and headed to Islington, briefly stopping around the corner from the Angel tube station. He walked briskly to the Asian mini-mart he used when staying in town. He would need plenty of coffee and other basic supplies to keep him going in the house. Although the property was used by a variety of Office staff, no-one ever seemed to leave fresh milk or other items useful for the next visitor, but then nobody knew who would stay or when. There were cleaners who visited weekly; vetted and cleared but not tasked to do more than ensure a supply of clean sheets and that the bathroom and kitchen were respectable. He suspected they had military backgrounds as the rooms were always spotless. On the rare occasion their paths crossed, there was a polite exchange of pleasantries but all understood no more was required or expected. He would never find out who they were or anything about them.

He returned to the car and drove the last half a mile to the Georgian terraced house in Britannia Row and parked in a vacant residents space. He removed the valid parking permit from the glove-box and stuck it to the windscreen. He wondered if the neighbours were intrigued by the comings and goings. The anonymity of London and the transience of much of its populace helped obscure, but the Office kept an eye on adjacent properties ensuring no-one took more than a passing interest in the house's temporary occupants. Mater stepped from the car, carrying his small snatch bag and his supplies. He double checked he had locked the vehicle before climbing the steps to the front door. It was now dark, but the house was lit inside with curtains drawn on the first and second floors. Although the door was in shadow, Mater knew exactly where to insert the key. A new visitor would be delayed, fumbling to gain entry, giving the cameras, discretely secured to the eaves, more time to record in either natural or infra-red light. He entered and after automatically turning to check the street, closed the reinforced door behind him.

He called out, not expecting a reply, but heard the sound of a TV blaring in the ground floor lounge. The house lights came on at dusk and curtains drew automatically. The TV suggested the lounge was occupied with the high-backed sofas turned at an angle. From the outside an observer would not know that the license fee paid annually was for no-one's benefit. The small kitchen at the back had French windows. These could, in warmer weather, be opened onto a paved patio, hidden by a tall fence and a retaining wall. Mater dropped the carrier bag on the kitchen table, his snatch bag to the floor and filled the kettle. While it boiled, he used his phone to contact the Office again. By the time the kettle clicked off, a meeting with Control's number two had been arranged. Control, it seemed, was not available, spending the evening at a reunion in his gentleman's club. Mater knew, whatever the crisis, the chief would continue life at his steady pace; no fuss or bluster, always living up to his name.

Mater emptied his bag on the bed of the first bedroom at the back of the house, immediately above the kitchen. A shower, a change of clothes and he would still have plenty of time to wander through Islington's alleys, admiring the antique dealers' shop windows, before dining at the 'Taverna Lago di Como'.

Just before eight, Mater sat down in the alcove with a bottle of Ricossa Barbaresco 2009 and two glasses, courtesy of the restauranteur. Red wine Mater's choice and most agreeable but not too expensive for the Maître d' to donate. If Mater leaned forward a little he could observe the arrival of guests.

A smartly dressed Simon appeared as agreed, five minutes behind Mater. At the bar near the front door, Simon told Signor Bellita that he was expecting to join Graham Johnston for dinner. The Signor took Simon's coat and accompanied him to the back of the restaurant. Bellita always accepted bookings from Mater in the name of Graham Johnston; it was simply a name. Similarly, Mater didn't know whether the Italian was really a member of the famous Lugano Bellita family as he had professed to be but it mattered not. They had a professional relationship. The diners, once served, would be left undisturbed to negotiate their business or discuss any other affairs that two middle-aged gentlemen might be involved in.

They ordered from the limited set dinner menu. It was simpler and the bill would end up on Office expenses: neither would wish to appear extravagant. Indirectly they were tax payers too.

Mater thought Simon looked much older and more rotund. Simon considered Mater older too but as fit as ever. Mater poured them both generous glasses of wine. While waiting for the first course, they exchanged pleasantries but Simon seemed on edge, irritated and impatient. Mater had worked with him regularly but had never quite fathomed him out. A member of the small executive team who Control usually instructed to brief Mater's unit on their next mission. It was typically Simon who offered Control's congratulations when they returned after a successful operation but that was the extent of their contact. There was a mutual respect between them but their backgrounds, so different, had ensured that a certain coolness persisted over the years. Friendship between Office staff was, by necessity, bound to be limited and generally discouraged. However, Mater and his agents had endured so much together they inevitably developed a closeness between them not extended to anyone further up the management chain. He couldn't ever be privy to the details of Simon's origins, but surmised Simon had enjoyed a privileged upbringing and probably benefited from a Russell group university education. It was also clear to Mater that Simon was not a military man. Simon's life, as much as Mater knew it, a complete contrast to his own.

Simon apologised that Control was unable to receive Mater's report personally but reckoned he would understand. He did. *Perhaps*, thought Mater, *Simon, being called to work late at short notice, had been forced to cancel his own evening arrangements thus explaining his demeanour.* Mater noted Simon liberally sprinkled salt on his primo; a wild mushroom risotto. Not good for the blood pressure. For the second time that day he wondered if this public servant too, would not reach pension age. As they ate, Simon asked Mater to report on his day's work.

'In summary, there are a number of troubling aspects to Mick's untimely and unexpected demise, Simon.'

'Go on M.'

'The location was unlikely to be familiar to Mick and the suggested sexual activity prior to death surprises me. I knew him for years. It doesn't fit.'

'Is that all?' Simon sounded somewhat disappointed. He had read the file before leaving the office and had made similar conclusions. 'Nothing from the Brighton Police's records?'

'Well, one detail presents an enigma, but it's probably irrelevant.'

Simon stopped chewing and put down his cutlery. He took up his glass of wine and sipped, waiting for Mater to continue. He always listened, filtering titbits from the chaff, but knew from experience that if Mater had found something he considered out-of-place then it was worth being attentive. Mater pulled out the photograph taken in the bedsit from the side of the armchair where Mick's body had lain for the many days before discovery.

'You've seen this, Simon?'

Simon nodded. He was reluctant to look at the picture again, especially over dinner. The risotto was good, and he wanted to keep a healthy appetite for the courses to follow. Mater pushed the photo across the table, took up his fork and pointed with it to the Coke can. 'I don't think it contained Coca Cola.'

Simon looked baffled. 'Carry on M, please.'

'It was not manufactured in an established drinks factory. I don't believe it held a soft drink at all. My hypothesis is that maybe, just maybe, it was filled with something to subdue Mick. Perhaps a liquid or possibly a gas? I don't accept the Police's conclusion of death by misadventure. It may have been an accident but I'm not convinced he was alone when he died. As far as I'm concerned, his loss remains unexplained.'

Simon raised his eyebrows and indicated that Mater should expand on his theory. Mater reminded Simon of the events surrounding the Russian theatre siege. After he had finished, Simon took up the salt and dusted the food in his dish again. On a normal day, Mater's idea would have seemed bizarre but Simon had information that made this day anything but normal. He was concerned for all Office staff, himself included. Mater might be clutching at straws but, for now, the Office would grasp any possible clue.

'Your response, Simon, please?' Mater wondered why Simon deliberated for so long.

'M, we have a problem, a major one.' Simon was holding his glass, swirling the contents around and around. 'What I'm going to tell you will be relayed to all the operatives in your team personally.' He paused again as if struggling to express what he had to say next.

Mater's anxiety returned. He took a large swig of wine and wondered whether, with government austerity measures, they were about to be disbanded. He rapidly discarded the notion. There were too many current threats to UK PLC and the establishment surely wouldn't allow it.

Simon looked directly at him. 'You will be aware that our computers have been somewhat leaky recently. Well it's been more than a dribble. There's been a significant security breach; we've been hacked big time.'

The message Mater received back in Kent suggested a hiccup but this sounded like something far more serious. He was stunned, although the training kicked in and he managed to avoid a change in facial expression, as if someone had administered some rapidly acting Botox injections. *It wasn't possible,* he thought, not quite believing what he had heard: the Office's systems were constructed to be completely separate from the web with secure links to their sister agency, GCHQ and other friendly agencies.

Simon allowed a moment for the bombshell to sink in and continued. 'Must be an internal job making it all the more concerning.'

'What information has gone, Simon?' Mater asked gently, but he already knew what was coming. He just needed confirmation.

'I will only deal with your team M. We believe the complete database containing all your details is no longer secure. In essence, who you all are, where you live, what you eat for breakfast, even the size of your shoes may be out there, available to the highest bidder. Your aliases blown.'

'Or maybe,' interjected Mater, 'In the hands of an enemy who wants to seek revenge, cause mayhem and destroy the reputation of the Office. So are you implying that our lives are in imminent danger, Simon?' Again, he already knew the answer but wanted the official line and needed to know what the Office's solution to this unprecedented problem was.

'M, as you have intimated, we also believe Mick was murdered. The questions are: Who did he meet prior to his death and what were his actions in the days between his last contact with us and when his body was discovered?'

Silence fell between them. Mater struggled to take it all in. Mick murdered. This had been his conclusion, but he hadn't dared voice it to himself or to Simon. Exposed; all five of them. No, he corrected himself. The remaining four: Charlotte, Liam, Tiny and himself. Years of effort building aliases, sacrificing old friendships and many loving relationships. Alternative lives for the good of the country and the sanctuary of the team. All under threat. It appeared they were all in immediate danger. He was angry, but it was an emotion he had learned to inhibit. Anger led to poor decision making, and he was going to have to make some of the best decisions he had ever made just to survive.

'Why didn't Control inform me earlier, Simon?' Mater spoke quietly but firmly, modulating his voice.

'We didn't know ourselves until mid-afternoon when the GCHQ boys finished their analysis. As soon as the problem was confirmed, we agreed to tell everyone, as you would expect us to. Everyone in the Office is naturally deeply concerned.'

Mater nodded. 'We are where we are,' he mused. 'And how is the Office intending to deal with this?'

Signor Bellita appeared at the alcove holding the second course, one plate in each hand. He seemed troubled. 'Gentlemen, is the risotto not to your liking?' he enquired. 'You both have hardly touched it but it seems you've enjoyed the wine.'

Mater looked up and forced a smile. 'Delicious Signor B, but we haven't seen each other for a while so keep forgetting to eat! But, if you have it, more wine would be marvellous, the red is excellent.'

Bellita knew Mater better than his guest would ever realise. This regular customer was bullshitting, but he played the game the same way he always did. Offer compliments, provide copious alcohol and withdraw when guests appeared troubled. 'Another bottle will be with you shortly. Call me when you would like the next course; I will ask chef to make it fresh for you.' *Business may be good, business can be bad,* he thought, *but it's still business.*

Simon reached for the remaining rosso and emptied it equally into the two glasses.

Mater repeated his question. 'What is the Office going to do?'

Simon had prepared carefully. Mater, as team leader, would feel responsible for the others, but Simon would insist they disband immediately, avoiding any contact between them until the Office deemed it safe. They were all to disappear; become dormant agents who might never have any true value again. The Office would look after them anyway it could. Not to do so would break one of its cardinal rules. The situation would be, as far as Simon was concerned, similar to when an operative retired. There had always been an understanding: a new permanent identity, enough money to appear generous and a mutual promise of secrecy until death. He couldn't suggest this to Mater because that's where the similarity ended. In the current circumstances, there appeared to be an insider who had created mayhem. Trying to hide human assets was not going to be a routine task, perhaps impossible.

'The boss has put Anthony in charge. He'll collate all the information there is so far and make arrangements for you and your team. It might be a misnomer M, but we are sending you to another safe house. There will be someone keeping an eye on you and ensuring your daily needs are met. This person is a signatory to the act, worked with the service decades ago but retired from active duty years before chips and computers were employed. It's the best we can do.'

'For how long?' demanded Mater.

Simon began to answer but was interrupted when the next bottle of wine arrived. He thanked Signor Bellita and poured. 'Truthfully, we have absolutely no idea M. We will keep in contact as necessary using traditional methods only; revert to tried and tested ways of communicating but you need to move very soon, ideally tonight. We all hope the problem is dealt with rapidly and if anyone should be able to sort this mess out, Anthony should.'

Mater emptied his glass. The alcohol calmed him but his head swam. He didn't know if it was the wine or the realisation his whole way of life had instantly changed or perhaps both. Now he knew why Control had a meeting at his club this evening leaving the difficult conversation for Simon to conduct. He felt betrayed. If this was the end of his career, with all the implied attendant residual risk, then he would have liked to have discussed this face to face with the man who had been his mentor. He more than likely would never see or hear from Control again.

He leant out from the alcove and beckoned to Signor Bellita. 'Signor B, the bill please. I'm sorry but we have an urgent appointment and need to leave. The prima was as delicious as ever. I'll be back another evening, hopefully soon, for the secondi.'

The restaurateur nodded but didn't believe a word. Something in Mater's tone of voice told him that nothing would ever be the same again. Perhaps it was the last time he would welcome Mr Johnston to his restaurant. 'It is, and always has been, a pleasure sir,' he responded truthfully.

Simon took a Taverna Lago di Como business card from the napkin holder on the table, neatly wrote an address on the reverse and slid it across. 'M, this is what you need. You will be expected. Go carefully, take precautions and we'll watch over you the best we can.'

Mater picked up the card, read the address, memorised it and then slipped it into his pocket. Although he rarely did, he couldn't risk forgetting. The two men rose. Mater drew some notes from his wallet and tucked them under his plate. The bill had yet to arrive, but he knew the cash would more than cover it, with a very generous tip on top. He would miss his evenings at the Taverna but he needed to be certain that if he returned, he would be welcomed as if nothing had changed. Signor B. held Simon's coat for him from behind. As he did so, he looked to Mater and shrugged his shoulders as if to say 'what will be, will be'. As the men turned to leave, he grasped Mater's hand firmly. 'In bocca al lupo' were his parting words.

You might be wishing me good luck but 'to go into the wolf's mouth' might be more apt than you may ever know, thought Mater, translating literally. He raised a wry smile. 'Thank you for your usual kind hospitality, Signor B.'

'Grazie, Mr Johnston. I do hope you visit again soon.'

Mater and Simon stepped into the cold, briefly shook hands and parted.

Mater returned to Britannia Row, stopping regularly to look in shop windows, checking he walked alone. At the house, he collected his few things, secured the building and walked briskly to his car. It was late evening and the London traffic had lightened significantly. Within the hour he passed Sawtry on the A1 motorway heading north, slipstreaming behind the train of lorries trundling in the same direction. If he could have driven all the way to Norton le Clay, he would have arrived just after midnight, but he needed to abandon the vehicle long before he left the main road. As he drove, keeping to all speed limits, he turned over the evening's conversation with Simon. For the Office to lose so many experienced operatives in one go could only mean that the threat was significant; to be taken seriously by all. Whoever, within the service, had revoked their oath of loyalty had wreaked havoc. Probably they would be caught eventually, but the damage was done. He considered each of his Office contacts, starting at the top. Few individuals had detailed knowledge of his team's activities. By necessity, others supported him: equipment officers, travel specialists and Foreign Office liaison staff, all of whom existed to smooth Mater's team's insertion into country. And, of course, there was a battalion of cleaners and tea ladies. History exposed many examples from the world of espionage where embedded foreign agents had bided their time before delivering their fatal blow. He racked his brains, visualising each person in turn, trying to see in their faces something amiss, recalling past conversations, looking for clues. Nothing. What about his superiors? Could it be Control, Simon, Anthony or even someone from his own team? But who and why? At dinner Simon had seemed genuinely shocked, though Mater reminded himself they had all been trained as well as any successful actor who trod the boards of West End theatres: crocodile tears came easily. The never-ending conflict was who to trust and who not to. Trust too many too often and eventually you present your opponents with an open goal. Trust no-one ever, and you freeze, unable to act or react. *But where does the balance lie,* thought Mater, *when one of your best lies in a morgue?* For the first time in a very long while he felt exposed. The repeated successes of his unit had endowed them all with a sense of invincibility. This needed to be checked before every new mission: Mater knew from bitter experience that events could turn out badly and without warning. The consequences for him so terrible that their memory frequently surfaced; almost overwhelming him. Psychiatrists would probably have diagnosed him with post-traumatic stress, but he had little faith in the caring professions and had decided to fight his demons in his own way. He pushed the rising memories to the back of his mind and turned his thoughts to Mick. *The poor bastard, dead in a grotty room in a seedy part of a seaside town in his home country. Not the hero's demise that might have resulted from so many service operations. No heroic retirement, no gong.* Under current circumstances, even as a close mate, Mater couldn't visit Mick's ex. Unable to do the honourable thing and inform her, in person, what had happened and what a fantastic guy he had been; greater than she would ever know. Circumstances may have caused their marriage to fail but their relationship, although increasingly intermittent, had remained strong. He wondered whether as Mick's absence lengthened she had given up on him, simply believing that he must have found a new lover. He vowed, when the time was right, he would find her, explain and probably reveal more than he should. He would make sure she knew her ex-husband had been very special.

Chapter 3

At junction 33, Mater turned off the A1, joined the M62 motorway and headed to the Ferrybridge Services. He pulled off the highway and entered the services' carpark, seeking a space far away from the few other cars parked near to the cafés and shops. He switched off the engine and tugged the lever under the steering column to release the bonnet catch. He turned on the car's interior lights, placed his belongings on the passenger seat and then thoroughly checked the front of the vehicle for anything that might link him to it. In the glove-box, he located a torch and stepped outside. He opened a back door and then the boot, reassuring himself he would soon be untraceable. He lifted the bonnet and using the torch proceeded to disable the engine, detaching a wire from under the electronic control system. Now impossible to start, the fault would not be readily diagnosed by any roadside engineer; particularly in the dark.

Mater closed the bonnet, grabbed his snatch bag, and walked to the services' buildings. As he walked, he phoned the vehicle's registered recovery service, described where he was and explained that the car had broken down. He enquired as to how long it would be before someone helped. The call-centre girl advised him the evening had been busy, so she was sorry but he would have to wait at least an hour and should stay with the vehicle. Mater told her not to worry, finished the call, ignored her instruction and headed into one of the cafés for something to eat and drink. There was time to spare and with the Taverna primo digested long ago he needed topping up, ready for the night ahead.

On his way out of the services, he bought two of the new day's broadsheets and a chocolate bar. He would wait in the car, passing time reading the morning news. The papers could be useful later to fend off the cold should he have to hold up a while before making for his final destination. He liked to be prepared; have a Plan B.

The flashing orange beacons of the breakdown truck caught his eye as it slowly manoeuvred around the carpark looking for the ordinary white family saloon. Mater got out and waved as it approached. The driver stopped in front of Mater's car and hopped from the cab. 'Sorry for the delay sir, a busy night.'

Mater wondered if all recovery staff were taught a list of relevant excuses to be offered on arrival. He showed his insurance document and explained how he had pulled up, gone briefly to the toilet and found, on his return, the vehicle wouldn't start at all.

The mechanic oozed confidence. 'These motors? Usually one or two things. Have you on your way in a jiffy.'

Mater thanked him and smiled encouragingly, amused by the mechanics choice of language. 'A jiffy.' Only the British and specifically those of a certain age used that word. It was these details, unknown to so many of the Office's opponents that gave them away.

The mechanic opened the bonnet and set to work. Mater stood behind with his belongings and watched. He tinkered for a few minutes and then muttered. 'Thrown me, this one.' He frowned then dropped a spanner back into his toolbox before admitting defeat. 'Sorry. We'll have to tow you home.'

Mater explained that he had an urgent appointment in Manchester in the morning, so requested the vehicle be taken to its registered address in Hampshire. He would return to the services and book himself a taxi but was grateful that the mechanic had tried his best. The man was pleased his customer wouldn't be accompanying him: no small talk through the early hours. It took him only a few minutes to confirm with his boss that he should make the long trip south. He hitched Mater's car to his truck and drove away. Mater was alone and disappearing. Soon all traces of him would be lost.

Back in the café, he saw a table surrounded by men of various ages and build. Most of the lorry drivers clearly overweight: the consequences of an all-day everyday sedentary career and endless full English breakfasts. Mater interrupted their loud conversation, explained he had broken down, his car had been towed away and he urgently needed to reach Harrogate. Was anyone going in that direction and willing to give him a lift? Extra earnings were on offer. He held out two ten pound notes.

The drivers were not meant to allow strangers in their vehicles: over the years there had been hijackings and worse. But the man appeared harmless, his story credible and to Roddy, driving through the town anyway, it would not be much of an inconvenience. Someone else in the cab would make the time pass and help keep him awake. He wiped his plate with the remnants of a piece of fried bread and drained his mug of tea. As he rose he addressed the others. 'Onwards and upwards, mates.' He beckoned to Mater. 'Twenty quid, fine by me, although you'll have to cope with me choice of music. What's yer name, mate?'

'Tony,' replied Mater, 'Tony Milton.'

The two men left the warmth of the café, headed to the lorry park and climbed aboard Roddy's vehicle. The laden artic rumbled out of the services and slowly accelerated onto the motorway.

Roddy reached forward, turned on the cab's stereo, and slipped in a CD. Heavy metal from the last century began to thump out. 'Hope you don't mind, tough if you do'. He laughed, belly wobbling like a blancmange.

Mater laughed too. Roddy was right, it wouldn't be his choice but beggars can't be choosers and Harrogate was only an hour or so away. He would just close his eyes.

'What's yer business up here, anyway?' asked Roddy.

There was no reply. He glanced across. Tony fast asleep, or so he thought. 'No bloody stamina,' grumbled Roddy, 'No wonder this country's going to the dogs.'

Mater was skilled at cutting out the outside world when the opportunity arose: a few minutes respite would recharge his batteries. But with his eyes closed, all he saw was Mick's decomposing corpse and heard Simon's calm, controlled voice – '... the entire database containing the details of all your team members is no longer secure....' *We're all in the shit*, concluded Mater, *truly fucked*. He reflected on the years he had worked for the Office. In his late twenties, he had been enticed from a successful career in military intelligence by the prospect of working for an organisation that would guarantee adventure and a greatly improved salary; tax free. There were warnings about the downsides - leaving his past life, hiding the truth from his closest friends and family. In addition, there would be personal risks. The man who visited him at his Colchester base reassured him that the service hadn't lost anyone for more than a decade; not since the Berlin Wall fell. Mater didn't need the reassurances. He had few friends and early family life was always a struggle: Mother an alcoholic, parents arguing, fighting and ultimately divorcing. No siblings to share the burden. He had been envious of other children who were dealt a fairer hand. The lack of social stability took its toll, and he spent most of his youth rebelling in one institution after another. Without doubt the army was his salvation. He learnt to control his emotions, using the anger and frustration, which was ever present, to advantage. On active duty, he could kill without hesitation, finding the excitement of conflict relieved his internal stress. During battle, he was focussed and knew he would win. His strengths. coupled with a willingness to volunteer. did not go unnoticed. He was promoted up the ranks and often seconded to work with the Special Forces. By the time the Office came fishing, he was a Lieutenant with an enviable array of medals, bestowed not just for being there, but for going far beyond the call of duty. He accepted it would end sooner or later, either tending roses in a cottage garden or with a funeral accompanied by a military salute. His service attended by a few well-spoken, inconspicuous Office staff who would acknowledge each other, the contribution he had made, and then move on. There was no space for sorrow, pity or remorse. *It had been a good laugh, no better than that, pure fun,* thought Mater. He checked himself. *Forget it. It's not over, I'm not done yet.*

Heavy metal continued to blare out; Roddy accompanying. 1.45 am. The lorry turned off at the Wetherby junction and joined the A661 heading directly for Harrogate. He would be in time to make his delivery in town and manage a few miles of the return journey before taking a compulsory nap.

Mater, eyes still closed, noted the truck leaving the motorway. He remembered the road quite well. During the first few years of army life his regiment was stationed at Catterick, which lay to the town's north. Harrogate offered the squaddies evenings of light relief. Away from its elegant centre, they knew where to find cheap beer and girls, making the most of their time-off before being sent overseas to fight wars initiated, in Mater's opinion, by dubious government policy. He always wondered why the intelligence that swayed the politicians was so feeble. He surmised that it was an excuse: vital in maintaining good relationships with our friends from across the Atlantic. But he was part of the system, a loyal soldier and orders were simply that. He went with the rest of his unit and was lucky to survive. He opened his eyes, stretched and waited for a pause between tracks. 'When you get into Harrogate, drop me by the side of the road, just before you reach the Stray, please.'

'Sure, no problem. Have you somewhere to stay?'

'Yes, she'll be surprised to see me,' answered Mater, adding, 'If he's still there I'll have to boot him out.'

Roddy chuckled. He had no idea what Tony was up to but his passenger would soon be gone, he a little better off and no-one would be any the wiser. He really couldn't care less.

The truck pulled up beside the park as requested. Mater handed over the money, picked up his belongings from the foot-well and clambered down. 'Thanks Roddy. Drive safely.'

'You look after yourself. Be safe too,' said the driver, leaning across to close the passenger door and with a wave and a cloud of dust he was away.

'Little do you know,' murmured Mater to himself, 'Safe would be great.'

He was tired and cold but he knew it would be a while before the first bus left Harrogate for the village of Norton le Clay. He was tempted to find a taxi but taxi drivers often asked questions and remembered where they dropped their fares, especially at an unusual time of day. No, he would wait. A park bench for an hour or two would be welcome and he wasn't likely to be disturbed. He entered the Stray and headed to the bandstand where many years ago he had listened to a miners' brass band play on a sunny summer's evening. It was a heartening memory: laughing and playful children dashed around and around their parents who sat listening to the music. Old couples held hands, perched on benches, each displaying a plaque remembering a departed loved one. Others on bikes or pushing prams; passing by, paused to enjoy a few bars of the repertoire. The mines and miners were long gone. Mater wondered whether the musicians still performed, with younger members picking up the mantle. He felt it formed an integral part of England and her heritage, worth preserving, worth fighting for. As he reached the middle of the park, he was pleased and reassured to see the ornate Victorian bandstand was still there. He strolled to the nearest bench, placed the snatch bag at one end and opened the newspapers he had bought. He lay down, pulled up his collar, rested his head on his makeshift pillow and spread the newspaper on top of himself. He looked up. Despite the light pollution from the town he could make out familiar stars. He had spent many nights in the open on operations, using the heavens as a navigational aid or, when GPS was available, simply enjoying the spectacle. He didn't want to close his eyes but was tired and had to maximise his resources. He dozed; Mick's smiling face returning once again to trouble his rest.

A voice and a nudge woke him. He started but restrained himself from being physically defensive. He expected to see a policeman or a member of the local council parks staff, checking the Stray for misfits to be moved on. He slowly lifted his eyelids, noting a strong odour he recognised as the smell of the unwashed.

'What brings you here?' enquired the man, dressed in multiple grubby layers and insulated further from the cold by a straggly grey beard. 'I've been watching you for at least an hour.'

It was dawn, and the stars were fading. Mater rubbed his eyes, sat up and stretched before he answered. The newspapers slipped to the ground. He would stick to his story. 'Missed the last bus and can't afford a taxi, so thought a few hours here would do me before I go and visit my girl. She wouldn't like it if I turned up in the middle of the night, especially after I'd downed a skinful. Gives her time to throw out her other man too.'

The vagrant laughed heartily. 'As long as you're not going to take my patch, I'm OK with that.'

'Where are you from?' asked Mater. The accent challenged him.

'That would be telling,' replied the tramp, adding 'What about you? Where do you stay?'

It was Mater's turn to laugh. 'That would be telling indeed.' Mater shuffled to one end and beckoned for him to sit. 'Your bench,' he said.

They sat without saying a word, both listening to the dawn chorus; birds and traffic. Mater broke the spell. 'Lived here long?'

The tramp tugged at his beard as he spoke. 'Maybe too long. Dossed here and other places, from north to south. Never keen to overstay my welcome, get known. Like my own company.' He continued in full flow and Mater sat there; a sounding board. 'Held down a respectable job once and almost had a family, if she'd stayed. Yep, money, a house, a car even.'

'What was your work?'

'Believe it or not, designed, built and maintained mainframe computers, back in the late 70s. But with success came the drink. Working away from home and her. Finished it all off did the boozing. So here I am, but not unhappy with my lot.'

Mater didn't know whether anything he heard was the truth but it wasn't important. He had managed to avoid giving any more detail to his own story. He glanced at his watch. 6.17. The local bus services should start soon; time to find a proper bed.

'Here, buy yourself a cup of tea and a bacon roll for breakfast,' he suggested, as he reached for his wallet and handed over five pounds, along with the newspapers. The man might warm himself with tea or something stronger but it didn't matter to Mater. He was grateful to be have been allowed to sleep. That was enough for a reward. He got up, gathered his things and started to walk away.

'Thanks governor,' called the vagrant after him.

Mater waved his free hand but did not look back. He walked briskly towards the bus station, trying to encourage the circulation in his stiff limbs.

At first, the 7.04 service to Norton le Clay carried two people; Mater and the driver. The driver grunted when Mater handed over a note to pay his fare. Such passengers used up his change and the day had only just begun. It wasn't going to be a good one. Mater offered thanks as his ticket was thrust towards him and asked the driver to stop at the centre of the village. The driver grunted again and accelerated away before his passenger had reached the back of the bus and sat down. The bus passed other villages on its way to Norton le Clay, picking up school children and early workers. The school kids normally occupied the back but seeing the bench seat was taken by a hunched up old man, they chose to sit further forward. Soon, as ever, they were laughing and shouting amongst themselves. The stranger was quickly forgotten.

The bus pulled up at the village green as requested and the driver called to Mater, advising him of his stop. Mater stepped down as two more school kids clambered aboard and then watched the bus disappear in a fog of blue diesel fumes. He took in the scene. It was very quiet. The post office cum shop closed. A man working to the side of the local pub stacked barrels and crates of empties. The occasional car raced by, drivers perhaps already late for work or endeavouring to miss the inevitable rush to Harrogate. No-one noticed the newcomer as he turned away from the village centre and walked purposefully along Waterside Lane East towards Langley Hall, some three miles distant; hidden in its estate of forty-five acres. Mater visualised every detail of the route before it appeared; his almost photographic memory for maps as useful as ever. The wintry sun rose, warming him. The cold grey London of yesterday gone.

Finally, he strode up the long beech-hedge lined gravel drive to the front door, rang the bell, hoping that the resident or residents of Langley Hall were expecting him. There was the sound of dogs barking followed by a shout and then shoes tapping on floorboards as their owner approached. The door opened.

'Yes?' enquired the tall, heavily built, elderly man, elegantly dressed in a traditional outfit befitting of the country gentry.

'Randall, Philip Randall,' responded Mater.

'Ah, Mr Randall, I've been waiting for you, do come in.'

'Thank you; you must be Major Littlewood-Jones?'

Mater climbed the last step, entered and held out his hand. The Major clasped it and shook vigorously. For someone of advanced years, his strength surprised and impressed Mater.

'Indeed. Welcome, you are just in time for breakfast and then no doubt require a shit, a shower and a shave.'

Mater recognised the Major's severe tone as a product of decades of barking orders to subordinates which did not necessarily reflect the true man. The Major smiled broadly, his sun damaged wrinkled jowls sagged around a neat grey moustache, hiding a mouth with limited dentition.

'Spot on,' replied Mater, 'I'll add a fourth 's', if I may: sleep.' He was knackered.

'Spare room already prepped and ready for occupation,' clipped the Major. 'After me.'

As Mater followed along the corridor he heard growling and scratching at a closed door to his left. 'How many dogs?' he enquired.

'Just the two, a hunt hound and a German shepherd. Both as vicious as they sound. Living on your own here demands some security. I'll leave them locked away until you've had a moment to settle in and then introduce you. Assume you have no problem with dogs; they sense anxiety in those who don't like them.'

'No, problem with dogs,' confirmed Mater. He liked the animals but had been forced to kill a few during operations; one even with his bare hands. Not a pleasant experience for either of them.

In the kitchen, the Major indicated to his guest to sit while he cooked. There was a single plate. The Major, having been up since dawn, had eaten breakfast earlier. He placed a mug of steaming hot sweet tea in front of Mater.

Made in true NATO style, traditions never change, thought Mater. He sipped whilst enjoying the aroma of the full English being prepared: bacon and fried eggs. The Major served and then sat at the large old pine table opposite: probably as ancient as Langley Hall itself. As Mater tucked in, the Major drank from an identical mug, pausing intermittently to brief Mater on his role.

'I've known Control for many, many years. We worked together in a parallel service to yours, long before your boss transferred and rose through the ranks. We have lived by a mutual respect and trust, all underpinned by our loyalty to HM government and as signatories of the OSA.'

Signing the Official Secrets Act doesn't guarantee trustworthiness, thought Mater, remembering infamous past operatives who had betrayed their colleagues and country. Philby, Blunt et al. all characters the public were familiar with, but within the agencies lesser figures had been discovered, offering their services to the highest bidder or acting under duress. Would the source of the leak that compromised Mater's unit ever be identified or would he and the remaining members of the team run and hide indefinitely?

The Major continued. 'Control asked me to look after you. He tells me he believes you've led one of the service's most successful front-line teams and has no intention of losing you or anyone else. I have been provided with the financial resources to keep you here at Langley Hall until the problem, as he described it, has been resolved. You are requested to reside here until further notice.'

'A request, Major, or an order?' interjected Mater.

The Major sensed the frustration in Mater's voice. He knew from his own tenure that employees of the service when threatened were trained to go on the offensive.

'I think you should consider it an order, Mr Randall. The run of the house and estate are yours to explore but I recommend you do not venture beyond the boundaries. Enjoy some time off, but, of course, I can't, and wouldn't want to, stop you thinking and planning.'

Mater noticed the Major's smile had returned and there was a twinkle in his eye.

'None of us succeed without occasionally, out of necessity, breaking rules,' said the Major.

Mater felt reassured by his host's rebellious streak. It implied he had worked on the fringes of acceptable behaviour and would probably not stand in Mater's way if he needed to act without instruction. In the meantime, he would take up the Major's offer; rest and recuperate. Time to think. Time to plan.

Mater finished his food and sat drinking a refill of tea. The Major scooped chunks from a large tin into two stainless steel dog bowls lying on the kitchen floor. 'I'll let the dogs out. They'll be much friendlier with full stomachs. They need to get used to you. I don't mind them eating strangers but certainly not my guests.'

Mater watched as the hounds raced into the room and headed straight for the food, ignoring his still figure sat at the table.

'I'll show you to the annex, Mr Randall.'

Mater rose slowly and quietly. The dogs took no notice. *Pathetic guard-dogs if they can be bought off with a bowl of meat,* thought Mater. He followed the Major further along a corridor towards the Hall's east wing.

The Major opened a door linking the annex to the main building. 'Everything you need is here; shower, soap, fresh towels in the bathroom and this is your bed. In the adjacent sitting-room you'll find a radio and an old TV. You are welcome to visit my library off the hall and borrow any books you like. However, I'm afraid there is no telephone and Control requested I look after your mobile. Any messages from him to you, I will relay. Neither Control nor I want anybody locating you here and I am sure you don't either. I'm meant to be retired and rather enjoy the peace. Spare clothes in the wardrobe; probably won't fit but best I can do. Sleep well. Lunch is at one should you awaken and require it. Dinner is served at 7.30. I assume you cook. We'll take it in turns to create some culinary delights.' He turned to leave.

44

'Do you have any staff, Major?' enquired Mater after him, concerned that he might at some point bump into someone without prior knowledge of who or why they were there.

'I don't have a gardener or groundsman. That will be self-evident when you go outside. Pension doesn't stretch that far but I'll introduce you to Mrs Robinson who visits every Friday to clean and deliver groceries. You need not worry about her. She is even older than me and long retired from the service, reputation intact.'

'An active past?' asked Mater.

'Cleaning and groceries, Mr Randall, just cleaning and groceries.'

Mater set his few possessions on the dresser by the window. From there was an open view of the Hall's walled garden with its ancient orchard, the tree's branches twisted and bare. In front, vegetable patches containing the remnants of what looked like cabbages and sprouts and two lean-to greenhouses, most but not all panes broken. Beyond, hills rose in the north, obscured in part by a small wood. It was a tranquil scene. He felt safe within the walls of the Hall and under the care of the retired Major. He stripped off, showered, shaved and slipped under the fresh sheets, naked. The annex wasn't warm but compared to a park bench and newspapers this was luxury. As he fell asleep, a sea of faces raced through his mind portrayed as a series of mugshots; the internal film jamming with the image of Mick's swollen plastic bag enclosed face.

Mr Randall spent the next few days getting to know the Major and his dogs. The latter became friendlier and would even join him during his daily run around the estate. His host was reserved and the conversation between them remained courteous but superficial. The Major knew isolated details of his military career could be accessed by any Tom, Dick or Harry at their local library, so was willing to reveal something of his past adventures. However, Mr Randall's name was inevitably false and although he recognised his guest also had an army background, there could be no quid pro quo when it came to exchanging stories. The Major had enjoyed meeting with Control at his club; it was always a pleasure when the two managed to get together but he took Control's request seriously and his words to be accurate. The man staying, described as a valuable asset under immediate threat, needed to be hidden until further notice. He had no intention of letting his friend down; the less he learnt about Mr Randall the safer they both would be. Neither Mater nor he had any idea how long the current situation would persist.

The Major advised Mr Randall he would inform him if there was any news but to date there was none and perhaps, thought Mater, this was a blessing. He was sure someone would visit soon, deliver a folder of documents, giving him a new identity and a way forward. The Office would have to deal with the cottage and his personal effects, compensating him generously. The problem was there were some private items he never wanted to lose, and these he had concealed very carefully in his old home.

While he waited, Mater structured each day: reading books from the library, wandering the grounds with the dogs, enjoying the Major's company during mealtimes and keeping fit.

Chapter 4

Liam received the message to meet Simon not more than five minutes after Mater noted the contents of his. Simon had been tasked to brief everyone in Mater's team individually, to explain the problem that made their work untenable. The Office, under direct supervision of Control, determined that each operative needed to be move urgently to places of safety. With the severity of the threat, isolating each person should minimise the chances of further setbacks.

Although Control had overseen the recruitment of Mater's team, the line-up required to create an efficient and effective unit needed to be perfect. Mater considered Liam an obvious choice, brushing aside any managerial reservations. During many overseas operations, Liam's love of and educational success in languages endowed the unit with the ability to communicate with friendly locals. This proved especially useful in the Arabian Gulf and on several Russian missions. In addition, he could turn his hand to anything electronic or electromechanical and enjoyed being an amateur chemist. So, accessing computers, tinkering with motor vehicles and bomb making were skills often put to good use. Colleagues were naturally never informed he narrowly avoided youth detention because of his juvenile explosive exploits, but one experiment left him burnt and scarred; lucky to survive. Mater and the others suspected that the story of the burning pyjamas was baloney: they had seen the effects of high explosives on the human body. Running away from the garden shed device with too short a fuse taught Liam a lesson although maybe not the best. If you are going to play with big bangers always give yourself a longer fuse: a margin of safety. Those of a different disposition would have given up the fireworks altogether but Liam didn't. Mater admired this quality. When the team made a plan that they considered dangerous, Liam advocated caution but still tugged at the leash, itching for action. After recruitment within the service, Liam, with no prior military training, needed time to get up to speed. However, he had been a quick learner and Mater, recognising his aptitude and good interpersonal skills, remained patient. Although as physically fit as most other men, he was small and lightly built. More of a distance runner than a sprinter. Eyesight, poor since childhood, required him to use strong lenses, making his eyes appear large and alert, often likened to those of a bush baby. His visual impediment worried the selectors and mislaying his glasses nearly caused one or two disasters in the field. There had been little point in offering him extensive weapons training: it was soon evident that a submachine gun, with its inherent inaccuracy, was the only firearm for him.

On receiving Simon's message, Liam packed quickly, secured his flat and headed to Birmingham's New Street Station. He would be in time to catch the early evening London train, due to arrive at Euston at 21.50. A room had been booked for him at the St Pancras Renaissance Hotel, a ten-minute walk from the terminus. Simon presumed Liam would eat during his journey and so arranged for them to meet for a drink in the foyer bar which would be busy with businessmen and tourists. Liam had no idea what the meeting would be about or why so urgent. It didn't matter. He assumed the Office required the services of the team and that always enough for him to drop what he was doing. They had been here before many times; it wasn't unusual.

Liam checked in at the hotel: the receptionist warmly welcoming Mr Copeland as a first-time visitor. She informed the new arrival that room 23 on the second floor was booked for one night. The bill would be covered by his firm and so he didn't need to show a credit card. He obeyed Simon's instruction not to use any of his usual aliases but this had played on his mind as the train sped south. They all used temporary pseudonyms on occasions but these were typically weaker than an established identity with its comprehensive back-story. He decided what lay ahead must be a special operation or a change in direction for the unit. He couldn't know the latter was an accurate assessment, but for reasons he would soon glean. He picked up his bag and headed to the lift. Two men in smart suits were waiting for it. Something inside Liam advised him to take the stairs. He climbed three steps at a time. No-one followed. At the second floor, he followed signs to rooms 1 to 30 and heard the lift doors part behind him. As he reached his room and inserted the key, the two businessmen passed by.

'Evening,' he said.

Neither man spoke, but the taller smiled and nodded an acknowledgement.

He pushed open the door, and paused before entering, just long enough to see both men disappear into room 28, further down the corridor. He dropped his holdall beside the bed, drew the curtains, switched on the TV and raided the mini-bar, choosing a fresh orange juice. He would have preferred an alcoholic drink but there could be no booze until he learnt what Simon had in store for him. Only forty five minutes to go before their meeting in the foyer bar. *Perfect timing,* he thought.

At 11.00, Liam quietly left his room and headed back downstairs. He sensed someone was watching, but when he discretely glanced behind as he opened the door to the stairway, the second-floor corridor was empty. He breathed a sigh of relief. His ever-present caution always invoked a degree of paranoia when working for the Office. But he lived by the maxim; 'paranoia is a healthy state of mind'. This had served him and the team well.

Simon slouched in a large leather armchair near to the fire exit at the far end of the room, an empty chair facing him. A party of drunken guests stood drinking and laughing loudly. Liam walked past them without anyone taking interest and stood in front of his colleague.

'May I join you?' he asked.

Simon nodded and indicated for him to sit.

'Something to drink, Liam?'

Liam requested his second orange juice of the evening but accepted Simon's suggestion that something stronger wouldn't go amiss. His choice was replaced by a double brandy and Simon went to order a refill for his tumbler.

As he waited for Simon to return, Liam viewed his surroundings. Typical hotel bar with much leather and glass: a commercial attempt at luxury. At the opposite side to him, were further sofas and chairs casually placed around convenient gleaming coffee tables. Despite his eyesight, he made out two seated familiar figures, seemingly in deep conversation. *Wonder*

50

if they are discussing their next mission? he pondered. Simon returned with their drinks and sat. They clinked, took a sip and then set their glasses on the table.

'OK Simon, what's cooking?'

Simon briefly checked no-one was in hearing distance, although he needn't have worried. The noise from the group at the bar easily drowned out their conversation. He leant forward and started to talk, divulging the news in the same format that had been received by Mater. A summary of the problem, the background as known and the current situation.

'So, where are you sending me?' enquired Liam, on hearing the decision to disband and instruction to discard their existing identities.

Simon passed over a folded piece of paper with details of a safe house. Liam read it once and just as Mater had with his, slipped it into his pocket. It was a lifeline.

'Have you spoken to the others?' he asked.

'I'm in the process of doing so.'

'And the response from those who know? How did they take it?'

He didn't answer. He hadn't mentioned Mick, knowing that Liam's personality was more vulnerable than Mater's, who was, anyway, the team leader. He would find out eventually; probably sooner than later when the Office knew everyone was safely secreted away. Simon finished his drink.

'Any further questions?' he asked, before standing.

Liam took off his glasses and spent a minute polishing each lens. Finally, he looked up. 'Many, but I don't expect answers now. Your instructions are clear. One step at a time.' He drained his own glass, rose, and they shook hands.

'Good luck Liam. I know Control and the whole department appreciate your dedication. Who knows when we will next meet?'

'Thanks Simon. Here's hoping this mess is sorted soon. Perhaps, it's the organisation that needs the good fortune.'

Simon turned and walked out without looking back. Liam craved another whisky but resisted the temptation, needing to keep his wits about him. He wouldn't relax until he reached his designated safe house in Cornwall. Better to go upstairs and try to get some shut-eye before catching the morning 8.15 Great Western Intercity train from Paddington to Newquay. He intended to travel first class and enjoy the on-board dining; his reward for his contribution as a 'civil servant'. The country could afford to pay for a little luxury. As he left the bar, he passed the two businessmen he had seen earlier. Liam was aware that, as he strode by, they stopped talking to each other. *Perhaps,* he thought, *business folk have many secrets too; their commercial success threatened by industrial espionage.* As he climbed the stairs to the second floor, he corrected himself. No, not just businessmen, everyone hides something. But, unlike him, he doubted few spent the rest of their days looking over their shoulders. Once again, life was going to be challenging, but this he relished. Back in his room, he double checked that the windows and door were secure. Best he could do. Alarm set for 6am. Time for sleep.

Liam woke and got up long before six. He cancelled the alarm. It had been a restless night. His mind focused on the day ahead; there wasn't time to feel tired. If needed, he would catch a few winks later on the train going west. He was concerned that his elderly parents would worry if they did not hear from him. He was a dutiful son, telephoning regularly, even if work prevented regular visits. They knew his government post was important and forgave him. They believed he carried out research for the Ministry of Defence which often got in the way when he planned to call. Growing up during the Second World War and, being patriots themselves, they certainly didn't expect to be told what he did. They were simply pleased that he had a secure job, a pension and was working to keep the country safe. Simon had reassured Liam that arrangements had been made for all the team's friends and families to be contacted and given plausible explanations. It was hoped the absences would be brief.

He washed, dressed and packed. He rehearsed the Cornwall address in his head, removed the slip of paper from his pocket to check he was right. 'No dementia yet,' he muttered to himself. He tore it into pieces and as he flushed them down the toilet, thinking *I'll be dammed if we are all going down the pan. If the Office can't solve this, I'm sure M will have his ideas.* He would have loved to call Mater and the others but for now he would have to work alone, survive. After carefully checking that the room was clean, he picked up his bag and left, closing the door quietly behind him. A quick breakfast and then head off. If he arrived at Paddington early, the first-class lounge would be available.

He entered the ground floor dining-room. It was empty apart from a member of the hotel kitchen staff, an attractive Eastern European woman, who offered him tea or coffee. He ordered coffee and forced himself to eat heartily. *Need to keep those batteries fully charged,* he thought. Liam considered this a sensible precaution; in case a change of plans became necessary. He still intended to enjoy the services of the express's dining car later.

He finished breakfast just before seven, handed his key back at the front desk, confirmed there was nothing to pay and stepped out onto the Euston Road. He would catch the tube at Euston Square; only four stops from Paddington. It would be a long journey and fresh air and a stretch would be welcome before he joined the Intercity train. The London rush hour had already started in earnest. Cafés were opening, deliveries being completed; night workers heading home passed day staff rushing in the opposite direction. Liam crossed the road at Melton Street. He was wary of the fast-moving traffic and didn't notice the two men following him. The morning crowd was growing, providing cover for Liam but also for his pursuers. He headed into the underground, swiping his oyster card to gain entry. He had asked the Office whether this was traceable and been reassured. The passageway leading to the escalators was only partly illuminated. The few commuters using it sounded like tap dancers, their footsteps echoing down the tunnel and fading around the bend at the far end. Pasted posters advertising West End shows covered each wall. Liam briefly stopped at one. 'Last call for the mousetrap', he noted, 'Forty seven years run to finish.' *Must book it,* he thought. As he turned to continue, he found his path blocked by two familiar figures.

'Hello, Mr. Copeland,' said the taller of the pair.

The man spoke with a foreign accent but Liam, taken aback, didn't have time to work out the man's origin. A blow to his head floored him, his glasses and bag flew along the ground. Before he could deploy his self-defence skills, the tall man pinned him down. Liam felt a sharp pain in his thigh. He kicked hard and the other assailant cried out as Liam's shoe dug into his groin, causing him to stagger back. Liam directed a punch at the Adam's apple of the man holding him tight. He had been pleased that when he deployed this karate manoeuvre in the gym, the force shattered a pile of five terracotta tiles. Unfortunately, his attacker was equally skilled and saw what was coming. He twisted away just in time but in doing so, released Liam from his grip. Liam leapt to his feet, blood streaming from his nose and upper lip. The men backed off.

'Goodbye, Mr Copeland,' the tall man said, as both walked briskly away.

It was all over in less than thirty seconds. Liam bent down and searched for his spectacles on the floor. They were broken. He picked up his bag, held a tissue to face and headed towards the escalator, feeling out of breath. His holdall felt heavier and heavier and he struggled to walk in a straight line. *Must be the blow to the head,* he concluded, *It has messed up my balance.*

This was Liam's last thought. As he reached the escalator, his legs buckled, and he fell headlong onto the moving stairs that carried him down towards the platforms below. His bag remained at the top, blocking the path of fellow travellers who shouted out to him to watch out. Those observing Liam's fall believed he had simply tripped. No-one knew that as Liam descended he slowly suffocated, turning a dusky blue, as the drug injected into his thigh increasingly paralysed every muscle.

The ambulance crew called to the scene took over from members of the public trying to revive the man at the foot of the escalator. They were equally unsuccessful, carried the victim to the surface and then by slow blue light to the St Mary's University Hospital. The paramedics knew there was little point in rushing with this one. London Transport broadcast that an incident at Euston Square had closed the tube station temporarily but normal service was expected to resume very shortly. A short paragraph describing the event appeared in that day's Evening Standard newspaper and that was that.

The Accident and Emergency staff, on receiving Liam's body, declared death. They noted the minor facial wounds and the lack of identification amongst the deceased few belongings. They guessed that the inevitable post mortem would show a cardiac problem resulting in the collapse.

'Back luck to be stepping onto an escalator when you have a misfire,' remarked the senior charge nurse, assisting a young nursing student in the preparation of the corpse for the morgue.

Chapter 5

Simon wouldn't know that another agent had died until many days later. Liam's host in Crantock became increasingly concerned that her charge hadn't turned up within the expected time frame. After forty-eight hours, a coded message was posted in a sealed envelope back to an address in London, picked up and delivered to Simon in person by a runner. He sat with the opened letter at his desk and considered various possibilities. Maybe Liam, realising the consequences of the Office security breach, panicked and decided to make his own arrangements; rely on his own experience and take his chances. Unlikely. He tried to avoid considering the second option but reckoned he would have no choice but to assess its probability: Liam might be detained or even dead. The third possibility was also unpalatable; perhaps he was involved in the leak, escaping, with or without the help of others.

A thorough search of missing persons records, travel booking datasets, hotel reservation lists and hospital admissions eventually provided Simon the answer he would have preferred not to receive. The post mortem on the unknown deceased male concluded that he had probably suffered an irregular cardiac rhythm causing him to collapse. The heart and rest of the internal organs, including the brain, were structurally intact. The subsequent fall down the escalator explained, according to the hospital's resident pathologist, the broken nose, cuts to face and bruised left thigh. St Mary's Hospital informed the Police that a body of about 40 years of age was stored in one of their fridges, its identity unknown. They requested the Police carry out any investigation rapidly and arrange for its early removal to a local authority facility.

Simon's team picked up on the Hammersmith Police's involvement and quickly used their contacts in Scotland Yard to take over the inquiry. A second autopsy was ordered and the corpse's condition recorded as before. Toxicology came up negative apart from a little alcohol in the blood but neither legal or illicit drugs nor recognised poisons found. The Yard's specialist pathologist, did however, note a minute puncture wound in the centre of the thigh bruise. Probably also caused by the tumble although he couldn't be sure. He checked the hospital pathologist's description. The bruise was noted but the further injury missed.

'Bloody amateurs,' he muttered.

The new information rang alarm bells in the Office. On reading the findings, the 1978 London assassination of Bulgarian, Georgi Markov using a poison delivered by a pointed umbrella tip sprang to Simon's mind. He wasted no time in directly reporting his concerns to his boss.

Control listened without interruption. Two operatives from five dead. No clear cause of death for either but the information lost by the computer hack had halted the operations of his best unit and now decimated the team. He decided to suspend several ongoing inquiries and divert further human resource to investigate the deaths of his employees. He would also meet with Mater at Langley Hall, offer his personal condolences, explain the current crisis and see whether he had any ideas to solve the problem. A chance to catch up with Littlewood-Jones would at least ease the unpleasant nature of the task.

Usually he travelled in a style befitting his senior civil service position; chauffeur driven for shorter trips or by Army Air Corps helicopter for longer or more urgent journeys. The present situation demanded that a subtler arrival was required. No flash transport and no bodyguards. Just Control away for a weekend visiting friends, somewhere. He wouldn't inform anyone in the Office or his family where he was going. He would take an old-fashioned radio-pager with him. If needed, contactable but not directly locatable but he hoped this would be not necessary. A stay with the Major generally involved a generous dose of fine wine, acceptable dining when his friend cooked, followed by cigars and reminiscing.

After meeting with Liam, Simon's next tasks were to pass similar instructions to Tiny and Charlotte. Time pressures meant it was easier for them both to travel to London rather than him visit them which he considered a pity. He held a soft spot for Charlotte. There were mutual flirtations but their relationship never developed further. The nature of their work resulted in opportunities to meet being limited. Anyway, if they had ended up together, the management, with so much at stake, may have insisted on their resignation. Charlotte was, in Simon's opinion, the perfect potential partner. Intelligent, educated, multi-skilled, loyal, entertaining and quite beautiful with abundant black hair, dark eyes, a petite nose and delicate lips. He didn't know if she had a husband, boyfriend or other, whether she was straight or gay. They flirted but despite Charlotte's slightly rebellious streak, duty inevitably always supervened.

Charlotte joined Simon at the Tate Modern gallery café. For a weekday, it was busy, the chilly winter weather drawing in locals and tourists for a warming mid-morning coffee. They sat opposite each other on low plastic designer chairs, sculptural and easy clean but not comfortable. She guessed he chose the Tate because he wished to enjoy the current modern masters exhibition. He always hinted that he loved the arts although perhaps this was simply a ruse designed to impress her. However, when they met at 10.30, the time Liam should have been safely travelling to Cornwall, Charlotte noticed Simon failed to offer any compliments about her. She had even worn makeup and a rather revealing dress to tease him; attire she generally avoided unless required for work. It was true that, on more than one occasion, Charlotte's feminine form had been employed to attract or distract the opposition. Lured by her beauty, elegance and charm, the victim had been offered simple alternatives: cooperate, be arrested or worse. The rest of the team would be waiting in the background, ready to pounce, but sometimes her options were more limited, and she had to act alone. She had no qualms about ensuring her target would be permanently prevented from acting against the UK again. Such actions were routinely denied by the management in their briefings to ministers, who wouldn't have expected otherwise. The Home Secretary could stand and answer questions in Parliament without hesitation; his or her conscience clear.

Charlotte received Simon's news and digested his instructions calmly. This was a unique situation, but the Office had a solution, even if it appeared temporary. She was used to winning, and she believed that the service would find the leak and plug it rapidly. He, who knew more than he revealed, thought Mater's team finished and her optimism misplaced, but it was not in his remit to suggest so.

Charlotte's destination, she noted from the paper handed to her, was located in the Scottish Highlands, near to Blethybridge. She suggested, at this time of the year, it wasn't impossible for her to be cut off by snow there, making further face-to-face meetings difficult. Truthfully, she didn't care to be away from the glitz and glamour of city life for an indeterminate period. She suggested an alternative; staying with a reliable friend based in St Peters Port, Guernsey. Someone whom she had not visited for years.

'Why don't I go there?' she asked, 'There's better weather and French inspired cuisine.'

Simon pointed out that the only way to reach the Channel Islands in winter would be by commercial flight. This required some form of identification – the fundamental problem created by the IT leak. Private air transfer would also involve a passenger log.

'No,' he insisted, 'Control has given clear instructions. Make your way to the safe house rapidly using anonymous public transport. No contact until the Office communicates in person, leave no trail and keep your head down.'

'Worth a try,' she replied, adding seductively, 'Would you like to accompany me around the exhibition and then perhaps a light lunch? It sounds as if it will be impossible for us to enjoy each other's company for a while.'

Simon was tempted, but he was due to meet Tiny that afternoon on the other side of town. There could be no cock-ups on his part.

'Sorry Charlotte, not today, would love to, but work stops play.'

She understood. 'Last chance. Yearn for me,' she said, uncrossing and crossing her legs.

Simon smiled. 'You know I'll do that,' he replied, the image of her stockinged thigh embedding itself in his memory. With that, their flirtation and meeting ended.

Chapter 6

It was always easy to spot Tiny. Simon saw him striding towards him from the end of the street, his head floating above the sea of other faces meandering along Brick Lane. The nickname was obvious and inevitable but he had had others. At six feet five inches tall and built as an American footballer on steroids, he was pure muscle and bone and weighed more than twenty stone. Although still incredibly strong, the bulk now incorporated early middle-aged spread: Tiny failing to cut his calorie intake after being discharged from the Parachute Regiment. His size, on occasions, presented problems during his army service. Uniforms only just fitted, his red beret perched like a beanie on his shaven bonce. When fully kitted out, he barely squashed into the seat of a Hercules transport. In battle, he could carry vast loads: weapons, medical supplies and when necessary an injured comrade to safety. His role as a front-line medic gave him his first ubiquitous nickname 'Bones' but this changed to 'Bowels' after an unfortunate episode during training in Belize. There were other paras of a similar build to Tiny, so this name was reserved until his recruitment to the Office. Those fighting with him were reassured by his presence. He was highly trained, skilled, and brave. Other paratroopers knew if Tiny couldn't sort a problem in the field, he would rapidly evacuate any casualties, with little regard for his own life. He had a temper but learnt to convert his anger into useful actions. It surprised no-one that Tiny's efforts in the First Gulf War saw him become an early but deserving recipient of the military medal. A faulty parachute two years on resulted in spinal injuries fortunately without permanent damage. although they caused severe pain, required a protracted period of rehabilitation and stopped him parachuting. The senior officer who visited him at Headley Court Tri-service rehab centre offered him a transfer to a ground based role but Tiny was obstinate. He had battled through selection to join the regiment, fought with the regiment and struggled to recover from his injuries. It was the Paras or nothing. He tended his resignation and after leaving Headley Court twelve weeks later, returned to civilian life.

But Civvy Street wasn't for him. Frustration and depression had been finally countered by a chance meeting with an ex 2 Para at the British Officers Airborne Club's annual reunion at Brecon. During the gathering, the Colonel enjoyed drinks with some of the men; each unwittingly being evaluated for a potential new career. He had studied the service history of more than ten retired soldiers, all of whom with excellent credentials. However, without doubt, Tiny, if persuaded, would make the perfect choice. He caught up with him last. There had been the usual initial polite exchange of pleasantries: the relationship between senior officer and subordinates intact, but the Colonel wasted little time in bringing forward his proposal.

'It sounds as if you are missing your days of active duty,' he suggested, knowing this to be undoubtedly the case.

Tiny concurred.

The Colonel followed this with his offer. 'I have been tasked to find suitable candidates for a unique government employer. You are particularly well suited. I understand what they have in mind is not without risk but I'm sure it's something that you would enjoy; an opportunity to use your skills. I know few details but can recommend you for an interview if you want.'

Tiny wasn't stupid. He did not need to hear the Colonel's confirmation that one of the secret services was on a recruitment drive and he didn't hesitate.

'Yes, sir, I would be grateful if you would.'

'Good man,' answered the Colonel before moving on to chat to another veteran.

Simon and Tiny arrived outside the Aladdin Curry House simultaneously. Although mid-afternoon, the restaurants on Brick Lane were still doing a brisk trade in take-aways. But inside the lunchtime rush had subsided, and it really had been unnecessary to make a reservation. But Simon needed to be sure that he handed over his last instructions from Control without any minor administrative hiccups. Simon was a stickler for detail, an attribute that helped propel him from low level operative to middle management. He knew Tiny was always hungry, so as they sat down at the table in the window, he ordered the buffet lunch for two - Tiny could enjoy larger helpings. The food was served promptly, accompanied by tap water for him and a zero-alcohol beer for Tiny. Tiny had no inkling as to the reason for their meeting but preferred to have a clear head if he was to receive new orders. Simon didn't want to lessen Tiny's enjoyment of his meal, so decided to wait until post-lunch tea arrived before delivering his bombshell. Tiny would cope better with a full stomach. The last couple of days had been arduous and he would be glad when this final briefing with Mater's team was over. The Asian waiter left the pot for them to pour.

'Shall I be mother?' asked Tiny incongruously.

'Please, go ahead,' answered Simon.

Tea poured, Tiny picked up the cup but before drinking wanted answers.

'OK, meal's over, what else is on the menu?' he asked.

Simon took a large gulp of tea and began regaling the current problem, finishing by handing over a similar folded paper to those received by the others. He sensed Tiny restraining the rising anger inside.

'Fuck me,' Tiny muttered, 'You'd better catch the bastard or bastards soon, Simon.'

Chapter 7

Despite the time of year, Control would have wished to have driven his jaguar north; roof down with his beloved classical music blaring. Instead, he signed out a service vehicle; a silver-grey family estate, reliable, boring and uncomfortable.

At least the radio works, he thought, as he pulled out from the service's underground garage in Pimlico.

He deviated briefly from his intended route to stop at his favourite Vintners, picking up a recommended half case of St. Emilion Grand Cru 2010, paying in cash as always. Over the years, the shop's owner identified his likes and dislikes but wondered why this successful businessman didn't appear to own a credit card. But he visited regularly and paid, and that was enough.

Control wedged the wine on the floor in front of the rear seat alongside his weekend bag and hung up his suit carrier. *Six bottles should be adequate,* he decided. *We'll have two or three over dinner and I'll leave the others as a thank you.* He couldn't stay long.

He joined the North Circular traffic heading towards the junction with the A1. *Should be there in about five hours*, he calculated, Taking into account a couple of stops to empty the bladder. Must get the bloody prostate sorted.

At Langley Hall, the Major had been delighted to learn that his old friend was planning to call although somewhat disappointed it was to be a flying visit. Control, he learnt, would be travelling alone; unusual and disappointing. He would have liked to have seen his friend's wife but Mr Randall was staying and undoubtedly that was the explanation. At least Mrs Robinson would only have to make up one bed. He would inform her by telephone so she could bring in extra rations.

As instructed, he informed Mater about Control's trip, who wondered what developments had occurred to cause the boss to make the journey. He hoped, naturally, it would be good news but didn't think this required meeting in person. He assumed that if the problem in the Office had been resolved, then normal lines of communication would resume. No, too optimistic. Perhaps Control had decided to disband the unit and retire the remaining staff. Everyone knew he always spoke personally with those leaving the service, formally thanking them for their contribution and reminding them of their indefinite obligations. They would be handed a thick envelope filled with crisp fresh notes to tide them over until standard pension arrangements kicked in. Mater would be sad to leave but he understood.

Control's trip was uneventful and took him as long as he had anticipated, having kept just ahead of the Friday dash. The route was familiar, and he didn't need to use the vehicle's sat nav. In his own car, he had never quite mastered the on-board technology that automatically came with such advanced modern vehicles. Instead, he preferred the tatty volume stowed in the glove box insisting that nothing beats a traditional paper map. The lengthy familiar journey provided ample time for him to consider how he would broach events with Mater.

As dusk settled, he turned off the country lane outside Norton le Clay and passed between the ornate gate pillars guarding the entrance to Langley Hall.

Excellent, he thought, *Sun's over the yard-arm. I'm sure the Major will have a little refreshment waiting for me.*

He pulled up in front of the stone steps rising to the main door, switched the engine off, opened the car door and gingerly levered himself out. The noise of the engine was replaced by the sound of wind blowing through cedar trees and dogs barking inside. He liked the animals and they him. He stopped and listened for a few moments, stretching his stiff limbs. Current times were particularly challenging, but he had overcome many problems before securing his eventual appointment as chief. He would, with help, resolve this one too and would not let it ruin a bloody good weekend.

The Major clasped his friend's hand firmly. 'Great to see you, Paul', he said, his sagging wrinkles accentuated by a broad grin. 'Mr Randall is in the drawing room. I'm afraid we've already started on the Scotch but I am sure you'll catch up. I've put in you in the green bedroom suite. Join us as and when.'

Control deposited the wine in the hallway and climbed the grand oak staircase to the first floor. He liked the rooms the Major had given him. South facing with a small balcony; an early 20th century addition to what was essentially a Victorian pile.

As he entered his bedroom, he noticed the smell of lavender that masked the residual mustiness from non-occupancy. *Mrs Robinson has been busy here,* he thought.

69

The air was cool and damp but the cast iron radiator warm. It was a struggle for the Major to maintain the Hall and he was grateful that his friend had fired up the central heating ready for his visit. They coped with living rough when they fought side by side as young Sandhurst graduates, but now appreciated life's luxuries even if the Major's pension didn't stretch far. Control hung his clothes in the curved beech veneer wardrobe, selecting a tweed jacket and regimental tie for the evening. No need to change the cords.

Control entered the drawing room to see the Major and Mater sitting in front of a blazing log fire. Two large dogs lounged on a rug occupying the space between the chairs and the heat source. There was a third armchair reserved in the middle for him. Both men stood.

Mater stepped forward and reached out with his hand. 'Good to see you, sir, straightforward drive?' They shook hands.

'Pleased to see you too, Phil. Journey fine thanks,' his face offering no clues as to the reasons behind his visit. Mater noted the emphasis on the 'Pleased to see you too'. Whatever it was, he now doubted Control was going to be the harbinger of good news.

'Scotch, Paul?' enquired the Major, pouring a hefty measure without waiting for an answer and then refilled his own and Mr Randall's glasses. The three men sank into their chairs, politely chatting before the warming fire. The alcohol consumed during the evening would dis-inhibit. Despite this, no-one would reveal anything of note. They were all too experienced for that but the conversation would eventually turn to subjects which, in mixed company, would be definitely taboo.

'I'd better get on with creating dinner,' announced the Major, standing up and walking to the table at the far side of the room. He poured himself the third of the day and took the bottle back to Mr Randall.

'Gentlemen, please help yourselves, I will leave you in peace. You have important matters to discuss. If you need anything I'll be in the kitchen. You will not be disturbed.'

The door in the lounge closed. Mater pulled out the cork from the scotch and offered to re-fill Control's tumbler.

'No more for me just now, thanks Phil, but please help yourself.'

Mater declined, returned the stopper and placed the bottle on a side table. He waited for his boss to speak. Control twirled his glass, the little remaining whisky colouring the crystal as it whirled, staring intently at the flames roaring into the chimney. With his other hand, he reached down and stroked the nearest dog behind the ear. Mater sensed the chief was struggling to start.

'Phil, this is not easy. I'll tell you what I know. Then please ask me anything. I will answer your questions if I can.'

Retirement, here we come, deduced Mater.

'Liam's dead,' stated Control, 'Presumed murdered, I'm very sorry.'

Mater didn't hear a word beyond dead.

'You're joking, C', is all he could muster, forgetting his boss's position for a moment.

'Phil, I am not.'

'I apologise sir, I butted in, please carry on.'

'Liam's dead, probably assassinated.' Control repeated, pausing to allow the words to sink in, watching Mater's reaction before continuing.

'Happened not long after meeting Simon and receiving his safe house instructions. Looks as if he was poisoned with a rapidly acting drug injected into him. I directed a team to investigate and their CCTV video analysis identified two men who feature in footage from Liam's hotel. They are also seen along the route Liam took to Paddington and in Euston Square tube station where he was killed. They remain our main suspects.

'Then where did they go?' interrupted Mater. His teeth bit the inside of his lower lip. He tasted blood but felt no pain.

'That's the problem, Phil. They're seen leaving the underground and climbing aboard a number 73 bus heading towards Victoria station. We even have on-board images. They are clearly heavily disguised, but it is possible to make out some useful features. However, we lose them after they leave the bus, one stop before Grosvenor Place. I'm sure they were aware of the extensive surveillance around the Palace and at the railway station.'

'And the others?' asked Mater, 'Are they safe?'

'We believe so. You'll be relieved to hear that we've had confirmation that they in good hands.'

Mater was indeed reassured. Charlotte, Tiny and himself, separated and scattered. Safely hidden but how long would they have to lie low?

'Sir, I have a question, no, many questions but I'll start with the obvious.'

'Go ahead Phil. I told you if I have the answers I will give them.'

Mater's lip had stopped bleeding but throbbed. He swallowed a large slug of whisky, numbing his mouth and throat.

'Someone must have known about Simon's meeting with Liam or at least identified where he stayed and where he was heading.'

'Yes, it is likely they knew he booked into the Renaissance Hotel but he may simply have been followed after he left.'

'A broader question, boss: Are any other units within the service being subjected to this attack or has my team been singled out for this 'special treatment'?' Mater's cool was slowly fracturing, his voice sarcastic and tremulous.

Control hesitated briefly. 'The leak could have identified others. We anticipated after the Docherty incident we would face a much bigger problem, but it appears that yours is the only one to be attacked.'

'Up to now,' interjected Mater.

'Yes, you're right. To date there haven't been any incidents involving other units. In that respect so far, so good, but, of course, I am not complacent, Phil. Apart from believing it is only right and proper I should deliver the news about Liam in person and provide you with some clarification, I also need your help.'

'Clarification, sir', exclaimed Mater, adding, 'All seems as clear as mud to me.'

Control recognised the concealed stress. He spoke gently and with praise. 'Phil, I always value your contribution. Your attributes are admirable and your consistent efforts have helped the Office deal effectively with many threats. Others might have failed or given up when the shit flew, but not you. But we're up to our necks in it now but if you have any ideas of how we could solve this, I'm listening.'

Control reached across and picked up the whisky bottle. He went to pour for them both. This time, Mater did not resist. They sat quietly for a few moments, sipping the fine malt, taking in the peace that the sanctuary of Langley Hall offered. An owl hooted in the woods near to the house. The dogs hardly stirred on the hearth. It seemed, at that moment to Mater, the violence that had enveloped his unit was surreal; product of a bad dream.

Finally, the silence between was broken.

'Sir, I have an idea. Give me the night to think on it and I hope to have a proposal for you by the morning, at least the outline of a plan.'

Control smiled. 'Good man, Phil. If it has any potential, you can count on my full support and all necessary resources. We must nip this in the bud.'

'But,' said Mater, 'I have one further subject to discuss before we eat. When are Liam's and Mick's funerals to be held?'

Control, having failed to anticipate the question, shifted uneasily in his seat. 'I'm sorry, Phil, Mick has been buried already. The funeral was held last Tuesday. We couldn't risk bringing any of you into the open.'

Mater swallowed hard. He recognised that once you died that was it. But he wanted to do what was right. To comfort Mick's ex and tell her he had been a brave, reliable colleague and most importantly a true friend. He paused to take it all in and then followed up 'And Liam's, sir?'

'Not organised yet. The body can't be released until investigations are complete. For now, though, it would be unwise for you to attend. If circumstances improve, I will, of course, keep you posted.'

Mater's glass was about empty. He downed the remaining whisky and immediately poured himself another healthy measure.

'Thank you, sir.'

There was a knock and the Major popped his head around the lounge door.

'If it's a suitable moment, dinner is served,' he announced.

'Excellent, perfect timing, we've just finished,' responded Control, feeling hungry. The two men drained their whisky glasses, rose and headed to the dining room. Mater stood to one side to allow Control to enter before him.

'No please, after you, Phil,' he said, patting Mater firmly on the shoulder and guiding him in. 'My best agent needs to be fed first.'

As expected, dinner was not haute cuisine but acceptable. The Major mainly cooked for himself during the many years since his wife's death. He had learnt to create a limited range of dishes, most of which, he described as 'man food'. There was little subtlety in the presentation of the fillet steak and roast vegetables but plenty of calories, added to by the two bottles of excellent red gifted by Control. Desert was, it was agreed by all, surprisingly good. On finishing, the Major admitted it had been the creation of Mrs Robinson. As the evening wore on the conversation became increasingly light-hearted: Control and Mater managing to put more serious business to one side. They had no choice anyway; their host needed to be kept in the dark. Naturally the Major understood he could not be party to any aspect of his guests' work. He simply enjoyed their company. The three returned to the lounge for brandy and cigars, talking beyond midnight. At half past, Mater excused himself, leaving the older friends joking and laughing together. As he climbed the stairs to his room, Mater's thoughts turned to the idea that had evolved earlier. He would sleep on it, rise early, run and while exercising he hoped the details would fall into place.

Mater's night was not restful. Whether this was due to the alcohol, the information imparted by Control or the need to develop his plan, he wasn't sure. He had been plagued by visions of his team. In his dreams, he saw a line-up of them, armed and ready for action. As his eyes scanned across, looking at the familiar faces, red crosses appeared, obliterating first Mick, then Liam followed by Tiny and Charlotte. As the ink began to stain his own image he woke yet again, sweating. He recognised it as a dream that did not represent reality, but the threat to him and his remaining colleagues was certainly real. Mick's death remained unexplained but the cause of Liam's crystal clear. Mater rose from his bed and dressed. His running kit left something to be desired: old tennis shorts, long walking socks, a T-shirt from the Royal Horticultural Society; too small. The Major had provided the best he had. Fortunately, he had packed his own trainers. His head thumped, but he decided the cool air outside, coupled with an equally cold shower after his run, would help clear his mind. He quietly descended the stairs, padded through the kitchen past two sleepy hounds, opened the backdoor and stepped out into the bright winter sunshine.

On his return, as he turned the door handle, he smelt bacon and coffee.

'Good morning, beautiful day,' he said as he slipped off his muddy shoes.

The Major was busy at the cooker, frying. 'Morning Mr Randall, your boss is waiting for you back in the lounge. He requests you join him. I've poured you a coffee. Take your time; the food can be kept warm on the hob.'

Mater took the mug, noting with some irony, that 'Keep Calm and Carry On' was printed around it. *Wonder if C had chosen that one especially for me?* he mused.

As Mater entered, Control, once again in an armchair, looked up from a novel he was reading. 'Rarely get the chance in the mornings,' he said, closing the book and waving it in the air. 'Slept well, Phil?'

'No, not particularly, sir, but thank you for asking. Did you?'

'Like a log, always like a log when I'm here. Got anything for me, I'm all ears?'

Mater finished his coffee and began to summarise the current situation as he understood it. Control listened, occasionally offering a little more detail or background. A hack of the service's IT system had resulted in a limited leak of personal information including data about Mater's team. Two colleagues had died: one murdered, without doubt, the other's demise unexplained but foul play suspected. As yet, no suspect or suspects identified. It was assumed that an internal security failure was more likely than an external attack because of the unique separation of the computer systems. There were, however, two men, seen on CCTV who, in all probability, had been involved in Liam's death. Presently they were off the radar. It would be prudent to assume that there remained a severe threat to Charlotte, Tiny and Mater himself.

Control nodded in agreement, impatiently. 'And your plan, Phil?'

'I would like to return to my own home with Tiny and Charlotte. If our enemy has full information as to our aliases including our addresses, it's only a matter of time before they attack. I wouldn't be surprised if our houses weren't being staked out as we speak.'

Control butted in. 'We are, of course, keeping a watch in the environs of your homes but so far nothing unusual has been reported. I do ask for a daily sit rep.'

'But that's the problem, sir, if I may say so. If, we are victims of a rotten apple within the service, then quite possibly they know where and when monitoring is happening. But if they think the Office perceives the threat has passed, then conceivably they might choose to strike but we will be ready for them. This could be achieved by lowering the state of alert and re-establishing normal routines.'

Control sat thinking for a few moments, frowning. 'Still risky Phil. I'm sure you are angry but I sense revenge. Your actions should not be coloured by emotion.'

'You're right, sir, this is vengeance but right now we're sitting ducks. This whole affair, as you have explained it, has seriously damaged the Office's effectiveness. Rest assured I am not being emotional, simply practical. Of course, if you have an alternative approach in mind?'

He waited patiently for Control to decide. Control sat with his fingers interlocked and stroked his chin with a forefinger. 'Alright Phil, we'll go with your idea. It's clearly dangerous but as yet I've nothing better. I'll arrange for Tiny and Charlotte to be informed. When do want you to proceed?'

Mater was already itching for action. 'I suggest in three or four days. Gives the others a chance to sort things wherever they are and you, Chief, time to return to base and authorise arming us.'

'That sounds reasonable. I should inform them myself and check they are happy with the plan too. Give me a kit list and I will personally make the requisition and deliver it here. But whether you like it or not, I intend to arrange a back-up team to be in the near vicinity, ready to help out on your call.'

Mater was concerned. 'To do that, sir, involves more of your staff. If the traitor is still at work, then inevitably, the cat will be out of the proverbial bag. I would prefer if we took our own chances.'

Control knew Mater couldn't be persuaded, there would be no point in trying to change his mind.

'You are courageous, Phil, and maybe, sometimes a little crazy.'

'Definitely the latter, sir, but then I wouldn't be working in your organisation if I wasn't, would I?'

Control smiled broadly. 'Cheeky bugger. Get in touch with a regular sit rep, even if it's simply to confirm you're still alive; weekly would be fine. You should contact me via my radiopager using different public phones. Now, breakfast. Let's eat. The Major's bacon will be crisp and eggs solid.'

The Major was delighted that his friend was leaving only temporarily. 'I'll leave your bedroom as is,' he said. Control departed mid-morning, Mater's kit list safe in his bag. He wasn't used to being the subordinate in an operation; those days had long gone, but as he drove away, he realised he was really quite enjoying the concept. He was going to be busy over the next twenty-four hours and not at his desk for a change. It made him feel young again.

Mater was pleased too. He was appreciating the peace of Langley Hall but it couldn't last and he was keen to meet up with Charlotte and Tiny. There was also the matter of his secret belongings at the cottage. The Major was generous and loyal but Mater didn't wish to impose on him or his generosity for too long. Another day or two and he would be gone.

Chapter 8

Tiny and Charlotte were surprised by Control's visits. His proposal, as he described it, seemed fraught with danger and they assumed this was why he asked for their agreement rather than, as would be routine, issuing an order. Tiny smelt a rat.

'Sounds like something M dreamt up,' he said, 'Probably just wants to get back home and to his own bed.'

Control chuckled. 'When you see him, you can interrogate him yourself, Tiny,' is all he offered.

Charlotte was intrigued. None of the team had ever visited or stayed at each other's addresses. They limited their knowledge of each other's lives to facets that made their joint cover stories ring true and no more. If anyone were to be captured during a mission, then they would only be able to disclose the truths they knew. However, Mater always delivered so, with little hesitation, they agreed. They would meet and be briefed by him and then be ushered into his real life. Evidently, it wasn't going to be a routine operation.

On Control's return to London he held an urgent meeting with Simon and other members of senior management. They discussed, at length, the slow progress in the investigation to find the source of the computer hack and the anticipated effect of limiting operations across the board. The unanimous conclusion was the leak was localised, the head of the Office's IT team confident that the affected systems had been reviewed, secured and reinforced.

'Any further information about Docherty's death?' asked Control, his question directed primarily at the Forensics Division.

'Nothing new sir. The Coke can appears to be a red herring – no traces of toxins.'

'But its manufacture?' interjected Control.

The forensic scientist coughed nervously. 'I am sorry to report; we don't have an answer to that. We have no idea where it came from.'

Control looked surprised, but was keen not to detract from the real purpose of his meeting. 'Keep working on it, please Ken. This afternoon I shall brief the Home and Foreign secretaries. Our sister agencies will be there. They would not wish to hear that our operational capability is diminished. Gentlemen and lady, I propose we allow each of our teams to start work again. They should be told an atypical threat may persist and so should be even more vigilant both here and abroad. Consequently, if any individual wishes to withdraw their labour either temporarily or permanently, this should be permitted without a stain on their character or commitment. I must be informed at once if anything starts to go awry. These are interesting times. Any objections?'

The assembled remained silent.

'Excellent. Let's get to it and good luck everyone.'

As the team rose and made to leave, Control called after Simon. 'A moment, please Simon.'

They left the conference room and entered Control's elegantly panelled office. To the side of his desk a huge picture window offered a magnificent view of the Thames and its river traffic slowly floating by. Despite the armoured glass, the architects had decreed the head of service should not position himself directly in front of it. There was a limit to the builder's guarantee when it came to penetrating weapons. The desk always tidy and ordered, reflected his personality and work ethic. The rest of the room quite bare: photographs of earlier incumbents, low chairs around a modest coffee table, a cocktail cabinet in one corner and a large video screen on the wall opposite where he sat. He indicated to Simon to sit. Control remained standing as he spoke, occasionally walking to the window to gaze outside.

'When you met each of Mater's team, did you notice anything unusual, something different?' he asked.

Simon thought for a while. 'No, sir. Naturally they were surprised when told about the leak and, perhaps quite reasonably, expressed concern for themselves, their colleagues and others who knew their cover personas.'

Control paused and watched a rubbish laden barge being towed down river. 'The problem is I wonder if we are barking up the wrong tree. Our hypothesis is we've been the victim of an electronic assault but what if that assumption is incorrect, it being simply a way to distract us? What if,' he hesitated again, 'there is a traitor close to Mater? Are you sure, none of M's team could be responsible?'

Simon had considered this possibility himself and was ready with an answer. 'Sir, the tech specialists identified malware in the system and nobody from our specialist units ever visits the Office. It would be necessary for someone within M's unit to be in regular direct contact with staff at the centre. Obviously, I do accept each operative is very well trained in subterfuge. Even with my experienced eye the probability of anyone making a slip would be low. I have been watching for clues and seen nothing so far. Look at the Cambridge crew. Took years for the truth to emerge.'

'You're right. I just hoped you may have come across something that you hadn't wished to bring up at this morning's meeting.'

Simon felt slightly uneasy. *What was Control implying? Was he hinting at his own possible involvement?* He decided to change the subject. 'Good weekend, sir?' he asked.

Control was still staring at him but his mind seemed elsewhere. His face broke into a smile but Simon didn't find it reassuring.

'Excellent, thank you, most enjoyable.' Control gave nothing away. 'Thanks for your help, Simon. As ever, my door's open if you have anything to report. That's all.'

Simon got up, taking his briefing papers with him and walked from the room, gently closing the heavy door behind him.

Control set to work. He had the ministerial meeting later in the day but he also had to fit in a discreet trip to the armoury in Battersea. He pushed a button on the intercom on his desk and called in Elizabeth.

'Lizzie, be a darling, bring me a coffee and a decent snack. I need to go through my diary.'

'Certainly, sir,' came the immediate reply.

He noted the intonation in the 'sir'. He always teased Elizabeth by calling her Lizzie or Betty or Beth or Lisbeth but never Elizabeth. When first employed as his PA, it annoyed, even enraged her until she realised that it was his way of showing affection. The 'darling' bit the cherry on the cake but she always got her own back.

A few minutes later there was a knock on the door and she entered carrying a small silver tray laden with a steaming cafetière, a china cup and an apple.

'There you are sir,' she said placing it on his desk.

Control pointed at the fruit. 'Lizzie, what's that?' he demanded.

'Waistline, sir, waistline. You asked me to look after you to the best of my ability.'

Control snorted. He knew she was right. He was significantly overweight but fruit. 'How thoughtful Lizzie, so kind, thank you,' he said somewhat sarcastically. 'Please note, after the ministerial meeting this afternoon, I'm going to visit some of our London facilities, just to keep them on their toes. Today, anyone can contact me but, in confidence to you, I won't be available tomorrow or the next day. Blood pressure's up and Doc's recommended a few tests. I think they call it a 'well man check'.' He laughed, dismissively. 'Unless the proverbial really hits the fan, direct any requests to Simon or Anthony. I'll carry my pager again.'

Control had no intention of having his blood pressure measured now or in the near future. 'Bloody quacks', his position when it came to healthcare. He found it bad enough having the prostate investigated even if the finger probing was accompanied by the whistles and bells of private medicine. He had kept Elizabeth in the dark about that.

Much to his relief, the scheduled ministers' intelligence briefing passed without too much hassle. Control had expected searching questions relating to the Office's reduced activity, but he reported that his management team's opinion suggested the problem was well on the way to being resolved. Normal routines were being re-established. He noted raised eyebrows from representatives of the sister services and, of course, Sir Cyril Wentworth from 5 made a sarcastic comment but he could cope with a little teasing.

At half past four, Control commenced his lightning review. He really had only one target destination, but it was important that this didn't become obvious to his driver or the bodyguard travelling with him. The staff based at the bunker by Heathrow were surprised to see the chief. The facility was kept in readiness in the event headquarters became unserviceable. Its location near to the airport and RAF Northolt provided transport flexibility. Control explained to the bunker's occupants that he was performing a routine surprise visit so that he could be sure taxpayers' funds were being spent wisely. He asked a few pertinent questions and departed leaving everyone somewhat perplexed.

A fast drive followed, back along the M4 and around the South Circular Road to Crystal Palace, his car pulling up outside the new satellite relay station. The Thames building had its rooftop communications equipment, but this was exposed and deemed vulnerable. Landline links had been established with Crystal Palace duplicating the technology required for reliable contact with other friendly agencies. Their proximity made it easy for specialist technicians to maintain both. There were, of course, further facilities beyond London but today, for Control, the one nearby offered suitable cover.

His final request was to be driven to the service's combined garage and armoury. The armoury lay behind and under a service station built into three railway arches off the Portslade Road. It was a front, of course, offering good service to the local population and an even better response to Office demands. Within these caverns, experienced engineers, with backgrounds in motor sport, ensured Office vehicles were reliable, fast and adapted as necessary for special roles. A steel door was built into the back wall of the middle arch. It appeared to be welded shut. In fact, operation of an electronic key and knowledge of where in the room to place it, triggered the door to open quietly and effortlessly; sliding back on well-greased bearings. In addition, a grubby intercom connected the garage to the member of staff who beavered away in the armoury.

Control suggested to his driver and bodyguard that during this visit they take a break and find themselves a cup of tea. It had been a busy afternoon and inside he would be safe.

The mechanics were delighted to see Control. They were working on an old Volvo estate that had been souped up and armoured. They were, as ever, proud of their achievements and welcomed feedback from the boss. He demonstrated a keen interest in the vehicle, gave a glowing report and offered further encouragement. Although it was already mid-evening, they wanted to finish the vehicle's alterations. Control left them to it and moved over to the garage's office. Here he spoke into the intercom, softly uttering the required password and then walked to the back of the workshop and waited patiently by the reinforced door. After a few minutes it opened, fluorescent light from within flooding the entrance and the sound of jazz escaped through the doorway.

Stanley, the armourer, stood beaming. 'Great to have you back, chief, please come in. What can I do for you?'

'Good evening, Stan. Still listening to that stuff; always know when you're on duty.'

Stanley and Control had known each other for nearly three decades. Control, with his prior military training, had joined the Office with standard weapons knowledge. Stanley, who had already been in post for a few years, rapidly discovered the new recruit lacked experience with the unique firearms and explosives used in special operations. But Control had been an enthusiastic and quick learner, which pleased him. They soon became close friends within the limitations imposed by the job. Control's ultimate promotion stopped the armourer calling the boss by his first name; demonstrating his respect with 'chief'.

'Hope you are keeping well Stan and being let out occasionally. No windows lead to a lack of Vitamin D.'

Control explained that, in response to a question from a minister, he was carrying out a rapid review of Office facilities, but in short, he had a specific request. He glanced around. The armoury was full, each high powered standard issue or specialist weapon secured in its specific place in racks. With the temporary lull in service activity most of the armaments had been returned. It gave Stanley a welcome opportunity to carry out routine maintenance. He was, as ever, keen to help but concerned when Control handed over Mater's shopping list.

'Chief, this doesn't have any of the usual authorisation,' he said, turning the paper over and over in his hand.

Control had already considered this might be Stanley's initial response. It was fundamentally reassuring, but he needed access to the weapons. He decided to play the loyalty card first. Later, if necessary, he could issue an order.

'Stan, that's admirable; following the rules to the letter. I'll put that in my report. But, today is different. Within these walls, just between you and me, I need you do to something. I'm only asking you because we have worked together for so long. I have a unique situation that needs resolving urgently. I have operatives facing problems that are taxing them more than you can imagine. Makes my field work from days past seem like a picnic. I would be grateful if you would assist. Lives depend on it.'

Stanley thought for a while, unhappy about breaking regulations but keen to help his colleague and friend. 'What about the records, Chief? There are regular audits.'

Control placed his hand on Stanley's shoulder, trying to reassure him. 'Stan, there's to be no record. Records have dropped us into the brown stuff. We don't need more. My wellies aren't big enough! This stays just between us. You have my word.'

Stanley paused again. The end of his career was approaching, and he looked forward to a quieter life. 'OK, Chief, but if this goes tits up and I lose my pension, I'll be forever knocking on your door asking for handouts. Promised the missus holidays and sunshine in our twilight years and as you've told me, sunlight would do me good. When do you need the kit?'

'Later this evening, please Stan. Could you pack it all for me to collect here by eleven tonight?'

'Bloody hell,' exclaimed Stanley before checking himself. 'Sorry. Must be urgent. Of course, it will be ready. I suggest we meet outside. The garage will be shut and unless there's been a drama, the on-call mechanics should be tucked up in their beds. But when you come back, if the lights are on, park around the corner in Dickens St. Although there it is a bit more exposed, so take care.'

'Thanks Stan. This mission is really important and don't worry you will see the sun. Have to make sure none of my staff develop rickets. And when you do eventually hand in your resignation, I'll give you recordings of Mahler's complete works. That's proper music. See you later.'

He patted Stanley firmly on the shoulder and departed, the volume of jazz rising behind him as the steel door slid closed again.

Control asked his driver to drop him at his club in Park Place. He didn't enter but loitered in the foyer for a few minutes before turning around and heading back down the weathered sandstone steps into the street. He hailed a taxi, requesting it take him in the direction of his home. About a quarter of a mile from his London residence, he asked the cabbie to stop, paid, stepped out and walked home.

At his house, he unlocked the front door and poked his head into the living room where his wife Alexandra sat watching a drama on the television. She accepted, yet again, his apology for missing their wedding anniversary. He climbed the stairs to their bedroom and repacked his bag. When he came down, Alex was waiting to see him go. He kissed her, asked if he could borrow her Mercedes and without waiting for an answer took the keys from the desk in the hall and headed out again. He had been home less than half an hour. Alone once more, she curled up on the sofa, heard the car engine start in the driveway, sighed and with a press of a button on the remote control, returned to another life.

Chapter 9

The handover of the firearms and ancillary equipment from Stanley to Control went ahead as planned outside the garage and without incident. There was no sign of anyone else during the few minutes it took to load Control's wife's Mercedes red coupé. The kit was innocently packed in cardboard boxes labelled as car parts. If any nosey passer-by had noticed, they might have assumed the two men were involved in the motor trade; possibly handling stolen goods.

'Whatever, you're up to, good luck Chief,' were the only words spoken between them.

Control climbed back into the driver's seat, gave a wink and a thumbs up before pressing the ignition button and disappeared into the gloom of the lane. Stanley had no idea when his kit would be returned, though he hoped it would be soon as a check of the armoury by the Office's security staff was overdue.

The duration of Control's return journey to Langley Hall was as calculated. The routine use of the cruise control stopped him from speeding. His journey was punctuated by the two unavoidable 'prostate stops', as he referred to them. During one he bought a couple of sandwiches and the largest bag of crisps he could find. Neither Alex nor Elizabeth were there to scold him. He arrived, exhausted, just before dawn. All of Norton-le Clay's residents were asleep in their beds as the Mercedes purred quietly through the village. Even the Major's dogs struggled to muster a bark when he rang the Hall's doorbell. It was Mater who answered it.

'Welcome back, sir, successful trip?'

'Yes thank you, Phil. I have procured everything you requested. All in the boot. But I don't think it would be wise to leave it in the Mercedes.' He yawned. 'If you wouldn't mind, could you move it? I'll take my bag and then I am off to bed. I'm knackered. Please wake me when the Major makes breakfast. I can survive with little shut-eye but not reduced rations. Good night.' He handed Mater the car keys.

'Sleep well, sir, and thank you,' replied Mater.

Mater carried the kit to his bedroom. Opening the boxes alone in the early morning, he was like a young child who wakes on Christmas Day to find the filled stocking at the foot of their bed. Unable to resist the temptation, they open each present, laying them out in neat rows. Mater checked the contents against his mental list. Everything there: two suppressed Heckler and Koch MP7 A2s, each with four thirty round magazines and a single Brugger & Thornet APR 308 sniper rifle also fitted with a silencer and night-sight. Stanley had also provided plenty of ammunition, along with two sets of night vision goggles, three combat knives, a case of smoke grenades, radios and webbing.

He carefully repacked the boxes and climbed back into bed. *Well done, C,* he thought, *First stage completed. Now we're cooking.*

Mater and his boss descended to the kitchen mid-morning, finding the Major ensconced in the previous day's newspaper with two dogs curled around his feet.

'Good day, gentlemen. I hope you managed to catch up on your rest. I heard you arrive, Paul. Safe journey?'

Control felt re-invigorated and like Mater was eager to get proceedings underway.

'Yes, thank you, straightforward.'

'Good, good,' said the Major, 'I'll knock you up breakfast, leave you to discuss whatever and then we can reconvene for lunch. Coffee's in the pot,' he added, waving his arm towards the Aga.

Control didn't wish to offend his friend but time was precious. 'Thanks but I'll have to decline the offer of lunch. I'm very sorry I will need to depart as soon as I have had discussions with Mr Randall. Duty calls as ever.'

'Understood,' responded the Major, disappointed.

After breakfast, another of the Major's renowned fry-ups, Mater and Control returned to the lounge with mugs of coffee. Their host remained in the kitchen and opened his paper where he had left off. The chief spoke first.

'I hope I brought everything you requested. I intend to visit Tiny and Charlotte again and brief them. I suggest you three get together soon and travel to your home. This morning, I will drive us into Harrogate. There, I will hire a vehicle under one of my pseudonyms. This will be for your use during the operation. I have five thousand pounds of Office funds with me. Should be enough to keep you going. When you need more, page me using a public phone box, and we will arrange to meet again. Likewise, if you require anything else or have an update, contact me by the same mechanism. We have no idea how long this will go on for, or even if the bait will be taken. And, Phil, gentle with the hire car please. I don't want any unnecessary complications.'

Mater was keen to get started. 'Sounds good to me sir. If, Tiny, Charlotte and I were to rendezvous in Central Manchester would that fit conveniently with their current locations?'

'Would be fine. It doesn't matter where they are. They, I'm sure, will join you at a place and time of your choosing.'

Mater thought for a moment. 'Ok, let's make it in two days time at 2pm. Information desk, Manchester Piccadilly.'

Control freshened up in his bedroom, checked his false driving license, packed and joined Mater and the Major in the hall. He shook the Major's hand warmly. 'As ever, can't thank you enough for your hospitality and discretion. And once again, I'm sorry to be torn away so soon. Dinner on me, at my club, next time you are in London. Keep in touch. Mr Randall will be back shortly.'

The Major nodded. 'Always a pleasure Paul, never a chore.'

He watched the two men climb into the Mercedes and with a spin of wheels, gravel flew as it disappeared up the driveway, leaving shallow gorges. The Major, as a stickler for order, muttered to himself, 'Poor clutch control. Better get the bloody rake out.'

Less than an hour later, Control handed over his licence at the car rental desk. 'Don't worry about reducing the insurance excess,' he said, smiling brightly to the assistant. 'I'm a very careful grey haired driver.' He glanced across and raised his eyebrows to Mater.

'Are you planning to take the vehicle off-road?' asked the ever-helpful lady. 'There may be a cleaning charge, if you do.'

Least of my worries, thought Control. 'That's fine, I understand. You've been most accommodating, thank you,' he said, offering his credit card as a deposit.

'Perfect, Mr Somerville. The vehicle's full of fuel. Have a safe trip.'

Mater and Control drove the Mercedes, and the hired Toyota Landcruiser a mile or two before stopping in a layby on the outskirts of Harrogate. They shook hands, swapped vehicles and went their separate ways. Mater would be back at Langley Hall in time for a late lunch. Control headed to Scotland: he would visit Charlotte first before travelling almost the entire length of the country to give Tiny his instructions. He didn't enjoy driving long distances anymore but at least once he reached the highlands he could put his foot down; his wife's car had poke when conditions allowed.

Chapter 10

Mater spent the next day thinking and preparing. The assumption was that his operatives had been identified with all recorded details relating to their false identities exposed. This included their cover histories, financial transactions, private vehicles and home addresses. The problem was, as he viewed it, that after decades of living as another person, this other life had become real. So, although old friends and family contacts remained protected, those working as or near the agents were now under threat – as the two appalling deaths had clearly demonstrated. He considered the motive behind the attacks. Revenge was a possibility. They had certainly made many enemies over the years: terrorists, drug smugglers or foreign spies, some of whom were undoubtedly still alive and active. Or perhaps the data loss had been opportunistic; Mater and his team not specific targets but a convenient mechanism to disrupt the whole organisation. Either way, disruption had occurred, even if Control had taken the brave decision to restart operations. Mater decided to work on the premise that his unit was the primary target. He preferred his battles to be personal. If he was right, then it was likely that the attackers were from overseas, probably from one of the dozen or so countries that Mater had operated in. It was, therefore, also probable they would want to complete their mission within the shortest time possible and disappear. To stay in the UK longer than necessary risked exposure by accident or design. *So*, he concluded, *if there are to be hostile visits to any of our homes they should happen soon. And, if they call at my cottage, as I hope they do, we will be ready for them.*

On Friday morning he packed, intending to depart before Mrs Robinson made her weekly visit to Langley Hall. The Major kept out of the way. With the Landcruiser loaded and Mater having double-checked his bedroom suite for any personal items, he caught up with him, sitting as usual in the warmth of the kitchen.

'Ready for the off, Mr Randall?' he asked.

'Yes, I think so. Thank you again for your generous hospitality.'

'A pleasure, the least I could do. I have always been, and always will be, a patriot.'

'I'm sure you've demonstrated that many times over the years, Major.'

The Major stood up. 'I'll see you off the premises,' he said, 'Oh, and I have something for you.'

In the hall, he opened the drawer of the antique rosewood desk in which he kept his keys and the dog leads. From the back, he pulled out a Makarov 9mm automatic pistol and handed it to a surprised Mater.

'Souvenir; from my days living on the wrong side of the Berlin Wall. Please take the weapon. It is loaded but I'm afraid I only have the single magazine. Looked after me. It's probably why I am still here able to speak to you. My talisman. Whatever, you're working on; I hope it guards you too. You can give it back when you succeed.'

Mater took the gun, noting how worn it appeared. He checked the safety catch was on and turned to the Major. 'Thank you. I will indeed take care of it and return it as soon as possible. Good bye, Major.'

Mater climbed into the Landcruiser, slipped the pistol into the glove-box, started the engine and drove slowly away. As he headed up the driveway, he saw, in his rear-view mirror, Langley Hall's sole resident standing to attention at the top of the steps. To each side of him sat his dogs, obedient and motionless. The Major appeared to salute.

Mater activated the car's sat nav and entered the postcode for his chosen carpark in Boad St, adjacent to Manchester Piccadilly. Next, he switched on the radio and settled down for the drive across the Pennines. He aimed to be in the station, monitoring the information desk, no later than 1.50 that afternoon. No rush. Snow over high ground was forecast but the Landcruiser would cope with that.

Mater arrived in central Manchester in good time, the anticipated bad weather failing to cause delays on the motorway, and parked as planned. He had a few minutes to walk to the station concourse. He hesitated before exiting the vehicle. No-one seemed to have followed him into the car park but he opened the glove box, deciding to take the Makarov with him as a precaution. It was raining, almost sleet. Mater pulled his collar up and put his hands in his pockets. As he walked he could feel the grip of the pistol tucked into his trousers. It wasn't secreted in the ideal location should he need it in a hurry, but he felt reassured by being armed.

Once on the concourse, Mater bought a magazine in a newsagent and chose a bench a little way from the information desk with an unobstructed view of it. He noted a couple looking confused by the advice being provided by an assistant working behind the counter. Mater assumed they were from the Far East, perhaps Chinese. They were short and elderly. *Definitely doesn't fit the description of Liam's assailants,* he thought, relaxing slightly.

He opened the magazine and flicked through the pages, looking up every minute or so. Just before 2pm two familiar figures, each carrying a small holdall, independently approached the counter. They stood, one behind the other, forming a queue behind the Chinese couple, still struggling to understand the advice being given. Mater closed his magazine, rose and strode towards them.

'Can I help you?' he asked Tiny and Charlotte, 'I have information you might find most useful. Follow me.'

They both smiled; relieved that Control's instructions had worked. The three headed across the concourse and out of the station, Mater checking they weren't being followed, clasping his hidden weapon. He suddenly felt a tremendous responsibility. His team, or what remained of it, had been re-united and he was in charge again. Once they were safely in the car, there was communal shoulder slapping and they could speak freely. Mater reached inside his trousers, retrieved the pistol and asked Tiny, seated in the passenger seat, to return it to the glove-box.

'Interesting piece, M,' he said, turning it over in his hands, 'Where did you get it?'

Mater grinned. 'From a good friend who wishes us well.' He started the Landcruiser, drove to the exit, paid the attendant and merged with the mid-afternoon Manchester traffic.

'Nice motor,' commented Tiny, 'Yours?'

'On our pay? You're joking Tiny. No, hired by a Mr. Somerville AKA our boss. He's very worried that I'll scratch it.'

Tiny and Charlotte laughed.

'Least of his worries at this moment, I would have thought,' quipped Charlotte.

After they joined the M6 southbound, the banter stopped, and the conversation became serious. Mater brought up the deaths of Mick and Liam, asking the others to comment. It was important that each of them had the opportunity to express their feelings about the losses. Tiny was clearly livid and ready for revenge. Charlotte's response was more measured, her thoughts sorrowful and tinged with regret. But no doubt she felt guilty about being a survivor. Mater drove on, not commenting on or criticising his friends' opinions. When the discussion faltered, he stepped in.

'I'm also, as you might expect, both sad and angry beyond words. Stating the obvious, there's nothing we can do to bring them back. So we must direct our efforts to finding the bastards who did this, and deal with them in the way we have been trained to. As always, the boss would like them taken alive; handed over for interrogation. That is our primary aim, but if there is contact and we have no choice, kill without hesitation. It is likely that we are being targeted as well, so self-preservation comes first.'

Mater filled in details of the strategy he had outlined to Control. When he finished, he asked if there were any questions.

'Who in the Office knows about our plan?' asked Charlotte.

Mater was pleased that his idea had been changed from 'his' to 'our' plan. Joint ownership was more likely to lead to success. 'As far as I am aware, only the chief.'

'Does that imply there isn't back-up, no-one sitting in the wings, briefed, ready to help if needed?'

'Yep, precisely,' replied Mater. There was no point beating about the bush.

'Bloody hell, M, that may mean it's an all-or-nothing mission.'

Mater eyeballed Charlotte in the rear-view mirror. 'If you think we might have underestimated our enemy and could be killed, then the answer is naturally yes but I don't intend departing this world any time soon.'

Tiny butted in. 'Do we have a full tool box?' he enquired.

'It should be more than adequate. Everything is in the boot. We'll unpack and check everything as soon as we arrive.'

'When do we get there, wherever we are going?' asked Tiny, 'I need a piss.'

Mater decided to play a game with his colleagues. 'Twenty questions, all geographical. See if you can locate my home. Once you've got it, I'll pull over at the next services.'

It was late evening when they crossed into Kent, rock music blaring from the car's infotainment system. Tiny had coped with Classic FM for just over an hour until finally warning that unless Mater changed the bloody station, the whole mission was off. Mater obliged even though Tiny's choice would never be his own. *Need a happy team,* he thought to himself.

Mater's home village of Wormstead lay about halfway between the market towns of Maidstone and Ashford, with the latter's useful link to the Eurostar rail line. A paradigm of English rural life. A steady drive south-east along the familiar M2 and they would be there before midnight.

'We're almost there,' said Mater to the others, who were dozing. 'From the moment we arrive, we are to stay on high alert. I will drive the car through the village before entering Primrose Lane. We need to see if anything or anyone seems out of place. It should be quiet; the pub closes at eleven. Then I will stop at the end of the lane. There you should don the NVGs and arm yourselves with the MP7s. When we enter the driveway to the cottage, lights off, exit the vehicle just as it stops and check the perimeter of the house. You'll find a stone path runs all the way around. There is no external illumination; it is always safer in the dark and I love seeing the stars on a clear night. It was one of the main reasons why I chose to live in such an isolated place. Tiny, pass me the Makarov. I'll wait for you at the front door. When you reappear, I'll open it and then we will effect a rapid entry. Find someone inside, ask questions later. Understood?'

'Yes, boss,' came the simultaneous reply. This was a routine procedure for them all.

Wormstead was as expected, peaceful and quiet. Mater drove slowly, enabling the vehicle's occupants to check for anything unusual. He would have liked to have made a second run but if any residents' prying eyes peaked through gaps in curtains, they might become suspicious of a crawling car. It was a neighbourhood-watch zone and burglaries had been a problem for many. He headed out of the village for five miles to the junction of the B road with Primrose Lane, turned left onto the short farm

103

track which led to an open fallow field. He knew the area like the back of his hand.

'Right, we should be hidden here. Let's arm ourselves. The cottage lies at the end of a hundred metre track roughly half a click away.' The team got out of the vehicle, the frosty night winter air inducing clouds of vapour as they breathed.

'Bloody freezing,' commented Tiny. 'Hope your home has central heating.'

'You'll be lucky,' replied Mater, 'There's a stove, if you can be bothered to chop wood for it.' He pointed to the Milky Way. 'See what I mean,' he said, 'Makes it all worthwhile.'

The three went to the rear of the Landcruiser and opened its tailgate.

'The MP7s are in the medium sized boxes and the goggles in the shorter, fatter case there,' said Mater, pointing with a torch. 'When we're ready we must make sure the car's interior lights don't come on as we open the doors.'

Tiny and Charlotte checked their weapons. There really was no need. Stanley had done a meticulous job as usual. They each took two magazines, loading one. They tested the NVGs. Batteries full, straps adjusted. With the goggles activated, their world was instantly bathed in an eerie green light, as if an alien sun had risen too early. As they moved their heads to compensate for the reduced field of view, the countryside gave up its night secrets. An owl flapped past and in the far corner of the fallow field, deer grazed in the darkness, oblivious. Hills rose in the distance although the cottage itself remained hidden.

Can't see them, they can't see us, thought Charlotte.

'Should we take smoke grenades? We could fling one in as we enter, just in case,' suggested Tiny.

Mater snorted. 'Bugger off. I'm not having my house stained green and stinking. Right, are you two ready?' he asked.

His companions nodded.

'OK, let's go.'

They climbed back in the car with Tiny and Charlotte in the rear. If there was a pre-emptive strike, they had a better chance of surviving the initial assault: it would be Mater, driving, who was most likely to be hit. They turned off the vehicle's interior lights and opened then closed the doors, checking they stayed off. Mater drove slowly out of the farm track using his knowledge of the terrain and starlight to guide him home. He swung into the Cottage's driveway which rose and then fell, ending in the little dell where the cottage had been built all those centuries ago. Once over the brow of the hill, he switched off the engine and coasted. All three car occupants released their door locks and held the doors slightly ajar. Mater could see nothing parked on the drive and no light spilled from within the cottage. Tiny and Charlotte, with the advantage of the NVGs, concluded there were no signs of life in Mater's home. Mater brought the Landcruiser to a stop near the front door. Without a word, Tiny and Charlotte smoothly opened their doors wide, crept from the vehicle and headed around the building. As instructed, they followed the stone path, taking care not to make a noise, providing cover for each other. Mater stepped out and strode to the entrance, pistol in one hand, safety off, and key in the other. In less than two minutes, Tiny and Charlotte appeared beside him giving the thumbs up. They hid either side of the door as Mater quietly turned the key and gently pushed it. It opened a little and then stuck. *Shit,* he thought, *What's caused that?* He listened; still all quiet. He put his shoulder to the door and heaved. The pile of mail gave way and they were in, running room to room, checking and confirming. The cottage was empty. Mater pulled the curtains shut and switched on the lights. In the kitchen, Tiny and Charlotte removed the NVGs and made the MP7s safe. Mater placed his handgun in a sideboard drawer. It was cold inside but to Mater it was home and he was glad to be back.

'Welcome,' he said.

'Nice place,' answered Charlotte, looking around. 'Could do with a woman's touch but still attractive.'

'Sorry about the leftover washing up; had to leave in a hurry. I'll light the stove and make some tea. The wimp looks like he needs warming up', teased Mater, pointing at Tiny who had made himself comfortable in the armchair in front of the wood burner. He filled the kettle, found three mugs and continued. 'Once we've warmed up and watered, we'll pick straws as to who does the first watch. I will find my camouflaged one-man basha and some suitable extra clothing. You two bring in the rest of the kit from the Landcruiser. I suggest for sleeping, Charlotte chooses a bedroom upstairs, Tiny occupies the other and I'll doss down here on the sofa.'

The kettle clicked off, water boiled. The three sat at the kitchen table, cupping hands on the steaming mugs of black tea, sugar added.

'Service will improve,' promised Mater. 'Right, time to decide who is not going to enjoy the luxury of a duvet tonight.'

He took three matches and broke one. He held them out for the others to choose. 'Ladies first,' he said.

Charlotte tugged an unbroken match from his hand. Tiny reached forward and made his choice.

'Sods law,' he muttered.

'Who's a winner,' teased Mater again, 'Let's go over once again the plan as agreed. We'll try eight-hour OP shifts. I'll walk up the hill with you Tiny, show you the spot I have in mind and help you set up. We will need the APR with its silencer and night sight and a radio. I'll fill a thermos and find a little something to eat. Must keep a growing boy happy. Charlotte, you keep an eye from the cottage, using NVGs, until I return. Anything worrying; straight on the radio. In the morning, once it is light, Charlotte and I will lay out the audio warning system and then Charlotte can take the next stint. I'll lead you to where Tiny is hidden. After that, a trip into the village to show my face, pick up more provisions and to make it clear I'm back. The earlier the bait is placed, hopefully the sooner we can expect a bite. Our only regular visitor should be the postman; usually about 10.30 every day except Sundays. Be wary of anyone else. I'm afraid you two should stay out of sight at all times; no visits to the pub. Awkward questions could be unwelcome and if we are attacked, ideally, we want the bastards to believe I'm alone.' He looked up at the kitchen wall clock. 'It's 1.30 in the morning. Let's aim to have everything in place by 3.'

Mater and Tiny went outside and climbed the track that weaved up Burham Hill. Mater was aiming for a copse that clung to one side, three quarters of the way up, not more than 300 metres from home. The edge of the wood provided a clear view of the cottage, the end of the driveway and the junction of Primrose Lane with the village road. The intended observation post faced south-east, and weather permitting, the occupant should enjoy the sunrise, warming stiff limbs.

'Good spot,' whispered Tiny when they arrived. In almost silence, the two men rigged up the waterproof cover, camouflaging it further with vegetation until the OP merged into the terrain. They covered the ground underneath with bracken forming a natural mattress for its occupant. Tiny slid into his hideaway and set up the sniper rifle.

'Comfortable?' asked Mater.

'Fuck off,' replied Tiny, adding, 'Confirm it all looks good as you go back.'

Mater took the second set of NVGs, returned to the path and began to descend. Periodically he turned and scanned the hillside. Tiny remained hidden from view. He quietly spoke into his radio.

'You're invisible, Tiny. Charlotte will relieve you at 11 and I'll have hot water and a proper breakfast waiting for you. Take care during the exchange. The path is seldom used but you never know.'

Mater headed home, desperate for some shut-eye before he had to go into the village to show his face. He was lined up for the first evening / night shift and didn't want to risk falling asleep while occupying the OP. Charlotte heard Mater open the front door. She remained upstairs but as Mater walked back down, had moved to the other bedroom to scan the drive. He called to her.

'All's good, Charlotte. Let's turn in. I'll set an alarm for 9.'

'Night M,' came the brief reply, 'Sleep well.'

Mater opened the wood burner, filled it to the brim with seasoned logs and lit it. He lay on the sofa watching the flames gathering strength, waiting for the warmth of the stove to permeate through the kitchen cum living room. Within minutes he was asleep. On the hill above the cottage, Tiny saw smoke rising from the cottage's chimney. *Lucky bastards,* he thought, nestling down deeper into the bracken.

Mater struggled to wake with his alarm call. It was good to be home and briefly he wondered whether recent events had simply been a nightmare. He was impressed to see Charlotte standing, already dressed, in the kitchen area pouring tea. The smell of fresh toast encouraged him to get up.

'Sleep OK?' he asked

'Fine, thanks,' answered Charlotte, who having slept in almost every indoor and outdoor environment, had no problems in accepting the comfort of a proper bed.

Mater outlined the morning's activities. 'After breakfast, we'll place the radio-microphones beside the hill track and the cottage's driveway. They should pick up any movement or conversation, warning us if the occupant in the OP fails to. After that, I'll drive to Wormstead, drop in at the post office and the village store which will fire up the jungle telegraph. Mrs. Popplewell in the shop loves to gossip, so I'd give it a nanosecond before almost everyone knows the wanderer has returned. If anyone's on our trail, the scent should strengthen from now on. I should be back in time for you to change places with Tiny. I will need to show you where he is.'

Mater and Charlotte finished breakfast promptly. Mater called Tiny on the radio, checked all was OK and briefed him on the morning's plans. As he made to leave, he reminded Charlotte about the postman. 'My usual postie is very tall, is always dressed in shorts and has a ginger beard, but I suggest you don't answer if he knocks. Stay hidden upstairs. Back in an hour or so.'

Tiny observed the Landcruiser wend its way along the driveway and accelerate in the direction of Wormstead. Mater parked up beside the village green. He decided to visit the little store first. The owner, if not busy, would try to engage him in conversation for the day. The bell tinkled as he opened the door. The shop was quiet. A smiling face greeted him.

'Mr Slater, good morning. Nice to see you again. Are you well? Have you been away?'

Mater was prepared for the questions to come thick and fast. 'Morning Maggie, I'm fine, thank you and, yes, I've been abroad. I hope you're in fine fettle too.' And then to pre-empt her further enquiries: 'Upturn in the oil price has meant more work on the rigs both in the North Sea and the Far East. Excellent news for me although it will mean I'll be gone again soon.'

She beamed. 'You must love the travel.'

'Always good to have plenty to do, Maggie.' He changed tack. 'Now, could I have a couple of pints of milk, a loaf of bread and three croissants, please?'

'Three, Mr Slater, you'll have to mind your waistline or do you have guests?'

He looked her directly in the eye but did not answer. 'The croissants are your fault,' he said, placing a fiver on the counter, 'Too delicious.'

She laughed while he gathered his goods and left, the doorbell announcing his exit.

As expected, later that morning, the audio warning equipment picked up the sound of a small vehicle racing towards the cottage. Almost simultaneously, Tiny came on the radio. 'Red van approaching fast.'

Mater and Charlotte rushed to where the weapons were stored and each grabbed a submachine gun. Mater stood to one side of the front door while Charlotte headed upstairs to view the drive from behind net curtains.

'Relax,' she called down, 'Post van. Single occupant.'

She observed the postman sort the few letters to be delivered, climb out of his vehicle and walk briskly to the front door, whistling as he went. Mater froze as the door-flap opened and the circulars, which would go straight in the bin, tumbled onto the floor. The postman had noticed the expensive new car parked in the drive, thinking Mr Slater either had guests or had gone up in the world. He was correct in his assumptions about the former only. Five minutes after the postman drove away from the cottage, Mater and Charlotte walked up the hill to join Tiny. The audio warning equipment had worked. The early morning sun had given way to low cloud and drizzle; Charlotte wasn't looking forward to her stint at the OP but at least she would avoid the main overnight slot. As they climbed, she scanned the countryside rising above, trying to spot Tiny's hideaway. If she couldn't find it with her experienced eye, then she would be reassured that, once in place, no-one else could see her. At the edge of the copse Mater checked they were alone and directed Charlotte to leave the path. Finally, with less than thirty metres to go, she spotted the long barrel of the APR 308. Tiny had watched them the whole way.

'Thank god,' he called out, 'Think my limbs have turned to lead.'

'Good morning Tiny, anything to report?' enquired Mater.

'Nothing M, apart from the visit by your postie. Saw him coming down the drive from the moment he turned off the lane.'

Charlotte was a little concerned. 'How did you know it was just the postman?' she asked.

'I didn't, so I had him covered with this throughout.' He tapped the side of the APR. 'If he'd made any odd moves, I would have fired, but he was only armed with letters and a fine pair of shorts.'

Tiny yawned and turned to Mater. 'I hope there's some breakfast left.'

'Plenty, including a fresh croissant. Don't say I don't spoil you.'

Tiny slid out from under the basha and stretched. 'All yours, Charlotte. Let's go M, I'm frozen and famished.'

Charlotte checked the rifle's sights and settled down for the day. She had trained herself to observe and consider other things at the same time. It enabled her to stay alert. *Multi-tasking, that's why we women make such good operatives*, she told herself.

Over the coming days the team established a routine. They agreed to mix up the shifts a bit so that the stint spent on the hill varied. It would be miserable for the same poor individual to face many hours alone in the darkness. Shorter slots were planned if the weather turned truly grim. They observed the postman's regular visits but there were no other callers. Intermittently, Mater drove to the village for basic rations and further afield to Maidstone or Ashford when there were other needs or requests. During time off, they ate, slept, enjoyed television, played cards and drank a little. No-one over-indulged. To be inebriated might prove suicidal. They would all get very drunk if, no when, the plan succeeded.

Chapter 11

Thursday 2nd February began in much the same way as the previous thirteen days. Mater finished his night shift and handed over to Tiny. After lunch, he intended to drive into Maidstone to top up with supplies and make his second sit rep call to Control.

'Rush hour traffic permitting, I'll be back in plenty of time for Charlotte to take over from you. Anything you need?' he asked.

'A holiday,' replied Tiny.

'I'll see what I can do, but I thought you were really enjoying yourself here?' teased Mater.

'I've had better staycations,' growled Tiny. He was becoming frustrated and bored.

Mater walked away wondering, as he returned to the cottage, how long they could keep this up for. His confidence faltered. *Perhaps, my idea was crap,* he thought, *we might have to do this for weeks, months or even years.*

In Maidstone, Mater occupied a public phone box waiting for Control to ring back. The boss was pleased to hear from him and relieved all was well. Mater expressed his concern that he wasn't sure how long they could carry on without a break.

Control listened carefully but was emphatic. 'Slowly, slowly, catchy monkey,' is all he said.

'Speak to you in a week,' said Mater and replaced the receiver.

Mater drove home via one of Maidstone's smarter supermarkets where he bought various culinary treats with the aim of maintaining morale. The detour resulted in him getting caught up in the early evening rush made worse by torrential rain. He hoped the others wouldn't be too concerned, but he had no means of contacting them: no-one had used their mobiles since going into hiding.

Dusk was fast approaching as he drove down the lane back to the cottage. He noticed the kitchen lights were on. He cut the engine and allowed the car to roll to a stop, reached for the shopping lying on the passenger seat, and walked to the front door. It was unlocked. As he quietly opened it, he heard a woman's voice calling almost in pain. He tiptoed to the kitchen. A range of emotions swept over him: anger, disbelief, surprise and yes, even envy. Tiny and Charlotte were fucking. Charlotte was bent across the sink work surface, her trousers and panties around her ankles, facing the window as if urgently looking for the arrival of a guest, Tiny's bare buttocks thrusting from behind. They were both grunting and moaning but then Charlotte looked up and spotted Mater's reflection. She froze. Tiny immediately sensed the change in her demeanour and glanced behind him, expecting to be attacked.

'Sorry to disturb,' was all Mater could squeeze out, 'I'll go upstairs for a moment to allow you two lovebirds to sort yourselves out.' He knew he shouldn't be angry. 'After all, we all have hormones, even the bad guys, but it's going to alter the dynamics somewhat,' he said to himself. He sat on a bed for ten minutes before calling downstairs. 'Are you decent?'

115

Tiny called up to him. 'Yes, M, sorry.'

Mater joined Tiny and Charlotte in the kitchen and they carried on almost as if nothing had happened.

'I've brought some goodies. Thought they would cheer us up,' he said, emptying the carrier bags on the table. Mater decided to pull rank. 'Tiny you might have to wait for a further treat as you should already be up on the hill. So, what happened, apart from the obvious?' he asked.

Tiny explained that with the weather being so crap he had offered to knock up something hot for when Charlotte returned from her stint in the OP. They had hoped that M would have been home in time to join them but with the delay, Tiny had suggested they hand over in the cottage. And then one thing led to another.

'You certainly knocked up something hot,' Mater joked, adding quickly, 'Sorry Charlotte. Right then Tiny, better get out there. Radio in when you're in place.'

Mater made himself and Charlotte a cup of tea. They sat looking at each other, exchanging few words, waiting for the walkie-talkie lying between them to crackle into life, confirming Tiny's occupation of the OP. Suddenly there was a voice on the radio; not discernible as speech, but loud and almost a squeal. Less than a second later, an explosion ripped through the bathroom on the first floor and incoming rounds rapidly shattered the cottage's windows, peppering the internal walls. The noise was deafening.

'Fucking hell,' shouted Mater, 'On the ground. Get the weapons.'

The two of them scuttled as fast as they could across the room to the cupboard which acted as their temporary arsenal.

Glass and plaster showered down, cutting their knees and hands as they crawled. The cottage fell dark as flying debris took out the ceiling lights. Charlotte grabbed an automatic, Mater pulled on the remaining NVGs, tucked the pistol in his trousers, armed himself with the other MP7 and then passed her a smoke grenade.

'It's all coming from the front of the house,' he bellowed in her ear, 'Large calibre machine gun. Wait for the reload, throw the smoke out front and I will jump out via the rear living room window. Give me 30 seconds covering fire as I come around to attack.'

'Got it,' shouted Charlotte back.

She felt her way to the living room and waited for the incoming to stall. With the NVGs illuminating the scene, Mater spotted the windowless space at the rear of the cottage. Using the butt of his MP7, he knocked the remaining glass from the window frame and waited for Charlotte's command. Suddenly the firing stopped. She pulled the pin from a grenade and threw it through the hole where the window had been. It spluttered into life, spewing thick green smoke, which obscured the cottage as it swirled in the driveway. Charlotte pointed her MP7 around the corner, shouted go and delivered short bursts into the darkness right to left and back again. Mater climbed carefully through the hole and sprinted to the corner of the cottage. As he peered around, the smoke began to clear and the machine gun opened up again, lead pounding the cottage's walls and scattering randomly inside. Mater could see flashes from the attacker's weapon coming from the back of a van, its rear doors open. Beside the vehicle a man stood raising another weapon. *Fuck, fuck, fuck,* thought Mater as the man levelled an RPG launcher at the cottage. He squeezed the trigger on his MP7. The man holding the RPG crumpled, firing the weapon as he fell. The rocket passed over the house, exploding at the base of the hill. The machine gun released a further brief burst before its firer was thrown backwards in the van by the rest of Mater's clip. There was another spurt of automatic fire from within the cottage.

Mater called out to Charlotte. 'Keep down, stop firing.' He waited and then as silence descended on the scene crept forward. 'Attack, best means of defence,' he murmured to himself.

As he reached the van, he saw fuel dripping from the punctured tank onto the wet drive and a motionless body slumped against it; blood oozing from the chest. Mater hesitated. *Don't want to leap literally from the frying pan into the fucking fire,* he thought. The man lay quite still, breathing shallowly; blood spraying gently from his mouth with each exhalation. Mater rapidly searched him for weapons. He was unarmed. Next he checked the back of the van, his MP7 ready. The NVGs illuminated a scene all too familiar. He climbed in and over the machine gun, recognising it as an American M240. Towards the driver's cab lay the other assailant. He was missing most of his face and head, a black beard, neat and trimmed, covered his intact jaw. Brains, bone chips and blood coated the cab partition wall above the torso. Mater withdrew and returned to the man who was still alive. He appeared to be trying to say something but with every breath air hissed from his chest wound and his voice was weak and unintelligible.

'Charlotte,' shouted Mater, 'All clear. Bring me my camera now. Top right-hand drawer of the weapons cupboard. Hurry, Hurry.'

Charlotte fumbled in the darkness, cutting her hands further. She located the camera and ran to join Mater.

'The bastard's muttering, can you make it out?' he asked as she arrived, thrusting the camera into his hand. Charlotte put her face close to the man's and listened carefully, her cheek spattered by droplets of his blood. Her ears rang from the gunfire and RPG explosion. She shook her head.

Mater leant forward. 'Tell me what you want to say,' he demanded, 'Then I will attend to your wounds. Who are you? Who do you work for?'

He switched on the camera and videoed the man mouthing words. The dying man seemed to be endlessly repeating the same phrase but with each effort he grew weaker. Blood no longer sprayed from his mouth and nose but formed dribbles and small rivulets along his cheeks. Mater stopped videoing. He looked to Charlotte. 'He's fucking had it,' he muttered.

Charlotte nodded and stood up. Suddenly, the silence that had descended was broken by the sound of tearing metal as a high velocity round passed through the van's walls, missing Charlotte by less than a metre. She dropped to the ground again behind the van.

'Shit,' shouted Mater, 'That's coming from up there. That can't be Tiny. Oh fuck. Where's Tiny? The radio's in the house. You run inside. I'll cover you. Call him.' Mater leaned cautiously around the back of the vehicle. 'Ready, go,' he bellowed, emptying the remains of the magazine randomly towards the hill. He had no idea where the shot had come from. Clip empty, he darted back to the cottage, weaving across the driveway. A second incoming round ricocheted off the drive as he set off, causing

119

loose stones to fly into the air. He hoped it would take the gunman longer to reload than for him to sprint the short distance to safety.

Gasping for breath, he found Charlotte sitting on the kitchen floor with the radio held to her ear. 'Nothing,' she said, shaking her head, 'nothing at all.'

Mater and Charlotte both realised Tiny was in trouble.

'I'm going up there,' said Mater, without hesitation. 'You hold up here with the remaining MP7 ammo. I'll take a handgun and the other radio. I know my way around the side of the hill and can approach the OP without using the path.'

In the gloom Charlotte nodded. For the first time in a long while she was petrified; her fear overriding the pain of a wound to her right thigh and the multiple minor cuts to her hands and face. Mater crunched out of the cottage via the front door, moved along the side of the house, hugging its walls until he was able to dive into bushes. From there he found his way to the base of the hill and headed east before starting to climb. Where there was cover, he stopped to catch his breath and scan the land rising above; the NVGs bringing him a daylight view. Finally, as he neared the OP, he checked the safety was still off on the Makarov and crept slowly towards the hideout. He could just make out the basha covered in bracken. At twenty metres distance his foot caught on a tree root and he fell, hitting the ground hard. The NVGs rammed into his forehead, switched off, plunging him into darkness. The occupant of the OP leapt from their lair and started running away. Mater called out 'Tiny.' There was no response. He followed up with a blind shot, fumbled with the NVGs and the light flooded back in. He saw a figure reach the path, run up the hill and disappear. He fired again, more out of anger and frustration, knowing there was no hope of catching whoever it was. Mater cautiously approached the OP. He took hold of a corner of the basha and yanked it upwards, pegs flying out of the ground. Tiny lay there motionless. Mater dropped to his knees and leant over his colleague. The knife that killed Tiny had almost severed his head from his neck: a single deep cut exposing the vital structures connecting mind to body. Mater held his face in his hands. 'What a fucking disaster, my bloody fault,' he said to himself. The radio beside him crackled. He grabbed it and spoke to Charlotte. 'I'm really sorry,' he said softly, 'Tiny's had it. It's just you and me girl, now.' Silence, Charlotte didn't answer. 'The bugger who did it got away. I'll come down with the rifle. Cover me, please.'

Mater wrapped the basha around Tiny and picked up the rifle and spent cartridges. As he retreated, his legs felt like lead, his body numb and his mind confused. He didn't bother to check as he walked. The firefight was over and he had lost. Charlotte watched Mater's return; a lone figure silhouetted against the hillside, walking slowly, exposed. She rested the MP7 on the upstairs bedroom window sill trying to ignore the shaking that enveloped her frame.

Mater entered the cottage and called to her. She hobbled down the stairs, clutching the hand-rail and fell into his arms, hugging him tight, quivering. He stroked her hair, trying to comfort her. He had never known her to react like this but then they hadn't faced such a situation before.

'I'm terrified,' she said, pushing her face into his chest.

'Me too,' admitted Mater, 'We've played away so many times and won and now when it's a home game we lose.'

'What happened to Tiny?' asked Charlotte, regaining some of her composure, 'And what are we going to do now?' Her

121

thigh was throbbing badly and the right leg of her jeans increasingly blood soaked. Mater ignored the first question and had already decided on their next action.

'I'll fix the lights, we'll pack, leave in the Landcruiser ASAP, taking all the weapons with us. I need to contact Control.'

'And then, where do we hide, M? We've no idea if there are others who will go after us.'

There was an element of desperation in her voice, partly in response to the shock of the attack but aggravated by the slow ongoing blood loss. Mater searched in a kitchen drawer, found a torch and spare lightbulbs. He switched it on, climbed on the table and using, a handkerchief removed the metal remnants of the broken bulb, replacing it with a new one. The room was instantly lit, and the devastation caused by the machine gun became all too apparent.

'Looks like some DIY is needed,' he said, jumping down, trying to lighten the mood.

He looked at Charlotte who had collapsed onto a chair. 'You look bloody awful,' he said.

Charlotte was leaning forward clutching her thigh. 'Thanks a lot you bastard,' she said, adding through gritted teeth, 'I think I've been hit.'

Mater now focused, resumed his command. 'OK, undo your jeans and let's have a look.' He grabbed a clean tea-towel. 'I'm ready with this,' he said, holding it up for Charlotte to see. 'We can use it as a pressure bandage or tourniquet. You're going to be fine.'

Charlotte released her hand and quickly undid her jeans, wriggling on her chair as she pushed them to her knees. Mater reached forward and pressed the towel against her leg. She stifled a cry.

'Right I'm going to take this away and have a good look. Ready?'

She nodded. He slowly removed the home-made dressing. There was a long gash in her thigh, exposing the little fat she had under her skin but no muscle and no major bleeding, just a steady general ooze. They both looked at the wound.

'You'll live. Bloody close shave, could have been caused by a round or flying debris. Interesting tattoo though. Missed that the last time you dropped your trousers.'

Charlotte didn't respond to his further attempt at cheering her up. Guilt overwhelmed her. She and Tiny had failed Mater. They had, albeit briefly, succumbed to the boredom and the natural urges of human beings, resulting in failing the watch. Tiny had paid the ultimate price for a few moments of ecstasy.

Mater re-applied the dressing and told her to press firmly while he looked for something to secure it. He went into the cupboard under the stairs and returned with a roll of duct tape. 'Fixes everything,' he said encouragingly.

He tore off strips and secured the towel to her leg making sure the tape didn't go all the way around. *A tourniquet could save lives but it can also be dangerous,* he reminded himself. He was pleased he had remembered the first aid they had all been taught and periodically revised.

'Sorry,' he said, 'The jeans will have to come right off. Have you a skirt with you?'

Charlotte rarely wore a dress but always travelled with a range of clothes so she wouldn't look out of place at almost any function. 'There's one in my bag upstairs. Take it out and then throw in the rest of my things. I'll just sit here for the moment, if that's OK. Could I have some painkillers as well, please M?'

'Sure, hold on. We'll get you sorted,' he replied.

Mater worked fast. He wanted to get away within the shortest time possible, not knowing if a further attack was imminent. They had used most of their ammunition though now had the services of the machine gun but he wasn't sure how many 7.62mm rounds remained. He packed all the firearms and other equipment along with his and Charlotte's personal kit. Outside, working with a pair of NVGs, he stacked the bags and boxes on the ground at the back of the Landcruiser ready for loading. He opened a door and tried folding down the rear seat. It stuck and then he noticed the distorted lever and a bullet hole in the side panel of the car. He walked around the vehicle counting five entry points in total, all neatly punched out. Fortunately, there were none near the engine compartment.

'The fucking thing better drive,' he mumbled and carried on loading.

He would cover the holes with duct tape but considered even though both were silver, the car rental company might spot the damage. Control would be losing his deposit.

Sweating, he headed back to the house to collect Charlotte and the final item he wanted to take away with him. In the kitchen Charlotte watched Mater pick up a poker from beside the stove

124

and stab and scrape at the wall to one side of the cooker. Mater worked furiously, pulling plaster-board from the studwork. At last the hole was large enough for him to reach in and retrieve a green plastic briefcase, carefully wrapped, from the wall cavity.

'What's that?' she asked.

Mater held the case by its handle, dusting it off with his other hand. 'My other life, Charlotte, my real life. I'm not leaving it behind.' He used one hand to carry the lightweight case and offered the other to Charlotte. 'Can you stand ? I'll help you. It's time to go.'

The Landcruiser started as if nothing had happened and Mater drove at speed away from his home, through the village and towards Maidstone. He knew he might never see the cottage again but tried to blot out the evening's events, concentrating on delivering Charlotte and himself to safety. Charlotte, sat in the passenger's seat, felt the benefit of the analgesics. She held the Makarov pistol in her lap, loaded but with the safety catch on. Using the car's sun-visor's and wing mirrors she repeatedly checked they were not being followed.

By the time they reached the centre of Maidstone, the pubs and restaurants had emptied and the streets were almost deserted. Only a few individuals and couples remained, staggering to the taxi rank and night-bus stop. Mater pulled up beside the public phone box near to the library. He took a hand-full of change and left Charlotte guarding the vehicle. In the phone box, he inserted more coins than required and dialled Control's radiopager number. The automated message asked him for a message or contact number. He tapped in the phone's number and replaced the receiver before returning to the car to check on Charlotte. He stood outside watching a young woman vomit into a rubbish bin, her friends laughing and videoing her on their mobile phones. Pay day was taking its toll. *To think we risk our lives to protect all of this,* mused Mater. It was not the first time that doubt had crossed his mind, but he always pushed it away, justifying his work by considering the consequences if the country fell under the control of the bad guys. He also had to admit he had been addicted to the adventure with its adrenaline rushes. Until now, that was. Mater sighed. Here he was, late at night once again, waiting for his boss to return his call, middle aged, tired and on this particular evening nearly dead. Instead, he should have been sitting in front of the wood burner, enjoying a good book, growing fat and greying. His self-pity quickly vanished when his thoughts turned to Tiny and the others murdered: he had no reason to feel sorry for himself. Whether he liked it or not, he had a duty to them even if his commitment to Queen and country had faded. His thoughts were interrupted by ringing from the phone box. He went back in, picked up the receiver and gave the code-word.

'Good evening, Phil, all's well?'

Mater recognised Control's voice but also detected a slight irritation. It was after all rather late for a routine sit-rep. Control was soon to learn the day had been anything but normal. Mater decided to limit his summary to the absolute necessities.

'Late this afternoon, just as we were changing watch, the expected assault came. There are three corpses for collection and the entire site needs cleaning.'

Control butted in. 'Three Phil, do you think you caught them all?'

Mater paused. 'I'm sorry to report, sir, one of them is ours; Tiny is dead and unfortunately one of the attackers escaped.'

126

This time it was Control, who struggled to take it all in, atypically stuck for words. Finally he spoke. 'Are you and Charlotte safe?'

'Yes sir, we think so. We're OK but not sure what to do next.'

Control realised he had to direct Mater, help him make practical decisions. 'Right, the hire car may have been noted, so you'll have to get rid of that. Have you still got the Office tools?'

'Yes, all present and correct, and more besides but the house is devastated and surrounding area littered with spent ammunition.'

'Understood Phil. I'm extremely sorry to hear about Tiny. Stanley will be relieved about the weaponry. I'll ring you again in a few minutes. Stand by.'

Mater returned to the car, contemplating what he had just heard. He found it slightly strange that the boss seemed almost as concerned about the guns as his staff. It seemed out of character. Charlotte wound down the window.

'What did he say?' she asked.

Mater shrugged his shoulders. 'What could he say? I fucked up, and he knows it. He's acting in the most practical way possible, as always. He's going to call again shortly with instructions.'

A few minutes passed, and the phone rang. Mater answered it and gave the next code-word. Control began to speak. 'I want you to drive back to the A1 and leave at the Knebworth junction. Meet me in the car park of RTD Rewinders in the Arlington Business Park, east of the motorway. They are based at

Unit 15. For the sat-nav, the post code is SG1 2FP. If I leave within the hour, we should both be there between two and three in the morning. I'll be driving a dark green Renault traffic van registration SP15 4TL. We'll transfer the kit and I'll give you your next instructions then. All understood?'

Mater confirmed.

'Drive carefully Phil, I'm very sorry.'

The line went dead.

Chapter 12

Mater's and Charlotte's journey to Knebworth was uneventful. They sat in silence, both tense. Charlotte struggled to avoid being overwhelmed with guilt.

'I'm not making excuses,' she said at last, 'But why didn't our electronic surveillance devices warn us?'

Mater tapped his fingers on the steering wheel for a few moments before replying. 'No idea. Perhaps they were jammed. What concerns me is someone knew they were there and how to disable them. That implies either one of our own or another group with extensive knowledge. We're certainly up against it, aren't we?'

Suddenly a terrible thought flashed through his mind. He heard his internal voice repeat 'Someone knew, someone knew' and that person might just be the woman sitting beside him. Had Tiny been lured into his brief physical interaction with Charlotte opening up the opportunity for the attack? He discounted the idea. It was absurd. She could have died as easily as him. He breathed a sigh of relief. Don't be paranoid. They needed a fuck, that's all.

In the darkness, Charlotte winced from pain and anxiety. Mater switched on the radio, tuning into national and local stations to see if the events at the cottage had become public. He wasn't to know that residents in the village had been disturbed by the explosions. They had asked themselves whether it was gunfire but decided with so many bangs, it was probably only an early evening fireworks display. Charlotte, despite the numbing effect of the painkillers, remained vigilant, the handgun never leaving her lap. Mater drove at speed but within the legal limits to avoid attracting attention and was confident they weren't followed.

The sat-nav guided the Landcruiser to the Business Park. It was peaceful apart from the occasional loaded lorry revving up before heading for the A1. At 2.17 am they cruised past RTD Rewinders, looking for Control and checking for any other activity that might inhibit the exchange. A hundred metres after passing the entrance to the rendezvous, Charlotte spotted a dark coloured Renault van travelling in the opposite direction. Mater slowed to a crawl and watched it in his rear-view mirror turn off into the RV. He did a U turn and headed back. As they entered, he saw the stationary van, lights off, occupying a centre space in the carpark. He pulled up behind, illuminating the registration number with his headlights. All well. He switched off the engine but no-one emerged from the vehicle in front.

'Pass me the pistol,' he said. 'When I leave, are you able to slide across and be ready to drive off at the first sign of trouble? Don't wait for me.'

Charlotte nodded and passed him the weapon. Mater stepped from the Landcruiser and raised the gun in both hands. He guessed the van's occupant or occupants could see him approach in their nearside wing mirror but he was prepared to defend himself. He heard the driver's window lower, followed by a voice.

'Phil, gun down, C here.'

He recognised Control at once but kept the automatic ready as he opened the passenger door at arm's length.

'It's OK, Phil. I'm alone. Get in.'

Mater raised a thumb to Charlotte and climbed into the van.

'Are you alright?' asked Control, knowing full well his agent would be anything but.

'Feel like shit, sir, but thank you for asking.'

Control understood. 'Give me a brief sit rep Phil, please.'

Mater outlined the evening's events including approximate timings and details of the firefight. He didn't refer to the transient lapse in the watch. His boss listened attentively. After Mater had finished, Control's usual decorum faded.

'In our line of business Phil, you and I both understand when shit comes, it's often delivered in spades. But mark my words we will screw these fuckers and if we catch them rather than kill them, they will wish we had put bullets in their heads. Your unit has always worked on a long leash. As far as I am concerned that tether has snapped. I've already authorised a forensic clean-up team to deal with your home. It is inevitable they'll identify it as your house. I assume there isn't anything there I should be aware of that could compromise others.'

Mater considered the plastic case sitting in the back of the car. From now on his other life would have to travel with him.

'Nothing, sir.'

Control nodded his approval and continued.

'Right. We are going to swap vehicles. I will return the hired Landcruiser and the weaponry. You take the van to Langley.

131

The Major already knows he has two guests arriving. In the van you'll find a couple of 'pay as you go' mobiles. One's yours and the other Charlotte's. I bought them so they have no links to anyone at the Office. It is safe to use them to keep in touch with each other. Our Langley friend has been asked to hide your vehicle on his estate and organise for Charlotte to be attended to. Lie up for a few days, but we must use this time to devise a new plan. Contact me by the usual mechanism as and when necessary. If I don't hear from you within a week, I'll visit. Do you still have enough money?'

'Yes, thank you, but one thing needs following up.' He passed over the digital camera. 'I videoed one of the attackers just before he died. He was the guy who fired the RPG. He seemed to be repeatedly saying something but we couldn't make it out. I recorded him because I thought perhaps the analytical guys could work on it.'

'Let's hope so, Phil, we have few leads. Anything else?'

Mater thought for a moment, recalling the attack again. 'You remember I disturbed the enemy in the OP and he or she ran off as I approached and shot at them. I managed to fire a second time before they were out of range. I was pretty deaf from the firefight but I may have heard a shout at that point. Maybe, whoever was fleeing was trying to warn an accomplice or perhaps I was lucky and they were hit. Would it be worth checking the Accident and Emergency departments of local hospitals to see if anyone has been treated for a gunshot wound?'

'Sans doubt,' answered Control. 'I'll let you know if anything turns up.'

'Final thing boss, before we part. The Landcruiser isn't quite the same as when you hired it. I've stuck duct tape over the holes where the rain might get in. There is some internal damage from the rounds that penetrated. Ballistics should analyse the bullets lodged inside and also the cartridges retrieved from the transit.'

'Ah. Wear and tear. Do you expect me to sound surprised? I'll deposit the car in the Office garage when I drop off the weapons. They'll sort it and, don't worry; it will be on my tab.'

The two men climbed down from the van and walked to the Landcruiser.

'Hello, Charlotte. M told me you've been injured. It's good to see you looking reasonably OK. I'll leave him to explain the plan for the next few days. I intend to join you soon and debrief you formally then. But first we need to fix you up. If you would like to get into the van, I'm sure M, as a gentleman, will collect your bags. Look after yourselves.'

Charlotte managed a smile. 'We'll try to, sir, but it's proving rather more challenging than usual. A little good fortune might help.'

'I don't believe in luck,' said Control, 'Manage the odds and events will turn in your favour. We'll overcome this, I promise you.'

Charlotte was not convinced, although it was always encouraging to be on the receiving end of one of Control's pep talks. She smiled again and gingerly climbed out of the car. She was surprised when Control stepped forward and gave her a brief hug. She would have blushed but the earlier blood loss prevented it and she felt weak and dizzy.

133

'See you when we see you, sir.'

Control helped her into the van.

'You'll be as strong as ever within days,' he said positively, and closed the door to keep out the night cold.

The two vehicles drove back to the A1 and then parted. Mater and Charlotte headed north towards Yorkshire and Control set off in the opposite direction. Charlotte did not enjoy the ride. The seats were basic as was the suspension; bumping along, jolted and jarred. But she didn't complain. She was as relieved as Mater to be alive. He had described Langley Hall and its owner, and she looked forward to his hospitality. Each pothole passed meant they were one closer to a place of safety. A location that, as far as she was aware, was not known to the Office and therefore impossible to have been leaked.

The Major was woken by his dogs, who themselves had been disturbed by the sound of the van's wheels crunching along the Hall's driveway. They barked and scampered away to the front door. He had dozed in the kitchen, waiting to welcome his guests, whatever time they arrived. Paul had hinted events had not turned out as hoped or expected. The Major's visitors would likely be extremely tired and anxious. Because of his own experiences, he would not need further explanation. Two bedrooms were made up, and he had checked the heating worked in both. More importantly, as far as he was concerned, he found an unopened bottle of Scotch ready for them all to consume. He resisted the temptation to check its quality: a 1976 Balvenie single malt was bound to be good. He padded in his slippers to the front door, calling to his dogs to stand down and arrived just as Mater knocked.

'Hello,' he called, leaving the door firmly shut. 'How can I help you?' Mater recognised the voice.

'I'm sorry to disturb you, Major. Mr Randall here. I'm accompanied by Ms Hawick.'

It was safe to let them in.

'Welcome back, Mr. Randall.' He shook Mater's hand. 'Welcome Ms Hawick. Please, please come in.'

The hounds ran forward licking and muzzling Mater and then turned their attention to Charlotte. Sensing she was also a friend of their master, they waited to be patted and stroked. The Major realised Charlotte was in pain.

'Through to the kitchen, both of you,' he said. 'I've a little something to help make it better. Your boss told me you've had a rough time.'

Mater carried in Charlotte's and his bags, dropped them in the hallway, and followed the others. It all felt very familiar and homely. Once again, he wondered if he was getting too old for the work and should follow the Major's footsteps into retirement.

The three of them sat around the kitchen table making small talk. The Major didn't offer anything other than whisky to his guests. Even though it was already the early hours, and Mater and Charlotte were desperately tired, they didn't resist as their host filled and re-filled the crystal tumblers. It was an exceptionally fine malt and the alcohol, created that extraordinarily hot summer in '76, performed its miracles; suppressing Charlotte's pain, Mater's failure and their mutual loss. Both Charlotte and Mater were a generation younger than the Major and he found it difficult to keep referring to her as Ms Hawick. Eventually, with the spirit on board, he asked her what she liked to be called.

'Suzanne,' she replied, with just a little hesitation, 'But feel free to call me Suzie. Everyone does.'

To the Major, this was a lie. They were all playing a game where the rules were dominated by half-truths and lies. It had been years since he participated but he enjoyed playing now.

'Fine, Suzie, it is then. Please address me as Archie; much less formal than 'Major'. Tomorrow, I will direct you to someone who can tend to your injuries properly. As for Mr Randall here,' he said looking to Mater, 'No doubt he has a first or nickname. Willing to shed some light, Mr. Randall?'

'Phil,' answered Mater, his thoughts wandering back to the plastic briefcase and its contents. He was exhausted, suddenly keen to give up, reveal all and return to a former life. But, when logic stepped in and took over from emotion, he understood he had no choice. 'Yes, Major, I mean Archie, it's about time we all got to know each other better. 'Phil' would be fine. But I need to get to bed. Tomorrow, work starts again.'

With that he rose slowly, steadying himself with a hand on the kitchen table. He felt quite drunk, exactly where he wanted to be. A modicum of oblivion to water down the memories of a terrible day.

'Goodnight Archie, we'll take up your offer of medical help. Please wake me early. Sleep well Suzie.'

He left the two sitting, drinking measure for measure. *A fair contest there,* he thought as he climbed the stairs to his bedroom.

Despite the night's consumption, the Major had breakfast fried and plated by eight. He woke his guests, leaving each a mug of sweet hot tea beside their beds. Mater gratefully drained his and got up. He felt rough but forced himself to waken and get going. As he dressed, he tried to remember details of a nightmare he had experienced during his alcohol and fatigue induced slumber. He couldn't quite grasp it but something niggled.

Only a dream, he said to himself, If it's important I'm sure it will come back. He descended the grand stone staircase and joined the Major and Charlotte. She looked surprisingly well considering the whisky, lack of sleep and the injury she had sustained.

'Good morning, Phil, a new day', she said, smiling briefly.

He had always been impressed by her tenacity and once again he recognised the qualities that had made her an obvious choice for his team.

'Morning, Suzie, how's the leg?'

'Not so bad, I'll live. I'm not sure I need to be examined by the Major's quack.' 'We'll get it seen to, today,' insisted Mater, 'Can't afford for an infection to set in. Better it was cleaned and bandaged properly.'

The Major, without asking, placed a full English breakfast in front of him, who in return, pushed the Makarov pistol back across the table.

'Thank you,' he said, 'For both.'

'Did its job, eh?' said the Major.

'What do you mean?'

'Well, you're still alive and kicking, aren't you?'

Mater nodded. The Major seem to sense others had not been so lucky.

'If you need it again, just ask,' he said, returning to the cooker.

Over breakfast, the Major provided details of the private hospital in Harrogate and the name of the doctor he had contacted. 'He's a good friend and excellent physician. As far as my own medical needs are concerned, I've always been confident he adheres to the highest standards of patient confidentiality. Understands the need for discretion.' He winked at Mater. 'I took the liberty of booking you an appointment this morning. Bloody awkward having a guest nearly kill themselves while shooting on the estate.' He winked again, this time at Charlotte. 'You can use the wife's old car during your stay. Kept it ticking over after she passed on; a back-up for my vintage MG, just in case. It's a challenge to obtain spares for the old girl.'

Mid-morning saw Mater and Charlotte climb into a small yellow Nissan, garaged to the side of the Hall. A turn of the ignition key resulted in a cloud of sooty smoke but the ancient vehicle started first time. The Major, stood watching, pleased and impressed.

'Jap cars always reliable. Pity we had to fight them in the war,' he shouted. He waved as the car kangarooed away up the drive.

The Major's hand drawn map proved, as expected, easy to follow and accurate. Mater pulled up in the patient drop off bay and Charlotte climbed out.

'Call me when you ready to be collected. I'll park up and then walk into town for a stretch. Anything you need?'

She shook her head and limped up the steps and into reception.

The hospital receptionist was friendly and efficient. She informed Charlotte her appointment was due in five minutes. Dr Baird would see her, accompanied by a nurse. A coffee machine, free for patients, was stationed in the waiting area outside his clinic rooms. Charlotte hobbled along the corridor and had just sat down alone when a door opened and a balding, white coated gentleman popped his head around.

'Suzanne Hawick,' he called, guessing the dark-haired woman, sitting in front of him was likely to be his next patient. Charlotte struggled to her feet and nodded in his direction. 'Do come in. Nurse Johnston, please help this lady,' he said to someone behind him.

'I'm fine, thank you,' said Charlotte, doggedly determined to manage by herself.

With the nurse acting as a chaperone, Dr Baird asked Charlotte to lie down on the couch and lift her skirt, revealing the homemade bandage, now soaked dark red. He washed his hands and pulled on surgical gloves. The nurse opened a dressing pack.

'Let's have a good look. I will be as gentle as I can but if it hurts too much, please speak up,' he said, gently peeling off the tea-towel.

He carefully cleansed the wound and removed the clot from its base. Charlotte winced but did not complain. Dr Baird raised his eyebrows. The injury most interesting as was the tattoo.

'Bad luck to have a misfire with the shotgun,' he said. 'But it might have been worse.'

The doctor hadn't spent years working in military field hospitals not to recognise the true origins of such an injury. However, the innocent nurse stood beside him so he kept his thoughts to himself.

'Your wound requires a thorough clean, and it's essential I remove any dead tissue. It is fairly superficial, so do you think you'll manage if I carried this out under local anaesthesia? If you would prefer a general, we would have to send you to the local NHS hospital. They might ask questions.'

Charlotte decided she would cope. The nurse prepared the local anaesthetic, a bigger dressing and a suturing pack. Dr Baird washed again and put on a sterile gown. The anaesthetic injections hurt but were nothing compared to the original wound. Charlotte gritted her teeth and Dr Baird commenced surgery.

Mater wandered around Harrogate town centre with all its boutique shops and cafés. He periodically stopped to look in shop windows. He had no need for anything but admiring the displays gave him repeated opportunities to check he wasn't being followed. He turned a corner and found himself outside the famous Betty's tea shop. When stationed nearby, he had enjoyed afternoon tea there on many occasions, causing much amusement and teasing. 'The tough guy succumbs to cake and tea' or similar went the bait, as he recalled but he was quite content to enjoy some English traditions. If his friends in the regiment preferred to pursue others and get pissed during their leave that was up to them. More cake for him. Mater decided the tax payer, via the Office, could afford to treat him and spying an empty table in the window, he entered. The service, tea and confection were just as he remembered them. The whole experience imbued a longed-for sense of peace. An anonymous self-indulgent pleasure. His life seemed so full of contrasts. An hour spent observing the middle classes entertaining but the other customers had no idea what efforts were made to ensure their lifestyles continued unhindered. *It would have been nice to have treated Charlotte and the Major,* he thought as he paid his bill before being tempted to buy more cakes to take away. He would offer them to the Major when the kettle was boiled back at the Hall later.

Carrying his bag of treats, he decided to return to the hospital via the Stray. The warmth of the sun making it seem spring was coming early. As he entered the park, he saw the buds on the cherry trees were ready to burst and yellow and mauve crocuses weaved patterns on the grass verges. He looked ahead and saw a familiar figure ambling towards him, grey straggly beard swaying as he walked.

'Hello again,' called out the vagrant, 'We meet again. Did she let you off?'

Mater paused, considering his response.

'Don't you remember?' continued the vagrant, 'You told me you'd had too much to drink.'

'Hi,' replied Mater, 'Indeed I had. But, no, she wasn't angry and fortunately for me or him, if he had existed, there wasn't another man.'

They laughed.

'How are you?' asked Mater, with genuine concern.

'I'm well,' came the reply. 'Still enjoying my own company and the strong stuff,' he said, indicating a bottle protruding from his coat pocket. 'No-one bothers me; nobody knows who I am or why I'm here. A never-ending mystery. That's just how I like it.'

'You look in good form,' said Mater, lying, adding while pointing at the sun, 'You will be pleased spring is on its way.' He reached inside the bag he carried and took out the small box of cakes. He handed it to the man. 'You'll have to buy your own tea to go with these,' he said.

'Thanks very much,' replied the vagrant, eagerly taking the box from Mater. He weighed it in his hands and read the elegant label.

'Betty's eh, real class, you are a true gentleman. I don't know why I deserve them but I'm grateful. If you ever need anything when you're in my park, simply ask.'

With that, he shuffled away, clutching his gift. Mater stood for a while watching him go, thinking. His train of thought was abruptly disturbed by the mobile in his pocket.

'Must change that bloody awful ringtone,' he determined as he reached to answer it. 'One of Control's little amusements.' Charlotte had finished her treatment and was waiting to be collected. She told him she would be in the hospital reception area.

She passed the time flicking through a magazine, reading adverts for cosmetic surgery including tattoo removal. She smiled to herself. 'Tried that the hard way,' she muttered.

Mater arrived back within the half hour and brought the car around to the drop-off bay. He entered the hospital and found Charlotte sitting in front of the TV.

'Do you want me to find you a wheelchair?' he asked but the look on her face gave him the answer before she spoke.

'I'm not a bloody invalid,' she replied and stood up with ease. Mater was impressed, not knowing the local anaesthetic was still working its magic.

They passed the journey back to Langley almost in silence, disturbed only by Mater tapping his finger on the steering wheel. Charlotte noted that he seemed lost in thought. She wondered whether, as the originator of the failed plan, he was suffering pangs of guilt and recent events played havoc with his emotions and mind. She was correct in assuming their troubles were prominent in his thoughts but the main thrust of his brain's activity had changed. He was planning their next move. As they neared Norton Le Clay, Charlotte reached across and slid her arm around Mater's shoulders and squeezed gently.

'Penny for your thoughts,' she said.

Mater chuckled. 'Take more than a little seduction for me to reveal anything, but rest assured once it's clarified, you'll be the first to be told.'

Charlotte withdrew her arm. It was obvious now. Mater was working on a new tactic. She prayed it would be more successful than the last.

Chapter 13

Charlotte and Mater spent the next few days resting and recovering. The Major provided, as ever, tasty wholesome food, wine and whisky, and a welcome sense of security. Charlotte's walking improved as the pain settled: a review appointment with Dr Baird scheduled for Wednesday the following week. Mater resumed his daily run around the estate, the dogs joining him enthusiastically. He was keen to meet up with Control as soon as possible but realised his boss had many ends to tie together and things to cover up. He decided to wait before contacting him and wondered what the Office team had made of the scene at the cottage. They periodically listened to the radio news to see if there was any mention of bodies found in Kent. Control seemed to have covered all bases perfectly: there was none.

During breakfast, on the Sunday, the Major announced that his guests' boss had been in touch and would be visiting the next day. Mater was excited. He was starting to feel restless, ready to move on, resume the fight. He and Charlotte discussed events over and over, looking for clues as to who their assailants were, which organisation supported them, supplied arms, safe houses, finance and documents. They reviewed their overseas missions, considered enemies killed and new enemies made. They came up with theory after theory, but there was no conclusive evidence pointing to any specific individual or group. Perhaps, the computer records loss had simply identified an opportunistic target.

Control arrived in another hire car, on time in the late afternoon. He had wished to use either his own or his wife's vehicle but realised there was an increasing risk of compromising the Major and his guests. The Office was containing problems but not eliminating them. He was delighted Charlotte looked so well and Mater with a spring in his step. He decided, if the Major would forgive him, to hold a private meeting with the two of them in advance of dinner and before any alcohol flowed. The Major was not offended. He would stay in the kitchen until the lounge door re-opened. His culinary efforts could stew all night if necessary.

'You will be pleased to hear, Phil, that your cottage and grounds have been cleaned and repaired. It took a few days but I've visited myself and it looks like an excellent job has been done. The house is secure and being watched. I took the unusual step of involving 5. I decided for two reasons not to use our own people. First, frankly we still don't understand how the original leak happened and the unfortunate event at your home really falls on their turf. Second, I'm keen to avoid our guys getting wind of either the problem we face or learning too much about you and your background. The head of 5 kindly personally provided me with their detailed report. He was also generous in not criticising our apparent failings. Their team carefully combed the hillside for clues and to recover all the kit. Ballistics have determined the machine gun, although American, came from Eastern Europe, probably Poland. Apparently our transatlantic friends lost a container, with its load, during a NATO exercise there five years ago. The RPG launcher was even more intriguing. It's old and someone at some stage repainted it. The paint was made in Pakistan. Review of surveillance and military footage has, by chance, shown an identical weapon being used by Al Qaeda militants in Afghanistan during our early attempts to dislodge Osama bin Laden. It is possible, of course, that a number of these weapons were renovated in the same way, but likely this one originated in one of those two countries. This is all supported by your video, Phil. That proved very interesting. The audio was indeed challenging but 5's linguistics section managed to lip-read the poor bugger's final words. He kept repeating 'Allahu Akbar' followed by 'Antinal'. So, we seem to be facing yet another extreme Islamist group.'

Charlotte butted in. 'What is Antinal?' she asked.

'Of course, that was checked out. Bizarrely, it is an anti-diarrhoeal drug containing a medicine called nifuroxazide and is available in many countries.'

'Why did he say that? Perhaps it was a code name?'

It was Mater's turn to come up with a suggestion. 'I think you might be right. If it's taken for eliminating the shits, then what an apt title for an operation where you intend to kill those you view as your worst enemies.'

Control gave a wry smile.

'Do we know the nationalities of the two dead attackers?' asked Charlotte.

'The straight answer is no,' responded Control. 'They appear to have been quite professional in their activities. Absolutely zilch found to pin them down: who they were, where they stayed in the UK and so forth. DNA analysis of the bodies hints at an East European or Middle Eastern origin but that's it. 5 threw the net far and wide with respect to the one who got away.

146

A man with limited English and a gunshot wound was treated in the emergency department of London's Charing Cross Hospital the day after the attack. But his injury was minor, and he wasn't admitted. After treatment, he disappeared with nothing for us to follow up: the name and address he gave false. There were five other firearms related injuries recorded in the South East that week but none relevant. The van they used was stolen three days earlier. It was probably laid up somewhere as we can't find it on any CCTV recordings after its movement from North London to Kent. It is suspected they were prepared and waiting nearby, biding their time until the opportunity to strike arose. What I don't understand is how your watch failed and the opening presented itself? Any ideas?'

Charlotte glanced across to Mater who showed no emotion. Mater realised he had no choice but to offer an explanation. 'Boss, you suggest we were under surveillance for three days before they attacked. If true, that gave them information as to our routines and resources. We ran eight-hour shifts throughout. Maybe Tiny was caught short and needed a crap. Our normal routine, when manning an OP, would be to shit into a plastic bag and bring it home. But with each shift being only a few hours, I'd be surprised if he had to fulfil a bodily function, but perhaps he did. During that brief lapse they grabbed their chance.'

'But what about your other protection? You placed acoustic detectors around the cottage. 5 kindly returned the units. Didn't they work?'

Charlotte shifted uneasily in her seat.

'Clearly not. Maybe the damp winter weather caused their failure. Who knows?'

147

Control appeared baffled. He would ask Stanley to check the kit carefully.

To the assembled, all that had been said seemed plausible, but Mater had picked up on one facet and he would keep his idea to himself; at least until he could provide evidence to support it.

Control moved on. 'The vital questions are where do we go from here and how do we ensure your safety? Despite reassurances from within the Office, I'm still concerned. Even if we keep moving you between safe houses, but a traitor remains at HQ, it will be only a matter of time before your cover is blown. Then you become targets again. So what should we do?'

Control's difficulty in deciding on his next move provided Mater with the opening he was seeking.

'As you might expect, since we lost Mick, Liam and now Tiny, I've spent almost every waking moment thinking about my team. The problem is, as I see it, it doesn't matter how different our false lives are from our real personas, we are inevitably still identifiable; particularly if there an insider colluding with the enemy. Although life's records, electronic or otherwise, create the person we claim to be, they unfortunately also help those who would do us harm.'

It was Control's turn to interrupt. 'What you are saying has always been self-evident in this game. We simply try to minimise the odds against us. I'm not sure what this is leading to.'

Mater was impatient to explain. 'What if we didn't have any background? Operatives with no history either from within or beyond the Office?'

'Go on,' said Control, intrigued.

'Well, sir. The primary problem seems to have been someone accessing computer records. But if my team didn't exist on any system, then, however hard the enemy looked, they would find nothing. Indeed, a completely false trail could be created.'

'And who doesn't live in this modern digital world?' It was Charlotte's question, who, up to this point had listened attentively but thought Mater was losing the plot.

'Ah,' continued Mater, 'I wouldn't be able to guarantee their pedigree but a small part of the population lives on the fringes of society, often for years. Many, I surmise, had jobs requiring specialist skills but for one reason or other have been forced outdoors, literally.'

As Mater spoke, he visualised the vagrant in the park, so reticent to talk about his background except for mentioning he had worked in the computer industry. Mater was sure he didn't own credit cards or a passport, receive utility bills or have doctors and dentist registration or club memberships. He was anonymous.

'If I recruit agents from the down and outs, working far from all Office departments, rules and functions, then I might create a unit that could be used to strike. Afterwards they simply disappear. This would be the dream team to deal with the current threat.'

Mater paused, waiting for a reaction. The others sat for a while not saying a word, unsure whether Mater had gone mad or had come up with a brainwave. Charlotte concluded Mater's mind was slipping and lay back in her chair, watching Control. He frowned, tugged at his sagging jowls and stared at the fire, lit by the Major in the late afternoon. It was almost out. He pulled on a glove, poked the ash and carefully placed a large log on the embers. Immediately, flames began to lick up, swirling around and up into the chimney.

'Phoenix from the ashes,' announced Control. 'Sometimes I think you're quite crazy, Phil,' he said, 'But if anyone can pull this off, it would be you. If I agree to your mad-cap plan, we shall call it Operation Phoenix. I like that. Tell me more and then I will be better able to judge the feasibility of your idea.'

Charlotte looked at Control in surprise. She was incredulous. He wasn't really going to let Mater recruit staff for Her Majesty's Secret Services from the street's alcoholics and drug addicts; the dross of society.

Mater was delighted his concept hadn't been dismissed out of hand. He had thought through many of the details just in case he was given the chance to pursue it.

'I plan to join them, wandering from place to place, getting to know the characters living under our bridges, in doorways and on park benches. This usefully avoids the Office having to find me yet another safe house although currently the term seems to be a misnomer. Once on the street, I will listen to their stories and if someone has a useful background, entice them with the offer of a different life. Most, I'm sure, are likely to reject the opportunity to come into the warm and dry. However, I don't need more than three or four volunteers. It will take time and require a significant advance. From the moment I disappear, I mustn't buy any service or physical item with anything other than hard cash. It would also help a lot if you provided me with somewhere unknown to the Office where my recruits could adapt to their new lives. There they could detox if required and train for any future mission.'

150

'You mean like here, Langley Hall?' suggested Control.

Mater would have loved to stay, but the location wasn't right for his operation. 'Not here, but similar. Must be secluded and not impose on anyone.'

Control sat deep in thought for a few minutes and then finally made his decision. 'OK Phil, you have a provisional green light. I will need to create a cover story to extract a significant sum of cash from the Office finance department; a hostage release episode probably suffices. It is also necessary that we meet or at least keep in regular contact for you to update me. I cannot allow large sums of public money to be used without some sort of audit in place. It might all come out eventually which would be rather embarrassing.'

Not so embarrassing as to lose all the agents from my section, thought Mater, struggling to keep his mouth shut.

Control looked to Charlotte. 'Do you want to get involved in this hair-brain plan?' he asked. 'There's no three-line whip on this one. If you want me to, I can swiftly find you another place to stay and arrange a further identity.'

Mater stepped in before Charlotte could answer. 'I very much need a reliable person to man the base while I'm recruiting. A pair of experienced hands to assist with training would be invaluable too.'

Charlotte realised Mater was really begging for her to join him. Without her he would struggle to hold it all together.

'Thanks for the offer, C,' she said, 'I'll think this over for a while but will probably go with Phil. I can't simply hide when

151

we've lost three of our own. To be frank, I'm desperate to retaliate.'

'OK, good girl,' said Control, 'But remember revenge is emotionally charged and emotions generally don't sit well with our activities. Take great care.'

Having agreed to help in principle, now it was Charlotte's turn to question Mater's plan. 'My first concern is how are you going to deal with any drug, alcohol or mental health problems?'

Mater had already considered this. 'Potential candidates may need to be clinically evaluated and offered help to get them off the booze or whatever they poison themselves with. I've read about specialist clinics where patients are rapidly weaned from their addiction. I wondered whether the Major's physician friend could point us in the right direction. If they can't stay drug free and sober, then we return them to where they came from. No-one will be told the real purpose of their invitation to a new life until we are confident they are suitable.'

Charlotte voiced her next worry. 'What about arms and weapons?'

'We'll try to play the enemy at their own game and buy them on the black market. If that doesn't deliver the goods, then we may need to create a cover story to assist Stanley in organising a long-term loan.'

Control interrupted. 'Avoid the black market, Phil. You risk being targeted by many organisations. We, our sister service, as well as customs, the national crime agency from this country and also foreign bureaux watch the arms merchants continuously. No, if you recruit successfully, then I will work with Stanley to make sure you have what you need. The first task is to find a suitable location for your base. The obvious choice is somewhere like Dartmoor or Sutherland in the North-West Highlands. I plan to return in a few days, hopefully with the cash and perhaps by then we can put more meat on the bones. Any further thoughts at this point?' He looked to each of them.

'May I ask about the funeral arrangements for Tiny?' asked Charlotte quietly.

Mater knew the answer even before Control spoke.

'I'm sorry Charlotte. It is to be held this coming Friday in Hereford. The Office will be represented but I cannot allow either of you to break cover to attend. It's better that you are from now on, as Phil suggested, totally invisible. I shall put it around HQ that you both disappeared on my instruction. Without my input, elements within may start looking for you either out of concern or because they consider you were involved in your colleagues' deaths. No, let's keep it simple. Let slip this and that; help the rumour mill rumble on. As far as I am concerned, you've had enough, decided to resign; fading discretely back into normal society.' He placed another log on the fire. 'Right, unless there's anything else, it's time to catch up with the Major. Can't leave him to drink himself under the kitchen table alone.'

Control ensured the rest of the evening was entertaining and passed without reference to anything that had been discussed earlier. But the Major had incite. He recognised that repeated visits from his old friend and the presence of his two charges could only mean the security service's current work was unusually challenging and difficult. But, as a staunch patriot, he would help as and when he was able. If this meant simply providing a roof over their heads, he was content to do so. He would not ask questions.

153

Control departed long before breakfast with the intention of being seated at his desk early; he had lots to do. Mater and Charlotte went to work piecing together the details of his proposal. At this stage, they had no idea if he would recruit anyone suitable or how long it would take. But in the meantime, they would find and establish a base and devise a training package. Charlotte's outpatient appointment with Dr Baird was booked for the next day. She agreed to ask the understanding consultant, as she described him, if he would be willing to help in their search for a detoxification service. The Major gave them permission to borrow his computer which they used to search for a hideaway.

Mater had a further plan he was going to have to admit to.

'I'm going to Hereford,' he announced.

Charlotte looked up from the monitor, a mixture of surprise and concern etched on her face.

'Surely not,' she said, 'We both heard, and I assume understood, C's orders.'

'I viewed it more as a recommendation,' retorted Mater. 'He won't know I'm there. I will watch from a distance.'

'If you upset Control, he might pull the plug on your mad-cap project,' warned Charlotte.

'You're right, but I've missed Mick's and Liam's send offs and just need to be sure Tiny at least is given the ceremony he deserves. I'll only be away a couple of days.'

'On your head be it,' said Charlotte, shaking her own and returned to the internet.

154

It didn't take Mater long to find out when and where Tiny's burial was to be held. If Tiny had been a current SAS member, the regiment's recommended funeral directors would have been secretive, but the town's other funeral company was more than helpful when he phoned them. They had no reason to suppose that Mater wasn't a work colleague. He had been, of course, but not quite in the area described. To his Hereford friends and neighbours, Tiny had been simply a local guy who few people knew but was thought to have been employed in financial services. They believed he commuted to London regularly and occasionally travelled overseas to negotiate contracts. To die from a stroke at such an early age surprised many; perhaps his job had been more stressful than they imagined.

The Major was aware that his guests were searching for new accommodation and working on something important. He was, therefore, most willing to loan his wife's old Nissan to Mater again. He agreed it would be easier to visit potential sites by car and although he quite enjoyed the company, he looked forward to having his own space back. Mater's request for a pair of binoculars was easy to fulfil; it was natural that Mr Randall would want to check the neighbourhoods.

Chapter 14

On Wednesday, Mater drove Charlotte back to the Harrogate Hospital. Dr Baird was delighted to see that Charlotte's wound had not become infected and was already healing.

'It was fairly deep and so may take months to resolve fully. It is likely you will be left with a scar, I'm afraid, and your tattoo will never quite be the same.'

Charlotte pulled up her trousers and asked if she could speak with Dr Baird alone. The nurse who had chaperoned her looked affronted, but he waved her away with a request for a cup of tea.

'I have a brother,' started Charlotte, 'He's the black sheep of the family because of his problem. It's a bit embarrassing talking about it.'

Dr Baird wasn't quite sure what she was getting at. 'Go on,' he said, 'You can talk to me in confidence.'

'Well, he's an alcoholic. I'm struggling to find a way to help him. He failed multiple attempts at rehab and his attendance at Alcoholics Anonymous short lived. Recently, I read about private clinics providing treatment where the patient is rapidly weaned off drugs or alcohol. The results sound encouraging. Do you know anything about this?'

The consultant had heard a little from his anaesthetist. The concept was discussed amongst theatre staff a few months ago when they teased the sister in charge about her over-indulgence at a hospital celebration.

'You're right, a few doctors have attempted this with only partial success and it is potentially very dangerous. I believe patients have died as a consequence. I'm not convinced main stream physicians working in the addiction field are comfortable with the research being undertaken in this area. Are you sure you would want your brother to be subjected to it?'

'Things are desperate,' answered Charlotte, 'If you are able put me in touch with anyone who can help I would be most grateful.'

Dr Baird considered her strange request carefully before making his decision. 'I will ask next time I'm in theatre. I work with the same anaesthetist each week.'

'Thank you. That would be most kind. There's one other thing though. Please may I emphasise the need for discretion. My brother is well known and whoever helps him must do so in strict confidence.'

Dr Baird smiled. Something didn't quite hold together with Charlotte's story. She sat before him, a patient out of the blue, asking for advice about a specialist area that lay way beyond his clinical comfort zone. She had been recommended to visit him rather than the local hospital by his old friend the Major, probably because of her near miss with a high velocity gunshot. He decided to be bold.

'Do you want to tell me how and why you were shot?' He smiled at her encouragingly.

Charlotte stood up and reached out to shake hands.

'No,' she said firmly, shook his hand then walked away. At the door she paused. 'Thanks for your assistance. If you are able to help my brother, I can be contacted via Major Littlewood-Jones. Good morning.'

Dr Baird watched her leave and sat thinking, intrigued.

Chapter 15

Tiny's funeral was scheduled for Friday at 11 am , so Mater decided to drive to Hereford on the Thursday afternoon. He knew the city quite well, having worked alongside both the SAS and SBS during his military career and his tenure with the Office. He booked for one night only into Holme Lacy House, an elegant Georgian country hotel, and arrived just in time for dinner. It lay a few miles from the centre, far enough to minimise the risk of bumping into someone who had known Tiny.

At the reception desk, a pretty young lady, whom he guessed originated from France, welcomed him. He asked if he could pay in cash up front as he might have to leave early the next morning. The receptionist was a little surprised but as he was willing to settle up now she didn't ask for a credit card as security. Mr Randall seemed a typical English gentleman, and they were generally reliable.

That evening, Mater dined alone. As expected for the time of year there were few other guests and he enjoyed a surprisingly delicious meal, undisturbed. Straight after eating he retired to his room alternating between watching television and revising his plan for the new team. He slid into bed intending to relax by enjoying a film but tiredness forced him to switch off the TV and he fell rapidly and deeply asleep.

He woke at six, keen for a run, but knew he needed to keep a low profile. Instead, he decided to take advantage of the

159

hotel's swimming pool for his morning exercise. Situated in the south wing of the ground floor with large picture windows, it offered beautiful views of formal gardens and the Brecon Beacons in the distance. The pool's smooth unbroken surface reflected the blue of the spring sky. Mater dived into the clear cool water, fracturing the reflection. He powered up and down for a few lengths and then dived deep, swimming underwater until he could go no further. Desperate for oxygen, he pushed off the bottom and shot to the surface. Taking great gulps of air, he looked outside. A man strolled alone in the grounds, stopping periodically to look at the shrubs and ornaments. Mater's eyes, stinging from the water's chlorine, struggled to focus. The man was undoubtedly familiar and his presence made Mater dive under again and swim as fast as he could to the far end; out of view of anyone. He clasped the pool's ladder, panting. *Surely not,* he thought. *Hereford has so many hotels. If that's who I think it is, why in hell did he choose the same place to stay?* Mater tried to convince himself it was a coincidence or just bad luck but he didn't really believe in luck; good or bad. In his opinion, it was always safer to assume events, however strange, were planned. He checked nobody had joined him, climbed out, wrapped a towel around himself and walked rapidly to the changing rooms. He wondered if he should abort his mission but was desperate to know why the man in the garden, if he was who he suspected it might be, was there. It would be safer to stay in his room, call room service for breakfast, and not emerge until he left for the cemetery. At 10.15, having packed and dressed in his dullest outfit, he went downstairs, passing reception on his way out.

The receptionist called to him as he dropped his key on the counter. 'Bonjour, Mr Randall,' she said radiantly, 'I hope you

160

slept well. You didn't need to leave so early after all. But, I am sorry, there is a small extra charge for the room service.'

Mater fumbled in the inside pocket of his overcoat, drew out a twenty-pound note and handed it to her.

'Oh no, Mr Randall, the extra is only five pounds, I will have to find you change. Would you like a receipt?'

Mater was anxious to get away. 'No thank you. I don't need one. Keep the rest as a tip. I have enjoyed my stay here immensely.'

The receptionist blushed. 'That is most generous, sir. Have a nice day,' she called after him as he reached the revolving front doors. He heard her good wishes although, despite the bright sunshine, didn't expect it to be at all enjoyable.

Mater strode swiftly to the hotel carpark, frequently looking around surreptitiously but the man he had seen earlier wasn't there. He climbed into his car and drove off. The journey to the main cemetery in Westfaling Street took less than thirty minutes. He spent another five searching for a suitable place to park until finding one near to a secluded spot from where he hoped he could view the burial. The service was due to start soon.

Mater watched as pall bearers emerged from the Saxon church carrying a plain coffin, followed by a small group of darkly dressed, well wrapped up figures. Even with the binoculars, it proved difficult to make out the faces. Some familiar, most not. Control was definitely present and possibly Simon. In the middle of the graveyard, the minister mouthed words for a while and then Tiny's coffin was lowered into the ground. Shortly after, the crowd ambled away in the direction of the cemetery's carpark leaving a single woman standing still by the grave, head bowed.

Mater struggling with his own emotions, found it hard not to shed tears. *Who is she?* he wondered. *Must have been someone special.* He sighed, packed the binoculars in their leather case and headed back to his car.

'Hi, Phil,' called a familiar voice.

Mater briefly froze and then realised he had no choice but to play along as if there had been nothing unusual about his behaviour. He turned and faced the man as he approached. Now his suspicions about the man from the hotel grounds were confirmed. 'Hello Anthony, how are you?'

Anthony smiled. 'OK, thanks. Looks like you were doing the same as me.'

'What's that?' asked Mater.

'Watching Tiny's funeral, of course. The boss told me I didn't need to go, but I wanted to be here. I assume, naturally, you shared the same wish.'

Mater felt distinctly uncomfortable. He had disobeyed Control's instruction, but it seemed odd for Anthony to do so as well. Although the two of them went back a long way, the same couldn't be said about Anthony and Tiny. The whole purpose of Mater's team was that it operated in virtual isolation with minimal links to mainstream Office staff. Mater's communication tended to be with Simon, Anthony only involved when Simon was otherwise engaged.

'Well, perhaps we should just keep it between us, what do you say?' said Mater, not wishing to become embroiled in a lengthy conversation.

Anthony nodded his agreement.

Mater turned and started to walk away.

'Good luck,' Anthony called after him. '3 - 2 isn't a bad result but maybe not for a home game?'

Mater nearly froze but his professionalism made him focus on forcing one leg in front of the other. He didn't respond, acting as if he hadn't even heard. How did Anthony know the score? Control had indicated he asked 5, and 5 alone, to investigate and cover up. No-one from the Office apart from him involved. *It is possible,* thought Mater, *Anthony has connections in 5 but there have been too many coincidences.* The word 'Antinal' floated into his mind.

When he reached the little Nissan, he looked back just in time to see Anthony drive off in a white BMW coupé. Mater jumped in, started the engine, did a U turn and followed at a distance. He assumed Anthony would recognise his car because evidently he had been at the hotel. Anthony, though he had flown a desk for years, had been trained like all operatives in the arts of pursuit and evasion. Mater needed to be very cautious tailing him. As Mater drove, the voice within his head kept repeating 'Antinal'. He now suspected the fanciful idea that had come to him when Control first mentioned the drug was true. 'Antinin' is Czech for Anthony. The dying man wasn't talking about some shit stopping medicine at all. He was saying 'Antinin' not 'Antinal'. There must be an East European connection.

Anthony's car weaved through the city centre, the morning shoppers and pedestrian lights impeding his progress. Finally, he pulled into a public carpark next to the city's library. Mater drove one hundred metres past the entrance and stopped on double yellow lines. He grabbed his hat from the rear seat, climbed out and headed straight back towards the carpark, pulling

163

his coat collar up and hat down. He didn't notice the traffic warden preparing a ticket. As Mater entered the carpark he saw Anthony leaving it, on foot, at the far side. He quickened his pace until he could keep Anthony in his sights, merging in and out of the crowd. At a crossroads, Anthony went right. Mater, about fifty metres behind, turned the same corner no more than thirty seconds later but Anthony was nowhere to be seen. Mater carefully scanned ahead and then returned to the crossroads. He checked each exit but as the minutes passed, he knew his quarry would be further away. He walked back to where he had lost sight and spotted a coffee shop. *Had Anthony gone in?* Mater looked through the café's window, half expecting to see a familiar face mocking him. Most of the window seats were occupied but none by Anthony. The customers, sipping their drinks, wondered who this strange man was spying on them from the street.

'Bugger. Where's the bastard gone?' he said to himself.

He decided to go into the café to check. It was busy, and he was out of luck. He gave up. The chase over. It was almost lunchtime, breakfast seemed a long time ago, and he was hungry; he might as well top up before leaving Hereford. Armed with a steaming cappuccino and a ham and cheese panini he sat himself down at the last vacant table looking out into the street. He took a sip of coffee and thought about his surprise encounter. *Who knows what he is really doing here? Maybe I'm going crazy. Perhaps, he had simply driven into the city centre to buy something or sightsee.*

The previous occupant had left a copy of one of the local papers. Mater picked it up and, while drinking, checked the obituaries. Tiny's funeral wasn't listed. Occasionally, he glanced over the paper to watch the world pass by. A van was parked across the road on the pavement, its driver loaded boxes onto a trolley. Behind him, a small mosque, its modern middle-eastern architecture and twin minarets somewhat incongruous in the old English city. Being Friday midday, increasing numbers of visitors entered, most but not all appearing as if they originated from the Indian subcontinent. Mater surveyed the scene with natural curiosity. He felt slightly jealous as the worshippers met outside the mosque, chatting together and united in their beliefs. Sometimes he wished he believed in a deity. But having seen so many terrible things happen in the name of religion, he couldn't take comfort in the concept of a god. He drained the last of his coffee and got up, ready to leave. He looked out once more. The delivery man finished unloading and drove away. A few worshippers were already leaving. Mater almost choked. Anthony emerged from the building, seemingly deep in conversation with two men, trotted down the steps to the street. *Clever bastard,* thought Mater, as he grabbed his hat, pushed past other diners and rushed to the exit. As he opened the café door, he saw a car pull up and the three climb in. It drove off at high speed. He ran into the street, trying but failing to catch the registration number.

'What the hell is he up to?' Mater muttered to himself.

He would have to decide whether to own up to Control that he had been to Hereford and then question the boss about his suspicions or pursue his hunch alone. Either way, the situation was becoming more complicated by the day.

At his car, Mater tore the parking ticket from the windscreen, screwed it into a ball and then stopped himself from throwing it into the gutter. If the fine wasn't paid, the Major, being the car's owner, would shortly receive a summons and this might draw unwelcome attention. No, he would discretely give the

Major the cash to cover it. *After all,* he mused, *it will simply be a case of the redistribution of public money.*

He started the engine and drove out of the City, heading north east. He would be back at Langley by the evening, even with a stop or two. There was no rush. Tiny had been buried but his sacrifice had given Mater something to work on; a definite lead. As he drove, he mulled over the day's events. There were many questions but few answers. He hoped Charlotte's doctor had been helpful. They needed to get on and ahead in the game.

Chapter 16

Back at Langley Hall, Charlotte discretely quizzed the Major about Dr Baird. She had been slightly unnerved by what she viewed as his excessive interest in her wound. The Major was reassuring, detailing more background to his relationship with the consultant.

'Don't worry,' he concluded, 'If you want advice from my friend, you can do so in the knowledge that he is most discreet. He has, how should I put it, inside understanding. If he is able to help, he will.' He smiled and checked his watch. 'Time for a cup of tea, Suzanne; we can't wait for Mr Randall.'

Late afternoon, the phone rang in the lounge, making the dogs howl in unison. The Major called to Charlotte. 'It's the doctor, he would like a word.'

She took the receiver but waited until the Major left the room before speaking.

Dr Baird was succinct. 'I have been contemplating your request and made enquiries. It is possible, but it would be wise to discuss it with you in person. I suggest I call at Langley Hall. I know Major Littlewood-Jones would be quite happy if I visit. Would tomorrow morning about ten be alright?'

Charlotte wanted to confer with Mater first, so hesitated but before she could answer Dr Baird broke the silence.

'Ms Hawick, you can be sure I fully understand the requirement for absolute secrecy. Unless I hear from you otherwise, I'll be with you at ten prompt.' He hung up.

Charlotte called Mater on his mobile. She was anxious. The strength of Mater's plan lay in the players' anonymity but she concluded it would be impossible to change novices into professionals without help although the doctor's involvement might make the ship leak again.

Mater was approaching a parking layby when his phone announced an incoming call by its irritating ringtone.

'Still haven't changed that racket,' he grumbled, as he pulled over to answer it.

Charlotte described her conversation with Dr Baird and his intention of visiting. 'I can put him off, if that's best?' she said.

Mater, had also realised they were going to need help. 'No, let him come. We'll have to think a bit more about your brother. I might get in touch with Control and ask him to vet the doctor before tomorrow. I have news for you too, but it should wait until I'm back.' He didn't want to try to explain his encounter with Anthony until he sat face to face with her.

'How's the leg wound?' he asked with genuine concern.

'Healing nicely, thanks. The doctor's pleased with it. Drive safely.' With that she ended the call and returned to her search for a suitable future home.

Mater drove on, looking for a public phone, cursing the rarity of them in the modern world. He needed to page Control as soon as possible to give the chief enough time to run a check on the good doctor before the next day's meeting. He imagined

Control must have reached London unless he had other tasks to perform in Hereford. He turned off the main road and after passing through three villages spotted a familiar red phone box. The routine would delay his journey but he would sleep better that night knowing a little more about the ever helpful Dr Baird.

Control was not altogether surprised by Mater's request. He too had concluded that Mater and Charlotte would struggle to achieve their goal without expert help.

'I'll text you with anything useful,' he said. 'Should give you an answer within the hour.'

Mater didn't mention Anthony.

As Mater neared Harrogate his phone pinged. Once again, he pulled over and picked it up. The message was reassuring. Dr Baird was not only trustworthy but had in fact been an employee of the service, albeit years ago and on a temporary basis. The text reminded Mater that once a signatory of the Official Secrets Act you were tied by the law for the rest of your days. He felt it was their first lucky break and recognised, once again, he had the Major to thank; this time for the introduction. In the town, he stopped at an off licence, where, using a little more of the Office's financial reserves, he bought his host a bottle of his favourite malt.

He set foot back in Langley just as the Major was serving the first round of evening refreshment.

'Excellent timing,' the Major said as Mater dropped his bag in the hall. 'What's your poison? Looks like you might benefit from a sharpener, Mr. Randall.'

The Major had tried to refer to Mr. Randall by his forename but without alcoholic lubrication, his age and position made him revert to the more formal.

'You don't know how much I need a drink, Archie. I've brought you something to at least partly replenish your supplies. It's a minor token of thanks. I remain very grateful for all you are doing for Suzanne and me.'

'No gratitude required, but the malt is, of course, most welcome. We shall enjoy it together when you succeed in whatever endeavours you are undertaking. Just tell me when I should open it.'

'I certainly will, but I fear the bottle may have aged somewhat more by then.'

'Be optimistic Mr Randall, full of hope.'

The Major's encouragement prompted Charlotte to step in with her positive news.

'Phil, could I show you something on the Major's computer before we settle down for the evening? It requires an early answer.'

The Major took this as his cue to return to the kitchen to pour the drinks and begin dinner preparations.

Charlotte beckoned to Mater to pull up a chair. 'I've enquired into leasing a hunting lodge near Lochinver in Sutherland,' she said. 'Looks promising, possibly perfect, but I need to confirm the booking as soon as possible. What do think?'

Mater scanned the details. He agreed, it seemed ideal. An isolated collection of buildings, lying roughly halfway between the little West Coast port Lochinver and the village of Inchnadamph with good access to the main road connecting the two; the accommodation extensive with plenty of space for teaching, garaging vehicles and storage of equipment. A small wood bordered the main lodge to one side, the loch on the other and the whole site surrounded by mountains. It would be easy to protect and provided a variety of terrain for training. There were three outbuildings: Mater envisaged one being converted into a temporary medical clinic and the others, being somewhat ramshackle, perfect for urban warfare drills. He suggested to Charlotte that she confirm while they had the reservation in front of them but she just looked at him and shrugged her shoulders.

'Yes, Phil, let's book it now but how? Neither of us has a credit card or should use it even if we did. We're living in a cashless society. This is going to be challenging.'

Mater thought for a moment. 'We'll have to ask the Major yet again for his help. If he covers the deposit, we can reimburse him and pay the balance in cash. Provided we are generous on all counts, then hopefully few questions will be asked. I'll call him in.'

The Major was more than helpful. 'I've been a little, how should I put it, a little naughty,' he said, after Mater had explained the urgency of their request. 'You won't place me in an awkward situation because I've kept open my poor deceased wife's accounts, including her credit cards. When my own credit standing falls into disrepute, I simply carry on using hers. I keep things ticking over and conveniently signatures aren't used on-line, only passwords, and we never kept secrets from each other.'

Once the reservation was confirmed, the evening progressed in its customary fashion: a heady mix of eating, chatting and laughing in a thickening alcohol induced haze. Mater, Charlotte noted, was indulging more than usual. She had been waiting for him to volunteer his news but knew she would have to wait until the Major retired to bed: it would be imprudent to do otherwise. He had sounded agitated on the phone but she hoped the distortion was due to poor mobile reception. At a quarter past eleven, the Major announced he was going up, encouraging his guests to enjoy the rest of the after-dinner brandy without him. Mater and Charlotte wished him good night, waited for the door to close and his footsteps fade. Mater reached for the bottle but just as he was about to refill their glasses Charlotte grasped his wrist and forced it back to the table. She held on.

'You've had enough, Phil. Tell me what's up. You weren't quite yourself when you rang me earlier.'

He managed a token smile.

'I'll stop drinking but you might want more when you hear about my day.'

She relaxed her grip, and he poured a modest tot into her glass. He started at the beginning with his first sighting of Anthony, then described Tiny's funeral and the surprise encounter, the pursuit and finally his observations at the mosque.

'You lost him?' asked Charlotte, somewhat incredulously.

'He had help. Goodness knows what's going on? But there's more.'

Mater explained his Antinal-Antinin theory and then sat in silence waiting for Charlotte's reaction. She took a large sip of brandy.

'Oh, shit,' she said.

'Yes indeed,' responded Mater. 'Anthony's possibly a shit and we're definitively in it over our ankles. The whole show looks pretty shitty.'

Charlotte picked up the bottle and dispensed them both a measure.

'Keep calm and carry on, M. But do you, do we, inform Control?' she asked.

Mater had spent much of the journey back to Yorkshire wrestling with this and reached a conclusion.

'Not yet. Let's give Anthony the benefit of the doubt. What he said about attending the funeral might be true and the hotel just a coincidence. And the mosque? Perhaps he was following up some lead or other.'

Charlotte snorted. 'More shit, Phil, bullshit. You don't make multiple random throws with the darts and they all hit triple twenty. There are too many coincidences. Anyway, if there is a problem at that mosque, 5 would be actioning it, not one of our seniors. You should inform the boss.'

'Give me a little time,' replied Mater. 'If I can track Anthony down, I will find out what he's up to.'

'And how, assuming you locate him, will you get him to speak?'

Mater was evasive. 'I'll manage. I doubt it will be pleasant. He won't enjoy it, but he'll talk.'

The next day Dr Baird arrived exactly at ten. The Major welcomed him in as an old friend and introduced him to Mater.

'Ah, I wondered if you might be Ms Hawick's brother,' he said, as he shook Mater's hand.

'No, just a colleague,' responded Mater. He wasn't sure what the Major had revealed, if anything, to the doctor about his house guests.

The Major invited everyone into the kitchen.

'Morning coffee for all?' he asked. 'I'll leave a pot on the table and take mine through to the study then you two, no three, can discuss things in strictest medical confidence.' He chuckled as he poured his own, took a biscuit and left the room. He was quite enjoying all the skulduggery.

Mater and Charlotte were reassured by learning the Major and Dr Baird knew each other so well. They sat down and Mater served. Dr Baird was the first to speak.

'Do you mind if I vape?' he asked, 'I've been trying to give up my tobacco habit ever since I was discharged from the army.'

Charlotte was amused. They were asking for advice about dealing with addictions from an addict.

Puffing clouds of eucalyptus flavoured nicotine rich vapour, Dr Baird turned to Charlotte. 'Ms Hawick, I wasn't expecting someone else to be sitting in on our discussions. Are you OK with this?' He waved his hand through the fog in Mater's direction. She nodded. Dr Baird continued. 'Let's cut the pretence. Who you really are or what you're involved in is your business. I don't need to know. If you belong to one or two

174

particular organisations, which I suspect you do, then I hope I can reassure you. Like you, I am a signatory to the act. You can rely on me to keep secrets. I was employed in a variety of active and advisory roles for, how should I put it, Her Majesty's Special Services.'

Mater was pleased the doctor had hinted at his past commitments, connections and loyalty.

Dr Baird continued. 'In order for me to assist, some background would be useful, but if I ask a question too far or pry too deep, please let me know. I won't be offended.'

Charlotte took over. 'Thank you, Dr Baird. We've carried out checks and would be delighted if you helped us. But I should clarify one or two things. I have a brother but unlike the one described. I hope you'll forgive me. The gunshot wound. I'm sure you guessed correctly; a very close shave, literally, with a high velocity round. To be frank, a bit too close for comfort. You may have interpreted my lack of enthusiasm for seeking medical care from anywhere but yourself as a sign that our current project is exceptionally secret. You would be right. We are tasked to recruit new staff but unfortunately some candidates have addiction problems and these personal issues must be dealt with before employment is offered.'

Dr Baird put his hand up, indicating she should stop. 'Enough. This already sounds quite bizarre. Can't you find anybody suitable without these complications?'

Mater stepped in. 'The people we are targeting possess unique skills. There is no-one else. Obviously, if their addictions cannot be managed, then they will be deemed unsuitable for the job. And naturally, they would be free to choose whether to participate in any treatment proposed and the work that follows.'

'OK,' continued Dr Baird, 'Let me explain. My understanding is the programme typically involves inducing a coma for about a week, during which the patient withdraws from all alcohol or drugs. This requires them to stay in an intensive care environment which, I must warn you, is very expensive. Sometimes specific antidotes are given depending on which drug they are addicted to.'

'Cost won't be an issue,' advised Charlotte, butting in.

Dr Baird carried on. 'So, you will need to access or establish an intensive care set-up with all necessary medical and nursing support. All staff would have to be prepared to accept one aspect that is unpleasant and unpredictable.'

'That is?' asked Mater.

'There is a significant mortality risk associated with this treatment. So high, that it has been abandoned in mainstream medical practice. Makes the ethics difficult and anyone involved might be putting their career on the line if it goes wrong. Is it worth it when there's always the risk the patient may relapse?'

'Doesn't sound very encouraging,' concluded Charlotte.

Dr Baird sighed and rolled his head side to side. 'Well,' he said, 'It depends on how important that individual is to your work and how urgent it is to rid them of their vice. Only you can answer that. Most of what I said I gleaned from my anaesthetic colleagues, one of whom has worked in this area during his time in America, where it remains quite popular. Would you like me to put you in touch with him?'

Charlotte decided Mater and her needed to discuss things further before making any decision.

'Thank you very much, Dr Baird. I think I understood everything, most educational. Can we get back to you if we want to go ahead?'

'Of course, call me at the hospital anytime. I'll find Archie for a brief chat and then I need to be on my way. Lives to be saved and all that.'

The Doctor stood up, reached forward and shook their hands. 'Good luck and take care.'

Charlotte watched the door close and then turned to Mater.

'Well?' She said.

He had already considered the options. 'Perhaps we use the establishment of a medical clinic as cover for renting the Sutherland Lodge? If we involve Dr Baird further, we would be relying on him to help with the detox facilities, doctors and nurses. It all seems rather complicated. But we could open our little hospital, so to speak, run the programme and then close it down immediately afterwards, sending the staff away with adequate financial reward. That should shut them up.' Mater saw Charlotte shaking her head.

'Won't work unless they are Office staff,' she said, 'We can't rely on others to keep mum and obviously we can't use employees of the service. It is better you go on your recruitment drive. If you find anybody suitable and willing, we ask Dr Baird and his anaesthetist to cure our candidates using their own proper facilities. If we pay enough, I'm sure all the good doctors would be delighted to help.'

'Agreed,' said Mater. 'Let's divide the workload. I suggest you sort out the Lodge facility. We can still pretend it is to be used as a rehab or fitness centre. In those posh magazines, you periodically see large private houses advertising themselves as retreats for the rich and famous. Keep in with Dr Baird until I have found someone who needs his help. I shall concentrate on recruitment and Anthony. I must find out what he's up to before we go too far with our plans. We need to know whether he is involved or can be eliminated as a suspect.'

Mater and Charlotte decided to tackle their tasks immediately. Mr Randall informed the Major that he would soon be leaving again and asked if it would be alright for Suzanne to stay. The Major replied, with a twinkle in his eye, he would be delighted to have a young woman staying in his home, keeping him company.

The next morning, the Major was surprised by the quantity of food that Mr Randall ate. Mater, not knowing exactly how the coming few days or weeks would pan out, thought it sensible to leave with a full tank. After breakfast, he packed his bag with a few spare clothes, toiletries and tucked in a wad of cash. He put on his thick coat and hat, checked his mobile was fully charged and went to find the Major. He found him sitting in his study behind an elegant walnut veneer writing desk, catching up on paperwork.

'Ah, off again, Mr Randall. I'm going to start making wagers on how long you will be gone.'

'Not long, if you keep on feeding and watering me so well,' answered Mater.

'You'll need this,' said the Major, pulling open the top drawer of his desk and taking out the Makarov. 'Can't have you wandering out into the big bad world without it, can we? I'm sorry there isn't any more ammunition, only four rounds remain, but perhaps you can lay your hands on some more.

Mater wasn't sure he wanted to roam the backstreets of London or anywhere else armed. If discovered, the weapon could bring him into contact with the authorities. But, it just might, as the Major suggested, save his life. He took the gun, wrapped it in an old T-shirt from his holdall and placed it inside the bag.

'Thank you Major, once again. Don't worry too much about Suzanne; she is very capable of looking after herself.'

'About that, Mr Randall, I have no doubt. Look forward to seeing you again soon. I'll try to save you a dram from the scotch you gave me but if you're away too long, I'm not making any promises.'

Charlotte drove Mater to the railway station in Harrogate. As she pulled up at the drop off bay, she asked. 'Do you know where you will go?'

'Yes, but I should keep it to myself. I'm going to deal with the brown stuff sticking to my shoe and then afterwards go AWOL from everything and everyone. Don't worry, I'll be in touch.'

He grabbed his bag, blew her a kiss and without looking back strode into the station. Charlotte waited a few moments before starting the engine unsure whether she would ever see him again.

Chapter 17

Mater bought himself a second-class single to London. *Cash is good. No-one asks who you are or why you are going: they just want your money,* he told himself, as he handed over a note to pay.

The next train was due in a quarter of an hour; his new life about to begin. He felt a mixture of trepidation and exhilaration. It pulled in on time and he climbed aboard.

'Here we go,' he whispered to himself, 'Do or die.'

Mater sat alone: the carriage less than half-full. During the journey, he formulated the plan for the coming days. He would rent a room in a cheap tourist hotel, buy a sleeping bag and more warm clothes from a charity shop and start living on the streets. He had often slept rough on missions but rarely in the urban environment. It would be sensible to spend a night here and there, meeting the dispossessed, asking questions and making offers to potential recruits but it wasn't necessary to slum it all the time. He didn't want to become tired either: fatigue led to mistakes and he couldn't afford any errors. Creating an opportunity to question Anthony played on his mind. He was convinced that something was going on but Anthony, being skilled in the art of evasion both physically and verbally, would be prepared even if he cornered him. It was preferable that Control didn't get wind of his concerns just in case he was wrong. He considered other familiar Office employees, questioning whether any of them might be involved. In addition to Simon and Control, he crossed paths with admin staff, computer specialists, cleaners and maintenance crews but was sure he hadn't antagonised anyone. *No,* he told himself, *Don't throw the net too far and wide. Concentrate on each suspect in turn. Follow up the leads you have and only change direction as new information comes to light. Anthony first; he must prove his innocence.*

As the train sped through the North London suburbs towards its final destination, Mater found the solution. If he enticed Anthony to a meeting, he would use his recruits to carry out his dirty work. A first test of their abilities and commitment. He was eager to get going, wondering whether his scheme really had any mileage.

After the express pulled into the terminus, Mater sat waiting while his fellow passengers, impatient to get off, stood in the aisle clutching their belongings. He was pleased no-one seemed to take any interest in him. As the last passenger walked away to the carriage door and disembarked, Mater picked up his bag and followed. He stepped down onto the platform, bumping into the train's maintenance crew who waited to climb aboard and prepare the train for its return journey. Mater ambled towards the exit. No ticket checks. Nobody noticed the middle aged unshaven traveller with the heavy grey old coat and hat, carrying his world in his hand.

Outside the station, a man, of similar age to himself, wrapped in a grubby blanket, squatted on the damp pavement, insulated from it by a square of cardboard. An infinitely patient and loyal dog lay beside him. Mater hesitated in front of them. The man shook a paper cup in Mater's direction in hope, his face full of resignation. Mater reached into his pocket, deposited a few coins and wished him well. The man checked the cup and his expression changed to one of surprise. He beamed at Mater.

'Thank you and a good day to you, sir,' he said, his voice hardly audible above the passing London traffic.

Mater smiled back and walked on, wondering whether he had just abandoned a potential recruit.

First things first, he thought as he approached a nearby parade of shops. Most were up market boutiques, Kings Cross, at last, up and coming but inconveniently so for him. He was about to give up when he spotted a charity shop at the end of the street. He entered and began searching through rails of second-hand clothes. As he rummaged, a middle-aged lady volunteer dressed in a blue merino wool jumper and expensive Harris Tweed skirt scrutinised him closely. He took a small pile of items to the till. The posh assistant noted the cost of each and starting totting up.

'As you have more than five things here, you get a ten percent discount,' she said, eyeing her customer up and down. He didn't look like someone who needed to buy others' cast-offs.

'The charity helps prevent and treat cardiac disease doesn't it?' said Mater, handing her cash. 'It's a worthy cause. I don't need the reduction, thank you. Please keep the change as my donation.'

Her suspicious demeanour softened. She smiled, folded his new clothes and slid them into a carrier bag. He thanked her and walked out: the shop assistant would never learn about Mater's irreparably broken heart. He strolled along the streets in the vicinity of the station, keen not to stray too far from it. If he found a base nearby, the option to flee London, back to the safety of Yorkshire, would remain.

Mater found suitable accommodation more than one hundred metres from Kings Cross. Low key, an anonymous establishment whose residents included businessmen struggling to make deals and ends meet, passing trades people and tourists seeing London's sights on a shoe string. When Mr Sutcliffe booked in, the hotel manager insisted on payment up front; cash all the better. If necessary, his three day stay could be extended simply by paying for extra nights the evening before he would be due to leave. Breakfast would be available in the basement, self-service with as much coffee or tea as you like from the machines. He was advised in no uncertain terms that subletting or inviting guests in who proffer special services was strictly against the rules. If required, he should avail himself of the many walk-in facilities located in the neighbourhood. This was not news to Mater, but he thanked the manager for the advice, playing the innocent temporary workman pulled in to do a job in the West End.

Mater's third floor room at the back of the hotel was dingy and dirty with a view of the neighbouring building's brick wall. He wasn't convinced the bed sheets were fresh, certainly not ironed. In principle, this didn't bother him. Out of necessity, he had hot bedded for much of his life but as he had his sleeping bag with him, he unrolled it on top. At least the room was warm and dry: he would be able to sleep. It was early evening. Tonight, he would find a quiet café and then perhaps enjoy a film. Tomorrow, his search for human resources would begin.

Mater got up at six, washed and then dressed in his rough second-hand clothes. In the basement breakfast room, he placed a chipped mug under the tap of the coffee machine. It whirred briefly and

183

delivered a steaming hot brown liquid that, on tasting, he couldn't decide was tea or coffee. He helped himself to three plastic wrapped croissants, pocketing two and eating the third, washing down the rubbery item with the contents of his mug. One other resident, wearing overalls, ploughed through the same basic meal while reading a red-top newspaper. He ignored Mater and Mater him. Mater finished breakfast and headed upstairs, collected the few belongings he would take with him onto the streets and then left the warmth of the hotel. He decided his search should start near to his base but if fruitless, other London railway termini might deliver richer pickings.

He made his way back to Kings Cross station. Yesterday's man and dog had gone. Perhaps they had been moved on or sought shelter from the incessant drizzle that the grey sky deposited on the City below. With cash, he bought himself an Oyster card which gave him ready access to London's entire transport network. If necessary, he could avoid spending hours in the cold and wet by hiding in the labyrinth of the underground. The London pavements around the station buzzed with pedestrians vying for space, automatically negotiating their safe passage through the throng. There was the continuous roar of traffic that many suppressed with headphones, taking their owners to more peaceful places. Others, rather miraculously, avoided collisions despite being glued to their mobile phones. Mater stood for a moment, resting against the concrete wall of the station and observed the mass of humanity flowing in all directions. He wondered what they all did, what drove them. His eyes followed one or two individuals: a pretty young girl with waist-length brown hair that swayed from side to side as she passed, her short sheepskin boots sodden. A man marched past protected by an old fashioned light grey raincoat, clutching his briefcase in one hand, a folded umbrella and newspaper in the other. Mater tried to guess their jobs, destinations and purpose. They might be office workers or shop assistants, bankers or politicians, actors or dancers. He checked himself. Or perhaps just like him, living with a different persona, a surrogate life, an assassin or spy or both. It was impossible to tell.

Monday morning. He would give himself until Thursday to find volunteers who would want to swap their familiar existence for his proposal. A change that might alter their lives for ever. He picked up his belongings and wandered around the back of the station. For years the area had lain dormant, the efforts of the Luftwaffe still visible in the propped-up buildings that lined the cobbled streets covered in a thin layer of tarmac that had fallen into disrepair. The industrial warehouses circled by barbed wired and broken-bottle topped walls were gradually being replaced as the manufacturing base of the British economy eroded. Kings Cross, a hub for the desperate, the addicted and the destitute but Mater knew that it was changing with gleaming new office blocks rising, serviced by elegant walkways. However, he hoped the location's reputation as a sanctuary for the homeless and dispossessed persisted. London thrived but many of its citizens were left behind; struggling with little cash, often mental illness and complicated backgrounds. Mater intended to make offers that might help but only to the right person or people. He couldn't solve the social inequalities that were so evident even if he had wanted to. He had his own personal agenda from which he would not deviate.

In front of one steel and glass building, he spotted someone who was sheltering under the overhang of the first floor, sat on the pavement but protected from the cold ground by a filthy mattress. The man, wrapped in a blanket, rested his back against the polished concrete wall, holding the ubiquitous cup while simultaneously stroking an obedient whippet. Mater sidled over. The man held out his cup and pointed to a sign resting against his feet that indicated both dog and owner were hungry.

Mater shook his head. 'I'm in the same position as you, mate. Merely looking for somewhere warm, a place where I can lay up without being bothered.'

The man nodded, understanding. 'Just arrived?' he asked. 'You don't look like you've lived on the street for long.'

Mater was surprised by the man's perceptive skill. He thought quickly. 'You're right,' he said, 'I'm new to this game so any advice you can give me would be most welcome.'

The man looked Mater up and down before beckoning to him to sit beside him. Mater perched himself on a corner of the mattress, hoping that any lice or flees present would be numbed by the cold, unable to leap across. He reached out to stroke the dog wedged between them. He expected to smell the familiar odour of the unwashed but was surprised by a pleasant perfumed scent of lavender.

'You'll need one of those. It's obligatory,' said the man, pointing at his pet. 'Tugs at the heartstrings and useful to keep you warm and safe. A perpetual hot-water bottle on legs. We're coming into spring but I tell you last winter was harsh. Not everyone survived.'

Mater didn't answer. He had experienced the effects of days of exposure. He found it more demanding than the heat of the desert or the permanent damp of the rainforest. Once the cold penetrated, the discomfort infiltrated your every thought and even the simplest of tasks became almost impossible. Years earlier, his unit had nearly been overrun in the Afghani mountains when their ability to fire weapons and operate radios degraded. The memory made him shiver. He tightened the belt on his coat and tugged down his woolly hat.

The man broke the silence. 'Where're you from?'

'Just north of London,' replied Mater. 'Came by train. Penniless but managed to fare dodge.'

The man grinned. 'Well done. It's us against the system or perhaps the other way around. I'm always pleased when I pull one over the bastards who caused me to end up where I am now.'

'What happened?' enquired Mater.

The man didn't answer but offered advice instead while gently stroking the dog behind each ear, causing the creature to sigh and stretch out.

'I suggest you're careful what you tell people. Good folk live in our community but also those who screw you. Then there's the mad, the druggies, and the simply lost. You never quite know who you're dealing with.'

Mater persevered. He noted the man's appearance, guessing that despite the weather beaten skin he wasn't older than thirty. His shabby clothes were offset by a clean shaven face and neatly tied back long black hair.

'And you. To which group do you belong?'

The man laughed. 'Good try. Let's simply say that I consider myself unlucky. A poor throw of the dice. Can happen to anyone, anytime.'

Mater nodded with understanding. His own life had thrown up both welcome and unwelcome surprises. His thoughts briefly drifted to his early career in the service. Images of family and friends long departed rose into his consciousness. He fought to suppress them. The man was right. You never knew when you would be dealt a bad hand. His focus returned to the man beside him. Well spoken, clean and tidy: not as Mater had expected. Educated perhaps; an enigma.

'Unlucky, how so?' he asked gently.

The man screwed up his face but continued to caress his dog using the motion as therapy against the anger rising within.

'Stop digging,' he replied. 'Only let me say, I worked in one of these and was doing exceptionally well.' He slapped the glass and concrete tower. 'The higher you go, the further you fall and I nearly reached the top even though I was young. Then the crash. Job gone, and for many others too, but somehow some wangled their way back in. For me, no such luck.'

'I am sorry,' said Mater.

'Don't be. It's dog eat dog out there. I often think I'm better off out of it. Now I have time, plenty of it. The world rushes by, its citizens riding life's carousel at an ever faster pace and are they satisfied?' He pointed towards the people scurrying along the pavement. 'Do they look happy?'

As they passed, Mater looked at their bowed heads; everyone ignored the two men and the dog. No-one smiled. It was a good question. He considered his own position. *Content?* He had no doubt in the past he had been very happy. Life seemed to have smelt of roses as strong as the flowery scent that wafted from beside him but now it was different. He couldn't resist the excitement of his work. It was his addiction. And there were moments with his team of unrestrained laughter, but actual joy, pure bliss, that had disappeared long ago.

'You're right,' answered Mater, 'They don't appear pleased with their lot but perhaps they have hope. Optimistic tomorrow will be better than today. Isn't that something worth living for?'

The man chuckled. 'That's the common mistake we all make.'

He changed the subject. 'My advice to you is straightforward. Think carefully before you follow in my footsteps.' He waved his arm towards the people on the street in front. 'It's your choice but if you're fortunate to have a tie to their world, don't let go. Once it's severed, the fall never ends.'

'Advice noted. But, given the chance, would you want to come back inside?' asked Mater, taking advantage of the opening.

The man laughed again. 'No, bloody hell, no. Despite the discomfort and the dangers, I'm settled. As I said, I have time and when it's all over I won't care and nor will anyone else. Why ask for more?'

A coin dropped into the paper cup, still steadily held in his outstretched hand, interrupting the flow of his thoughts. He thanked the donor.

'See,' observed Mater, 'Someone cares.'

'Maybe or perhaps they are just assuaging their conscience.'

Cynical but quite possibly true, thought Mater. He knew this man, whoever he was, did not fit the description of those he needed. Time to move on. London's streets crawled with potential recruits. All it would take would be one lucky break. He would hang around Kings Cross for a while and when he needed a rest, his hotel room, although basic, was there to provide comfort and sanctuary. He stood up.

'Where do you recommend I try to sleep tonight?' he asked.

The man pointed north. 'Walk about a mile in that direction and you'll see a couple of disused warehouses off Goods Way, backing onto the railway line. Sometimes I stay there. It's a bit busy, but you should find a dry space and you get used to the trains running all night. We might bump into each other again. It's been a pleasure to chat. Good luck.'

'Thanks,' said Mater, 'Good luck to you too.' He patted the dog again, stood up, brushed himself off, picked up his few belongings and walked away back towards the railway station. There he would buy himself a coffee and then go underground; respite from the cold and damp.

He wandered onto the concourse of the terminus and joined a queue at the nearest café. The line of travellers shuffled their bags along the tiled floor with their feet. Mater could make out a range of languages being spoken: French, Italian, unfamiliar tongues from the Far East and an American version of English. The sound of the Americans talking loudly grated, their all too public conversation barely drowned out by the regular tannoy announcements advising train departures and the need to keep luggage safe to avoid destruction. As he reached the front of the queue, a firm hand grasped his shoulder. He swung round preparing to defend himself using the skills he had practised so often that they could be deployed automatically and only just managed to suppress his reflexes. Two British Transport police officers loomed over him despite his own significant height. One had his baton drawn. Mater realised at once this was not the time or place to demonstrate his abilities.

'Move on,' growled the officer, brandishing the steel rod.

'I'm only queuing for a coffee,' protested Mater. He heard a tutting from the customers behind him.

'Yeah, yeah, yeah. The standard line. Listen, nobody wants their bags rummaged in by you or your type. Come on. Let's go.'

His colleague pulled out a pair of handcuffs. Mater knew he couldn't afford to protest further. He had a job to do; far more important than hunting petty criminals.

'Okay,' he said. He bent down to pick up his belongings. A large black boot held the strap of his bag to the floor. He looked up at its owner who stood motionless, grinning. From behind him a voice called out.

'Leave the poor man alone.'

An old lady, smartly dressed and carrying a Gucci handbag, stared at the officers.

'Here,' she said, handing over her cup of coffee to Mater, 'Have mine and this.' She opened her bag and searched inside before withdrawing a twenty pound note which she gave to him.

'Thank you very much. That's most generous, you're so kind,' said Mater, accepting both gifts.

He smiled at her and then smirked at the police officers who released their grip from him and his belongings and then took a step backwards. With his free hand, Mater gathered his things and walked slowly towards the entrance to the underground.

'Someone cares,' he said again, this time to himself.

He decided he would use the tube to visit the location where Liam had met his fate. He wasn't sure he should, but it was only a couple of stops down the line and it might reinvigorate his enthusiasm for the task he had set himself. The police officers' actions hadn't surprised him but it had been disappointing all the same. Once again, he speculated whether it was all worth it: working to protect a society that he increasingly considered divided and uncaring. A fleeting trip to Euston Square might upset him but it might also make him angry. Bad things and bad people infuriated Mater, drove him on. He knew from bitter experience great personal loss tries to destroy you, emptying you of energy and determination. But he had taught himself to convert this void into controlled hidden fury, motivating him to work ever harder to do what he perceived to be right. He realised his enemies likewise believed in their cause but he had to trust his own values. They made him willing to risk his life fighting those organisations that suppressed others, either in their own communities or beyond, dominating by force rather than dialogue. To this end, he had honed his skills as an Office operative and ended up a trained killer.

He caught the next tube, barely aware of the brief journey while he contemplated his first morning on the streets. He tried to imagine what Liam had been thinking as he made his way to escape London, seeking safety in the West Country.

At Euston Square, he stepped from the train and walked slowly to the escalator hall. He stopped at the base of the down escalator, standing to one side to allow passengers to pass. He didn't expect to see any residual sign of the drama that had unfolded there so recently and indeed there was none. Each user of the escalator stepping on the very spot where his colleague had died, oblivious. Mater watched as the metal steps tumbled under the floor reappearing at the top, ready for use.

What goes around comes around, he thought. *Every square yard on the planet must have witnessed, at some time, a dramatic event, either good or evil. It was only a matter of waiting.*

He closed his eyes. There was Liam standing there, beckoning him to step onto the up-escalator, reassuring him it was safe. He felt himself sway and quickly opened his eyes again. The escalator was devoid of users and Liam had disappeared. The anger he yearned for rose within him but then he heard the sound of a lone busker emanating from above. He stepped onto the escalator. At the top, melancholic music drifted from a side passage. He made his way towards its origin. Wary of the location, he took extra care to make sure no-one followed as he entered the tunnel. The volume of the saxophone grew as he turned the corner. The saxophonist sat on a camping chair, instrument to lips, rocking gently. Mater recognised the song: 'Baker Street'.

Wrong station but nice rendition all the same, he thought.

He stopped in front of the performer; a girl, so young she could have been his granddaughter. The paper at her feet carried the predictable appeal for funds. She looked at Mater but continued to play without hesitation. He stood silently listening as the tune echoed along the tile-lined tunnel, simultaneously sorrowful and uplifting. She finished playing and lowered her instrument. Mater clapped; the sound of his clapping rippling through the tunnel.

'That was excellent,' he said.

'Thank you,' replied the girl, indicating with the saxophone the note in front of her.

'Worked this patch long?' asked Mater, keeping his distance from her, aware of the age gap between them and his own appearance. He didn't want to unnerve her. It was a daft question but somehow he hoped she had been there when Liam died. Perhaps her music had comforted him but maybe also, just maybe, she had seen something that no-one else had. The girl looked anxious.

What did this man mean by working? I'm not a prostitute but a talented music student trying to make ends meet, she thought before saying. 'I simply play my saxophone to practise and for others to enjoy. If I earn extra cash, all the better. Student life is tough.'

'Are you studying music?' asked Mater with genuine interest.

'Yep, at the Royal College but as I say there's little support. You're not some kind of policeman about to prevent me from doing what I do, are you?' She looked at Mater, pleadingly, wondering if the tramp like figure was an undercover officer.

Mater decided to come to the point. 'No, no, not all. Your playing is lovely but I wonder if you can help me. You see, a close friend of mine died in this very station recently. Perhaps you were here when it happened. I was told he succumbed to a heart attack

194

and simply collapsed on his way to work. I just need to know he didn't suffer.'

The girl eyed Mater carefully. He seemed a nice man, genuinely sad. She didn't think she could help but felt she should respond.

'I'm sorry about your friend,' she said and thought for a moment before recalling she had been present when there was a medical emergency a little while ago.

'I was at the station but not at this spot. I had just arrived, planning to busk during the morning rush, when this guy fell down the escalator. It carried him all the way to the bottom. People gathered round and called for help but I stood back and watched. To be honest, I'd no idea what to do and they appeared to be doing all they could for him. Eventually, paramedics appeared and took him away. I didn't play that day.'

'Thank you,' said Mater, 'It must have been distressing.'

She paused, not wanting to cause upset. 'It wasn't really. It seemed like in a movie. Everyone characters in a drama as I simply looked on. After-all, I didn't know him or anyone else. I half expected someone to call 'cut' and your friend, if it was him, to stand up again. Some stunt he performed though! Oh, I'm sorry. I didn't mean to say that.' She looked down.

Mater took his opportunity. 'It's OK,' he said, 'By chance did you see anything else that seemed different, appeared not quite right?'

The girl looked up again, considering his question. Once more, she wondered who he really was.

'Are you a policeman or what? You don't look like one but...' she trailed off.

Mater knew he had to give her something if he was going to receive anything in return. 'Sort of,' he said. 'The man you saw fall was a very close friend. His name was Liam, but he was often in some kind of trouble. He was always so fit that I find it difficult to accept he died from a heart problem and just wondered whether he had been pushed down the escalator? So, I thought I'd try to find out even though it won't help him now.'

The girl sat in silence for a bit, tapping the keys and levers on her saxophone, searching her memory of the day's events.

'I did see something that surprised me. As your friend fell, people shouted out but at the top these two tall guys simply stood there. They didn't run down after him, quite the opposite: it was almost as if they were blocking the escalator, trying to stop others using it. When he reached the bottom, I looked up again, and they had gone.'

'Most interesting, could you describe them better?'

'Well, as I said, both were tall, smartly dressed guys, grey suits, oh and one had really blond hair, almost bleached white. That's why I could see it from where I stood even though they were quite far away. That's about it, I'm afraid.'

'Thanks, you've been really helpful,' responded Mater. He delved into his pocket and took out the twenty pounds he had received earlier.

'Here,' he said, 'Good luck with your studies and thanks again for the music. You play beautifully.'

196

The girl eyes sparkled with delight. She grinned. 'Thank you so much,' she said, snatching the note, 'And I am truly sorry about your friend.'

Mater nodded and walked back along the tunnel.

'What goes around comes around,' he repeated to himself. He briefly visualised the kind face of the elderly lady at Kings Cross before the image was abruptly interrupted by the blurred CCTV images of Liam's murderers.

Chapter 18

Mater spent the afternoon wandering across much of central London, passing through tidy parks and by famous landmarks. In Regents Park, he heard the animals in the zoo complain about their lot. After walking north up Primrose Hill, he stopped to enjoy the magnificent view of the city's skyline. He noted several of the park-benches were occupied by the poor and dispossessed, their few belongings gathered around them. The majority slept or just stared vacantly into the distance but a few sat muttering to themselves and their demons. Everywhere, empty cans and bottles lay scattered at their feet and overflowed from rubbish bins. From time to time he dropped a coin or two in the owner's preferred receptacle and attempted to strike up a conversation. The responses he received varied from a grateful nod to a mutter, often almost unintelligible but usually, although not always, in English. Many slept, he assumed either because of inebriation or as they caught up after a night attempting to keep warm. And then there were those who seemed simply crazy: rocking back and forth or completely immobile, dumb, unaware of him or their surroundings. Yet others ranted and swore incessantly, ensuring their patch remained devoid of human beings; everyone nervously skirting around them. He thought he knew the city well, but this was one facet that had passed him by. It resembled an open air asylum.

If I lived my life again, perhaps I should have been a social worker or even a psychiatrist, he wondered.

As the sun dipped towards the horizon, he wandered back to the Kings Cross area in order to find the warehouses where, hopefully, he could stay the night. There, he might find at least one potential candidate for his new team. He had had little luck so far. On the way he picked up food and filled his bag with beer and a bottle of vodka. If the community was going to accept him, he guessed he would still have to pay for his bed. If he had learnt anything during the day, it was that this parallel world he had entered lived by its own rules and customs; the citizens just as territorial as any middle class home counties neighbourhood.

At Kings Cross, he spotted the man he had seen when he first arrived, lying on the ground in exactly the same place, still guarded by his dog. Mater paused briefly in front of him. Despite the traffic noise, he heard snoring. He bent down to make a cash donation but withdrew his hand quickly as the creature snarled.

'I'm trying to give not take, stupid animal,' he said, returning the money to his pocket.

He turned the corner and walked north along York Way, passing the office block where he had sat that morning stroking the whippet. The dog and its owner were gone. He hurried, watching carefully for the turning for Goods Lane, keen to find the warehouses before it was completely dark. Ahead of him a dark figure made slow progress, weaving from side to side across the broken paving stones, struggling with its burden of plastic carrier bags. When Mater drew level, the man's appearance and belongings suggested he might be heading for the same destination. The man breathed heavily, rapid gasps interspersed by an intermittent coarse cough that ended with him spitting into the road. His left leg appeared to struggle to keep up with his right, the foot dragging along the ground.

'Evening,' said Mater, 'May I help you with your bags?'

'Top of the day to you too,' came the reply, the broad Southern Irish accent clearly recognisable despite the slurring of his speech. 'Kind offer, but I'll manage.'

The man's fists clenched the thin plastic handles, callouses on his palms preventing the material from cutting into his hands. He slowed further. It was a challenge to walk and simultaneously make conversation with this stranger.

To Mater, he seemed very old though tough and determined. Mater continued. 'I'm looking for the disused self-storage warehouse where I can doss down for the night. Do you know where it is?'

'I guessed right. Follow me. Name's Patrick but don't call me Paddy.'

Mater chuckled inside. *Had to be,* he thought, blurting out before he could stop himself: 'Truly your name or simply one that fits?'

The man didn't take offence. He began to laugh himself, the effort halting his progress along the pavement. His thin frame shook. The laughter ended with a coughing fit and the production of a blood stained glob that streaked down the front of his filthy frayed coat. He wiped his bearded face with his sleeve. Still short of breath, he turned to Mater and looked him up and down before asking. 'And yours, what's yours?'

'Phil, just Phil.'

'OK Phil, I will show you where we go and I'll accept your offer to help me. Bloody leg's had enough. Should have had it chopped off a long time ago but when it's your own, it's a difficult decision.'

'What happened to it?' enquired Mater, keen to keep the conversation flowing.

'Who knows? I visited one of those drop in doctor clinics years ago. They told me to stop smoking. Said it was messing up my arteries. How does that work then? A fag in your mouth, smoke in your lungs. Now that explains my breathing but how does it reach your legs? Can't manage a ciggy anymore. Bloody doctors. They haven't got a scooby doo.' He coughed again.

Mater noted the cockney slang. 'Been on the streets for long?' he asked.

'More years than you've had hot dinners. I'm nearly fifty and came here in my teens.'

Mater was surprised; around the same age as himself. He had assumed Patrick must be over seventy. Clearly the lifestyle and the smoking had caused a lot of damage; the combination remorselessly finishing the man off. He picked up three of Patrick's four bags, adding them to his own limited possessions. The two men set off again. Mater made sure he kept to his companion's snail's pace.

Dusk fell, the footpath barely illuminated by the few working street lamps, supplemented by the dying rays of the setting sun. Around the next corner, the dark shadow of a large warehouse loomed in front of them, set back from the road by an overgrown vehicle park. The complex was surrounded by a high fence topped with rusty barbed wire. They passed the main gates, heavily padlocked and adorned with signs warning of guard-dogs and security cameras. Mater pointed to the signs as they slowly ambled past.

'Bullshit,' commented Patrick. 'We're almost there. The good thing about those signs is they help keep others out. Those of us in the know have used this place for ages and we don't want trouble from anyone.' He looked at Mater sternly before coughing again. Mater wondered if it was a coded warning to him not to rock the boat.

At the far end of the site, an alleyway left the road and tracked the perimeter fence. Mater followed as they entered. A few paces on, Patrick put down his remaining bag and pulled at a small loose section of chain-link, creating an opening. He waved Mater through. With both men inside, the fence sprang back into position.

'Welcome to our home. You'll find it quite busy here and don't expect everyone to be welcoming,' Patrick warned.

He guided Mater to a steel side door, the padlock and its hasp long gone. On opening it, Mater heard the murmuring of voices. By the glow of a single low wattage bulb he made out at least ten people who turned in unison to face the new arrivals.

'Evening all,' announced Patrick, 'This is Phil. He's looking for somewhere for tonight. He's my guest.'

The mumbling grew louder as if the occupants of the warehouse needed to make a decision. Mater stood still, watching and waiting. If he had to, he could leg it before anyone could catch him. He was glad that, unlike Patrick, he maintained his fitness. Eventually the chatter died down and a lone voice spoke.

'OK Patrick. Welcome Phil. By chance did you bring any booze with you? If you have, let's consider it payment for your reservation.'

Patrick interjected. 'Hey, come on. Phil's one of us. He's only recently arrived.'

'One of us, is he? Are you sure?' replied the spokesman.

'I simply say we should be a little more generous.'

Mater waved to Patrick. 'No, it's fine. I've brought a bottle with me and would prefer to share it, if that's OK with you?'

He opened his bag, took out the vodka and placed it on the wooden box in front of the assembled men. The spokesman reached forward and examined it. After adjusting his cracked spectacles, he held it up to the dim lamp.

'Blimey,' he said, his grin exposing a few blackened rotten stumps, 'It's the real thing, not some cheap crap.'

He looked at Mater. 'How can you afford this?' he queried suspiciously before concluding, 'One night Patrick and then it's better he moves on.'

Mater spoke up. 'Thanks a lot, I'm grateful. Patrick is right. I'm new and finding my feet but I promise you I mean no harm. Just show me where I can lay my head and I will be on my way when it gets light.'

He cursed himself for the vodka. Branded was a mistake. A detail but potentially significant.

The spokesman stood up. He was tall, broad and very heavily built. Someone, Mater surmised, able to defend himself and the group if he had to. *No wonder he's the leader of the pack,* thought Mater, The man led Mater to the far side of the room that had once served as a manager's office, treading carefully over a line of old blankets and sleeping bags. He pointed to a small bare area of floor.

'Your spot, guest facilities,' he said, 'In the night, if you need a piss, make sure you go outside and don't wake the rest of us. A couple of guys here regularly have bad dreams and if you disturb them, all hell might break loose. Understood?'

'OK,' replied Mater. 'I'll bring my stuff over here and then may I join you for a drink?' He was keen to break the ice.

The spokesman grunted. 'As you brought the booze, of course.'

Mater collected his belongings and laid his sleeping bag out close to, but not touching, the damp wall. He planned to edge in on the conversation, gain their confidence. He had no idea whether anyone present might be useful to him but hoped to find out. Within the short time it took to make his bed, the vodka had been shared amongst all, leaving just a little for their visitor. The men huddled around the wooden box they used as a table. Some perched on wobbly old chairs, nearly as legless as their owners, while others sat on the floor. They made space for Mater. He picked up the chipped glass containing his share and raised it with a toast.

'To my hosts and their generosity.'

He sipped the vodka and watched as his companions drank theirs; most draining their glasses, one or two savouring the luxury. Mater noted that three of the assembled didn't talk but simply seemed to stare vacantly at him. He wondered if they were fearful, mute, from overseas or insane. The effects of the alcohol loosened the tongues of those willing to speak. The conversation turned from discussing the day's events to the telling of increasingly lewd jokes but was often interrupted by the roar of trains tearing along the mainline nearby. Even the spokesman laughed and managed a smile in Mater's direction. Mater was surprised no-one asked him about his origins or why he was here but whenever he made tentative enquiries into the background of anyone, he was stonewalled. There was clearly an unspoken code of secrecy that everyone present adhered to. Perhaps, if Mater hadn't been there, they would have been more open but he would never find out. As the evening wore on the group thinned as individuals wandered off to their beds. At about eleven, Mater excused himself, briefly stepped outside for a pee and then carefully climbed over those sleeping to his own pitch. He was tired. He slid into his sleeping bag and listened to the mixture of sighs, snores and rustling.

The sound took him back to his first experience of barracks. Young soldiers pressed together. During those days though, there were the added sounds of the occasional recruit who cried with homesickness or carried out furtive acts of masturbation, fulfilling the universal need of youthful men. Then, there had been an implicit rule that nobody complained about the others' behaviour. Teasing and banter always allowed but everyone understood it was only a matter of time before they would be caught out doing the same. The exception in Mater's case was that, when young, he had not been homesick once. That feeling of emptiness arrived much later and followed tragedy. He felt unwelcome memories return and willed them away by concentrating on the days to come. Tomorrow, he would leave and make his way to another rail terminus. He was confident that if anywhere could provide rich pickings, it would be near a station.

At dawn, Mater was the first to wake. He levered himself out of his sleeping bag and stretched. The bare floorboards had taken their toll on his body, muscles restrained by the bag. He had slept surprisingly well though; dry and quite warm. He was grateful he hadn't been forced to sleep outside in a doorway. He quietly packed his few things and once again stepped gently over the shadowy forms curled up in a line. At the box table, he stopped and took out the cans of beer he had been carrying, leaving them in a neat stack as a gift. He pulled open the door and briefly glanced back.

Poor buggers, he thought, *Can't we do better than this?*

He heard Patrick's distinctive cough.

'Good luck,' whispered Patrick.

'Thanks and you too,' replied Mater, surmising the man who had helped him would not be long for this world. He stepped outside, found the opening in the fence and returned to the streets and his quest.

Back once more at Kings Cross, he took a tube to Victoria, squashed in with the silent morning commuters. He took the escalator to the surface and was glad to walk out into the open air; the cool damp tinged with the diesel fumes from London's buses and early delivery lorries. He walked around the back of the station and headed to Ecclestone Park, not more than five minutes away.

As he entered the park, the noise of the London traffic faded and he heard song birds hidden in the park's bushes and trees. Mater spied a man lying alone on a bench wrapped up like a mummy, tell-tale empty cans and bottles scattered underneath. Mater approached, bent down and gently nudged him. There was a grunt and the man, wrinkled and tanned, opened his eyes and stared at Mater.

'What do you want?' he demanded in a slurred voice, scowling.

'Just checking you were OK,' answered Mater.

The man relaxed a little. 'I'm fine,' he grunted, eyeing Mater up and down before asking. 'Are you one of those do-gooders relieving their consciences; about to offer words of wisdom and advice or have you something of more practical use for me?'

Mater chuckled. He delved in his coat and handed the man a five-pound note who pocketed it without a word.

'Neither,' he said. 'I'm someone who's following in your footsteps. Where's the best place to stay and meet folk such as yourself? It's my first time on the street and I might need advice.'

The man coughed. 'Everyone gives advice to us here,' he said. 'Some like it; others wish to be left alone. There are those happy to roam while others stay put. And many, like me, simply get pissed to forget.'

'Forget what?' asked Mater.

'If I told you I would be remembering, wouldn't I,' replied the man, angrily.

Mater apologised but carried on probing. 'How long have you been living like this?'

The man rolled himself over into a sitting position. 'More than fifteen years. Can't really recall what it's like to live indoors. You get used to it and the booze keeps out the cold. Blame the fucking army for much of it. You bloody serve and then when they've done with you, out you go with not a lot to keep you on the straight and narrow.'

'The straight and narrow?' repeated Mater, delighted to learn of his past connection with the army but concerned by what followed. 'So have you been a guest of Her Majesty then?'

The man was taken aback by Mater's intuition. At first he didn't respond, but reached down and fumbled under the bench, his hands searching for a plastic bottle, half-full of white cider. He placed it to his lips and emptied it without taking a breath. They sat in silence for a few minutes, both waiting for the alcoholic top-up to take effect. Eventually, the man spoke.

'Yep,' he said, his rambling even more slurred. 'Done for GBH. The fucker deserved it. Mouthing off about the military and misplaced loyalty and so on. You can't walk into a squaddies pub in Deal, say things and expect people like me to just sit there. What did he know? Stupid idiot. Crazy to pick a fight with an ex-soldier, someone trained to kill who had knifed three and probably shot many more in Iraq. I tell you, close combat is a truly fucking awful thing. One of the guys I killed squealed like a stuck pig, shouting in his own tongue for a few moments before keeling over. The others snuffed it quietly. Fucking war. You never forget.' The man was surprised to see Mater nodding, understanding. 'Yourself?' he asked.

Mater ignored the question and responded with his own. 'Are you still bitter, about the army, I mean and all that?'

'No, it's long gone but when you've lost everything, job, family, home, you sometimes wonder what might have been.'

Mater seized his opportunity. 'I've not been completely straight with you,' he said.

The man looked alarmed. 'What do you mean? You're not one of those save all souls God squaddie types, are you, or from the Police or the Social? I've done nothing wrong since I was let out from prison. I served my time.'

Mater smiled and softened his voice. 'No, none of those, but I might be able to help restore your self-esteem, though I need to know whether you want to get off the booze.'

The man was baffled. 'You're a strange geezer,' he said, 'Wandering over here, making me blab about my past then offering to help me but for what? Are you planning a bank raid or something? What's in it for you?'

Mater had expected this but he couldn't offer much of an answer; certainly not now and probably not for some time to come.

'I'm offering you a chance to rebuild your life. It demands persistence and commitment and at the end of it there may be a job. I can't give you details yet but I guarantee that you are very likely to be perfectly qualified for the post. You will have to trust me and me you.'

The man returned the cider bottle to his mouth and tried to extract the last drops of ethanol, squeezing the plastic container in desperation. Mater reached forward, clasped the bottle firmly and steadily pulled it away.

'You can do better than this,' he said quietly. 'What is your name?'

'Pete. Pete Stoneham. And yours?' said the man looking up at Mater, still standing above him as he sat on the bench.

'Mr Sutcliffe, Phil Sutcliffe.'

The man sighed, closed his eyes and dragged his wrappings tighter around him. Mater realised he had to make some sort of immediate proposal, a concession or he would lose this one to the next liquid fix. 'If you're interested, I'm staying for a few days at the Kings Cross Inn Hotel. You can catch me there but I'll pass by here again to check you're OK. Us military men need to look after each other.'

The man opened his eyes again and smiled, revealing broken brown teeth. 'I rather guessed you were an ex like me,' he said, 'I'll consider your offer. It might be worth a punt. If you come back, and I say if, then I may join you unless it risks me a stint inside. But I'm going to spend at least one more night sleeping rough; it's my way.'

Mater reached down and patted him on the shoulder. 'Good. I'll return tomorrow for your answer and I truly believe you could do well.' With that he walked away.

A hit. Here's hoping, he thought, uncertain as to whether Pete Stoneham would be there when he returned. Mater had the rest of the day to investigate Mr Stoneham's background before confirming his offer. Assuming it was his real name, it would be possible to check his military past simply by looking him up in the records held at any public library. First Mater needed coffee, and then he would hole up in the nearest library to check any paper or computer records he might lay his hands on. He strolled back to Victoria station, knowing there would be a choice of cafés and the tourist information centre there should be able to direct him to a library.

The nearest library at 160 Buckingham Palace Road occupied the lower two floors of a grand Georgian building; the interior elegantly panelled with floor to ceiling shelving, all stacked full. If Mater had removed a volume, a dust cloud would have cascaded down, caught by the light let in by the large bay windows. But he had joined the modern age and asked the bored librarian, playing patience on her own computer, to direct him to a public machine with internet access. She pointed towards a door at the far end, disappointed once again that her knowledge of books and libraries were no longer required.

The rooms with books had been empty, almost desolate, but the computer room buzzed. Visitors of all ages tapped away with variable ability. Mater looked for a vacant computer not overlooked by another browser and spotted one in the corner. No password necessary, he set to work. It took less than half an hour to track down the records of three ex-military Peter Stonehams but none seemed to fit the man's history. Two of the three had completed their service before the first Gulf War. The third served in the Logistics Corp and was unlikely to have fought on the front line.

Mater sat back, rocking on his chair, tapping his finger on the desk. Then it came to him. The fight in Deal. Hopefully he would be lucky and find details of the assault that led to the stretch in prison. There must be local newspaper reports. It would have been the type of thing to excite a budding journalist, hoping to move on from the parochial. Mater keyed in his search. The East Kent Mercury proved to be the rag that gave him the answer. 1993, two years after the end of the war, page five halfway down: Peter Steedman, ex-soldier, found guilty of causing grievous bodily harm, sent down for eighteen months.

Cautious bugger. Steedman is Stoneham, but maybe caution is good, thought Mater.

The trail went dead after 1993. He couldn't find any further reference to a Peter Steedman fitting the description of the man he had met. He returned to the service records. There was only one candidate. Corporal Peter Steedman, Royal Anglian Regiment, 1985 to 1993, dishonourable discharge; deployments to the Middle East, Cyprus and Belize. Awarded the military medal for acts of extreme front-line bravery during Gulf War One. Mater was delighted.

'Bullseye and with the first throw,' he whispered to himself, switching off the computer. 'Now all I have to do is persuade him to join my band of merry men.'

As Mater left the library, he thanked the librarian: he had found what he wanted. She looked up and said he was welcome, unsure what she had done to contribute to his successful visit.

Mater decided he would see if his luck would hold by approaching the next homeless person he encountered. If he was rebuffed, then he would take the rest of the day off and continue his mission with a return visit to Ecclestone Park the next day.

He passed by Buckingham Palace. As he weaved through the tourist throng, he contemplated the incomprehensible social divide between the Palace's residents and the homeless he had met. Years ago, he had sworn allegiance to Her Majesty but now his heart felt closer to the abandoned serviceman he had just met. He was no longer sure who exactly he was fighting for, but it was his job and he was loyal.

He crossed Green Park, all familiar territory, and headed into Mayfair. He wondered whether you got a higher class of vagrant in Mayfair, collecting guineas in their cups rather than asking for pounds. He stopped briefly to look through the showroom window of Stratstone's car dealership: showcasing the latest Aston Martin models, polished and gleaming. Mater chuckled to himself. James Bond motors. Only the CIA could afford posh wheels. The Office salary barely covered the cost of living but it was good to dream now and again.

'Going to buy one?' called a voice to his left.

Mater started slightly. He hadn't noticed the young woman, almost a girl, sitting on the pavement a little further on. She was hunched up, lank matted hair falling in front of her face, her hand caressing a patient mongrel tucked in beside her.

'Wish I could. How about you?' he said, at once realising the absurdity of his question and hoping she wouldn't take offence.

'Fuck off,' said the woman, laughing, 'But if you give me some money, I'll start saving.' She reached out with her free hand, exposing lines of sores stretching from her wrist up to the sleeve of her T-shirt.

Mater thought she must be cold, wearing so little, but she didn't seem bothered. He looked at the wounds and recognised the needle puncture marks.

'If I give you money, will you let me save you?' he asked somewhat melodramatically.

'Fuck off,' she said again, still with her arm outstretched.

Mater took out a note from his pocket and placed it in her hand. 'Here, something for the dog,' he said, knowing exactly what the money would be used for.

She laughed again, and he walked away.

Mater ambled slowly back through the West End to his hotel, looking down alleyways as he passed by; keen to spot fresh human resource. He seemed out of luck. *Perhaps, everyone's been moved on; dossers aren't good for the tourist trade.*

By the time he reached Kings Cross it was late afternoon. He realised he hadn't eaten since breakfast and so joined the take-away queue at a burger joint within throwing distance of his base. The food was still hot when he sat on his hotel room bed, staring through the window at the brick wall.

His thoughts turned to Corporal Steedman. Why was it there were men who could kill and others who couldn't? And why was it killers were divided into those who coped and those whose lives fell apart? Which was he? Was alcohol the crutch that if kicked away would cause him to fall or would he regain his strength; his self-esteem. If he joined Mater, only time and the detox treatment would tell.

Mater finished his burger and washed it down by placing his lips under the running cold tap in the en-suite shower room. The taste of London's water did not impress but compared to some liquids he had survived on during missions, it was quite acceptable. Fleetingly, he remembered Liam, wondering if he had stayed at the same place, imagining the fear he must have experienced when he realised he was being followed. He decided to call Charlotte to tell her the recruitment process had started and to check on progress at her end. He was keen to find out if the Lodge was on track and whether she had been in touch with Dr Baird.

Charlotte answered her mobile within five rings, recognising it was him calling. 'I'll pop out of the kitchen,' she said, 'The Major, and I are just enjoying a pre-dinner drink.'

Mater visualised the scene. Life at Langley Hall had taken on its own special routine and he quite missed it even though he had only been away a day or so. He wondered if it was a sign of getting older. A few moments later her voice returned.

'Great news, the Lodge has accepted our reservation. We can have it for four months and extend as needed; monthly after that. I've reviewed the facilities and made enquiries as to how near the neighbours are. Looks encouraging on both fronts. How are you getting on with your good-for-nothing drop-outs?' she teased.

'I also have potentially, positive news,' answered Mater. 'First target looks promising. I will find out tomorrow whether we have a goer. I suspect he might benefit from the Dr Baird treatment. Have you heard from the good doctor?'

'No, but there's no reason to contact him again until we have confirmed patients requiring treatment.'

'OK. Enjoy your evening. Pass my best wishes to the Major,' said Mater.

'Enjoy yours too,' replied Charlotte. 'Hope the pavement isn't too hard.'

Mater, held his mobile to the mattress, bounced up and down on the bed, making it squeak.

'What's that noise?' asked Charlotte anxiously when Mater returned the phone to his ear.

'Noise, what noise?' he teased back. He wasn't going to tell her that at this stage, at least, there was no point in suffering. 'Speak to you soon,' he said and hung up.

The next morning, Mater made his way back to Ecclestone Park. Near to his destination, he bought two cups of coffee and four fresh bacon rolls, keeping them warm by placing them in his coat pockets. In the park, everything appeared as it had done the day before, except when he reached the bench it was vacant. He looked around. All was peaceful apart from the incessant noise of London's traffic, punctuated by regular fly pasts as aircraft dropped height during their easterly approach to Heathrow.

Mater sat and placed the coffee cups on an arm of the bench. He rummaged in a pocket and took out a bacon roll. Just as he put it to his mouth, a voice called out.

'I'll have some of that, Mr Sutcliffe.'

Mater swung round. Pete Steedman emerged from bushes beyond the flower bed that bordered the park's path, tugging at his trousers. He tiptoed across the flowerbed avoiding the crocuses and early daffodils.

'Sorry,' he said, 'Was just having a piss.'

'No problem,' responded Mater. 'Here, I've brought you a couple of rolls and coffee for both of us. I don't know how you

216

take it but I suspect white with lots of sugar would be traditional for an ex-military man.'

Pete joined Mater on the bench, wolfed down the food and sipped his coffee. Mater waited until Pete had finished eating before asking. 'Where are the bottles, where's your stuff?'

Pete sat bolt upright, turned to Mater and performed a joke salute. 'Thought I'd better tidy and spruce things up a bit, sir, ready to begin a new life; being an ex-military man, as you described me, and all that. When do we start?'

Mater was encouraged by Pete's enthusiasm and trust and decided to capitalise on his desire to get involved.

'That's excellent, I'm delighted. I will help you to the best of my ability and hopefully, if you are successful, you'll find your new job rewarding. Now though, you could assist me with your local knowledge.'

'My knowledge of what?'

'Well, my plan is to create a team of three or four to work with me. I want to support those who having been living rough for at least ten years, preferably much longer. But I need volunteers with particular experience and backgrounds.'

'Ex-soldiers, like myself then?' butted in Pete.

'Most likely but not exclusively. I'm looking for, how can I describe them, unique skills. At this stage, it would be best that, if you have contact with anyone who you consider trustworthy, you introduce me. Then I'll decide whether I should make them the same offer as I did to you.'

Mater decided not to reveal he had learnt more about Pete's background believing that if Pete discovered, at this point, Mater had investigated him, he might be alarmed.

Pete laughed, rocking backwards and forwards. 'Trustworthy, us!' he exclaimed, 'Dossers on the streets, alcoholics, druggies, ex-cons; society's misfits. Trustworthy, huh? Well, you're the boss but a strange one.'

Mater thought about his own role, realising that he too was a societal misfit. He sipped his coffee. Finally he said, 'Do you have anyone in mind, Pete?'

Pete stopped laughing and looked Mater squarely in the eye. 'Bloody hell mate. You are serious, aren't you? Sure, I know some guys. I can introduce you.'

'Thanks. And yes I'm serious, but the business is serious too.'

'OK. As long as it doesn't end up with me doing another stretch, nothing illegal, then let's get on with it. I'll collect my things; they're in the bushes behind.' He stood up and tiptoed back across the flower bed.

Mater considered the legality of his actions. The Office's activities were always portrayed to the public as being carried out within the bounds of the law but he had been involved in other actions. Hidden from scrutiny; secret and deniable.

Pete returned carrying in one hand two grubby but robust supermarket bags stuffed full of old clothes and blankets. In the other, he grasped a large tatty women's handbag emblazoned in chrome with the Chanel logo; the contents clinking as he walked. As they strolled to the park exit, he winked to Mater.

'Keep my valuables in there,' he said, holding up the handbag.

Mater understood. He hadn't yet seen Pete drink any alcohol that morning but it couldn't last.

'Where are we going?' asked Mater.

'We'll go south of the river and visit Waterloo. I've a couple of mates there who I catch up with once in a while. Roughly my age, similar time spent on the street and same problems.'

'OK,' said Mater, 'Lead the way and if we pass a suitable shop, I'll buy you a Bergen for your stuff. I'm not walking with you all day if you're going to carry a glitzy handbag. Can I carry one of your carrier bags for you?'

'No, I'll manage,' answered Pete, keen to show his physical strength and independence.

The route took them past the Houses of Parliament and across Westminster Bridge. They paused briefly in the middle, surrounded by tourists taking pictures of the iconic building.

'Our elected masters are all in there,' commented Mater, then thinking to himself, *Little do they realise how hard we work to keep them and what they represent safe.*

After they entered the concourse at Waterloo station, Pete stopped outside a mini-supermarket.

'Need supplies,' he said turning to Mater and asking, 'You wouldn't happen to have any spare change guv'nor, would you?'

'Cut the crap, Pete. If you're needing booze, just say so and I will provide.'

Pete was a bit offended. 'Who says it's for me? Can't visit without taking gifts, can we?' He smiled, and the mood lightened.

'Of course, silly me,' said Mater, handing over a ten-pound note. 'But if you want something for yourself, ask. It's all part of the deal.'

Pete disappeared inside the shop, leaving Mater watching over their things. Waterloo was noisy and bustling, almost unintelligible announcements echoed along its vast glass covered cavern, adding to the din. Nobody took any notice of the tramp that waited patiently for his companion to buy his liquid fix. Pete emerged, the handbag bulging.

'Right,' he said, 'We need to go out at the far end and hopefully, just there, we'll meet Jock and Hefty.'

Mater wondered how many people Pete knew who shared his lifestyle. A whole new mini-society was opening up to him. He acknowledged that sometimes, those living like Pete did so out of choice, but he couldn't help thinking the country should do better for its citizens.

As Pete had predicted, two characters sat propped up by the stone wall beside the station's entrance. The glazed canopy above sheltered them from the weather and they were warmed by the stale breeze wafting from the station. Pete greeted his friends.

'Hello, boys,' he said, 'How goes it?'

To Mater, it was obvious which one was Hefty. Even seated, he was a giant, with long wavy grey hair and bushy eyebrows that had retained their brown colour. Mater noted he

220

was surprisingly clean shaven but his clothes were filthy and demonstrated the wear and tear that constituted the uniform of the homeless. In his mind's eye, Mater recognised the same build in Hefty as Tiny's. Only the nicknames were different. The other man appeared younger, much smaller, quite nervous, almost timid. The two reminded Mater of the organ grinder and his monkey. They looked up at Pete, who having reached into his Chanel bag, proffered cans of special brew. They each grabbed one and opened them straightaway with a simultaneous hiss.

'Things are good thanks, Pete,' said Hefty, putting the beer to his lips. He emptied the can and then asked, 'How's it in Victoria? And who's this geezer with you?' gesticulating, with the empty can, towards Mater.

Mater stood quite still and simply smiled.

'A new friend, a helpful friend,' replied Pete. 'He kindly paid for the refreshment.'

Jock, reassured by Pete and grateful for the alcohol, relaxed then piped up, his Scottish origins evident.

'He paid, you say. Why, what's in it for him? There's never a free lunch.'

Mater felt it was time he introduced himself and tried to ascertain whether there was any mileage in pursuing either of the men. 'My name's Phil,' he said, 'Phil Sutcliffe. I'm here to offer help to folk who have fallen on hard times.'

Hefty, his tongue loosened by the drink had heard this all before. 'What a surprise,' he said sarcastically, 'There's always someone, wanting to assuage their own conscience, pretending to care for the likes of us; living in life's gutter. Well, I don't want God, charity or the Social Services.'

Mater was impressed by his use of language: an education lay behind this somewhere. 'I'm not offering anything for free,' he said. 'All gifts have a price.'

Jock, irritated by the wordplay and emboldened by the drink, decided to take control of the situation. 'OK,' he said, 'Simply explain what you want and what you are offering in return. Then we can decide if we are interested but if you're a journalist, the answer's no, I'm not.'

Mater chuckled. The last thing he wanted was to publicise his activities.

'What's so funny?' asked Jock, once again irritated; wondering whether to end their conversation.

Mater didn't wish to cause offence but was limited in what he could divulge. 'Sorry,' he said, 'I'm singing from the same hymn sheet when it comes to journalists. Everything I say must be kept secret. My interest in talking to you is selfish but may benefit you too. To start with, I need to know more about each of you. How long have you lived rough? What brought you to this point? What jobs you have done in the past? That type of thing. I won't take notes. It all goes in here and stays there,' he said, tapping his head.

Pete joined in. 'It really is OK. I've told Phil who I am and a bit about my army days. You can talk to him.'

Almost true. Partial truths make the best lies, thought Mater, patiently waiting for either to speak.

Hefty opened his mouth first. 'Any more beer?' he asked. The contents of a single can, diluted in Hefty's heavy frame, had only a minimal effect. Pete reached for another in his bag and gave it to Hefty.

'There's plenty more where that came from,' said Mater, kneeling.

Hefty opened the second can, emptied it in one long swallow, and then started his life story. He pulled up his sleeve, revealing a large dark tattoo and thrust his arm towards Mater.

Classic, thought Mater, *An anchor. Won't have been in the air force then.*

'More than twenty years at sea,' said Hefty. 'Roughly half with the Royal Navy and half the merchant. Engineering, electronics and weapons maintenance. Civvy side: mainly communications and computer stuff. Didn't start out in the forces. Got a degree in something quite useless and after graduating there were, surprise surprise, no jobs. Certainly none in Hull or nearby. I had to look after my elderly parents so was keen to stay put but eventually they told me to get on my bike, in a manner of speaking. Passed the recruitment office one day and really out of simple curiosity, turned back and walked in. Before you know it I'd signed up as a rating. May '76, it was. The beginning of that glorious hot summer. The Navy trained me, set me off in a new direction. My parents died within weeks of each other while I was at sea in the Far East. We still had Hong Kong in those days. On reflection I suppose the drinking started then, in the forces, following Mum and Dad's deaths. Finally, they suggested I bought my way out. The Navy gave me a glowing reference that helped me into the Merchant Fleet but they never helped me with the drink. I was married by then with two youngsters. The missus coped when I was away but it wasn't good when I came home. I owe her, I owe them all an apology but I'll never be able to give it. Eventually she kicked me out; the court awarded her and the boys everything and I scarpered off to sea again. My final job didn't last long. Pissed too often. Arrived back in Southampton, got chucked off the boat with the clothes I stood in and a little cash to keep me quiet. Made my way to the big city and I've been here for nine years. Bumped into Jock inside a month and we've been best mates ever since.'

Mater listened attentively, remembering every salient detail for future reference. He recognised the signs of loyalty and a history of discipline but was concerned by Hefty's descent. Could he be brought into line or was he a lost cause? Irrespective, it looked like it would be either both Hefty and Jock or neither of them. They clearly watched each other's backs.

Hefty dried up. 'Over to you, Jock,' he said, putting the empty can back to his lips and sucking noisily for the last few drops.

Jock coughed nervously and shifted position. Mater suspected it was going to be more difficult for him to talk.

'I'll start with the bad bit,' said Jock, his speech slurred, 'It will be easier if I deal with that first.' He was aware he was about to tell his audience something that he had only ever admitted to Hefty. 'I killed someone,' he said bluntly, 'In cold blood.' He stopped.

Hefty laid a broad hand on Jock's shoulder. 'It's OK, Jock, go on,' he said.

Pete looked surprised but remained silent. Mater was impassive. They all waited while Jock regained his composure.

224

'The bastard demanded more and more. Once you're in debt, the bloody mafia types get a grip on you, offer to bail you out and then fuck you over, time and again. Prefer the alcohol addiction to the gambling one. Don't do that anymore. Not after bashing his head in with my hammer. See a casino or an advert for that new online gambling and all I see are brains splattered across my kitchen floor. I walked out there and then; never went back. They probably sold my flat to pay my debts but at least their enforcer isn't bothering any other poor so and so now. No, I've no regrets. But I suppose I'm really on the run and always will be. I made sure I didn't leave a trace, not a single footprint. No credit cards, no passport, no contacting old friends or family.'

Much of this was music to Mater's ears. A man who had disappeared, was capable of killing and who sounded as if he had nothing to lose. Drinking simply to forget. Mater stepped in.

'I'm sorry,' he said, 'Sounds as if you've had a rough time.'

'Que sera, sera,' responded Jock.

Mater needed to know more. 'What did you do before you made your hasty exit?' he asked.

'You're not going to believe this,' said Jock, 'But I was a customs and excise officer. Started at the bottom, rummaging through dirty underwear in some poor bugger's holiday suitcase; confiscating a box here, a carton there, of contraband fags or excess bottles of duty free spirits. Probably where the basic problem began. Sometimes we shared the stuff out. Providing the numbers looked right at month's end, no-one noticed the little extra we kept for ourselves. Moved up the ranks and following further training was employed by the narcotics team. Surveillance and drug busting. It was bloody good fun although dangerous at times. Best bit was when we caught a suspect and needed to make them squeal. You could do what was necessary and nobody asked questions, providing you got useful info. That's the first time I learnt a lot about how organised crime works. Eventually, with the gambling and the spirits it all unravelled. I must have tried every brand of drink from the entire world but you can't be allowed to use the drug squad tools if you're worse for wear. Might shoot the wrong one or shoot even when they've surrendered. Mind you, it would be the best thing for those cunts. If you live like me and Hefty, you see the miserable effects of their industry every day.' He paused.

Mater broke the silence. 'How long ago was all this, Jock?'

'Oh, years, I've lost count,' he replied evasively. 'I was here when Hefty turned up. He looked like a great lost bear so I gave him advice and suggested places to stay. All you need is somewhere dry and warm when the weather is rubbish, enough cash to keep you topped up and a story for the authorities when they bother you.'

'So, when did this happen, when were you forced leave in such a hurry?' persisted Mater, keen to clarify how long Jock had spent walking the streets.

Jock began to look agitated again before giving in; it was so far in the past, perhaps it really didn't matter anymore. 'Few dates stick in my mind except Sunday 26th March 1989. He assumed I would be in on a Sunday, nursing my head and my losses. Thought he'd catch me when I was down. But he got more than he bargained for that day. As I say, I've no regrets.'

226

Mater had heard enough. He didn't want to upset Jock further. The backgrounds to both men were potentially suitable for his purposes and he decided he had plenty to go on to check them out. 'Thank you,' he said, 'I'm grateful to you both.'

Pete stepped in. 'You haven't made your offer, Phil. You should. These are good guys.'

Mater agreed. He explained, as he had to Pete, the chance of a new life, help with their addiction and the prospect of employment; doing something useful, exciting but anonymous. Finally, he asked if they had any questions and waited for their response.

Jock was the first to speak. 'So, who are you, some kind of policeman?' he said, 'You're not the bloody salvation army, that's for sure.'

Mater laughed. 'Close,' he said, 'But I can't give you a straight answer at this point. If you come on board, all will be made clear in time. I might not be in a position to tell you everything now but neither will I lie. All I can say is I'm convinced you are both qualified to be considered for selection. You can, of course, opt out at any point and return to this.' He waved his arm around in the air indicating Jock and Hefty's abode. 'But I believe you can succeed; you have the pedigree I'm looking for. Think it over. I'm staying here.' He handed over a card that he had picked up in the hotel reception. 'Just ask for Mr Sutcliffe. If I don't hear from you by tomorrow evening, I'll try elsewhere.' Mater gave each man a twenty-pound note. 'I know what you are likely to buy with the cash,' he said, 'But try purchasing some vitamins as well. If you join me, you'll need to be fit.'

Mater left the three men sitting and chatting, no doubt discussing the stranger who had appeared amongst them. He had certainly been different; concerned for them but keeping his distance. They belatedly realised Mater had encouraged them to give up major parts of their life stories but they had learnt almost nothing about him. Jock was especially worried that the man was a private detective, employed by the gangs from the past who, by means unknown, had tracked him down. But they were all tired of running, exhausted by years of hiding. Pete summed it up.

'I've no idea what he's really up to but he seems OK; maybe even a good 'un. We've all taken risks in our lives. This is just the next step. I'm going for it. In for a penny, in for a pound, I say.'

Hefty nodded his agreement adding, 'If there's any funny business, there's three of us and only one of him. I'm up for it too. Tomorrow, we should meet him again at the Cross, together.'

There was no way Jock would go back to the street without Hefty. Somewhat reluctantly he agreed to join. Pete was sent off to buy more drink, so they could celebrate together in their own style.

Mater walked back through the station concourse, disappearing amongst the travelling public. He was delighted with his good fortune. He thought the initial recruitment drive might have taken weeks if not months, but looked as though it could be completed in days. He sent Charlotte a brief text. 'Three fish biting', it said. 'Excellent work', came the reply. He walked on thinking about the men. He had to make a decision. If they were all willing to work for him, then he needed to consider how many more people he should approach. It was a difficult question. Ideally, he wanted a trained team of five but could manage at a stretch with four. It was likely that at least some recruits would fail or withdraw. Failure might happen early as efforts were made to stabilise their lives and return them to a more traditional existence. Losing recruits at this stage would not be an issue because they wouldn't yet be aware of the ultimate goal. The challenge would be more acute later, once serious training had started or even been completed. Someone walking out, trained in weapons, communications, reconnaissance and survival and given, inevitably, a big hint as to whom they were working for, would present a real security headache. Mater came to the unpalatable conclusion that they might not be allowed to leave; they might have to disappear, permanently. He pushed the idea to the back of his mind and made his way to the Waterloo public library, opposite Lambeth North underground station. There he would attempt to verify the stories and backgrounds of the 'Waterloo boys', as he had decided to call them.

The library was physically very different from the one in Victoria, architecturally modern, all concrete and steel but the staff seemed just as bored. The computer room, quieter and lighter, gave Mater the privacy he needed. He had the whole afternoon to research. The two dates mentioned by Hefty and Jock provided significant leads. Mater searched for Naval recruits Hull, May 1976 and the records listed four names. One was excluded straightaway as he had become a submariner. Separating Hefty from the other two proved easy. Only one candidate jumped ship before completing their full service and that was Chief Petty Officer Gordon Bateman. It was recorded that CPO Bateman had worked as an engineer. Next Mater hunted for references to a Gordon Bateman in the Merchant Navy, looking for someone whose work involved engineering, computers or similar. Soon Mater felt he knew Hefty much, much better. Gordon Bateman, born Hull, July 14th, 1968, currently a resident of Waterloo Station, London. Mater moved onto Jock. He typed in 'Murders, 26th March 1989'. Nothing. Mater scratched his head. Perhaps the body wasn't discovered that day, maybe even months later. He extended the range of dates and multiple reports filtered onto the screen. If necessary, he would plough through them all. Perhaps it would be more efficient to check Customs and Excise staff records in the National Archives first, searching for employees who left the service at the end of March 1989. There was a list of eleven men and women. Within it, he found two Johns but only one of them had been seconded to the narcotics branch. *John, aka Jock, McLaren, you must be my man,* thought Mater. He returned to searching, trying different years in succession: 'Missing persons March 1989'. 'Got you,' whispered Mater to himself, not wanting to attract attention from others sitting in the library. The reference read: 'McLaren family, originally from Glasgow, now living in Dover, appeal for information as to the whereabouts of their husband / father who disappeared from home on March 26th, 1989.' Mater was impressed by Jock's ongoing attempts to throw him off the scent. Jock had employed the hammer on a Saturday not a Sunday although this mattered little to the recipient of his blows. Mater wiped the search history from the computer, logged off and left.

Once again, he congratulated himself for the ease which he had located potential recruits. He decided he would contact Control, give him the encouraging news and celebrate with a drink or two. Near to the library, he spotted a vacant red public phone box. He entered, inserted coins and dialled Control's pager. It had started to rain, so he decided to wait inside until Control rang back.

A couple appeared outside, the man sheltering the woman with his coat. Mater ignored them and pretended to be busy looking something up on his phone. The man knocked hard on the window and shouted angrily, 'Are you going to use it or not, mate?'

Mater smiled politely and shrugged his shoulders.

The man opened the door and repeated his question.

'Entschuldigen, was sagen sie, ich verstehe nicht?' said Mater, trying to appear confused and perplexed.

'Bloody tourists, bloody nuisance,' grumbled the man and let the door slam shut.

Mater smiled again. The man raised his middle finger and ushered his partner away.

'Up yours too,' whispered Mater. The phone rang. Mater picked up the receiver.

'Good to hear from you Phil.' Mater detected relief in Control's voice. 'Report please.'

'I'm in London. I've met three men. They seem enthusiastic and could prove to be excellent choices. I wonder if we might meet to discuss.'

'Certainly, I am free early this evening but have concert tickets for later. It's mid-afternoon already, but can you manage five thirty outside the Blue Bar, in Wilton Place, Belgravia? If you have positive news, I'll stand you a glass of fizz.'

'I'll be there but you'll have to excuse my attire.'

'Look forward to seeing you,' concluded Control, and the line went dead.

Mater was pleased Control would make time for him at such short notice. He welcomed the opportunity to update the boss, hoping that his rapid progress would impress. He also needed Control's unwitting assistance in carrying out the next phase of his operation. Mater walked past a tobacconist's and caught sight of his reflection. He stopped to examine himself more carefully. His coat and hat looked damp, grey and drab. He was unshaven and the combination was already making him resemble the street life he had met. He raised a sleeve to his nose and sniffed. The smell wasn't good. *Yes, it wouldn't take long to slide down into the gutter, not sure how this will go down at Control's choice of champagne bar.* He started walking again, disappointed that he didn't have time to return to Kings Cross and spruce himself up.

Mater wasn't certain where Wilton Place was and found himself asking a vendor of the Evening Standard, shouting the headlines to the passing pedestrian traffic. The man gave him directions. Then as Mater thanked him and went to leave, offered some advice. 'You might find they move you on if you try to stay around those parts. They're all nobs in Belgravia.'

Mater smiled and thanked him again, thinking that he must truly be looking rough.

He arrived with five minutes to spare and waited patiently outside. A tall doorman in black tie watched Mater for a minute, scowling, before he could no longer resist the temptation to assert his authority. He sidled down the steps to the pavement and stood face to face with Mater.

'Bugger off,' he said, 'We don't want people like you pestering our customers.'

'Bugger off?' repeated a voice from behind, 'No need for any of that, Mr Rotherhyde. This gentleman, despite his appearance which I admit is somewhat disconcerting, is with me.'

The doorman turned and instantly recognised the regular customer. 'I'm terribly sorry, sir. Welcome back to the Blue Bar.' He glared at Mater, hesitated, and then added as he performed a cursory bow, 'Welcome to you both.'

Mater responded by doffing his hat. Control looked at Mater and winked. As they walked up the steps he muttered, 'He's right; you really do look a mess.'

'Do I?' said Mater, 'There's me thinking I've just come from Saville Row.'

'Sarcasm doesn't become you,' commented Control. They both chuckled and entered. Control directed Mater to a table tucked away in a corner. As it was late afternoon, the bar was devoid of other customers but Control was keen to talk out of earshot of the staff. With Mater seated, he returned to the bar. Mater watched as Control conversed with the young smartly dressed man who stood behind it, polishing glasses. It was obvious they knew each other. Mater assumed Control visited regularly and wondered whether the bills appeared on his Office expense sheets. The barman reached for a bottle of champagne from the fridge. He placed it on a tray, along with two tall champagne flutes. He went to pick it up, intending to deliver it to his customers' table but Control, thanking him, waved him away and brought the silver tray over himself.

'Can't stretch to anything too special,' he said, 'We'll keep that for when your mission succeeds.'

'Any champagne for a tramp like me is a treat,' responded Mater, 'And I welcome your optimism which I hope, no, believe, is justified.'

Control popped the bottle and filled the glasses, passing one to Mater.

'Tell me where you've got to,' he said.

Mater provided a succinct report, describing, without providing names or any other identifiable information, the potential recruits, the training base and medical support. Control listened intently, watching as the bubbles grew on the side of his glass, rise in streams to burst on the surface. Mater stopped and took a sip. Control nodded.

'Good. Rapid progress,' he said, 'Excellent effort.'

'Thank you, sir,' said Mater, 'Any developments at your end?'

Control shook his head. 'Unfortunately none. We still haven't been able to identify Liam's, Mick's or your attackers but the work continues.' He fell silent.

Both men sat sipping the champagne. Mater was disappointed. He had hoped that the Office, and or 5, had made in-roads into his problem. It might have allowed him to abandon his plan and return to something approaching a normal life. It was not to be. He put down his glass.

'I have a request,' he said at last.

'Go ahead,' replied Control, always anticipating demands from his team leaders.

Mater reached inside his coat pocket and pulled out an envelope, sealed with Sellotape and with nothing written on it. 'I need you to post this envelope to Anthony, anonymously. I, naturally, don't have his address.'

Control looked surprised and troubled.

Mater placed the envelope between them.

Control left it there and topped up the glasses. Eventually he spoke. 'Should I be told what's in it?' he asked.

'I wish I knew,' Mater replied, 'You see, it's not from me.'

Control was confused. 'Not from you. Then from whom?'

Mater waited and then played his final card. He smiled, drank more champagne and winked at Control. 'I've been asked to keep it all secret, but maybe you've been aware of the dalliance between Anthony and a member of my team. She reassured me there isn't anything pertaining to the current situation, just personal stuff. I told her I would be seeing you. Naturally, if the two of them meet, it must be on neutral territory.'

Control picked up the envelope and sat fingering it. He returned Mater's smile. 'The naughty boy,' he said, 'You know the organisation generally frowns upon such relationships.' He sighed. Anthony and Charlotte had both delivered very long and loyal service. He felt they were both reliable beyond question. Things happened between people sometimes. He took the envelope and slipped it inside his jacket. 'As long as nothing interferes with our work or anything appears on expenses. I'll print an address on it, and post it, first class, on my way home. He'll never know we've been acting as cupids.' Control emptied the remaining champagne into Mater's glass and stood up to go. 'I'll leave you to enjoy a few more moments of luxury before you have to venture out into the cold again. I must get going. The wife will be dressed in her finery and twitching; too often I'm late for some social function or other. Today, if I hurry, I might just manage to impress her. Always worth trying to earn brownie points.'

Mater stood, thanked his boss, watched him drop the barman a tip and depart. He sat down again and picked up his glass. The champagne was really very good. If this lifestyle automatically came with promotion, it might be worth the responsibility. He was pleased the next part of his plan was falling into place though the timing was becoming crucial. Another piece of the jigsaw; it simply had to be fitted together in the right order. He took out his phone and texted Charlotte, feeling slightly guilty that he hadn't forewarned her. The brief message read: 'The boss is aware of the 'very personal relationship' that exists between you and Anthony. He's OK with this but I suggest, if he makes enquiries, you act accordingly. Best Wishes. M'

Mater assumed Anthony would receive the letter in the next day or two. No doubt he would be surprised by its contents but Mater was sure he would take the bait. If Mater's suspicions were correct, then Anthony would not miss an opportunity to demonstrate his prowess for spying and the chance to impress Control and the senior Office team. It would help cement his position as a reliable and effective operative. Now Mater had to ensure that the homeless men he had met were willing to participate in a little test. If they refused nothing would be lost, but the uncertainty surrounding Anthony's loyalty would persist.

He returned to the hotel where he waited, hoping for a call from reception announcing the arrival of Pete, Jock and Hefty. Twenty hours until the deadline passed; time enough to develop the test and get some rest while living off room-service pizza.

Chapter 19

Mid-morning the next day the phone beside Mater's bed rang. He pointed the remote at the TV to silence it and picked up the receiver. The hotel receptionist sounded alarmed. 'Mr Sutcliffe, three, um, rather unusual gentlemen are asking for you. They say you're expecting them.'

Mater smiled to himself, imagining the odours that had accompanied the men's entrance into the foyer. It wasn't a smart hotel but not a doss house either. He thanked the receptionist and made his way down as quickly as possible. He didn't want them to attract any more attention than was absolutely necessary. In reception, Mater's visitors sat motionless and silent in a row, occupying a plastic covered low sofa by a large window facing onto the street. A variety of grubby overfilled bags lay at their feet. They were not a good advertisement for the hotel.

The receptionist saw Mater enter and gesticulated to him. 'Your guests are seated over there,' he said, adding optimistically, 'I assume you will be meeting them somewhere rather more private.'

Mater looked at the men and immediately understood the receptionist's concern. Removed from the street they seemed out of place and uncomfortable. Mater realised he had his work cut out. He was going to have to shepherd his new flock with all their historical baggage, both physical and mental, managing their futures to his advantage.

He walked over to them and greeted them. 'I'm so pleased you decided to come,' he said, smiling, 'Please follow me.'

Jock and Hefty turned to Pete, clearly waiting for him to make the first move. Pete nodded, smiled back, revealing a mouth desperately calling for the services of an oral hygienist, and got to his feet. The others rose. Mater waited patiently while the men gathered their belongings and then led them to the stairway and up to his room. Once all were inside, he closed the door and asked everyone to sit where they could. He had ignored the odour that had accompanied them from the foyer but now it was necessary to open a window. With the group seated on his bed, Mater felt he should waste no time before providing them with further information. He remained standing in front of them like a teacher or a preacher about to give a lesson. He was practiced in the art of detailing a future mission but on this occasion he knew he had to divulge just enough to keep the men on board. At this very early stage, he would not reveal anything that might compromise him, Charlotte, Control or anyone else from the Office.

'Thank you again for meeting me here,' he began. 'I have been fortunate to come across three individuals who seem to hold similar loyalties to my own but have sadly fallen on hard times. I'll outline my proposal. Much of this you've already heard, but it's worth repeating so that you can be in no doubt what my offer is and where you stand. Naturally, the decision to join or to quit is entirely yours. You are at liberty to resign any at time.'

He paused. 'I'm the boss of this outfit. Like you, I have served my country and remain committed to doing so. Actions undertaken are my overall responsibility and although periodically their legality might seem dubious, the morality of my work is not in doubt. However, and this is an important proviso, I have no intention of carrying out tasks that might result in anyone, including me, ending up in court or prison. As a crucial part of building this team, you must gain control over your reliance on alcohol. Assuming this proves successful then you will undergo further training to enhance the skills you once had. Obviously, you must have asked yourselves, why I chose losers, as many might describe you, when surely other more suitable candidates are available. The answer is simple. I need individuals who nobody knows exist, staff who are anonymous but with useful and relevant backgrounds. Since abandoning your former lives, none of you have left a clear trail of who you are or where you have been. The work I'm involved in is sometimes arduous, not infrequently boring but can be inherently dangerous. The reward, though, is the involvement in a project serving this country and Her Majesty. It gives you the chance of a better life; rejecting a self-destructive path and finding new purpose. The financial compensation is mediocre but secure. If you are still interested, I will ask you to take part in an initial task: let's call it a selection test. Your performance will show me whether you have potential. If, in my opinion, you fail at any stage, it will be my decision and mine alone to fire you.'

Mater stopped, waited for the information to sink in before offering his audience the chance to respond. 'Any questions?' he asked.

Jock was the first, any inhibition loosened by the blood alcohol level in his veins. 'So, Mr Sutcliffe, are you a spy?'

Mater was a little taken aback though not entirely surprised by the question. It had arisen many times in the past and he had his answer ready. 'Thanks Jock. If by spy you mean someone who craves inside knowledge that would be of advantage

240

to themselves or an organisation they serve, I suppose I am. By that definition aren't all businessmen, market men or commodity traders, politicians, gamblers and crooks spies, using information to further their aims; whether for financial or other advantage or to exact revenge? I am willing to tell you that I do need information and plan to use it to retaliate.'

Jock nodded with understanding but stared hard at Mater. 'I guessed from the outset you weren't really one of us. You should learn from my experience that revenge, retaliation, vengeance or whatever you call it, can end with terrible long term consequences. Righting a wrong, managing a loss, often delivers unexpected penalties. You may fail and fall, just as we did.' He waved his hand, indicating his friends seated beside him.

Mater understood the message. He had lost more than Jock might ever discover but had managed to keep his head above the water, however deep it was or fast it rose. He thanked Jock for his advice and turned to the others.

Hefty reached into one of his carrier bags and took out a large bottle of cider. He brandished it in front of Mater. 'You and I both know I can't live without this. I would love to be free of it. I think we all would. So, how are you going to perform this miracle?'

Mater was keen not to appear infallible. It wouldn't look plausible.

'I've access to a rehabilitation service that I've been told has been very successful with people like you, but not absolutely guaranteed to help. I'm not a medic, so cannot give you all the details but I understand that the treatment you might be offered would only be provided with your full consent. You would need to demonstrate abstinence before continuing with my group so, I'm afraid, I would expect you to accept the doctor's recommendation.'

Hefty, resisting the temptation to open the bottle and take a swig, reluctantly returned the cider to his bag and nodded his understanding.

Finally, it was Pete's turn. 'You hinted at a preliminary task; a selection test as you put it. Can you tell us more?'

Mater hesitated. 'Yes, but not yet. All in good time Pete. However, you won't need to be off the booze for this first job but you mustn't be out of your minds either. Any further questions?'

Each man looked to the others. All three shook their heads.

Mater followed up, seeking confirmation. 'Are you all still game?'

The men checked each other again. Pete nodded followed by Hefty and Jock.

'I'll take that as a yes,' said Mater.

'What happens next?' asked Pete, who had clearly taken on the role of spokesperson.

'OK,' said Mater, 'From now on I need you to clean and smarten up but keep the names that you use so well to hide yourselves. You can use my shower and afterwards I want you to go out and buy new clothes but don't throw out your old ones; they could be useful. Oh, and a visit to the barbers wouldn't go amiss.' Mater handed each man a small wad of cash. 'Once you look a little more, how shall I say it, respectable, I will book you rooms in a hotel close by. Don't worry; the bill will be covered by me. I suggest we pretend to be workers pulled in to help at a building site in nearby Camden, so don't be too concerned if fingers and nails are still stained. Oh, and it goes without saying, from now on everything we talk about, absolutely everything I tell you, is kept secret… forever. Understood?'

'Yes boss,' came the unanimous reply.

Mater moved forwards and shook each man's hand. 'Phil will do. Welcome to my world.'

Chapter 20

Mater guessed that Anthony would receive the letter in the next day or two. By then he expected to be ready with a small team prepared to carry out their first assignment. As he played it out in his head, the whole scenario felt surreal. The stakes were high. If his hunch was right, their actions might save his and Charlotte's lives and go down in the Office annals as a textbook example of a successful mission. If he had got it wrong, then it most likely meant he would be pushed out into the cold with no protection or support from his colleagues. If he fouled up, his only hope would be that no-one, except Control, would know who was behind the anonymous men who carried out his plan. Mater's survival would then depend on Control's personal loyalties and he might be forced to choose: him or Anthony.

The letter was waiting for Anthony when he arrived home late from the Office. Hidden amongst the many circulars littering the carpet by his front door, he almost threw it away. Brown, printed address and uninteresting caught his attention. If it had been offering something he knew he wouldn't want, an enticement of sorts would have been advertised on the outside. Even the taxman's correspondence announced its arrival without discretion.

Anthony took the letter through to his kitchen, poured himself a large gin and tonic and using a skewer, carefully slit open the envelope. He sat down, drink in one hand and typed message in the other. He read it several times and then checked the back of the paper and the envelope to see if there were any clues as to its origin. A London postmark and nothing more. He was surprised, intrigued and troubled in equal measure. He put the glass to his lips and drained it. He had never expected to hear anything more about the organisation mentioned, having assumed his previous informant, long deceased, had provided enough material for the Office to eliminate the group. During that operation, he had always been confident of success although others described it as arrogance. He didn't care: the Office and the minister had been delighted. It was his running of the agent that landed him promotion. But this letter implied there were remnants who had escaped, gone to ground, and were preparing to operate again. He was being offered fresh information by a new contact, no doubt looking for a significant financial reward and lifelong protection. Most tempting; once again, a fresh opportunity to impress his boss. And it might prove very useful, especially now. *But how*, he wondered, *did the author of the note know where to send it?* This worried him. He poured himself another, stronger, drink. As far as he deduced, knowledge of his home address could only have originated from within the Office. Someone was helping but breaking the rules. If he decided to meet the person at the allotted time and place, he needed to be cautious. A conversation with Control beforehand would be sensible.

Anthony struggled to sleep that night, trying to distract himself by watching television into the early hours. He couldn't be sure whether what lay ahead was a trap: revenge for the blow he dealt all those years ago. But, if genuine, it might proffer further success and enhance his reputation as a reliable and effective member of the management team. It would certainly do him no harm, quite the opposite and show that, despite his age and seniority, he retained the ability to deliver results at ground level. If wrong, physical injury or even death might result. He played the choices back and forth in his mind, his decision remaining balanced on a knife edge. The discussion with Control should help him decide. He would make a point of catching the boss first thing the next day.

Chapter 21

Control was working at his desk, enjoying his first cafetière of the day, preparing his sit rep for the afternoon's weekly meeting with the minister. The agenda for the daily morning conference with Simon, Charles and Anthony lay typed up on the tray alongside the coffee and hazelnut cream wafers kindly brought in by Lisbeth. They were his favourite. *Was she buttering him up before requesting yet another unscheduled holiday?* As Control picked up a wafer and popped it into his mouth, Lisbeth announced, via the intercom, that Anthony had arrived, requesting a chat. With his mouth full of biscuit, Lisbeth just made out her boss's request to send him in with an extra cup.

Shortly after, there was a knock on the door and Anthony walked in.

'Good morning Anthony, do sit down. Coffee?' asked Control, holding out his hand for Anthony's cup. He looked at his middle manager and added, 'You look like you could do with a strong one. Bad night?'

'Thank you, sir,' replied Anthony, seating himself opposite his boss. 'I rarely sleep soundly these days; believe it's a function of age.'

Control nodded with understanding. His position didn't allow it, but each day he was tempted by an afternoon nap that could offer respite from the fatigue he suffered after each disturbed night. Forty winks would be so invigorating; he might even impress the wife by not nodding off during one of her favourite operas. That would be a first.

'How can I help you?' asked Control as he poured coffee. He didn't offer him a wafer.

Anthony reached across, took the cup and sat there with it in his hand on his lap, stirring it slowly with a silver spoon. 'I've just received, out of the blue, an interesting letter,' he said. 'It was waiting for me when I got home yesterday evening.'

Control tipped his head to one side, encouraging his subordinate to continue.

'I've no idea how someone accessed my address and I don't recognise the style of the writing although it must have been posted in this country.' He looked anxious.

'Go on,' said Control, thinking 'you liar'.

Anthony raised the porcelain cup, drank some coffee and continued.

'If it's alright with you, boss, I would like a day or two off. The contents of the letter have offered me an opportunity I am reluctant to let pass.'

Control smiled to himself. *Anthony, you really are a naughty boy,* he thought. He recognised Anthony's divorce had concluded many years ago and didn't consider it unreasonable that he was searching for a new partner. Control reminded himself that although generally frowned upon, close relations between Office staff had inevitably happened before and, on occasions, been tolerated. The closed world they all operated in sometimes strengthened such partnerships by the mutual understanding of the stresses and strains they all worked under. But he was duty bound to enquire further before allowing an employee time away whether it be one of his senior staff or his secretary.

'Do you wish to tell me what this is all about?' asked Control expecting Anthony to be evasive.

'Of course. You recall the Derwent operation.'

How could Control forget? It was he who had used the results of Derwent to support Anthony in his promotion. His action hadn't been totally altruistic as some of the gloss brushed off onto him, adding to the clamour for his own elevation to Director General.

'Yes, of course, Anthony, your masterpiece as I once described it,' said Control smiling, but wondering what Anthony's cover story was leading to.

'It is possible the group involved has re-formed. I have a chance to find out more, hopefully before they, if it's all true, can cause us or anyone else problems. I want you to know what I'm dabbling in, just in case.'

'Just in case?'

Control, wondered why Anthony tried to be so clever when a simple 'I need to visit an ill elderly relative would have sufficed'.

'In case I'm away for longer than expected. Should I disappear?'

Control sat without answering for a moment. There was something in Anthony's approach that he, as an experienced interrogator, found disconcerting. Anthony appeared to be telling the truth. *If so, what was Mater, as the letter's courier, up to?* 'Do you want me to organise some back up?' he asked, concerned.

His deputy's arrogance shone through. 'No thanks, I'm sure I'll manage. This is a first meeting, scheduled in two days. It's arranged to take place in a public location, here in London. I don't expect any nasty business. However, you should note the leak of my personal address. Perhaps, it came from the same source that damaged Mater's group.'

No back up, none at all, thought Control. *Of course the two lovebirds wouldn't want to be observed, let alone disturbed.* He was reassured but decided to push matters a little further. 'Would you like me to add your new challenge to this morning's agenda?'

'No, there isn't much to discuss as yet. I'll let you know what I find out before we involve others.'

Control nodded his agreement having expected that response. If Anthony's version was actually truthful and Mater had been the unwitting messenger, inevitably Anthony would want to keep his cards close to his chest. He had always given the impression of being a team player but underneath remained truly competitive. If there was kudos to be gained, he would want it all for himself. There was danger in letting Anthony play the game by his own rules but he had delivered in the past. If he was simply creating cover to avoid detection of his desire to fuck Charlotte, then Control looked forward to hearing his subsequent report with all its lies and deceptions.

Anthony finished his coffee, stood up and thanked the boss for his time.

As he left, Control called after him. 'Good luck Anthony, keep me informed.'

As the door closed, Control selected another wafer and repeated his parting words quietly to himself. 'Good luck Anthony.' He seemed to be saying that to too many of his staff. The organisation shouldn't run on luck but increasingly and worryingly, facts were being replaced by theories and supposition. He felt the Office was not in the best place.

Chapter 22

At Kings Cross, Mater booked three single rooms in the nearby Point A Hotel under the name of the Construction Partnership Agency: 'Providers of skilled tradespeople at short notice'. He had posted some coins into a booth inside a branch of the stationers WH Smith, creating business cards advertising the same. He would distribute these between himself and his workers, giving them something to use as an opener to their cover story. He purchased dark blue overalls, guessing their sizes. On the internet, he found a local clothes repairer/embroiderer who, for a few pounds and within an hour, stitched 'CPA' logos on them. He needed the men to be adequately prepared so that they had the best chance of succeeding in their first task. Finally, Mater, wanting to hear what went on during their test but needing to stay hidden himself, visited the Spycatcher store in Portman Square. The shop staff were discreet, and it hadn't really been necessary for him to explain that he required the body microphone to help him secure a business deal. They had heard all the excuses in the world before and were also quite used to customers paying in cash. He returned to his hotel and waited for Pete, Hefty and Jock to arrive.

Mid-afternoon there was a knock on his door and he recognised Pete's voice. He let the three in, each carrying a selection of new carrier bags that they placed on the floor beside the rest of their belongings. One of the bags gave a familiar clink as Jock laid it down. He glanced at Mater, embarrassed.

'It's alright Jock,' said Mater reassuringly, 'I don't expect you to be angels.'

Jock smiled meekly.

'OK men,' said Mater. 'Let's get you fitted out and then I'll brief you on your task.'

Washed, shaved and dressed in clean fresh clothes, each man was almost unrecognisable. They looked at each other in amazement and to their new boss for approval. Mater checked that the sale tags from all the new garments had been removed. It had been years since any of them had worn new things. He reached into one of his own bags and distributed the overalls, apologising that the fit was unlikely to be ideal. His guesswork, however, he noted as they put them on had been accurate.

'Right,' he said, 'You look great but not yet perfect. I want you to take these coveralls away with you and find somewhere discrete to dirty them up a bit; a minor tear here or there would help. You should also choose a trade that you can waffle on about even at a basic level. I need you to be able to bluff your way out of trouble.'

'Trouble?' questioned Pete, 'Would you care to enlighten us?'

'Coming to it,' replied Mater, recognising that it was necessary to keep them on side. 'Now for your mission brief. Please sit down and feel free to sample something from Jock's bag as I talk.'

Jock rummaged in the carrier that contained the liquid refreshment and handed a can to each of his friends. He offered a fourth to Mater who shook his head.

Mater began. They all listened intently as he explained how he wanted them to detain a middle-aged man and question him about possible links with criminal gangs or terrorist groups. Mater would provide a list of questions to start the process and also a body microphone so that he could listen, from a distance, to the target's replies. Their subject, he warned them, would be skilled at evading capture and deflecting their questions. He expected the target to arrive at a specific location at 9pm the next day. Mater would confirm it was him and then the men were to move in and apprehend him. Mater had identified the area would be busy with people eating out or going to the popular theatres nearby. This should reassure the target but increase the risk that he might escape. It was important the public didn't get involved or even realise that something unusual was occurring. There were many backstreets leading off the main thoroughfare and in one Mater had located a closed delicatessen that would be easy to enter and use for their purpose. The plan involved rapidly moving their man away from the crowd to isolate him so the discussion could take place unhindered.

'Discussion,' piped up Hefty, 'You mean interrogation. Sounds as though this could become quite unpleasant. What's this guy done wrong?'

'It is possible that he's responsible for a number of British subjects' deaths. It is very important that he provides information,' answered Mater.

'Then inform the proper authorities,' responded Hefty loudly, concerned about what he might be letting himself in for.

'I am the proper authority,' retorted Mater quietly.

The room fell silent. Hefty looked Mater squarely in the eye. The other two men gripped their cans of beer and watched, wondering what was coming next. Finally, Hefty broke the silence. 'How do we know you're not lying? That this isn't all bullshit? Maybe the man you want us to deal with, on your behalf, is the good guy and you the enemy?'

'You don't,' responded Mater without hesitation. He looked to each man in turn.

'There are lies, some big, some white. And there is truth and trust,' he said. 'If I tell you that I believe the man I am interested in has been involved in the murders of my friends and colleagues that is the truth. You have to decide to trust me but if you don't, hand over the clothes and cash I have given you and walk straight out now. Anyone who works for me must have complete faith in my actions. As I have indicated, you are always free to go.' He fell silent again, examining the reaction of each man, waiting to see whether he had convinced any or all to stay. To Mater's relief, Pete was the first to speak.

'I'm in,' he said, 'I'm willing to give this a try. If it all turns out to be bullshit as suggested by Hefty, then we can, as you say, walk away. Providing we don't hurt the guy, we shouldn't worry. He won't know who we are or where we've come from.'

Precisely, thought Mater.

'But boss,' continued Pete, 'Why can't you speak to him?'

Mater was prepared. 'Quite simply Pete, because this is all a part of your selection process, your interview if you will. If you perform well, there'll be other more challenging and

255

rewarding missions to be carried out later; after you have had further training.'

Pete nodded, memories from his army days flooding back. Mater acted like a superior officer; reassuring and encouraging, making men do things they would never consider doing of their own accord. The other two recruits, having faith in Pete's judgement, agreed to continue.

'Thank you,' said Mater, 'I will have that beer now you were offering, Jock, and then I'll put more meat on the bones.'

Chapter 23

At 8.55pm, Mater seated in the window of the Natural Bean coffee shop, saw Anthony walk to and stop at the junction between Earlham Street and Drury Lane. He appeared to take an interest in the display in the gentleman's outfitters that occupied the corner; showcasing traditional English hunting and fishing attire. The evening pedestrian traffic passed him by. Mater turned around to speak to the workman sat at the next table.

'Have you any sugar?' he asked.

Pete stood up and brought the bowl to Mater.

'Target wearing long dark coat, standing alone, looking in J.G. Livingston's shop. See him?'

Pete nodded, left the sugar with Mater and headed outside.

Under the bright street lights, Mater observed a man dressed in overalls cross the road, approach Anthony and engage him in conversation. Mater switched on his radio and adjusted the earpiece. He fiddled with his phone lying on the table ensuring the blue tooth connection recorded what followed.

Pete stopped in front of the window beside Anthony.

'Have you read the Evening News?' he asked.

Anthony turned around. 'I'm an Evening Standard man myself,' he answered.

'I have news for you. Please follow me,' said Pete. He walked around the corner into Neal Street, Anthony following a few steps behind.

Mater rose and left the café, listening intently as he, in turn, crossed the road. Roughly one hundred metres further on, Anthony, passing a small alley, failed to spot two further men dressed in overalls standing back in the shadows. A few paces later, Pete stopped, enabling Anthony to catch up. Pete smiled.

'I suggest we go in here to have our chat,' he said, pointing to the delicatessen, its windows whitewashed. Anthony looked at the empty premises and then Pete, alarmed.

'I would prefer it if we returned to Drury Lane. There's an excellent wine bar nearby.'

Mater could sense the tension in Anthony's voice.

'Here will be fine,' called someone from behind.

Anthony swung round to face Hefty and Jock. He was stuck. Jock took a key from his pocket and opened the padlock securing the front door. Their work earlier in the day ensured that it was quick and easy to enter the empty premises.

'After you,' said Hefty.

Anthony stepped through the doorway followed by the team of three. Inside it was almost dark; the streetlights, filtered by the whitewash, providing the only illumination.

'Please sit,' said Pete, indicating a chair in the gloom, placed in the middle of the room.

Jock pulled up another behind Anthony's, its back resting against an old empty glass food cabinet and dust laden customer counter. Pete stood in front. Hefty remained at the door, blocking the exit. Anthony decided to take control of the situation.

'You have information for me, I assume,' he began, 'And no doubt you want something in return. Probably quite a lot. Well I can assure you that if what you tell me is useful, the people who employ me will pay handsomely for it.'

Pete butted in. 'You're right. We do want something but it is information from you we need in return for,' he paused, 'us allowing you to leave.' His speech was calm, low and threatening. Anthony made to stand but found himself restrained by a firm hand pushing down on his shoulder.

'Who are you? Who do you work for?' he asked, his voice wavering, losing its confidence.

'We ask the questions,' retorted Pete.

Anthony snorted. 'We ask the questions, we ask the questions,' he repeated, laughing, hardly believing what he was hearing. 'Are you some sort of comedians? Only a bunch of comics or actors from a corny thriller could come up with that line.'

Pete ignored the riposte and decided to waste no further time. 'What does Antinin mean to you?'

Anthony stopped laughing. He swallowed hard and fought to suppress a tremendous urge to empty his bladder. He gripped the chair. He wanted to stay silent but recognised he had to offer something before they would release him. He would try, if he could, to turn this unpleasant experience to his advantage. 'Antinin' played again and again in his head as an ear worm. He tried to suppress it.

'It doesn't mean anything to me,' he said, 'Can you enlighten me? If you tell me more, I might be able to help.'

'It's Czech for Anthony,' said Pete. He paused, watching for a reaction from the man seated motionless in front of him.

'So?' said Anthony, relaxing his grip of the chair. He smiled at Pete. 'I'm really not sure what you are asking me. I don't know what you are talking about.'

Pete hesitated, uncertain how to continue. Anthony noting the man posing the questions apparent indecision, increasingly believed the men who had in effect abducted him, were amateurs. His confidence returned. 'I'm wondering if you have picked the wrong man. The letter you sent me implied you had information about a particular Middle Eastern organisation. I was hoping you did. It sounds as if you haven't and instead are looking for something I clearly can't deliver. But I'm most interested to find out how you learnt about the group mentioned in your note.'

Hefty had heard enough. Mater had warned them that their target would be clever and resilient but the longer this went on the greater the risk that they might be discovered. He decided that time was slipping by and a more traditional approach to extracting information was required. He moved forward and stood between Pete and Anthony, towering over him.

'Tell us about Antinin, you little shit,' he demanded.

Anthony looked straight at Hefty, struggling to keep his cool.

'I've told you it means nothing to me.'

Hefty tried again. 'I'll ask you once more, who or what is Antinin?'

Anthony shoved the hand from his shoulder and stood up. 'Fuck off,' he said, 'Enough. You can't help me and I can't help you. Meeting over.' He made to move towards the door but Hefty was too quick, pushing him hard back onto the chair where Jock's arms reaching from behind held him firmly. Hefty pulled out a roll of duct tape from his overall's and proceeded to secure Anthony to his seat. Anthony noted the smell of stale booze.

'You're not leaving, not yet,' he growled menacingly, as he wound the tape around and around. Outside, less than fifty metres away, standing at the edge of the alleyway, Mater listened in.

'Just keep demanding answers but don't hurt the bugger,' he muttered to himself.

In the shop, Pete returned to his questions.

'Who do you work for?' he asked.

'I'm a civil servant, working for Her Majesty's government; Foreign Office,' came the reply, Anthony hoping he might unnerve his interrogators.

'We know,' said Pete calmly, 'Who else?'

Anthony decided to keep his silence. He wished he had taken up Control's offer of some back up but he was on his own and would have to rely on his training to cope. The questioning could last for hours and it could become painful. But the Office wouldn't have selected him all those years ago if he had crumpled when it got a little rough. *No*, he determined, *his experience would see him through. The trick would be to give these men just enough to satisfy whoever they worked for and to make them believe they had succeeded.*

'Who else?' repeated Pete just before Anthony felt a blow to the back of his head, delivered by the man standing behind him. Jock had also decided it was time to move things on. Anthony tried to detach himself, mentally, from his present predicament. He imagined he was watching a classic spy film and the hero, played by himself, resisted the efforts of his interrogators, ultimately defeating them by guile and cunning. He let his mind wander, ignoring the repetitive questions. The pain caused by the intermittent blows was bearable but he purposely called out after each one, pretending it was severe and adequately effective in encouraging him to reveal information. Mater listening in, knew that Anthony would be a tough nut to crack but hoped that he would make just one small mistake. One simple error would give Mater the proof he needed to confirm his suspicions. Pete pulled out a blurred printed image derived from a mobile phone video. It showed a man's face, eyes half closed and covered in blood. He held the picture in front of Anthony, took a torch from his overall's pocket, and illuminated it.

'Do you recognise this man?'

Anthony dug a fingernail into the wooden arm of the chair, the duct tape preventing him from moving his hands further. He hesitated. To Mater, his finger pressing the earpiece hard into his ear, the hesitation was long, much too long.

'No,' answered Anthony, 'Whoever he is, poor chap looks in a terrible state.'

Jock, from his experience as a customs officer, also picked up on the delay and the lack of disgust or concern that the photo should have caused. He decided it was time for him to act, his anger simmering as a consequence of Anthony's failure to cooperate.

'I think we need to jog your memory,' he said.

There was a table to one side of the counter, fixed to the wall. Jock asked Hefty to drag their subject to it. Anthony's eyesight had adjusted to the darkness. The wooden table was bare apart from an old fashioned bacon slicer. He felt nauseous, hoping that the electrical supply to the shop had been cut, or the thing was broken. Jock told Hefty to grip Anthony's right arm as he released it.

'Right,' he said, 'We're going to fix your hand to this machine and then perhaps you will consider being a little more enlightening in your responses.'

Anthony tried to pull away but the two men overpowered him and quickly secured his hand to the dirty delivery plate. It lay at right angles to the round rusting blade, still contaminated with green rancid congealed pork fat.

'You fucking bastards,' he murmured.

'Heard that,' said Jock, 'Bet you hoped the power was off. Us, all sitting, nicely together, in the dark. No such luck mate.' He flicked the switch on the appliance and it whirred into life sounding to all like a dentist's drill as the electric motor revved up.

'Better tape his mouth,' said Jock, pulling a length from the roll of duct tape. 'Mustn't wake the neighbours.'

Mater heard it all and felt sick himself. He knew from Jock's background that he might carry on and use the machine. He also realised that if he had got all this wrong, then it would be the end for him and probably worse. Control would put two and two together and an injured Anthony would finish him off.

Jock proceeded to advance the spinning blade towards Anthony's fingers. Anthony's heart raced, and he felt warm urine leak into his pants. The blade met its target, slicing off layer upon thin layer of fingertip, blood spraying from the severed tip. Anthony screamed behind the seal of duct tape, wrestled with his restraints, desperately trying to take in enough air through his nose. Jock pulled the machine back and watched blood pulsing from Anthony's middle finger, most of the tip beyond the end knuckle gone. He waited while Anthony heaved in his chair, sweat pouring from his forehead.

'Right you fucker,' he said, 'I'm going to remove the tape from your mouth shortly. I want you to be a good boy and not make too much noise, then I will ask my friend to pose his questions again. You may wish to answer this time or your piano playing days will definitely be over.'

Anthony didn't find the old joke entertaining. Pete stepped forward and wrapped some tissues around the stump of the finger, helping stem the flow of blood. He placed the photo on the table in front of Anthony.

'Who is he and who did he work for?' he asked, speaking softly and calmly.

Anthony was confused and in severe pain. He shook and sweated; the perspiration inside his clothes mixed with the urine that had involuntarily escaped, soaking his trousers. His tormentors no longer seemed like the amateurs he had assumed them to be. He concluded they wouldn't stop until they had something tangible, something credible to take back to their masters. But who did they report to? Somehow, they had known it was him they needed to catch and question. But at this moment, none of this mattered. He had to finish this and get away before they did serious damage or even killed him. He swallowed hard.

'His name was, is, Jiri Skopek.'

'Good boy,' said Pete, 'That's better. Tell me more. Where was he from? Who did he work for?'

Jock held his finger over the slicer's switch, ready to flip it at a moment's notice. Anthony's resistance crumbled.

'He came from the Czech Republic; I don't know who he worked for.'

'You don't know?' sneered Jock, his finger twitching. Anthony looked at Jock, his eyes pleading for mercy. He remembered his trainers saying there comes a time when you may have to give in. Everyone would forgive you when that happened.

'No, no, please stop,' he cried, 'I really don't know anything else.' He realised, somewhat to his own surprise, he was begging for the torture to end.

Mater, listening only fifty metres away, had heard enough. Anthony had almost certainly incriminated himself and now he needed him alive to help him track down the rest of his group and any organisation behind it. Mater sprinted the short distance to the Delicatessen and banged hard on the door. He listened momentarily as all fell silent inside and then ran back to the alleyway.

Jock's finger on the switch had frozen. He glanced to the others and then Anthony. 'Who the fuck was that?' he whispered.

'Could be the owner, someone trying to break in or the Police,' suggested Pete. 'Let's keep quiet for a few minutes and then leave.'

He turned to Anthony. 'The interview is over. Thank you for the information. If we need more, we know where you are. We'll let you go shortly but please don't try to be clever. To follow or endeavour to find us would have dire consequences for you: it won't just be no more piano playing.'

Anthony breathed a sigh of relief. He was disappointed in himself and his inability to cope with the violence. He thought he should have done better. The pain in his hand was terrible, but he was alive. He consoled himself in believing he had given little away. He longed for the fresh night outside air and the relative safety of the London crowds.

Jock unplugged the bacon slicer. Pete picked up the photo and replaced it in his pocket.

'When we walk out of here,' he instructed Anthony, 'You turn left and don't look back. We will, of course, go in the opposite direction. Better get that finger dressed properly; you don't want it to become infected.'

Using a small knife, he cut Anthony's restraints.

'One final question before you leave. Are you a religious man?' he asked.

266

'Not particularly,' replied Anthony quietly.

'Not Christian, Sikh, Buddhist or perhaps a Muslim?'

'No,' said Anthony, 'In my opinion religion is for fools.'

Pete nodded in agreement. He turned to the others. 'Ready? Let's go.'

Jock moved silently to the front door and listened; his presence hidden by the whitewash. All was quiet. He gently opened it and peered out. The street was empty. He beckoned to the others. Hefty stepped forward, helped Anthony to his feet and then roughly propelled him to the entrance. Jock pushed the door wide open and Hefty gave an Anthony a firm shove, causing him to stumble out onto the pavement.

'Goodbye, thanks for your custom,' he called after him.

Anthony didn't dare look back. He walked quickly, holding his injured right hand in his left, passing the alleyway where Mater stood motionless and unnoticed in the shadows. He concentrated on burning the image of his assailants' faces into his memory.

'I'll get you, I'll get you all,' he muttered to himself.

He failed to notice the dark figure emerge from the alley and follow him at a discreet distance.

Mater wondered whether Anthony would immediately report back to the Office, bluffing his way with Control. It would be easy to explain that the attempt to gain new information concerning the Derwent terrorist group had failed, and he had been injured during the process. Anthony would still be on the inside, working to discover who had been behind the letter with its bogus invitation. It would only be a matter of time before Mater and possibly Charlotte were identified. But Mater had missed a critical part of Anthony's thinking. As the wounded man walked through the West End's theatreland, it occurred to him that those operating against him, having access to his postal address, must be Office staff. Further, as he was targeting one group in particular, it was likely the same were targeting him.

Mater, you bastard, he thought.

Arriving at Chancery Lane tube station, Anthony joined the throng of evening revellers heading home. Mater following on the opposite side of the road, crossed, dodging taxis and buses and entered the underground. He worked hard to keep track of Anthony as he passed through the ticket gates and descended to the eastbound platform. The station was busy, helping Mater hide his presence. As the train pulled in, he checked that Anthony boarded before swiftly jumping in just as the doors closed. Anthony sat, head bowed, his injured hand hidden from view in his pocket. No-one seemed to notice the staining on his clothes from the blood and urine; the dark grey of his coat concealing the worst of it. As Liverpool Street station approached he stood. Feeling lightheaded, he steadied himself by holding onto a metal handrail with his good arm. The blood continued to ooze from his finger soaking the lining of his pocket. He knew he needed help. The small crowd of fellow travellers around him, also waiting to get off, ignored him, assuming his unsteadiness stemmed from an overindulgent evening. Mater watched his quarry in the internal reflection of the carriage windows. At Liverpool Street, Anthony changed to the Metropolitan Line, again heading east. Mater wondered where he was going. Could it be to his home address? It certainly wasn't the Office. Once again, Mater was fortunate that the carriage Anthony and he boarded was almost full, providing Mater cover even if he didn't realise Anthony wasn't checking whether he was being followed. At Whitechapel, Anthony staggered to his feet again while Mater remained seated until the last moment. Fewer passengers alighted and Mater made sure that when he got off, he initially headed along the platform in the opposite direction to Anthony, only turning back when his quarry entered the side exit tunnel. Mater quickened his pace. He needed to leave the station in time to see where Anthony went next. He guessed Anthony would go to the London Hospital to have his injuries attended to. Mater reached ground level, exited the station and crossed the busy Whitechapel Road. Anthony, he calculated, aiming for the hospital, should be to his left, heading to Cavell Street. Mater couldn't see him. He quickly turned and looked west, spotting Anthony, now more than one hundred metres away, walking straight back along the Whitechapel Road towards Central London. Mater hurried after him wondering if he had been seen. He had to get closer in case Anthony jumped onto a passing bus or hailed a taxi. Mater needn't have worried: Anthony was hurrying to his destination, paying little attention to anti-surveillance. Less than two hundred metres on and he stopped, briefly checked around, and then climbed up the steps of a large grand building, instantly recognisable as a place of worship. Mater watched as Anthony disappeared inside the magnificent East London Mosque; its ornate brickwork, twin minarets and classical dome distinguishing it from the adjacent dull grey tower blocks.

You're not going in there on Office business, thought Mater, *but your own. Time to speak to Control.*

When Mater returned his hotel, Pete, and the others were waiting for him in the foyer, their overalls gone. The night receptionist had recognised the men on their arrival and was

269

initially astonished by the change in their appearance. Over the years he had seen many strange goings on; nothing really surprised him anymore, so he took little further interest. Mater walked straight over to his team and asked them to follow him to his room for a debrief. With the bedroom door closed, Mater turned to the men, seated as before in a row on his bed.

'Well done,' he said, 'Very good work. You achieved what I hoped you would. I recorded everything I needed. However, in the future, if you can avoid dissecting your prisoners but simply use threats, the evidence suggests they tend to give you what you want eventually.'

Jock interrupted. 'Boss, my own experience told me this one was going to be a tough nut to crack and we couldn't hang around too long. Anyway, he seemed a smarmy bastard and I'm afraid I took a dislike to him.'

Mater agreed that Anthony tended to rub up some peoples' backs the wrong way. 'I understand,' continued Mater, 'I'm sorry if I startled you by banging on the door. We could have done with a two-way radio but I didn't want your subject to think anyone else was involved.'

'You know him, don't you,' stated Pete, staring intently at Mater, who considered his response carefully before replying.

'Yes, I know a little about who he is but less about what he is up to. Your interrogation helped me a lot. You have passed the test and you can, if you want to, move to the next stage. Are you all still in?'

Pete, seated between Hefty and Jock, looked right and left, waiting for his friends' decisions. Both nodded and Pete answered on their behalf.

'Yes, we're up for it. To be frank, I thought it was rather exciting, even quite good fun, almost a game.'

'Excellent,' replied Mater, 'But please be aware that the game, as you describe it, is likely to become much more serious, more dangerous and it may not be so enjoyable. But let's not worry about that now. Time to celebrate.'

He moved across to the bedside table and extracted a bottle of champagne from underneath, along with some plastic cups.

'Sorry about the lack of crystal but the wine should still taste good. Courtesy of my employers,' he said, thinking, *I don't see why Control should have all the rewards.*

As Mater handed out the fizz, he saw Jock's hands shake as he reached for his cup, almost spilling the drink. Mater realised then that Jock would probably have to be the first candidate for detoxification.

Chapter 24

Early the next morning Mater contacted Control by the usual method. He didn't expect Anthony would return to work but, just in case, he wanted to deliver his information first. They arranged to rendezvous near the London Eye and then walked together along the South Bank of the Thames; the public environment demanding they changed the subject of their conversation each time they passed others who also enjoyed the pleasant weather and fresh Spring air.

'You suggested we meet urgently,' said Control. 'Give me an update.'

Mater had not slept well, trying to decide on how best to inform the chief about the potential traitor positioned so close to the hub of the Office's work.

'The organisation has a problem,' began Mater.

'Only one,' joked Control. 'You seem to have suffered rather more than that recently.'

Mater didn't join in with the frivolity. He continued. 'Yes, maybe just one.'

Control stopped and turned to lean on the concrete wall beyond which the muddy tide of the Thames ebbed east relentlessly towards the sea. He looked across the water, scanning the magnificent city skyline. Mater joined him, leaving his boss some personal space although close enough so his words could be heard but not discerned by anyone else. Control waited for Mater to expand on his comment.

'I'm sorry to report, sir, I believe Anthony may be involved or even responsible for the attacks on my unit.'

He allowed a few moments to pass, giving his boss time to digest the unsavoury statement. He knew he had to back up his allegation with something concrete.

'I have the beginnings of a new team and, as a part of their selection process, I tasked them to ask Anthony to explain a few things. Once encouraged to do so, he gave some interesting responses.'

'You did what?' interjected Control, almost hissing.

His boss's anger was tangible and Mater suddenly wondered if he had made an awful mistake but there was no going back.

'In Czech, Antinal is Anthony and Anthony is Antinal,' he said.

Control turned to face Mater who continued to watch the flow of the river. 'Phil,' he said, 'You better have some bloody good evidence to support such an accusation. How the hell did you persuade Anthony to speak to your men?'

Mater kicked the wall, feeling the pain as his left big toe felt the resistance of the concrete.

'The letter, sir. The letter I asked you to forward. It offered something to Anthony he would find even more attractive than Charlotte.'

Control shook his head slowly.

'Go on,' he growled.

'Well,' said Mater, 'There isn't much more except...'

'Except?' enquired Control, struggling to listen to Mater's every word, waiting for the whole picture to be revealed, before considering the consequences.

'I wonder if he is receiving help from members of our Muslim community.'

'You wonder what?' responded Control, 'What makes you think, I mean wonder, that this could be a possibility?'

Mater realised he would have to explain when and where he observed Anthony entering the mosques. There was no point in not confessing that he had visited Hereford. He needed to lay all his cards on the table and let Control decide whether his was a winning hand. He described in detail meeting Anthony at the funeral, repeating Anthony's strange comments, the tail to the mosque and the departure by Anthony in a car driven by others. He recited, verbatim, the contents of the letter Control had unwittingly posted which led to the violent interrogation of one of his senior officers, right here in his own capital. Finally, Mater detailed his second tailing of Anthony through the City to the East End ending in his quarry going to ground in another mosque. Mater stopped and waited for Control to consider his report. He listened to the sound of the river traffic, added to by the urban hum emanating from the opposite embankment, intermittently interrupted by a swooping gull's squawk or the chatter of pedestrians.

Control coughed and began in a low rumbling voice. Mater had rarely seen Control so angry.

'So, you disobeyed my order to stay away from Tiny's funeral. And you involved me in your plan, without my explicit consent, to entice Anthony to a place where it sounds as if he suffered at the hands of your recruits. To top it all, I suspect none of whom has ever heard of, let alone signed, the Official Secrets Act. I'm waiting for you to produce hard evidence to support your somewhat serious, and that's an understatement, contentions.'

'I apologise for the subterfuge,' replied Mater, 'But there is evidence. I recorded Anthony's discussion with my men.'

Control butted in. 'You mean your interrogation by proxy involving violence. You and I understand anyone will say what you want them to once the thumbscrews are tightened.'

The mention of thumbscrews brought back the sound of Anthony squealing as the bacon slicer carved into its target finger. Mater swallowed hard, suppressing his own rage.

'I've lost valuable members of my team, colleagues with whom I've worked for years, facing every kind of danger. You understand I can't sit and simply hide to save my own skin from a similar fate. I do not, or rather did not, hold any personal vendetta against Anthony but I'm sure he is involved directly or indirectly in the piecemeal destruction of my unit. Why he's doing this, is another question. If he is innocent, then I would expect him to appear in front of you, sir, clamouring for my head. But if I'm right, I suspect neither you nor anyone else will see him again, unless I find him.'

'Unless... he's already dead. Is he?' enquired Control, fixing his dark eyes to Mater's.

Mater stared back at his boss. 'He is alive and out there, sir, and in my opinion, extremely dangerous.'

Control continued to concentrate on Mater's expression. He had spent years learning to discern the truth from lies. A simple increase in blink rate, a brief avoidance of eye contact, or an unnecessary swallow could reveal more than any spoken word. Mater remained expressionless, but he saw the tension in his boss's face; the masseter muscles in his cheeks repeatedly contracting and the reddening of the wrinkles rising from his neck as the anger within him rose. Finally, Control reached his own conclusion and spoke.

'Get the bastard, Phil. Destroy the outfit that he is part of and bring him in. Carte blanche. But, and it's a very big and clear but, if you've been barking up the wrong tree you know whose head is going to roll.'

Mater nodded before speaking again, softly this time. 'I will need your help, sir,' he said.

Control regained his composure. 'Of course,' he said, 'Let me buy you an ice-cream and we can talk about your next move as we walk back.' The two men straightened up and strode together towards an ice-cream van parked on the pavement a short distance away. The air was cold but the warm sun ensured the man selling cones and tubs was rewarded with an ever-renewing queue of customers. They joined it but exchanged few words. Control chose for them both and handed Mater a vanilla cone with a chocolate stick.

'More treats on expenses,' he said, his smile returning, 'Don't say I don't spoil you.'

276

Control spotted a line of concrete bollards lining the edge of the paved pathway. He guided Mater towards them and, while licking his ice-cream, beckoned to Mater to rest on one. They were beyond earshot of the van and the crowd. He stopped eating.

'Tell me what you need, Phil.'

Mater was prepared. 'Clearly it is vital that Anthony isn't allowed to leave the country. I would be surprised if he returns to known addresses. It is much more likely that he will use his friends in the mosques to assist him so perhaps resource should be directed to watching those. If he surfaces, he might direct us to other active targets and locations. We've no idea if he is acting alone or has received help from within the Office or even 5. So, we should try to limit the number of operatives assigned to the task. I believe that during his interrogation he decided to offer information that was true, hoping it would be enough to stop the proceedings. In that he was right, but he might also have made his biggest mistake. We need to know everything about a certain Jiri Skopek. Skopek may be dead but his past actions and contacts, if in the records, could lead to those who worked with him; the other guy killed during the assault on my home, the man who escaped and those who murdered Liam, Tiny and possibly Mick. It's our best chance.'

Control listened carefully before offering his own thoughts. With his extensive inside knowledge and broad security clearance, Anthony represented a threat to the whole organisation. If anyone could catch him Mater could, but it was going to be a most arduous task; perhaps his greatest challenge yet.

'5 are already carrying out surveillance on the mosques for obvious reasons. They update me whenever they decide someone suspicious from the Muslim community is preparing to slip overseas to misbehave. If they do travel, they then fall onto our patch. I'll make sure they look out for Anthony too. However, the fact that he continues to visit mosques implies to me, that he doesn't fully realise the extent of 5's operations. So encouragingly, he probably doesn't have useful contacts in our sister service but to be frank I can't guarantee there still isn't a problem within our own. And if Anthony is lost to us, who knows who else? I expect he'll go to ground knowing we'll watch the ports and airports and hold a central record of his current Office aliases. I'll personally work on the Jiri Skopek issue. Give me forty-eight hours, then I'll contact you on your mobile from a pay phone. 'Phoenix rising' the codeword. Look after yourself and your new team.'

Control crushed the last centimetre of crisp sugar cone between finger and thumb, allowing the crumbs to fall and be dispersed by the gentle breeze, chased by a large flock of pigeons. He tightened his scarf and walked away. Mater waited, sat balanced on his bollard, until his boss disappeared; swallowed up by the perambulating throng in the distance. He threw the remains of his own cone to the birds, that briefly scattered, only to return at once, resuming their competitive struggle for food. He watched them fight. 'Anthony and your lot are just like pigeons, simply vermin,' he muttered. 'I will set my cats amongst you and feathers will fly.'

Mater returned to his hotel and decided he needed to update Charlotte. Events were moving at a faster pace than he had anticipated and they were going to have to speed up the training of their recruits.

Charlotte was pleased to hear from Mater. She had made great progress with Dr Baird, who had been more than helpful.

Apparently, he had shown increased interest in her detoxification plans although she couldn't be certain that his curiosity was not more about her than any potential patients. On occasions, the Major, who clearly had insight, had acted as an effective chaperone. Dr Baird's desire to examine her remained thwarted. The Lodge was vacant, ready and waiting. In essence, if Mater demanded it, the program could begin with the training schedule evolving over the coming weeks. Mater, in coded and guarded language, explained that there was indeed an urgent need to get on. He congratulated Charlotte.

'Well done. Excellent work. Your first students arrive within the next few days. Our naughty pupil has given away a secret or two and has skipped school. I suspect he has joined up with his rebellious friends. We can't let him abscond. The headmaster is on the case and will inform us if he finds out anything useful. Please tell the caretaker that I plan to visit, bringing the students with me so that he can sort out a dorm. I'll fill you in with the details then.'

Mater called Pete at the Point A Hotel. 'Get ready to move,' he said, 'We're leaving today. Our London work is done.'

Pete hesitated before answering. 'There's a slight problem, boss. The others are not in the best state. They're really pissed. I saw them only a few moments ago crashed out in their bedrooms. I think they've been on a bender using your cash.'

Mater knew it was only a matter of time before the overwhelming urge to drink would overtake the men's wish to reform.

'Can they walk and would they be amenable to a train journey?' asked Mater.

'Walk?' responded Pete, 'More like stagger but they are both surprisingly coherent.'

'Right, Pete, go back to their rooms, take away the remaining booze, help them pack and I'll be with you very shortly. The stag party is about to leave town.'

By the time Mater reached the men, Jock and Hefty appeared to be sobering up, such was their tolerance. Jock was almost apologetic, explaining that he had tried to cut his consumption but found the sweats, shakes and nightmares too much. Mater expressed some sympathy and wondered how Jock would cope when subjected to the formal detoxification treatment. Pete had been efficient in organising the team's belongings. Each man had a full holdall containing their new clothes but also carrier bags stuffed with grubby and tatty possessions accumulated over the years spent living rough. Mater looked at the pile and shook his head.

'I'm sorry boys; I'll need to check your stuff. Anything that links you to your past has to go.'

Hefty emboldened by the drink was not impressed and as Mater went to begin, stepped forward and grabbed his arm.

'Boss, you get us to do your dirty work but you won't let us keep our dirty kit? I've a few photos and one or two special things amongst that lot that I don't want to lose. No, I won't throw them away.' He squeezed tightly.

Mater used his other hand to release Hefty's grip. The contents of the green plastic briefcase briefly passed through his mind, images flashing by as in a hectic slide show.

'I understand Hefty,' he said gently. He turned to them all. 'Sort your stuff again and bin everything you really don't need. Anything personal or identifiable we will secure in a locker at the station. If you keep it with you, you increase the risk to yourselves and anyone connected to you via your belongings.'

Mater decided he had to re-iterate the potential seriousness of the men's involvement with him. 'This is no game. I don't want to give the man you met the opportunity of picking off you guys.'

The three looked at Mater. It was clear that he was deadly serious. Mater allowed the possibility of death to sink in and then continued. 'Remember, you can walk out now or at any time you wish.' He paused. No-one made for the door. 'Good,' he said, 'Let's get cracking.'

Each man emptied their bags and gathered together the few items of true personal value. Mater took possession of all that had been selected and placed everything in a single carrier bag.

'OK, take your things, I'll pay on the way out and we'll dump what remains in the nearest bin.'

At the reception desk Mater pulled out a wad of cash, settled the bill, and gave the receptionist a modest tip.

'Thank you, sir,' he said, rather taken aback but quickly pocketing the money.

'Job finished?' he asked.

Mater smiled. 'It's just begun.' He picked up his own bag in one hand, a carrier in the other and left, leaving the receptionist wondering what sort of employment paid before you worked; he would have liked a job like that.

Chapter 25

On the Intercity express from Kings Cross to York, other passengers deliberately sat far from the four men seated together. They were laughing too loudly and a collection of open cans of beer cluttered the plastic laminate table; empties rolled back and forth underneath it as the train followed the curves of the track. To the casual observer, Mater and team could be simply a group of fellow workers celebrating the end of a busy week or preparing for a good weekend away. Whatever their plans, they appeared a rough crew best left to their own devices. Even the ticket inspector made sure her necessary check was carried out quickly and without comment. Mater had tried to reassure her by smiling, but she interpreted his expression as a leer and hurried off down the carriage. He did, however, keep a tab on the quantity of ale consumed, aiming for his men to be happy and topped up but no more. He texted Charlotte: 'Students and master on board. Arrive Harrogate 17.15 hours. Please meet and collect.' She was bemused by his self-promotion to 'master'. She would rag him about that when the opportunity arose.

On arrival, the station in Harrogate was frantic as evening rush hour commuters dashed to catch their homeward bound trains. Mater and team descended from the York connection unobserved. The men, on Mater's instruction stayed together and kept quiet. They followed the boss out of the concourse to the pickup area where Charlotte waited patiently in the Major's deceased wife's car. She watched them approach in her mirror and saw Mater give a thumbs up. He lifted the car's small boot, and the men stowed their bags, obscuring the rear window. Charlotte leant across and opened the passenger door. Mater indicated to Hefty that he should sit in front. It was going to be a tight squeeze but Langley Hall wasn't far. As Hefty climbed aboard the suspension sagged. The others rubbed shoulders in the back. Charlotte shook hands with her passengers but said nothing. She started the engine and lowered the driver's window; the smell of beer somewhat overpowering. She was glad the journey would be short.

Less than thirty minutes later, the Nissan pulled up outside the front steps to the Hall.

'Welcome to Langley, I'm Charlotte but call me Suzanne here,' she said.

Hefty leant forward and stared through the windscreen. 'Blimey, some pad this,' he exclaimed, 'Do we go in via the servants entrance?'

Mater laughed. 'You'll meet the owner shortly. He's very generous. I'm sure you will be treated well, almost as a member of his family. You guys haven't had much luxury in your lives over the past few years so enjoy your stay here. I hope we can make life a little better for you in return for your efforts.'

The men climbed out of the car, stretched, and carrying their bags followed Mater and Charlotte to the grand entrance. Just as they reached it, the door swung open, and the Major stood there beaming, each fist clasping the collar of a dog. He eyed up his new visitors and then looked at Mater quizzically. Mater simply smiled benignly.

Motley bunch, thought the Major, but putting any concerns to one side, invited everyone in. 'Tea's in the pot,' he said, 'Unless you want something stronger,' he added, hoping.

'Tea would be perfect, thanks,' answered Mater quickly.

From behind him Jock grunted. The beer on the train had run out at least an hour before York and he had been looking forward to a top up.

The Major ushered everyone into the kitchen and invited them to sit around the old pine table. Mrs Robinson had kindly baked a cake that she expected to last until her next Friday visit but hadn't been aware of the impending house party. With tea poured and cake served, introductions were formally made. Mr Randall gave his recruits names just as he knew them. Their long absence from public life meant it wasn't necessary to invent new noms de guerre. The Major remained simply 'the Major'. After tea, he showed the latest visitors to their quarters. Although the Hall had a surfeit of rooms, on Charlotte's advice he placed them all in one. The Major didn't know that, for the men, a comfortable bed in a warm room were luxuries and a novelty yet strangely unsettling. Sharing a room would allay their anxiety and further strengthen the bond between them. As the men unpacked, Charlotte and Mater grabbed the opportunity to brief each other. Charlotte was troubled by the urgency expressed by Mater who indicated Jock should be offered the alcohol detoxification treatment post haste. Mater considered the other two to be physically and mentally more robust. He felt that they might even be able to start their training at the Lodge and be gently weaned from their dependence without specialist help. Both recognised Control wanted results fast. The longer it took to create the team, the greater the possibility that Anthony alone, or with others, would escape or worse, attack again. It seemed to Charlotte that their best chance of success was to make sure everyone achieved the required standards. Less than this would increase the risk of failure and danger to them all. She wasn't convinced that Mater was truly concerned for the safety of his recruits despite his protestations to the contrary. Following their discussions, Charlotte called Dr Baird.

'We have your first patient, doctor,' she advised.

'Excellent,' came the reply, 'When do you propose we should start the treatment?'

'I appreciate it's short notice but could you arrange for admission tomorrow?'

'Tomorrow?' exclaimed Dr Baird, 'I'll see what I can do. Unless you hear from me otherwise bring him or her to the clinic at nine o'clock. They should have only a light breakfast and can expect to be an inpatient for about a week. Oh, and the hospital will demand payment in advance.'

'And your fee?' queried Charlotte.

'My fee? Nothing. Duty calls,' he replied, adding in hope rather than expectation, 'But, maybe one day you can repay me in kind.'

Charlotte teased the consultant. 'You never know. We'll have to see, won't we?'

The next day's plan was discussed with Jock who much to everyone's surprise accepted the offer for help without hesitation. Mater couldn't decide whether Jock's understanding of what was proposed was blunted by the effect of the very drug flowing in his veins for which the treatment was required. But, although Mater was becoming attached to the recruits, the drive to resolve the Office's internal and external problems overrode any human considerations; he was rarely sentimental. In fact, at times he could be totally ruthless and the current situation demanded he act in a way that would optimise the chance of achieving their goal. If necessary, all emotion had to be put to one side: three down and outs were ultimately dispensable. Naturally, he would never tell them that.

The evening with the Major proved to be a little subdued. The new visitors trying to be polite and formal despite the Major, Mater and Charlotte all endeavouring to engender an atmosphere of camaraderie. Jock was particularly quiet during dinner, picking over his food as if it might be his last supper. The Major had been requested to provide alcohol but to limit his generosity. Mater also advised him to lock his wine cellar and spirits cabinet. He acquiesced to the request but kept a single bottle of malt hidden in the study for his personal consumption. He didn't feel it necessary that they should all have to suffer, especially the homeowner. At eleven, the parties bid each other good night. Jock, Pete and Hefty retired to their room but slumber didn't come easily to any of them. They weren't used to the silence and missed the familiar continuous rumble of London traffic. They chatted together into the early hours trying to understand how their lives had changed so dramatically in such a short time. Although he didn't yet know it, Jock missing sleep for one night didn't matter. He would soon be sleeping for longer than he ever had done before even if it was chemically induced.

Chapter 26

Dr Baird was aware the private hospital had been struggling financially for some time. He used this knowledge to his advantage when he suggested to its management that he could, with a colleague's assistance, establish a new service for those with addictions. It required quite lengthy periods of in-patient treatment in an intensive care environment. Intensive care was expensive and fortunately those seeking help had access to substantial financial resource. He added that the first patients insisted they remained incognito and in return for their discretion, the clinic and staff employed on this unique programme would be amply rewarded. Understandably, the finance director was excited by the potential mutual benefits of the good doctor's proposal and encouraged the others to agree.

At just before 9 am, it was therefore, not a surprise that the hospital receptionist welcomed Jock, though avoided asking him personal questions and omitted to complete the usual admissions paperwork. The man accompanying him carried a fat envelope in his hand addressed to Dr Baird. He handed it to her. Mater had, on Charlotte's advice, upped the clinic's reimbursement from the ten thousand pounds demanded, hoping that the extra payment would buy confidentiality. Jock's treatment certainly wasn't cheap. Jock and Mater were asked to wait in the reception area. Mater noted the absence of the typical hospital disinfectant smell, replaced by a fragrance emanating from the freshly cleaned carpets. A television, secured to the wall, advertised procedures and treatments that most would consider cosmetic; unnecessary for a healthy life.

He turned to Jock, grinning. 'Read any consent forms carefully Jock, otherwise before you know it they'll have stuck a couple of breast implants in.'

Jock looked up from the magazine he had selected from the array on the table in front of him, alarmed. 'Don't take the piss, boss. I'm finding this place a bit too posh and it makes me nervous.'

Mater patted him on the shoulder. 'You'll be fine,' he said.

A nurse approached them, friendly and professional. She explained she was here to collect Jock and show him to his private room. She was young and pretty but both men were disappointed to see she wore smart trousers and a short sleeved tunic rather than their idea of the traditional nurse's uniform. Her welcome and warmth relaxed Jock, and he stood up to follow her.

'Boss, you can leave me now, I'll manage on my own,' he said, giving Mater a wink.

Mater winked back and got up too.

'Good luck, Jock, hope it all goes well. I expect to see a new man when I pick you up in a few days.' He thanked the nurse for looking after his friend and left.

By the time Mater had returned to the Hall, Jock was already settled in his room. He had showered as instructed and had basic observations such as his blood pressure and temperature recorded. He lay on his bed wearing a thick warm bathrobe, flicking through the TV channels, aimlessly watching snippets of the daytime broadcasts. There was a knock on the door but before he could answer two men entered. One was dressed in a smart suit, the other wore theatre greens.

'Good morning Jock,' said Dr Baird, 'I hope you are settling in OK. May I introduce Dr Frank Heston. He will be in charge of your treatment which I believe is scheduled to start this afternoon. I'll leave you gentlemen to discuss things.'

Dr Baird left the room closing the door quietly behind him. Dr Heston sat on the chair beside Jock's bed, paper file in hand. An older balding man with a neat white beard, steel rimmed spectacles and a stethoscope strung around his neck. He took a pen from his top pocket and opened the file ready to record Jock's medical history. To Jock, he looked serious but professional and trustworthy.

'If I may, I'll take a few details about your past and current state of health,' began Dr Heston. 'Then I'll explain your treatment.'

Jock answered each question honestly but struggled during the discussion about his recent alcohol consumption. He simply didn't have any idea how much he drank. It never seemed to be enough. Dr Heston recorded 'excessive' in the notes.

'OK, now I'll describe what happens next and the potential risks. If you agree to go ahead, this afternoon a nurse will take you to the intensive care unit. There, once you're tucked up in bed, I'll insert a small tube into a vein and routine monitors will be attached to your body. Next you will be asked to breathe oxygen. Shortly after, an injection into the bloodstream will make you fall asleep. You'll remain unconscious for four days with an excellent team of nurses looking after you at all times. Then we wake you and hope your urge to drink will be gone.'

Jock listened carefully. 'And the risks?' he asked.

Dr Heston retained his serious expression. 'Significant,' he replied. 'As you withdraw from the alcohol, your body may struggle to maintain its normal functions. Blood pressure, pulse and temperature might become unstable and as you emerge from your sleep, you may fit.' He hesitated before whispering. 'There is a small but definite risk you could die.'

Jock nodded. 'I won't consent to that bit,' he joked. 'OK, where do I sign?'

Dr Heston closed the file. 'No need to sign anything. Dr Baird has explained to me you are simply to be known as Jock. The record I hold in my hand is only there to help me help you during your treatment. When that's over, it will be destroyed. The plan is for you to leave here cured and the hospital forget you ever came.'

Back at Langley Hall, Mater could sense the others' concern for Jock. He knew the men had watched out for each other during their years together on the streets where life's dangers were familiar and manageable. This new phase was an unknown entity and the journey they were making followed an unfamiliar path with a leader who was mysterious. They were also anxious to see if Jock's treatment would work; the result would influence their own decision as to whether they should go ahead or not. Mater decided there was little point in wasting the coming days simply waiting. Better to move the team to Scotland and begin training. It would distract them and allow the Major some space. Jock would join them soon enough. He caught up with Charlotte in the library and told her his plans. They would leave the next day.

The four were ready to depart soon after breakfast. The Major, as generous as ever, offered the car and handed back the Makarov pistol to Mater. 'Don't think you'll need this if you are travelling north, Mr Randall, but perhaps wherever you are, there will be grouse or rabbits. Somewhat powerful for such little beasts, but you might be left with a leg or wing for dinner. You'll be pleased to know I've found extra ammunition.' He gave Mater a small box containing thirty rounds. Mater thanked him again and apologised for intruding on his peaceful retirement.

'No apology necessary,' came the instant reply, 'Always ready to do my bit. Anyway, sometimes it's just too quiet here. Remember the door is always open, as and when you wish to visit.'

Driving away, Mater hoped to reach Loch Assynt before nightfall which would give him the opportunity to survey their new surroundings. Pete and Hefty weren't told the location of their next destination but were warned that it would be a long day. They had already experienced the car; it wasn't going to be a comfortable ride. Mater scheduled in a stop for lunch near to Edinburgh when he also intended to contact Control asking for an update and make his request for weapons to be delivered to the Lodge.

The traffic was heavy throughout the North of England until they turned off the main A1 artery and headed across the open rolling countryside of Northumberland. They sped past Otterburn training range, familiar territory for Mater and Hefty, climbed steadily to the border with Scotland, crossing late morning. The top provided a brief but magnificent view of the

Scottish Borders hills; their summits peeking from the valleys shrouded in mist. Hefty commented that it would have been a sight for absent Jock. The weak sun gradually burnt off the haze as the car passed through Jedburgh and reached the outskirts of Edinburgh.

Mater pulled up at the Kings Arms Inn as intended. He and Charlotte needed coffee and the others something stronger. They entered the pub to discover they were the only customers. It pleased Mater. He wouldn't have to worry about strangers approaching and engaging them in conversation. A rotund middle-aged lady wearing a grubby tight old fashioned apron took their order showing little civility and even less humour. Years of experience caused her to demand payment up front from travellers. Mater asked if there was a payphone and she waved her pencil, directing him without looking up from her note pad. Mater politely thanked her, understanding fully why the pub was so empty. He excused himself from the table and made his way to the phone.

To Mater's relief Control answered promptly.

'Phoenix rising,' he said when the line connected.

'Good morning Phil, all's well?'

'Steady progress, thank you. We will be ready to receive tools in a couple of days. Are you able to arrange delivery? I'll text you the coordinates.'

'Try my best. However, very pleased you rang. I have something for you. There is positive news about our Jiri, derived from our contacts in Eastern Europe. I would prefer to tell you in person.'

'Sounds encouraging. Please visit when you can; just tell us the date and time. You could come with the drop. Any update on our colleague?'

'None, I'm afraid. He must be in a burrow somewhere. Have to see daylight sometime. We'll keep watching.'

Mater returned to the table where the others had already finished their food. He looked at his plate: Two pale sausages perched on a pile of now lukewarm baked beans and soggy toast, and decided he didn't feel that hungry. Without sitting down, he tasted his coffee which was also cold.

'OK, let's go,' he said.

Charlotte looked up, concerned. 'What's the hurry?' she asked, 'Is everything alright?'

Mater gave her a thumbs up as he drained his cup. 'Everything's fine,' he said, reassuring her.

Back in Harrogate, for Jock, unconscious in Intensive Care, his treatment likewise proceeded smoothly. Three hours earlier, the nurse accompanied him to a private room in the ITU and he calmly climbed onto the bed. The ward nurses wired him to a variety of monitors. Dr Heston skilfully inserted a needle into a vein in his forearm, leaving a fine green cannula behind, into which the physician injected a liquid. Almost at once, Jock's hands stopped shaking, and he felt warm, safe and extremely relaxed. He smelt plastic as a mask was placed over his face filling his lungs with extra oxygen. He could just see Dr Heston pushing buttons on a small machine attached to the drip stand beside his bed. The doctor asked him if he was OK and he nodded. The pump bleeped and the large syringe loaded in it began to empty into Jock. He noted a strange cold sensation as the drug ran up his arm towards his brain.

God, I'm pissed, he thought as he drifted away.

The initial phase of his prolonged deep anaesthesia appeared to go as expected. Jock's vital signs remained stable, and the staff carried out the interventions necessary to support life in the now completely helpless man. Dr Heston passed an endotracheal tube down his throat and connected him to a ventilator. The nurses inserted a catheter into his bladder and another tube via his nose into his stomach, for feeding. Blood samples were taken to check his glucose and alcohol levels. Jock would begin withdrawing over the next day or two, oblivious to everyone and everything.

As the group drove over the Forth Road Bridge and headed towards the Highlands, Mater contemplated his conversation with Control. He wondered what new information the chief had. Mater would have to wait until he visited but decided he would not bring the boss to the Lodge. The barrier between his new team and the Office needed to be maintained for as long as possible. For now, he had no choice but to trust Control even though paranoia grew slowly and steadily in his mind. If Anthony could begin, without obvious reason, a vicious vendetta against him, who else might do the same? Were there others known to Mater working alongside his enemy? He glanced across to Charlotte, dozing in the front passenger seat, strands of her long hair waving gently in the steady breeze from the vehicle's ventilation system. Once again, he couldn't stop himself wondering whether she had set Tiny up. *No,* he thought, correcting himself as he remembered the intense battle at the cottage, *Don't be stupid, she was as likely to die as any of them that day.* He switched on the radio and the sound of classical music relaxed him.

'What's that bloody racket?' asked Hefty.

Mater chuckled, dispersing any fleeting thoughts of disloyalty. Somehow it didn't matter who travelled with him, they always complained about his choice of in-car entertainment. But he was driving and in charge.

'Once this represented the pop music of the day. Maybe I was born in the wrong century,' he said out loud, but mainly to himself and turned up the volume. Hefty sighed and returned to watching the mountains rush by.

Mater paused in Inverness for fuel, food supplies, coffee and a chance to stretch. He estimated they had roughly three hours to go and would arrive shortly before dusk. About one hour from their destination Mater asked everyone to look for a suitable location for a helicopter landing site. Near to the head of Loch Assynt Pete spotted a layby and suggested they drove along it to see if there was an accessible flat area nearby. The layby formed a loop lying between the main road and the north shore of the loch. Once entered, the bulk of it was hidden. Mater stopped the vehicle, and they all got out. The terrain sloped gently towards the Loch's waters, some thirty metres away. The ground felt spongy underfoot, but the shingle beach firm and there were no overhead hazards.

'Perfect Pete, well done,' said Mater. 'We will be able to close off the access temporarily and there is plenty of space for those clever pilot boys to land.'

Using his mobile phone, Mater recorded the LZ's GPS coordinates. The team of four paused to take in the fresh air and view. Late afternoon and the sun was beginning to drop towards the horizon causing the Loch's waters to shimmer with gold. If time had allowed, it would have been an ideal holiday location but Mater and Charlotte knew no-one was going to rest much from now on. Their real work was about to begin.

At the far end of the Loch, the heavily laden car turned onto a bumpy grass track which weaved its way uphill towards a large white two storey house. It was bounded by a conifer wood on one side and some stone sheds on the other. Mater pulled up in front. Doors opened and the stiff occupants emerged to air, cool and fresh. A gentle breeze caught the pine trees making the only noise. Peace and tranquillity surrounded them. The lodge lay about five hundred metres from the main road. Its position provided a view of the same for more than double that in either direction. There was no traffic.

Charlotte tried the front door. As expected it was unlocked. Keys and visitor instructions waited on the kitchen table along with a variety of brochures offering tourist sights and activities. Pete located the fuse-box and soon lights and kettle were on. They collected their belongings and supplies from the car and picked straws to allocate bedrooms.

As dusk fell, Mater and Charlotte explored the outbuildings. One had been set up as a small classroom with posters of birds and fish adorning the walls. It was clear the lodge had been used as an educational facility but probably not for studying the syllabus Mater had in mind. As Mater and Charlotte returned to the lodge they stopped to look at the stars that had emerged. The absence of light pollution allowed the night sky to show off its best.

Charlotte, trying not to break the magic, whispered 'Maybe we should exchange our mad lives for this,' she said.

Mater, his head and neck still arched upwards, thought for a moment. 'It is beautiful, the tranquillity, the calm, and one day, hopefully in the not too distant future, it will be possible to slow down but first…' he paused. 'I'm going to track down Anthony and if necessary, kill him.'

Chapter 27

The agent for the property appeared on the second day to collect the rent. Charlotte had spotted the old Landover crawling up the hill to the house five minutes earlier. The woman, dressed in a bright tartan skirt, Barbour jacket and wellingtons, spoke with a broad highland accent. She expressed her surprise but pleasure in receiving cash as payment for the first three months. It wouldn't need to go through her books. She explained she lived about ten miles further west should they have any problems and her farm sold fresh eggs and milk. She didn't ask questions. The Lodge had been used for many purposes; some, she surmised more legal than others, but as long as the guests paid, what went on was none of her business.

The next few days were spent establishing camp and getting to know the area. Mater drove into Lochinver to replenish supplies and send Control the coordinates for the helicopter drop. He spotted a phone box close to the quay of the tiny West Coast fishing port. Once bright red, the box was now rusty and battered, hammered by the sea-spray laden wind; many of its little window panes missing, allowing rain to flood in each time an Atlantic storm arrived. He was relieved the pay-phone still worked. Control responded to his pager.

'Settled in OK, wherever you are?' he asked.

'All's going well, thank you sir.'

Control repeated back the landing site coordinates, wished Mater well and the ended the call.

Mater decided everyone needed to improve their fitness and he initiated morning runs, exercises and challenging daily walks of increasing length. He and Charlotte progressively reduced the alcohol consumed by all, substituting a nourishing diet and plenty of sleep. Pete and Hefty, without really knowing it, gradually metamorphosed from the shells they had been almost back to the vigorous strong men of years ago. Mater was delighted to see his team gel.

Mater discovered he had to climb to the top of a nearby hill to receive a mobile phone signal. It wasn't the most convenient place should he have to break with protocol and make an emergency call to Control but it was beautiful, tranquil, quite serene. There, perched on a rocky outcrop, with a magnificent view of the Loch stretching into the distance, he watched a golden eagle soar back and forth along the mountainous ridge to his right. Briefly it flew close, just overhead, as if to check whether the man below was suitable prey.

If I was working overseas, thought Mater, *it would have been a vulture circling, waiting for my demise.* He laughed and called out. 'No chance, mate. Not yet.'

Back at the Lodge, Charlotte ran daily sessions on tradecraft while Mater taught self-defence and gradually introduced efficient killing techniques. Much was familiar from the men's previous careers and they rapidly acquired the basics. As the fog of Pete's and Hefty's alcoholic haze faded, their faculties sharpened and it became increasingly difficult for Mater to hide the identity of his ultimate employer or the background to the current crisis. It was over dinner one evening that Pete decided to confront Mater. It had been a tough day and everyone was seated around the kitchen table, quietly tucking in when Pete stopped eating and laid down his cutlery.

'The organisation you work for is in the shit, isn't it?' he said, without any preamble, looking directly at Mater.

Charlotte glanced across to Mater who chewed slowly and swallowed before resting his fork gently on his plate.

'Go on Pete,' he said, batting away the question, 'What's on your mind?'

Hefty continued to eat, but listened intently, as Pete began. 'It is clear to me that we're being trained for a covert mission. The tradecraft, the physical bit, have all the markers of classic security service training. I remember, when we first met, you were searching for those with military or similar backgrounds but who had essentially disappeared from normal public life. Anonymous men. Untraceable. We all fit the bill. So, I ask, why do you or your boss need to do this? Why not simply recruit using your standard routines or use experienced existing staff? To me, there are only one or two possibilities. Either you've lost confidence in those who normally surround you or.... or they no longer exist; they've gone.'

Mater thought for a moment. The success of his whole plan relied on building an effective unified new team. This required trust and for that, honesty between them. He wasn't at liberty to tell them everything but these men would soon risk their lives for him and they deserved respect and an answer.

'Right on both counts, Pete,' he said finally. 'I was intending to brief you in the morning but perhaps should do so now. Tomorrow night I'll introduce you to the chief of the UK's most important external security service. He's taking the opportunity to drop by when we receive our special equipment. We'll carry on with the work we've been doing but intensive weapons training will be added in to the program. I have complete confidence in him but, despite that, he won't be invited to come here. Even he hasn't been told exactly where we are staying and he certainly has no idea who you two are. The location of our current base is to stay secret.'

'Thanks boss, that's all I need to know,' said Pete and carried on eating.

The next evening saw the group collecting dry drift wood to build a large fire on the foreshore of the Loch. Earlier, they had parked in the layby, discouraging anyone else from using it by sealing both ends with tape and traffic cones found at the Lodge. Mater posted Hefty at the entrance and Pete the exit, just in case. The sun set a little after nine and Mater lit the fire, the welcome flames gathering strength, warming him and Charlotte. The helicopter pilot would be able to spot it from miles away. As the first stars appeared, they heard the sound of the aircraft's rotor echoing through the glen. Mater searched the sky, but the machine was flying lights off and it was impossible to see.

Back at the main road, a Dutch campervan slowly meandered along searching for a suitable place to park. The driver, from his map, expected a layby to be coming up, and he slowed, looking carefully for it, the vehicle's headlights illuminating the tarmac for more than fifty metres ahead. Suddenly, he became aware of a tremendous noise and wondered if his van's engine had developed a major fault. He was relieved to see the layby but was surprised by the sight of someone standing in the road between cones, blocking it. He pulled up, wound down the window and quickly realised the racket wasn't from his vehicle at all but the clatter of a helicopter approaching. The man at the barrier spoke politely but firmly.

'Sorry sir, you need to move on. Layby's closed. Search and Rescue exercise. You'll find other excellent spots a few kilometres further down the road.'

The Dutchman reversed back onto the main highway and slowly drove on, leaning out of his window hoping to glimpse the helicopter. 'Strange,' he said to himself, 'I can hear it but can't see it. How could that be?'

The Lynx Mark 9 gently touched down on the foreshore shingle, the downwash causing a mini maelstrom on the Loch's otherwise calm waters. Mater and Charlotte waited for the rotor to stop before approaching. They could see the green glint of the pilot's helmet mounted night vision and head-up display reflecting off his face. Another man sat in the co-pilot's seat. Mater opened the machine's door and offered a hand to Control, who clambered down.

'Welcome to Sutherland sir,' said Mater, 'Good flight?'

'Bloody uncomfortable but enjoyable all the same,' answered Control. 'Let's unload before we do anything else.'

Mater called to Charlotte. 'Change places with Hefty. We could do with his muscle.'

They slid open the side door of the Lynx and Mater climbed aboard. Under a net lay a pile of wooden and aluminium crates containing weapons, ammunition and other kit. There was also a cardboard box. He uncovered the load and pushed the cargo to the doorway. Hefty appeared and Mater heaved each item out of the helicopter into his and Control's outstretched arms. Soon the equipment was unloaded. Mater patted the pilot on the shoulder, thanked him and jumped down. Everyone stood back, the aircraft's engine fired, and the pilot took off with instructions to return in an hour. Enough time to refuel at one of the many emergency fuel dumps hidden across the highlands.

Silence returned to the Lochside. The team rapidly shifted the supplies the few metres to the layby and loaded the Nissan. It would take at least two trips to move everything. Mater decided he should introduce Control to his recruits and then they could make the first home run. While away, Charlotte and he could brief and be briefed by Control. Mater called the group together. They gathered beside the car, their eyesight adjusting to the dark.

'Sir, may I present two members of my new team.'

Control shook each man's hand in turn. 'Welcome to the club,' he said, still slightly out of breath from the weightlifting. 'I've been told little about you but I have great faith in Phil. He will look after you to the best of his ability. Your future service is greatly appreciated. I have brought you all a token gift,' pointing to the small cardboard box amongst the stack on the tarmac.

'Thank you, sir,' said Pete. The presence of Mater's boss, the helicopter and the weapons he found oddly reassuring. Any lingering doubts that Mater was a loner running a minor security outfit were dispelled. The hallmarks of official state backing were obvious.

Introductions over, Mater returned to the main task. 'OK, Pete and Hefty, you make the first trip home. Stash the kit somewhere secure, have a cuppa and come back later but I don't expect to see you before eleven. It will give the Chief time to brief me and get away.' In truth, Mater didn't want Control to know that the Lodge was located less than twenty minutes drive from the rendezvous.

Mater, Charlotte and Control walked over to the fire which with encouragement sprang back into life. The three of them sat down beside it. They heard the little car start and strain as it made its way to the main road, heading west.

'How's progress Phil?' asked Control.

'Very good, sir. Much better than I had anticipated. The team is coming together. They're learning fast.'

Control was pleased but also concerned. 'You have only Charlotte and these two? Is that enough human resource?'

'We have another. He's not quite up to speed yet but I'm still optimistic he'll join us shortly. Five is what I'm used to and is manageable. I accept there is little wriggle room should anyone fall by the wayside.'

'Well,' said Control, 'You need to be ready as soon as possible. I had a very informative meeting recently with the Czech military attaché at their embassy. Your Skopek fellow has come up trumps. He is, or I should say was, a member of a criminal organisation linked to an extreme right-wing mob well known to the Czech authorities. They have carried out surveillance on this group for years although successful infiltrations, let alone prosecutions, have been few and far between. They are a truly unpleasant bunch involved in drugs, people smuggling and assassination. It's my contact's opinion that failure to wipe them out is due to their leader's close connections with senior

304

government officials. Corruption seems endemic in that part of the world. My friend was willing to provide a list of suspects with photographs and other useful details. I suspect Liam's killers and Jiri Skopek are on it. Once your preparations are over, I think you should go fishing in Prague.'

'How reliable is your source?' asked Mater.

'Very,' responded Control, without hesitation. 'We go back a long time; in fact, to my days behind the iron curtain. He was working for us then. Let me know when you're ready and I'll sort out paperwork, transport and so on. If you are able to deal a blow to the Czech irritation, then many there will be delighted and helpful to you. It avoids the Czechs having to find their own clean guys to do the same. Something that clearly hasn't been possible up to now. I've left a small file in the cardboard box.'

'Any news of Anthony?' asked Mater, hoping.

Control shook his head. 'Not one single sighting. I thought he might appear in my office and try to bluff but not a squeak. 5 have made a special effort to look out for him but he's simply disappeared. My best guess is we missed him and he's abroad. Maybe also in Eastern Europe if that's where he recruited his lot.'

Mater was disappointed but not surprised. Anthony had all the skills needed to plan and effect his escape.

'Do you think he is directly involved with the Czechs or just paid them to do his bidding?' he asked.

'Your guess is as good as mine, but does it matter? He's crossed a line and there's only one way this can end. I'm relying on you. But I still can't fathom why. Why your team? Why now? Any ideas? I'm sure you've spent hours ruminating over it.'

This time it was Mater shaking his head. 'I've racked my brains but nothing has sprung to light. I always thought we had a reasonable working relationship, quite formal but professional all the same. Can you explain the visits to the mosques?'

'Yet another conundrum,' said Control, poking the fire with a stick. '5's observations suggest the mosques he frequented do have visitors of interest to them. So perhaps he obtained help there. It was certainly somewhere we wouldn't have anticipated him to go. But he would have known that if, by chance, 5 spotted him, they would have assumed he was working for us. As you know, despite my best efforts, there remains much rivalry between our two organisations and 5 wouldn't expect us to inform them of our every move. We should put that one on the back burner for now and concentrate on the Czech connection.'

'Anything else, sir?' asked Mater.

Control turned to Charlotte. 'Is he looking after you?' he asked with genuine concern.

'What do you think?' she replied, her smile lit by the fire's flames. 'Works us dawn to dusk like slaves for no pay but a promise.'

'A promise?' enquired Control.

'A promise of adventure and that everything will work out fine. No, I'm very happy working with Phil, thank you.'

Control unzipped his thick jacket and pulled out an envelope. 'This is for you,' he said, handing it to her.

Charlotte took it and tried to read the name and address on the front but the flickering firelight made it difficult. All she noted was the handwriting style. The scrawl seemed familiar.

'Chief, may I ask who it's from and where it came from?' she said, turning it over to exam the back, which was blank.

'Addressed to your home. Your real home. You'll have to excuse me but we've been intercepting your mail, as well as Phil's. I arranged for everything to be diverted to me. Most has been junk. The official looking stuff I've opened and dealt with but this looked personal, so I thought I'd deliver it directly to you.'

Their conversation was interrupted by the sound of the helicopter's return. The drum of its engine and rotor rapidly increasing in volume. Control stood up slowly, followed by Mater and Charlotte. Charlotte folded the envelope and tucked it in her pocket.

'Keep going, Phil, we will solve this,' Control shouted as the helicopter came in to land.

He patted Mater on the back and turned to Charlotte. She held out her hand but he didn't take it, moving in to give her a hug instead; something totally out of character. Until recent events he had never done this, but this was the second occasion Control had made physical contact with her. She didn't find it reassuring.

'Watch out for Phil and look after yourself. You are both terribly important to me,' he said, mouthing the words so close to her ear that she could smell his aftershave.

'Of course,' she replied and with that Control released his grip.

Landing as precisely as before and with the helicopter's engine kept running, Control waved, ducked his head, and dashed to the machine. He climbed aboard and immediately it lifted. He waved again but his farewell was wasted as the two on the ground shielded their faces from the occasional pebble flung in their direction by the down-draught.

Within a few moments silence returned to the Lochside. Mater and Charlotte walked the few steps to the layby to wait for the return of Pete and Hefty.

'Useful and encouraging update from the boss,' said Mater, 'But what was the hug about? I've never known him to act like that before.'

Charlotte shrugged her shoulders. 'No idea but I found it a little disconcerting.'

'Why?' asked Mater, laughing, 'Perhaps he's got the hots for you?'

Charlotte laughed too but didn't reply. She understood Control was desperate to resolve the Office's problem but there was an element to Control's concern for her in particular that made her nervous.

They had not long reached the remaining equipment, still piled on the tarmac, when they heard a car approaching at speed. Hefty and Pete were on their way back to complete the pickup.

Although it was nearly midnight by the time they were settled in the Lodge, the four opened the containers and checked their contents. Like children excitedly opening a giant box of fireworks, they carefully unwrapped and emptied each container, laying the items neatly on the floor. There were five familiar MP

7s, the same number of Glock 17 handguns and holsters, along with a large amount of blank and live ammunition. In addition, Stanley had supplied a case of grenades, PE 4 plastic explosive, detonators, cabling, timers and standard personal kit. A full set for everyone: body armour, helmets, gloves, balaclavas, infra-red light-sticks and NVGs. Mater was delighted. Every item requested appeared to be there. Finally, they noted the inclusion of cleaning equipment and tools. Clearly, everything was expected to be returned in perfect condition. The stores wizard had added in some extras with notes attached stating: 'Read all instructions before use'. Mater was amused. He had been in trouble with Stanley before for trying out new devices without fully appreciating their mode of action. Pete and Hefty were astonished by the sheer quantity of material.

'Bloody hell,' exclaimed Hefty as he looked over the weaponry, 'We've enough here for a small army.'

'We are, or at least will be, a small army,' responded Mater.

Pete was worried. 'Boss,' he asked nervously, 'What happens if this stuff is discovered by the authorities? We'll be for it.'

'Don't be too concerned Pete,' replied Mater, 'One call to the chief and we'll be in the clear, although it would mean the end of our shooting party. We just need to be careful.'

Finally, watched by the others, Mater opened Control's cardboard box. A file of a familiar design lay on top of a sealed package. He put it to one side and tore open the parcel. Inside, protected with bubble pack, was a bottle of vintage champagne on which Control had written: 'To celebrate your success'. Mater held it aloft. Pete's and Hefty's eyes lit up.

'Sorry, boys, not for now but we'll all enjoy it soon enough.' He carefully wrapped the bottle up again.

The team finally reached their beds in the early hours having carefully re-packed all the equipment and hidden it under a tarpaulin in the main store. Firearms training could begin.

Alone in bed, Charlotte held the envelope in her hands. She was now certain she recognised the handwriting, but it seemed to have been created by a shaky hand; perhaps written in haste, the ink forming spidery letters. The person whom she suspected had sent her the letter was elderly but had always been robust, retaining skills normally lost by most at a much earlier stage of life. She was troubled. She briefly considered Mater's letter to Anthony that had been post-mastered by Control. She sat bolt upright. Suddenly she had the notion that Control was involved more than she wished to believe and not in a positive way. *Could she be the potential victim of the same ruse?* She unfolded the envelope and opened it. She had guessed correctly. The letter came, she convinced herself, from her favourite aunt but the news wasn't encouraging. The writing was poor but the layout familiar, the message ending with a recognisable signature and an admonishment to be a good girl. Charlotte was upset to learn that her relative was so ill but her decline in health explained the deterioration in the handwriting and dispelled Charlotte's other anxieties. Mater wouldn't be pleased but she needed to make a brief visit south if she was going to see the elderly lady. It would be preferable to go before the team moved into action. Waiting until after they had completed their work might prove to be too late. She would explain the situation to the boss in the morning and hoped he would understand. She would only be gone for a couple of days.

While Charlotte read her letter, and considered how best to ask Mater for some time off, he was reading through the file from Control. Despite the poor translation into English, the various reports, derived from the Czech domestic security service, gave him what he wanted. As Control had indicated, it contained a list of names linked to the criminal gang suspected of working within the UK during the relevant period. Jiri Skopek's life history was there but Mater put to one side most of the papers, focusing his attention on the two characters believed to have killed Liam in the underground. The quality of the photographs was exceptional; the men didn't appear to be in disguise. Mater concluded they probably hadn't realised the authorities were on to them. There were details of their alleged illegal activities: drug and arms importation, human trafficking and assassination to order. Each man given a name with their address; all in Prague.

Excellent. Lovely city. Haven't visited in years; can't wait to return, thought Mater.

Chapter 28

Despite the short night, Mater rose early. Snores emanated from Hefty's room so he decided to allow everyone a lie-in. Downstairs in the kitchen, he was surprised to see Charlotte already sitting at the table, cup of tea in hand.

'Morning,' he said, 'Up with the larks, couldn't sleep or just wanting to get your hands on the kit again?'

Charlotte face failed to respond to his quip. She simply shoved the letter across the table in his direction. Mater picked it up and began to read. It was brief and to the point. He handed it back.

'You're going to ask me for a few days off, aren't you?'

Charlotte nodded. She hated letting him down; it rarely happened but when it did, it was always for a good reason.

'No problem,' said Mater, hiding his disappointment. 'If I had a close relative, asking me to visit before I departed on my final journey, I would hope they would make every effort to come. We'll miss you but cope. I'll put the boys through their paces with the weapons. Hopefully, on your return they'll be able to give you a run for your money when it comes to target practice.'

This time Charlotte smiled. 'Thanks, Phil. If you drive me to Inchnadamph, I can take the bus to Inverness and then the train south. All I need is one day in Essex with my Aunt and then catch the sleeper for the return journey to Scotland. Should be away three days max.'

'OK,' said Mater, 'Let's have a quick breakfast. Afterwards, you pack and we can set off. I'll probably be home before the others even surface. Let me state the obvious though. Do take care. I need you.'

Mater spent the rest of the day instructing Pete and Hefty on their weapons. The basics such as safety were familiar to them from their past and they quickly learnt to load, unload, strip down and rebuild both the sub-machine guns and automatic handguns. Live firing would begin the next day. On one of his runs Mater had identified a small disused quarry surrounded by Scots pines. It lay roughly a kilometre further along the track that led from the main road to the Lodge. It was unlikely that anyone would see or even hear them shooting in there. In the evening, he left the others relaxing in the lounge and climbed the rocky outcrop behind the Lodge to use his phone. He was keen to check on Charlotte. When the signal strength became strong enough, his mobile pinged with the arrival of a text. He was relieved it was from her but it simply asked him to get in touch ASAP. He sat down on a mossy boulder. The low cloud that had filled the glen most of the day had lifted though the mountain tops remained hidden and a light drizzle obscured the view further. He pressed the hot key on his phone to make the call, recognising her as soon as she answered it.

'Hi,' she said, 'I've been hoping you would get my urgent text.'

He noted the anxiety in her voice.

'Yes, sorry I'm late. Poor reception. Are you OK?' he asked.

313

'I'm fine. However, our good doctor called. Apparently, the Scotsman hasn't responded well to treatment. Something to do with him suffering many fits during and after his anaesthetic. He says they dealt with all of that but our friend doesn't seem to be the same person. His memory appears to be have deteriorated and his personality has changed.'

Mater was unaware of how tightly he gripped the phone. 'That's not good news. Do they think he will recover?'

'There's more and it's worse I'm afraid,' continued Charlotte. 'We may never find out. He's disappeared. They presume he climbed out of the window of his room. That was forty-eight hours ago. He's gone.'

Mater let the phone drop away from his ear and kicked a small rock lying at his feet. It bounced to edge of the ledge and tumbled over. At first, he heard it hitting other rocks as it fell and then there was silence. The drizzle began to penetrate, but he hardly noticed; instinctively zipping up his jacket.

'Phil, are you there?' Charlotte's voice brought him back.

'Damn it,' he said. 'Are the hospital staff looking for him?'

'Half-heartedly, I suspect. Maybe, as the treatment is somewhat experimental, they want to avoid any adverse publicity or perhaps our medical friend has concocted some sort of story. Who knows? Poor man. Are you going to tell the others?'

'Have to,' responded Mater. 'No choice. I need them to know they can trust me. We have to hope they find him or he really does disappear. We can't afford him blabbing about our operation. If he returns to the drink, there must be a risk of that.

314

Get in touch if you receive more news. I don't think there's much more we can do. I'll be available same time tomorrow. Have you seen your aunt?'

'No, I'm not there yet. Train delayed.'

Mater wished her luck, she him, and the call ended.

As Mater walked back to the Lodge in the gathering darkness, he became aware of the damp and cold but despite the conditions he didn't hurry. He faced a dilemma and wanted to resolve it before he reached base. If he told Pete and Hefty what had happened to Jock, there was a risk they would be angry, possibly resentful. His recommendation that Jock be put forward for the detox program had resulted in the three friends being split, probably permanently. If he concocted an alternative story, he would break his own rule to always deal in truths with his team, even if the information he gave was limited. The evolving bond of trust was vulnerable. Eventually he decided on a compromise.

The best lies, he reminded himself, *Are those seasoned with a little sprinkling of truth.*

As he entered the house, Mater heard Pete and Hefty laughing. He put his head around the lounge door. They each occupied a sofa, lying along them with their feet up, eyes glued to the TV. He was pleased they appeared so relaxed and offered to make tea. He returned with the pot, served and then sat in an armchair. He found their choice of program banal but he wouldn't interfere with their enjoyment. His news could wait. The sitcom ended and Pete switched off the TV with the remote.

'How's Charlotte?' he asked.

'Mater held the almost empty cup in his hand swirling the cold dregs in the bottom. 'She's fine. Not yet arrived at her destination but I still expect her to be back as planned. However...' He hesitated. The pause long. Both Pete and Hefty had learnt that with the boss this might mean not such good news was coming next. 'However, I have an update on Jock. I understand that his treatment has finished and went OK but he has decided to withdraw from our work.'

He waited for the information to sink in. Pete and Hefty looked stunned. They had supported each other for years and felt there had been an unwritten pact between them; to join Mater as one. Jock's behaviour seemed out of character. *Had they been betrayed?*

'That's really disappointing,' said Pete.

'Understatement,' grunted Hefty.

Pete continued. 'Do you know when he changed his mind or where he is now?'

'To be frank, no to both questions. I haven't managed to speak to him. I'm just aware that he has made his decision and left. I'm sorry.'

The next day the atmosphere was tense. Mater kept the two men busy with a series of vigorous exercises in the morning and target practice in the quarry during the afternoon. Little conversation passed between them and Mater guessed they were pondering the news he had given them. He became increasingly concerned that if Jock had changed his mind, the others might do the same. He would be back at square one with time ticking and Anthony, no doubt, using every passing moment to cover his tracks.

In the evening, before heading to the ridge to call Charlotte, he offered to cook dinner, making a special effort with the menu. He needed to spoil his recruits; show he valued them.

After they had eaten, he left Pete and Hefty once more watching television but the previous frivolity was gone.

As Mater climbed the ridge, the better weather made him feel more optimistic, grateful it was drier and warmer. Hopefully Charlotte would have some positive news. He sat down and dialled. Waiting for an answer, he spotted the eagle hunting again and for a moment he failed to pick up on the failure of his call to be answered. He tried once more, this time willing to hear her voice. The call diverted to voicemail. He left a message asking her to call him within the hour. Staying longer risked descending in darkness. His phone could be used as a torch but if it died, the walk back to the Lodge would be unnecessarily hazardous. He watched the sun dip below the horizon and saw the sky change from blue to black in the East and from orange to red in the West. A half-moon rose and alongside it Venus shone brightly. In the glen below, he saw the occasional light marking distant farms; the lights almost mirroring the stars appearing above. He repeatedly checked his phone but nothing. He checked the signal strength; it was fine. At fifty-five minutes, he called her again but no luck. He wondered whether there was simply a problem with her mobile but he knew if that was the case she would have found another way to contact him. It made no sense and made him anxious. He would have to try again the next day. After that, if she didn't respond, he would have to ask Control for help. Things were not going well but Mater had been in many difficult situations before and by the time he returned to the Lodge he had calmed down. *The leader must be ever the optimist,* he reminded himself.

The following day's training passed uneventfully although Mater struggled to focus and found the hours dragged by. He was anxious to complete the schedule early so he could make his call, trying to contact Charlotte one final time.

Once again, she didn't answer. He sat on his perch about two hundred metres above the Loch and held his head in his hands. The mixture of anxiety and despair returned, and he struggled to bat it away.

'Damn you, Charlotte,' he yelled. 'What's happened? I need you now more than ever. Please don't let me down.' The brisk breeze swirling around the outcrop, caught his words and whisked them away. Now Mater worried the aunt's message was forged and Charlotte in imminent danger. He felt he had good reason to be afraid for her. After all, he had used the ruse of a letter to entice Anthony to the meeting that resulted in his interrogation. It was imperative that he found, or at least contacted, Charlotte as soon as possible. He made the decision to drive into Lochinver that evening. He might catch Control before he retired to bed. The chief would forgive him for the late call.

After dark, Mater parked the car by the phone box and looked around before entering. No-one saw him. A small group of fishermen worked on the quayside making final preparations before their next departure at high tide. A man using the phone of no interest to them. The rest of the village was already asleep or living behind drawn curtains. Mater picked up the receiver. The line was dead. Then he noticed the vandalised wires hanging below. He sighed, once again questioning why he and others risked their lives for their fellow countrymen. He took his mobile from his pocket. He would have no choice but to break with protocol if he was to speak with his boss that evening.

A rather tired sounding Control answered his phone and wearily replied with the appropriate codeword.

'Sorry to disturb you Chief and call using my mobile, but I've lost touch with Charlotte. The letter you delivered was from her aunt who said she was seriously ill. I agreed to allow Charlotte time off to travel to Essex. That was three days ago, and we arranged to make contact daily. She is forty-eight hours overdue and I have no mechanism to locate her. You will understand why I'm concerned.'

He waited for Control to digest the news and come up with a suggestion. He knew Control had a range of resources available to him to find a missing person but the challenge would be to do it without arousing suspicion within the service. The boss might have to cash in a few favours.

'I'll get dressed and return to the Office,' replied Control with an audible sigh. 'I will ask the night staff to do some digging. Leave it to me but let's hope I can give you a positive answer tomorrow. Call me at midday.' With that he rang off.

Mater pushed open the door of the phone box and headed towards the quayside. The trawlermen had completed their preparations and were ready to set sail. He watched as they loosened ropes and then the powerful marine engine gently manoeuvred the rust-stained hulk away from the concrete pier. The navigation lights of the trawler faded into the distance. In his head, he wished them a safe and successful trip hoping that, in some strange way, someone else might be doing the same for Charlotte. His links to the past were becoming ever more tenuous and if she had truly disappeared, then he would be essentially on his own.

The next morning's training followed the usual pattern but Mater shortened the timetable so that he could speak to Control. He told the men to take the afternoon off: well-deserved R & R.

It wasn't essential to drive all the way to Lochinver to use his mobile, but he still wanted to minimise the risk of the phone revealing the Lodge's location, so headed east, inland. He turned off the main road onto a farm track and pulled up after a short distance. He could see Inchnadamph about a half kilometre away, the village looking unspoilt and seemingly devoid of life. The phone signal was good. At midday precisely, he made the call. Control answered promptly.

'We can confirm she reached Essex. Last seen at Witham railway station,' he began.

Control waited for Mater to comment but the line was quiet so he continued. 'There is some rather concerning information.'

Mater listened intently. *What could be more worrying than the apparent disappearance of the final member of his team?* Control seemed reluctant to speak but Mater needed to hear all the potential scenarios.

'Reasonably near to the last confirmed sighting there was a hit-and-run accident. Happened yesterday. The police are still working at the scene. The female pedestrian involved has not yet been identified. She wasn't carrying any form of ID and unfortunately, the body is in a bit of a mess.'

A lump stuck in Mater's throat and his heart raced.

320

'Phil, I think you should check it out and report back. I'll send a helicopter to reach you at 16.00 hours. Same location as the drop. The pilot will give you documents to allow you access to the scene and there'll be a car waiting for you to use. You'll be there with plenty of time before dark. Report directly to me after your visit.'

'Unfortunately, the body is in a bit of a mess.' The words repeated themselves in Mater's head adding to the fog of emotions. He struggled to answer and when he did, he could not stop his voice trembling.

'Yes, OK, will do, sir.'

He pictured the tattoo on her right thigh and the gunshot wound beside it. It should have almost healed by now but the healing process may have been abruptly halted. She had had a lucky escape at the cottage but it sounded as if her luck might have run out.

Chapter 29

The helicopter returned Mater to the beach by the lay-by, where Pete was waiting in the car. Mater said little but his expression told Pete that something serious had occurred.

'You OK, boss?' he asked as he set off.

Mater shook his head. 'Charlotte's gone, I'm sorry.'

'What! You're kidding me. She's abandoned us, let us down?'

Mater shook his head again. Charlotte had never done that. 'No, no, there's no easy way to say this, but she's dead.'

The car swerved slightly. Pete gripped the steering wheel, eased off the accelerator and brought the vehicle back to the right side of the road.

'Shit,' he said.

'Exactly,' said Mater.

'What happened, boss?'

'Looks as if she was run over. I suspect she was lured to her death. A fake letter; probably from the same person we delivered ours to. Touché.'

Back at the Lodge, Hefty took the news badly. He had grown quite fond of Charlotte. But perhaps importantly, if he ever had any doubt, her death meant Mater had been honest in his warning about the dangers they all faced. Within days they had been reduced from a team of five to three. One dead and another abandoned. He wondered how it would all end. Mater disappeared into the storeroom beside the kitchen and returned with a bottle. The others sat at the table, looking glum.

'At times like these, we need to break the rules a little,' he said, twisting off the cap and pouring healthy measures into three glasses. He slid a glass to each man and picked up one for himself. He stood upright in front of them.

'I don't know how it was for you, but when I was in the military if someone pegged it we met in the mess, got pissed on their bar bill, and started afresh the next day. After that; no further discussion. So, here's to Charlotte and to Jock,' he said, raising his glass.

Pete and Hefty stood and raised theirs.

Mater drained the whisky, thumped the tumbler back on the table and picked up the bottle, ready to refill. Pete and Hefty repeated the toast, tentatively sipped their drinks but didn't hold them out for more. Mater looked surprised.

'Not joining in?' he asked curiously.

Hefty spoke for them both. 'We're pretty well off the booze, boss. If we are to nail the bastard who did this, we need to be sober. Pete and I often talk about our future and consider our past and we don't want to go back.'

Mater screwed the cap back on the bottle. 'You're bloody good guys,' he said. 'Let's do this together. I'll tell the chief that we should be ready to start the hunt within the month. My best guess is it's going to be an interesting time in Prague.'

Chapter 30

Over the next three weeks the men's training continued apace, following a familiar but accelerated pattern. Physical exercise first thing, followed by time in the classroom covering tradecraft theory, radio ops, equipment maintenance, rules of engagement and terrorist and drug smuggling case studies. Mater acted as tutor, using his memory and experience. He was impressed by his own performance. Shooting practice occupied part of the afternoon; the various outbuildings and blank ammunition proving ideal for assault and urban warfare scenarios. He planned to begin night exercises once he considered the men to be competent and safe with the weaponry. Stanley's additions generated lots of curiosity. They included grenades containing an incapacitant with the warning that the effects were much more powerful than CS gas and could not be filtered by standard gas masks. There was a container filled with a special powder. When tipped into a vehicle's engine oil, it rapidly caused power to be lost as the abrasive eroded the cylinder heads. Finally, he had provided a range of everyday looking objects such as lighters and wallets, all of which contained explosive in a greater or lesser quantity; each accompanied by a caution not to confuse with the inert real items routinely carried in pockets. Periodically, Mater drove alone to Lochinver to collect fresh supplies. He pretended to inquisitive shop keepers and the petrol station owner that he was a writer temporarily living in the hills; the peace helping break his writer's block.

Pete and Hefty's proficiencies steadily improved and Mater's confidence in his men's abilities increased. He had transformed them from lost drunk souls into fit fighting men endowed with self-esteem and purpose although, in the limited time they had to train, they could never replace his absent colleagues. But for the single task that lay ahead they were well prepared, ready to give it their best shot.

Mater periodically updated Control on their progress. In turn, Control used his contacts to collate as much information as he could on the current whereabouts and activities of the Czech hitmen. They also helped him prepare the ground for the Czech authorities to allow the British team to enter the country and operate unhindered. Successful disruption of the Czech group by Mater and his men would be welcomed by the Europeans and enhance Czech-British intelligence cooperation. It also sent out a message to those attempting to damage the Office that their actions wouldn't go unpunished.

Control arranged to travel back to Scotland the day before their anticipated departure. He would deliver false IDs and wish them well. The helicopter would transport Mater and his men south to RAF Northolt where they would transfer to a plane for the brief flight to Prague. The Czechs offered to provide them with a vehicle on arrival and the loan of a safe house. But both Mater and Control were concerned that any leak within their Internal Security Service might compromise their mission and endanger them. Better they land in the Czech Republic and be met by an official from the British Embassy, who would be instructed to assist on request.

The day before Control's arrival, Mater ran through the Prague plan checking Pete and Hefty understood and accepted the risks involved. The weapons and other equipment were repacked and individual kit cleaned and readied. Mater decided the Office should treat the men to dinner in Lochinver. It would be a good opportunity to practice their cover stories. The writer with writer's block needed friends to visit from time to time. It would be quite natural to take them to the Caberfeidh restaurant in the High Street where the local seafood was known to be excellent.

That evening, Mater could sense nervousness in both Pete and Hefty. They had been virtually incarcerated at the Lodge with minimal contact with the outside world. Tonight, they were going to a place where they would have to start reintegrating, not as themselves but with new personas, playing characters created out of thin air; their lives might depend on their acting skills. Mater offered to drive in case either man decided they needed a drink to calm them. He would stay sober, observing their performance, ready to intervene if awkward questions were asked or other problems arose.

The restaurant formed part of a small hotel lying at the furthest point from the harbour, with an excellent view of the same, the sea and islands beyond. As the men were shown to their table at the window, the evening sun illuminated the diners and the horizontal rays penetrated the adjacent bar, casting a warm glow. A waiter approached clutching menus.

'Good evening, Mr Thornton,' he said to Mater and handed over the menus. 'How's the book coming along? The whole village is intrigued and wants to read it.'

Mater laughed. 'When I've finished it, if everyone buys a copy, I'll be a very happy man and have to come back to celebrate.

Unfortunately, though, the story has yet to be completed. The writer's block has faded but I may move locations to finalise the ending.'

Pete and Hefty listened attentively. They were impressed by Mater's ability to appear so relaxed. However, they could read the subtext and understand the subterfuge of his conversation. Mater's story, they knew, might or might not end happily but the end was nigh and they were going to be a part of it.

The waiter smiled. 'I can bring you drinks or you can order at the bar,' he said.

Pete stood up. 'I'll go the bar. What would you like?' he asked.

Mater waved his hand to Hefty. 'I'm driving. If you fancy a beer, they say the local ale is good.'

'Lime and soda, with ice, for me please,' said Hefty, ignoring Mater's temptation.

'I'll have the same,' said Pete, 'And you Mr Writer?' he asked Mater quietly, with a twinkle in his eye.

'For me, half of the Skye Red,' replied Mater, grinning.

Pete stood at the busy bar waiting to be served, listening to a lone piper playing a highland lament that emanated from speakers hidden amongst the extensive malt collection. He was about to place his order when someone slapped him hard across his shoulder, accompanied by a greeting that made his stomach form knots.

'Corporal Steedman, my word, what brings you here, you bastard?' said a rather drunk, portly, weather-beaten man of similar age.

Pete turned around, coming face to face to the man and his own past. His mind raced. He knew exactly who had addressed him. The last time they met was in the pub in Deal all those years ago. After their fight, Pete had been arrested by the military police, called by the proprietor and that was the end of his career. Now here he was again, pissed and mouthy. Pete crushed the twenty-pound note into a small ball in his hand. He turned back to the bar without answering and attempted to order his drinks. He felt another blow.

'It is you, I know it's you. Not so brave now are we? You bloody soldiers. A stint in clink clearly did you good,' taunted the man, so loudly that other drinkers put down their glasses and took an interest in the developing commotion.

Pete turned again to face the man, intending to deny everything and carry on as his alias. He was surprised to see Mater appear behind him, lean forward and whisper into the drunk's ear, his mouth so close that no-one else could hear the soft words spoken in a low threatening voice. The man didn't look at Mater, but drained his glass and staggered from the bar. Mater looked at Pete.

'Sorry, dinner's off. We have to go. I'll tell Hefty.'

As the three men hurried back to the car, Pete couldn't contain his curiosity. 'What did you say, then?' he asked.

'I told him to bugger off, otherwise I would kill him. GBH for his sort sometimes isn't enough but he has created a slight problem for us. You never know who he might talk to when he sobers up. We need to leave as soon as possible.'

The three men hastened to the car.

'Would you have killed him?' asked Hefty, as Mater opened the doors.

Mater climbed into the driver's seat and declined to answer. He needed to tell Control to advance their travel by twenty-four hours. They were going to have to work hard to have everything ready. The celebratory dinner would have to wait.

Chapter 31

During the following evening, a lone workman stood guard in the closed off lay-by beside Loch Assynt as two others ferried containers and bags from the Lodge. The warm damp air caused clouds of early season midges to rise from the surrounding heather. They made the task uncomfortable and irritating but the men barely noticed as they swiped their hands across their faces; all focused on being ready by nightfall. Before leaving the Lodge for the final time, Mater checked that all the buildings were clean; no evidence remaining of their real purpose in occupying the holiday accommodation. He left an explanatory note for the owner on the table along with payment in cash for the outstanding tenancy.

As darkness fell, Mater sat at the water's edge spinning stones, one after the other, out across the flat calm water where they sank into the peaty gloom. Pete and Hefty manned the layby. On cue, they heard the sound of a low-flying helicopter making its way up the Glen, a distant hum at first but rapidly intensifying as the screaming of the jet turbine and rotor echoed back and forth from the surrounding mountains. Mater cracked the disposable infra-red light sticks and laid them out on the chosen area of level firm ground; each marking the corner of a triangle. He walked to the furthest point of the landing zone, turned towards the Loch, grasped a stick in each hand and began to wave them side to side above his head. The LZ would be visible to the pilot but no-one else. As the noise rose to a crescendo, Mater could just make out the silhouette of the aircraft against the black moonless sky. The machine manoeuvred like a giant flying beetle, its power magnificent yet threatening. Slowly it descended causing the Loch's dark waters to stir. As it touched down, Mater stopped waving the invisible beacons and held them in front of him. The pilot shut down the engine and total silence returned. The co-pilot's door opened and Mater watched the familiar form of Control climb down, wearing night vision goggles and carrying a bag.

'Good evening Phil, everything ready to go?' he asked, as they shook hands.

'Yes, sorry about the rush. I couldn't be certain that our cover wasn't about to be blown.'

Hefty appeared leaving Pete, with the car, securing the layby. Mater slid open the side door of the helicopter and the three men worked as fast as possible to load the containers and bags into the cargo bay. They communicated by gestures alone, their eyesight adapted to the darkness.

Within minutes the task was done. Mater wiped sweat from his forehead and turned to Hefty. 'Right, collect Pete and we'll be on our way. Remind him to leave the car keys in the ignition.' He walked the few steps to Control, stood motionless at the edge of the Loch, enjoying the tranquillity of the scene. 'We're ready to go, sir.'

'Excellent,' he said, 'I've brought you a present from our mutual friend.' He reached down, unzipped his holdall, pulled out a small automatic pistol and handed it, grip first, to Mater.

'The Makarov,' exclaimed Mater. 'Thank the Major for me, next time you see him. I'm not sure if I'll be able to do it myself.'

'That's sounds rather pessimistic,' commented Control, 'You don't have to proceed if you don't want to or you're not adequately prepared.'

Both men stood in silence for a few moments, Mater contemplating the mission and Control wondering whether he would indeed lose the final member of his unit.

'No, we'll go. As ever, attack is the best means of defence. And to be frank, I'm out for revenge.'

'Don't let retribution colour your judgement,' counselled Control.

Mater ignored the comment and gave Control a piece of paper.

'These are the directions to, and instructions for, the Lodge. It is unlocked. You'll find the Major's car in the lay-by, key in the ignition. Oh, and I have something I want you to look after for me while we're away.' He bent down, picked up a green plastic briefcase and handed it to Control.

'Certainly Phil. Should I know what it contains?'

'It's personal stuff, sir. I would prefer if it wasn't opened. If on this occasion I fail to return, please destroy it along with all its contents.'

Control shook Mater's hand. 'You'll be back Phil, of that I am sure. Go and give them hell. I look forward to debriefing you.'

He turned to Pete and Hefty and shook their hands in turn. 'Your boss tells me your training has come along in leaps and bounds. He has every faith that, as a team, you will succeed. I believe he's right. When you return, Her Majesty's Government will reward you admirably. I wish you every success in your mission.'

The three climbed aboard the helicopter and the pilot started the engine. As the rotor gathered momentum and the black silhouette slowly lifted, Control stood watching from a safe distance, contemplating the fate of the men inside. He wasn't convinced the odds were in Mater's favour, concerned the whole operation was propped up more by hope and luck rather than expectation. And so far there had been scant good fortune.

Seated in the Lynx, everyone wore active noise reduction headphones, protecting them from the screaming of the jet turbine and the incessant throb of the rotor. They enabled communication but only Mater and the pilot spoke. Hefty and Pete sat behind mulling over the task ahead, watching the number of lights below gradually increase as they headed south away from the Highlands. Once they were at a safe altitude, it was the pilot who broke the silence.

'I know I shouldn't ask, sir, but I'm sure it was you and your team I delivered to El Kabur. It's good to have you back on board. Another hot holiday planned?'

It was inevitable that by returning, at least partly, to his past Mater would be recognised because there were few pilots who had the required skills and security clearance. He simply had to bluff as he had done so many times before.

'Ah, I thought you were familiar. What a relief to have someone so experienced piloting us. I've never enjoyed low level night flying. Gives me the heebie-jeebies,' replied Mater, side-stepping any further discussion as to the reason for their journey.

The pilot chuckled and briefly allowed the aircraft to drift side to side, swerving through the darkness.

'But weren't there five of you in your unit including a woman?' he asked.

Mater was about to stamp on the pilot's intrigue when their conversation was interrupted by radio contact from Air Traffic Control.

'Air Ambulance flight 239. Handing you to ATC West Drayton. Continue at current altitude of 130, destination Northolt.'

Air ambulance, thought Mater. *Cunning Control. Disguising our aircraft and purpose. Using civilian ATC, guaranteeing priority in air-lanes.*

Below the helicopter, the blackness rushed by, increasingly punctuated by street lights as the population density rose. Finally they saw the bright orange glow of London emerging in front. Mater began to feel the exhilaration that always accompanied him as he embarked on a mission. Others might be fearful, but he enjoyed a sense of anticipation. That excitement could, if left unchecked, interfere with the need for cool calm decision making and he had learnt to manage it; relishing the moment before forcing his mind to focus on the task ahead. He knew it wouldn't be long before they arrived at a place where distinguishing friend from foe would be difficult and dangerous.

With the runway lights of RAF Northolt shining brightly in front, the pilot switched on the Lynx's navigation beacons, no need to hide their arrival. Northolt was routinely busy with air traffic and the landing of a Lynx next to a civilian Learjet was not an unusual sight. A casual observer on the base would simply think it was a member of the high brass being shuttled to a NATO meeting or similar. However, if they had continued to watch, they would have been surprised by the movement from one aircraft to the other of so many military packing cases, a modest arsenal. High-level meetings demanded security but weapons carried by bodyguards were small, discrete and hidden; this was evidently something else.

Mater, Pete and Hefty worked fast to move the helicopter's payload to the jet. The two aircraft were positioned to minimise the task and to hide the activity from prying eyes. Transfer complete, Mater turned to the helicopter and gave the thumbs up to the pilot, who returned the gesture and restarted the Lynx's turbine. Moments later, it rapidly ascended into the night sky. Pete and Hefty had installed themselves in the leather executive seats of the millionaire's dream machine. As the helicopter ascended into the night sky, they craned their necks to watch it through the small porthole windows. Mater climbed the few steps, pulled up the door and locked it. He moved forward to the cockpit where the crew were making final preparations for their departure.

'Good evening, sir,' said the co-pilot. 'Vaclav Havel Airport, Prague, correct?'

'Correct,' confirmed Mater, 'And don't spare the horses.'

The pilot and co-pilot both grinned. When the taxpayer was picking up the bill, they didn't need an excuse to burn Jet A1 excessively.

The co-pilot checked the flight plan. 'Flying time will be approximately ninety-five minutes, sir. Please strap in, sit back and enjoy. There's food available in the rear of the cabin and the bar is fully stocked though I expect you're on duty.'

Mater sat down opposite his two men and fastened his seat belt. 'Ready?' he asked, 'The real work is about to begin. This is your last chance to back out.'

Pete and Hefty eyed up the luxury jet's interior, trying to comprehend the contrast between their current existence and the lives they left behind only a few weeks before. They looked at each other.

'I'm good to go. You too, Hefty?' asked Pete, tightening his belt.

'Yep. I'm ready,' responded Hefty, 'Let's do it.'

With take-off clearance confirmed, the pilot taxied the aircraft to the runway and without stopping pushed the engine throttles fully forward. The passengers were thrust back into their seats as the plane accelerated and after only a few hundred metres it pitched upwards then climbed rapidly. The streetlamps of London once again merged into a seemingly never ending orange glow, circled by a necklace of vehicle lights travelling along the orbital M25 motorway. To Mater, the scene seemed comfortingly familiar but as the city drifted away behind them his thoughts turned to the task ahead. He was now reliant on the Embassy staff, two untested recruits and the accuracy of the information provided by Control's contact in the Czech secret services. Previously, when embarking on missions, he had always been extremely confident, having weighed up the odds and ensured they were in his favour. On this occasion, he concluded the probabilities were against him but he was compelled to try, to push on. If it went tits up, most likely all of them would be returning in diplomatic body bags. He reached across the aisle and opened the bar, feeling the need for some Dutch courage.

'I'm going to have a drink,' he announced, 'Would you join me?'

Pete and Hefty both nodded.

'Make it a small one for me,' requested Hefty, 'Mustn't let you down.'

'Same for me, boss,' said Pete, 'I've no wish to foul up and I certainly don't want to end up dead because I can't shoot straight.'

Mater placed three crystal tumblers on the table and poured a modest measure of whisky into each. He picked up a glass and made a toast.

'To our success and your long and healthy lives.'

The small team clinked glasses and downed the whisky as the aircraft flying at Mach 0.8 darted across Europe.

Chapter 32

As the sun's rays returned to illuminate the cockpit, the pilot dipped the Lear jet's nose. The aircraft rapidly descended from its cruising altitude of forty-five thousand feet towards the darkness below. Prague was shrouded in low level cloud.

The dozing passengers were woken by the co-pilot requesting they tidy the cabin and tighten their seatbelts. They expected to land in twenty minutes. Mater handed Pete and Hefty their new passports.

'I've always wanted to be a diplomat even if it is only as a clerk,' mused Pete as he flicked through the pages to discover where he had visited before.

Control's contacts had performed well, creating temporary believable false identities for the team.

'I'll better that,' chirped Hefty, 'I'm one of the ambassador's replacement chauffeurs. What about you, Phil?'

Mater grinned. 'Top trump to me. 'Military attaché'. Possibly a bit too close to the truth but at least it makes it easier for me to bluff my way out of trouble if I have to. It's quite reasonable that we are travelling together but if problems arise, I'll do the talking. You two just flash your passports and explain how much you are looking forward to working in the Czech Republic and maybe also sampling the delicious famous beers brewed there. I'm anticipating that with the embassy man greeting us we will simply be whisked through the General Aviation Terminal. After all, we're all part of the European Union.'

Beneath the cloud, the Lear jet levelled off, the runway lights clearly visible, looking like two lines of sparkling diamonds, piercing the grey dawn enveloping the city. With permission to land, a minute later the plane's wheels burnt the tarmac. It rapidly left the runway, taxiing to a halt next to a black van close to the GAT. From the window, Mater saw a man wearing a large fur hat climb from the vehicle and stand beside it; his scarf wrapped around his face. The pilot gave the all clear to open the aircraft door. Mater turned to his men. 'I'll check our reception party before you get out. If I raise both arms as if I'm surrendering tell the crew to head straight back to Blighty. If all's OK, I'll give you the thumbs up. Got it?'

Pete and Hefty nodded. Mater unlocked the aircraft's door and the steps automatically deployed, allowing the outside cold to penetrate the cabin. The cocooned luxury quickly faded and with it Pete and Hefty's exuberance. They watched Mater approach the man and noted, encouragingly, that after a few words the two men shook hands. There was relief when Mater stuck a thumb in the air. Pete and Hefty unbuckled and stepped out. They joined Mater who introduced them. The embassy man's task was to drive the new arrivals to a rented apartment and advise them they were to be loaned the van so they could move equipment as and when. The diplomatic plates would ensure unhindered passage during their visit. The middle ranking official knew better than to ask questions, he simply gave and followed instructions. The four, helped by the flight-crew, worked fast to transfer the bags and containers from the aircraft to the vehicle. Daylight supplemented by the terminal's lights made them conspicuous and all parties wanted to leave this relatively public arena. The Learjet's crew wished to take off as soon as possible and Mater's team keen to hide away in the anonymous flat.

Van ready, Mater thanked the pilot, and climbed in. Pete took the seat between him and the driver while Hefty sat in the closed rear compartment of the vehicle, perched on a box. The driver hoped the gate security guards wouldn't be interested in checking the van's contents; human or otherwise. What none of the van's occupants knew was that the Czech Internal Security Service had been contacted by the embassy. ISS had acquiesced to a request to allow the visitors free movement into and around the city. They would, of course, watch with interest where the men went and what they did but would only intervene if their actions were deemed, in the broadest sense, undiplomatic. The van stopped at the barrier and, following a cursory examination of the men's passports, was waved through. The three in the front breathed a collective sigh of relief.

'I hope it's not far to the apartment,' said Mater, 'I could do with some food and sleep. The batteries are nearly flat.'

'You'll find it ready for occupation, sir: fridge and freezer full, heating on, beds made. There's a garage adjoining so you can load and unload unseen. When we arrive, I'll give you all the keys and make my way home by public transport. It's remarkably reliable. I use it every day.'

'I assume our accommodation has been chosen because it's somewhere off the beaten track?' commented Mater.

The driver nodded. 'It's in District 4. Popular with expats, people working in central Prague; a truly mobile population whose residents come and go all the time. You shouldn't be bothered by anyone. Nad Koloni is just off Jeremenkova Street which offers easy access to the Vltava embankment and hence the city centre. As you are probably aware, our embassy is situated in the Central District. It's only about three kilometres away should you need us. If you want to explore further, find your bearings, this van has sat nav of course, but you might do better buying a public transport pass. As I say, trams and buses are efficient and many people speak English so you won't get lost. I assume you don't speak Czech.'

'Ne,' answered Mater, thinking their driver would make an excellent estate agent should he be considering a change of career.

'We're here,' said the driver, slowing the van as it approached number 16.

The daily commute had yet to begin, so the street was still quiet. With his right hand, the driver reached into the car-door pocket and found a remote control. He pointed it at the double garage, pressed the button and its door swung open automatically. Carefully, he reversed into the dark cavernous space and the ceiling lights, detecting the vehicle, came on. He switched off the engine and handed Mater a bunch of keys.

'Anything else you need?' he asked.

'Ne, dekuji,' answered Mater.

The driver laughed. 'I'm impressed. Practice a little and you might pass as a local. Enjoy your 'holiday', sir.' He opened the driver's door, climbed down and walked away.

Mater and Pete moved to the back of the van, unlocked it and Hefty clambered out, the bright fluorescent lighting blinding him for a few moments. Mater pressed the remote and the garage door closed silently. Pete and Hefty retrieved the three personal bags from the stack in the van. Mater reached down, unzipped his, took out the Makarov pistol and checked it was loaded. He fumbled with the keys, eventually finding the one needed to open the internal door to the flat. He slowly turned the key and pushed, weapon ready.

'Not happy, boss?' Pete asked anxiously.

Mater stopped and whispered. 'From now on, I won't be until we have achieved our goal and return home safely. Trust no-one and that includes the embassy staff and the Czech authorities. That way we stay alive. We could be set up at any point. Wait here while I check it's safe.'

Mater held the Makarov with both hands, raised and steady. He silently stepped from the glare of the garage into the gloomy flat; the street lamps, still lit, casting a pale orange glow in each room.

A few minutes later, he returned beaming. 'Looks good and the fridge is indeed full. Let's have breakfast and then I'll take the first turn at keeping guard. You guys crash out for a bit. Enjoy it because there won't be much rest from now on, I'm afraid. When you wake, we'll hold a planning meeting.'

The main entrance to the first floor accommodation was accessed via steps running up the side of the garage. On top of it, an open plan kitchen/dining/living room. The bedrooms and a single bathroom led off from this area. At the front, large sliding French doors opened to allow access to a patio forming the roof of the garage. Pete and Hefty chose their rooms and retired to bed. Mater pushed an armchair far away from the glazed front area, well out of view. He sat down and listened and watched, turning the Makarov over and over in his lap. He could hear cars being started and the occasional shout from the street. He checked the time. The working day had begun. Nine to five routine for many but not for him. He had often wondered if his irregular lifestyle had taken its toll. His hair had greyed and then thinned prematurely and, although he had never smoked, his face was wrinkled and creased as if he was at least ten years older.

Perhaps, he thought, *my arteries are similarly worn, waiting to fur up completely or rupture at a moment's notice.*

He checked his watch. He would allow the men three hours of unbroken sleep then they would drink coffee and plan, after that he would have to rest. It was imperative they completed their work as fast as possible but to succeed they all needed to be alert. He yawned uncontrollably, fighting the craving to close his eyes; relying on the daylight flooding into the room to stimulate him. He tried to focus on finalising the briefing agenda but his mind struggled to separate what was to come from the many, often traumatic, events of the past weeks. His thoughts drifted back to the plastic briefcase he had asked Control to keep safe for him, his memories of its contents lucid. Irrepressible anger rose within, suppressing the urge to doze. He had chosen this career with all its warts and would see this mission through. He would win again or likely die; his future binary.

Chapter 33

At 08.30 precisely, he knocked on the bedroom doors before entering and delivering each man a mug of steaming strong sweet tea; NATO style. He had read somewhere 7.22 was the ideal time to waken. This however, he assumed, followed a restful night in a normal life; neither applied to them.

'Breakfast in ten minutes with a briefing at zero nine hundred,' he informed the shapeless lumps, hiding under their duvets.

He recognised the authority in his own voice; the requirement for precision and order. He had managed to channel the anger he felt earlier into a positive fervent desire to solve the Office's problem.

Mater returned to the kitchen area and began making breakfast, hearing the men carry out their ablutions. Hot drinks and food ready, he sat down and waited, the file delivered by Control lying on the table beside him. Pete and Hefty joined him.

'Morning boss, thanks for the tea,' said Hefty, sounding surprisingly chirpy.

'OK, let's eat. I'll pour the coffee,' said Mater.

Just before nine, Mater picked up the Office document and held it aloft calling the meeting to order. 'This contains all the information necessary to complete our mission. Before I open it,

I must remind you that the work you are about to undertake is covered by the Official Secrets Act. No-one has asked you to sign anything but be in no doubt the OSA still applies. After our task is done, you will never be at liberty to discuss it with anyone beyond the three of us sat here. Do you understand?' Pete and Hefty nodded. Mater continued. 'OK, some brief background. Until very recently, my unit was one of the most successful in the history of British intelligence but has since been taken apart piecemeal. Every member of my team has been murdered. It appears that a leading player in this attack is or was a senior employee of the service. His position would have allowed him access to personal info about my operatives, enabling his agents to do their dirty work. You met him in London, forcing him to confess enough, in my mind, to confirm his guilt. Further, it seems that he, or whoever he works for, has been engaging members of the Czech criminal fraternity to carry out the assassinations. The lack of controlled borders across Europe has made it easy for these people to move freely to and from the UK. My boss, through his Czech Internal Security Service contacts, has ascertained the authorities here would be delighted if the characters, that have caused so much trouble, were quietly eliminated. Such gangs are also a thorn in the side of the national government here. They have effectively given us the green light to operate under their noses. This file holds lots of detail, including the last known addresses of the men both agencies believe killed my friends. We shall watch those locations to see if they are still being used by them. If confirmed, my intention is for us to kill the bastards. Simple as that. The exception is Anthony who ideally should be brought home to face British justice. The chief would welcome a long chat with him before any trial took place. But if he resists or fights, then he risks being subject to the same penalty as the others. The

Czech's are keen too for a message to reach all these Mafiosi types that they cannot act with impunity.'

Pete butted in. 'The obvious question is why? What made Anthony change from being a loyal public servant to perhaps the organiser of an assassination squad?'

Mater thought for a moment. 'I've been pondering that one for a while but really don't have an answer. I would love to ask him myself but I'm not sure I will ever have the opportunity.'

It was Hefty's turn to speak. 'So, that's why you chose us. Clearly no connection with your parent service and essentially no recent ties with anybody or anything. Random and anonymous.'

'Anonymous yes but random, definitely not,' answered Mater. 'Your backgrounds are ideal and quite early on I realised you could be trained for this mission. Anthony would struggle to find you. Even my boss knows almost nothing and unfortunately the only other person who was party to my plan was Charlotte. No, when it's over you'll have two choices. Either continue working for queen and country or quietly and discreetly slip back into society, living a new life of your choosing. Control has indicated you will be admirably rewarded either way, enabling you to rebuild your lives.'

'Does the Czech ISS know we're using this flat?' asked Pete.

'I think we should assume they do. It is possible, although I have found nothing to confirm this, that we are being listened to and watched. If you need to discuss something that doesn't relate to the current operation, please write it down and show it or we should arrange to meet somewhere in the city, away from prying eyes. Irrespective, I repeat, they have given their consent and could simply be interested in our modus operandi.'

Mater opened the file, pulled out some papers and photographs then spread them on the table, revealing details of the men they were to hunt down.

'So we have three addresses to consider. If we are lucky and can identify our targets, we will take them out simultaneously or in rapid succession. We cannot afford to allow one to alert the others.'

'What about Anthony? Is he here, in Prague?' asked Pete.

'Who knows, but if he is here, then I have an idea where I might find him. I hope I do. It's become personal.'

Pete looked worried. 'You say the Czechs know where we are. Can you guarantee there isn't a rotten egg within their organisation who could either warn the targets, or perhaps worse, make an unwelcome visit here?'

Mater knew the score. There was no purpose in being evasive.

'The simple answer, Pete, is I can't guarantee anything. It's possible that we could be attacked and therefore during periods when we stay here someone should be permanently on guard, armed and ready. We might indeed find the birds have flown the nest and they may have recruited others to protect them. In this game, nothing is ever quite what it appears to be and the future always uncertain. I'm forever trying to minimise the risks but realistically I expect that someday I will be dealt a bad hand. During operations, I live from moment to moment, never at rest but dare I suggest it, it's bloody exciting and to win even better.

My intention is to reconnoitre the three addresses to work out if they are in use. If so, we need to identify the occupants and then, if they prove to be the characters we are looking for, we will plan our assault. If lucky, we might catch them all together or may have to split up and deal with them individually. The latter approach is far less attractive because it requires meticulous timing and they are extremely dangerous, clearly ruthless.'

'OK,' said Hefty, 'I'm up for the fight. When do we start?'

'There is no reason to delay. I suggest we discreetly visit each address as soon as we are all ready. We'll use public transport for the reconnaissance trips as recommended by our embassy friend but we need a hired a van for the attack. If it proves lively, the diplomatic plates on our current vehicle might generate awkward questions for the Foreign Office from the local police or even the media.'

Mater, Pete and Hefty spent the next few hours studying maps of Prague, memorising the topography of the three addresses; internet satellite imagery provided them with immense detail. One house, near the centre of the city faced a small café. The café would be an ideal place to sit, drink coffee and observe the property. The second, located in the suburbs was almost surrounded by an industrial estate. The third, and perhaps most promising property, might prove the most challenging. It appeared to be a farmhouse on top of a wooded hill with views across distant fields and, from the aerial image, clearly protected by a high fence and gates. Such was its position that, in times past, a lord might have built his castle there. Mater hoped the wood offered ample cover for reconnaissance and if necessary, assault. His major concern was that it lay only a few kilometres from

Vaclav Havel Airport, offering a potential escape route from the country.

After lunch, Mater, leaving the others alternating between guarding and resting, set out on foot to find a tobacconist to buy three weekly public transport passes. He kept the Makarov hidden in his coat pocket; reassured by the regular thump of the weapon against his body as he walked. He made sure to minimise the risk of a successful tail despite believing it was unlikely his enemies were aware of his presence in the city. Czech security was probably watching but if they were, they were making an excellent job at being invisible. The tobacconist showed no interest in Mater who, speaking almost no Czech, managed to make his request for the tickets understood in German. Prague always popular with tourists meant Mater and his team were unlikely to arouse suspicion from the local population.

With a pass in his hand, Mater jumped aboard a number 118 bus heading towards the centre and the Green Motion Car and Van Hire company depot. The bus was not busy but Mater saw buses travelling in the opposite direction crammed with commuters escaping home early.

At the Vltava embankment, he stepped down and queued with others for the number 3 tram going north. The tram clanked into view and with a squeal of brakes stopped to discharge passengers. Mater waited politely as the queue disintegrated and everyone tussled to board, all hoping to secure a seat. Mater climbed up and found a space to stand just to the side of a doorway. It was a good place to be; if necessary, he could alight at any time. He spent the journey periodically leaning forward to check where he had got to. Despite the packed carriage, no-one chatted, each passenger absorbed in tapping on their mobile phone or reading a newspaper.

He spotted the car hire yard, descended at the next stop and as the tram clattered away checked that nobody followed. All clear. He entered the depot and produced his diplomatic passport and associated driving licence. The customer service agent, a tall pretty girl with blond hair and full lips, spoke perfect English. She expressed surprise that he wasn't using their competitor who held the embassy account. Mater explained he was making a personal house move within Prague and he didn't really want his employer to know. In confidence, he told the agent, the British Foreign Office wouldn't approve of him having a girlfriend in every port. So he planned to quietly shift his belongings across the city but added that now he had met the woman assisting him, maybe he would change his choice of partner. She blushed and then advised him in no uncertain terms that wasn't her style; after all Mater appeared to be old enough to be her father. Mater laughed but expressed disappointment. The rental assistant hurriedly prepared the required paperwork, spending little time checking the documents he had offered and handed him the vehicle keys. Mater thanked her, apologised for being so forward and departed.

He found the navy blue Volkswagen T5, climbed in, programmed the sat nav for home and set off into the busy rush hour traffic; driving carefully to avoid any incident or, worse, accident. Without doubt, such a misfortune would throw his plans into disarray. Nearing Jeremkova Street, he cruised around until he spotted a suitable nearby side street with free parking. He parked the vehicle. Every couple of days he would move it to another spot so as not to arouse suspicion from local residents. As he walked back to the flat, he checked periodically that he journeyed unaccompanied; always comforted by the hidden automatic.

At the flat's entrance, he rang the doorbell, buzzing 'P' and 'H' in Morse code as agreed. Pete, sitting on guard, recognised it but went to the door with his Glock 17 pistol at the ready, just in case. He eyed Mater through the door's spyhole, checking he was alone. Training had taught him to take no chances. Mater seeing the spyhole darken as Pete's eye closed to it, blew a kiss in its direction. Lowering though not holstering his weapon, Pete let him in.

Pete roused Hefty and over a mug of tea, Mater up-dated his team. He decided they should reconnoitre the target properties that evening using the dusk and commuter rush to their advantage. Each man would visit one location, finding their way there and back by public transport. Working simultaneously, they would impede any tails and hopefully find out which, if any, of the addresses were being used. Pete was assigned the first; the house opposite a small café situated in District 9 on Kondanska Street. Hefty was allocated the second; the residence on Za Drahou Road, accessible by foot after a twenty-five-minute number 22 tram journey starting in the Central district. Mater chose the secure property on the hill. Out of the three, if there was going to be any trouble, this was the most likely, and he considered he would be best placed to confront it. Each would observe for as long as it took to see if it was occupied and to make mental notes as to the layout and possible obstacles. When the time came to attack, it would almost inevitably require a forced entry but the more information they had beforehand the easier their assault would be; maximising surprise. If the properties appeared empty then checking the refuse bins, growth in the gardens and seeing if mail was piling up would help suggest whether the place had been used recently. They agreed that they would return by two in the morning irrespective of what they had discovered. If any of them didn't appear by then, it was to be assumed they had encountered problems and the others would move from the flat, using the hired van. If detained, they should try to contact the Embassy, falling back on their 'diplomatic' status to assist them. Small arms were to be carried, concealed but ready: trouble might be only one wrong foot away. The planning meeting ended.

Mater rustled up a simple early supper during which there was little conversation; everyone contemplating the task and dangers ahead. The gaming at Loch Assynt seemed a world away. The foe they chased was now real and held the advantage of operating on home territory. To Mater this situation was familiar, but Pete and Hefty were naturally nervous, maybe terrified. The boss, noting the air of anxiety, tried to reassure.

'Remember guys, living and working on your home patch can make you overconfident, often complacent. I expect they are enjoying a routine normal life, unaware of our presence in the city. No doubt they operate with some care and attention but it's impossible to maintain your guard day after day after day. Sometime, somewhere they will slip up. We simply have to hide in the shadows and bide our time. Once we confirm where they go and where they stay, our opportunity to strike will present itself. Then we'll act swiftly and decisively before they know what's hit them.'

Mater listened to his own words as they flowed. It was like he was back with his regiment, giving his squad an early morning motivational speech just before an assault. His skill at encouraging his troops to attack even when the odds were unfavourable was legendary. In another era, someone might have asked him to write speeches for Churchill. Instead, he had been tapped on the shoulder with an offer of a quite different career and army life had quickly faded into distant memory.

As dusk fell, the front door of the flat opened allowing the sound of the city's traffic to enter. Three men joined the street and walked to the tram stop at the end of the road. The evening was chilly, becoming frosty, and they wore dark thick clothing as if they were out for the night. The sweltering summer typical of Eastern Europe was only a few weeks away. But spring was being tugged between the winter just passed and the season to come and currently winter retained its grip. They were glad when the bus appeared and mounted the few steps into the warm, ignoring the residual smell of the thousand or more travellers who had ridden that day. It was almost empty as it headed into the city but they sat apart, no longer communicating either by word or facial expression. They operated alone.

At the river embankment, they got off the bus and waited for a connecting tram, joining fellow travellers heading into the central district for the evening. Huge barges, laden with coal, slowly passed by behind them, working their way up the Vltava River, their green and red navigation lights brightly piercing the grey drab dusk. Finally, the no.3 tram clanked into view. They all climbed aboard, mingling with the other passengers. A group of younger people at the back of the carriage sat singing and laughing. Everyone else ignored them and each other. A couple of stops further on and two plain clothed ticket inspectors boarded and began to examine everyone's passes. Mater pulled his out and nodded inconspicuously to his team. The foreigners, interspersed with the locals, produced their tickets on demand and the inspectors moved on.

In the Central District, all three men descended from the tram and went their own way, regularly checking they were not followed. Mater's experienced eye told him that no-one tailed him; the Czech Internal Security Service appeared to be giving them a free hand. Pete and Hefty were less self-assured, although they understood what they needed to do and tried to suppress any anxiety as it gnawed inside them. They did what Mater had instructed them to do, uncertain whether amongst the many surrounding faces there existed a real threat.

Pete caught the no. 2 tram to District 10 and got off about one hundred and fifty metres from Café Jen. He planned to spend the evening there, drinking coffee and pretending to read the thick book he carried. The café would stay open until eleven when he planned to briefly visit the property opposite. He approached the café from the same side of the road as the house, using the opportunity to make a first pass of his target. As he walked by, he saw it was dark inside but noted two security cameras high up on the front wall, their detection lamps glowing a dull red. He noted the rubbish bins hidden from view in an alley to the side. He crossed over the street, doubled back a few paces and entered the café.

The interior was welcoming: warm but simply furnished with plain wooden tables protected by plastic tablecloths surrounded by chairs with colourful cushions. There were five other customers, enjoying hot drinks and cold beer. To Pete, they seemed to be holding a meeting and only briefly looked up at him as he entered, triggering a small bell, before returning to their hushed discussions. He sat down in the window, placed his book on the table and laid his overcoat on a nearby chair, making sure his hidden weapon could be reached easily. A young waitress approached and seeing the book's title grasped the opportunity to practise her English.

'It good story?' she asked, pointing at his book with her pencil.

'So far, most interesting and rather surprising in places,' answered Pete, smiling.

The waitress didn't know Pete had yet to open the paperback but was instead referring to his own experience since he left London those few weeks ago.

The waitress nodded. 'You on holiday in Praha?'

Pete hesitated. 'Sort of, more an adventure. I like exploring and it's a beautiful city with wonderful people. You are lucky.'

She grinned, pleased with the compliment. 'You want coffee or strong drink?' she asked, pencil poised above her notepad.

Pete felt the urge to accept the offer of a glass of Becherovka or similar. The liquor would give him some Dutch courage but he resisted the temptation just as he resisted the impulse to flirt further with the attractive woman standing over him.

'A pot of coffee please, very hot.'

'Sure,' answered the waitress, her English tinted with a false American accent, 'I make it very hot for you.'

'If only,' sighed Pete under his breath, and picked up his book.

He glanced across the street. The house opposite remained unlit. A steady stream of traffic passed by, the density of which gradually fell as the minutes then hours ticked by. Every now and then, he stopped reading, and stared out of the window, checking. To a casual observer it appeared as if he was simply digesting the story unfolding in the pages of his novel. Pete drank his coffee slowly and then ordered more which arrived with a complementary piece of Medovnik. The rich honey cake would be stale by the morning, so the waitress thought she would give it away and maybe encourage her lone customer into further small talk. Pete smiled as she placed it in front of him but rapidly returned to his book, deterring her. Disappointed, she retreated to the kitchen to watch television. The other customers, the formal part of their meeting over, had moved on to wine and spirits. They seemed relaxed and jovial. Pete understood nothing of their conversation but the loud friendly laughter was somehow comforting. They were living in separate worlds.

At a quarter to eleven, the waitress emerged armed with a broom. She began to brush the tiled floor, deftly creating neat piles of crumbs by each table. As she passed Pete's she handed him his bill.

'We close very soon,' she announced. 'You pay now, OK?'

Pete looked up and picked up the paper. The total, he felt, was ludicrously modest considering he had occupied the café for the best part of two hours. He delved into his pocket and withdrew a five hundred Koruna note. He gave it to her.

'Keep the change,' he said.

'All of it?' she replied, looking puzzled.

'Yes, it's for you, your tip, thank you, the cake was delicious and you can have this. I've finished it. He handed her his book.'

The waitress smiled instantly, forgiving him for denying her an extended English lesson. She rapidly pocketed the money and moved on, clutching the book and her broom.

Pete stood up, put on his coat, turned up the collar and went out alone into the silent street. He strolled for ten minutes in one direction before turning around and walking back to the target house. He had timed it perfectly. As he approached, he paused to watch the waitress lock the café doors for another day. She hurried off down the street oblivious, determined to catch the next bus home.

He strode swiftly to the house and dived into the alley beside it. As quietly as he could, he lifted the lids of the three bins, one by one, inspecting the insides. They were all empty. He gently replaced them and then pulled up his collar further and lowered his face before sidling around to the front. Next to the main door was a mail box, stuffed full, with letters and circulars spilling onto the ground below. He picked up all the loose items and tucked them inside his coat. He was keen to explore the outside further, but the CCTV unnerved him. He stood motionless for a few moments and listened. No noise. Realising the cameras would have recorded his presence already, he decided anyway to try to access the rear of the building. But as he made his way along the side of it he found the path blocked by a tall metal gate topped with spikes and razor wire. It wasn't a typical suburban home. A

358

neighbour's dog began to bark. Accepting defeat, he walked briskly back to the street, glancing right and left before re-joining the pavement. He headed towards the tram stop rehearsing in his memory the features and layout he had observed, wondering how the others had fared. He would be back at the flat within the hour.

Hefty had waited ages for the connecting number 22 tram to arrive. He was concerned that when he reached his destination, he would have little time to carry out any reconnaissance before catching the last tram back to the city. His target lay in a poorer area. He doubted the locals would welcome him so late at night, wondering why this foreigner was wandering their streets, far from the tourist zone. As the tram pulled up one stop before Praha-Hostivar station he jumped down, brushing past two young men standing in the doorway who scowled at him. They sported shorn heads and black T-shirts and, it seemed to Hefty although he couldn't understand, that they swore at him. Luckily, their confidence to take matters further was tempered by Hefty's obvious bulk. Working his way along the Za Drahou Road between the main rail line and a trading estate, he looked for a turning to his right into Sterboholska Street. After nearly five hundred metres he spotted a tatty street sign covered in graffiti advertising a local neo-Nazi group, the street name just visible. He spat at it and hurried on looking for the building he had viewed on the internet's satellite image. As the warehouses petered out, the road became enclosed by a high fence on both sides, beyond which was clearly a construction site where homes and offices were being built. He walked on until, under the glow of the few functioning streetlamps, his path was blocked by a padlocked gate. He stood for a moment wondering if he had made a wrong turn. Then it dawned on him; the computer images they had all studied earlier were already months, if not years, out of date. Prague, prosperous and growing was also changing and development inevitable. The older houses, derelict industrial sites and the surrounding countryside were now making way for the new.

'Well that reduces our options,' he muttered to himself, as he turned to go back.

Nearing the junction of Sterboholska Street and Za Drahou Road he saw a group of people waiting. As he approached he counted five individuals, all dressed identically. Each appeared to be carrying a length of timber or steel pipe. He recognised two of them from the tram, with their distinctive shaved heads and black shirts. Evidently, they had recruited their friends and followed him. Hefty stopped about ten metres from the group who patted their improvised weapons in their outstretched hands. He slipped his right hand inside his coat pocket and felt the hardness of the automatic's grip. He carefully wound his fingers around the gun, slid the safety catch off and gently placed his index finger on the trigger. The men in front of him were half his age. He imagined being their father trying to steer them to an honourable life but disappointed in his failure to do so.

'Gentlemen, what can I do for you?' he asked slowly and politely, his breath forming a visible vapour in the freezing air, knowing whatever it was, it wasn't likely to be deliverable.

One of the group stepped forward and answered in broken English. 'What are you doings here? Nothing to see here. Tourists not welcome. We are members of the Delnicka Straa. We rule Praha. You must pay us to be here.'

360

Hefty listened and watched intently. He hadn't heard of the Delnicka Straa but guessed correctly that it was probably the name of a far-right organisation. He spat on the ground.

'I'm giving you nothing,' he growled, adding menacingly, 'I suggest if you want to live, you leave straightaway.'

The one who was obviously the ring leader laughed and then shouted something to his friends in Czech. They joined in with the laughter, increasing the tempo of the rhythmic beating of their weapons. Suddenly the leader broke from the group and ran towards Hefty. He didn't manage five meters before being thrown backwards as a shot rang out; the steel pole he had brandished flew upwards and clattered to the tarmac beside him. Smoke curled from a small hole in Hefty's coat but immediately after firing he withdrew the weapon, ready to fire again. He held it in both hands, steadily waving it side to side, pointing the barrel at the other four assailants in turn. The fallen youth clutched his groin, rolled around in severe pain, screaming in Czech and his limited English. 'My balls, my balls', were the only words Hefty could understand. Hefty had tried to hit him in the thigh but the bullet had found its mark higher up. He stepped back a few paces, maintaining the distance between him and the thugs. Again, he spoke slowly and clearly.

'Right, you little shits,' he said. 'Your mate needs to go to hospital or he might bleed to death. Help him and leave. If anyone tries to be clever, I will kill them. Do you understand?'

Hefty wasn't sure the others did, but the gun didn't need translating; its potential universally understood. To the young men, Hefty was a giant, armed and obviously willing to inflict serious damage. They moved nervously forward and together

361

dragged their now silent friend away to a nearby car. His body had gone limp as blood seeped between his fingers and trailed along the dusty road. Hefty watched them drive off at speed and then ran as fast as he could back to the tram stop.

Bugger, he thought, *the boss isn't going to be pleased.*

Mater's evening proved to be more successful than Pete's and less dramatic than Hefty's. After leaving the others, Mater found his way to the main bus station where he caught a number 161, destination Vaclav Havel Airport. The airport lay almost at the border between Prague and Central Bohemia so he had plenty of time to plan his reconnaissance and contemplate what might follow. The bus was busy with young tourists, who travelling as economically as possible, carried backpacks and cheap plastic hand luggage. There was an excited air on the vehicle as they regaled each other with stories of their holidays in a variety of European languages. Mater felt slightly jealous of their happiness and apparent innocence. He remembered how, as a younger man, he had been fuelled with optimism and hope. He had joined the army with the expectation of righting wrongs and securing the peace but that spark had soon been dampened when he first saw action. The image of flies eating into the rotting bodies of the innocent dead in Afghanistan had imprinted itself in his brain and had never left. The frontispiece in an album full of ghastly reality. He wondered what ambitions the youth of today held and how many would have their dreams shattered before they had really begun. He looked out of the window as the suburbs rushed by, pushing his own grim memories back into the distant past.

The bus driver, in response to Mater's earlier request, pulled up at Tuchomerika and indicated it was his stop. Mater had, in German, explained he was visiting a friend, but hadn't been there before. The driver had been a little surprised. It was rare for his passengers not to be travelling to the airport. Even more unusual to drop someone so late in the evening, in darkness, in the rambling countryside. Mater thanked him and stepped from the warm fug into the cold night. As the bus drove away, he turned east following the edge of the road, trying to avoid the many potholes that pitted his route.

Roughly three hundred metres on, he found the overgrown lane which he expected led to the farmhouse; surrounded by trees and perched on a hillock. With no vehicles in sight, he darted into the undergrowth. He waited while his eyesight adjusted to the gloom before slowly climbing the hill, taking care not to trip or break branches underfoot. Halfway to the summit, he encountered a chain-link fence secured to the ground by concrete posts, the top angled outwards to deter climbers. Mater removed his boots and tied them to a loop on his coat. He took off his socks and stuffed them into the pocket with the Makarov. He inserted his big toe into the highest link he could reach and then using hands levered himself up. The strong wire dug into his feet prising his toes apart. Mater ignored the pain and methodically climbed, negotiating the overhang with experienced ease. The fence was topped with a single strand of barbed wire. He pulled out his socks and wrapped them, in turn, around the fingers of each hand. As he reached to pull himself over the barbs, his coat caught, tearing it and the Makarov slid from the inverted pocket. Mater swore quietly to himself, listening as the weapon made a dull thud on contact with the ground. He was balanced on top but now unarmed. He paused to consider his options. The Major wouldn't be pleased to lose his lucky charm. He could go back down and retrieve the gun but his hands and feet were cut and bruised. He wasn't sure he would be able to repeat the climb more than once. He decided to continue, descending partway down the other side before allowing himself to hang briefly by his arms before dropping the last few feet. A small branch emitted a loud crack as he snapped it underfoot. He froze, holding his breath while he listened. An owl hooted somewhere to his left but there was no other noise to cause alarm. In the distance, he heard the drone of traffic and overhead a fully laden aircraft, recently departed from the nearby airport, steadily climbed into the night sky. Mater sat down, nursed his sore toes and replaced his socks and boots. He searched around for a suitable stick and fixed it to the mesh marking his crossing point. He intended to climb back out at the exact same place and find the pistol. He clambered up another seventy-five metres and ahead, through the thinning trees, saw the lights of the farmhouse. Maintaining a low profile, he edged his way forward until he had a clear view of the building. Most windows were darkened by drawn curtains or blinds but light spilled from what appeared to be the main public rooms. The sound of a classical guitar, played skilfully, wafted in his direction. He recognised the tune but the composer's name escaped him. Suddenly the music stopped, and he heard at least two people arguing. Mater watched as shadows danced on an internal wall, trying to figure out how many residents were involved in the verbal contretemps. He crept out from his vantage point, crawling across a lawn, then a stone patio towards the house; always out of sight. Reaching it, he listened to the voices, still raised in anger. The sliding glass doors were slightly ajar. Mater caught more of the conversation. The Czech spoken by one of those inside was slow and uncertain. Intermittently the same voice reverted to English. He swallowed hard. Little doubt - it was Anthony's. He cursed himself for not climbing back over the fence. He was within a few feet of his quarry. With the Makarov and the advantage of surprise, he could have entered through the open French windows and possibly ended it there and then but that opportunity was gone. He listened intently, straining to work out what the argument or discussion was about. The Czech threw him but Anthony was clearly concerned about a CCTV recording made earlier that evening. Something had put the wind up him but Mater had no idea what. Mater had heard enough. The farmhouse contained his prime target. Whether the other assassins resided there, he couldn't tell. He crept around the house making mental notes of the position of doors, windows and downpipes, taking care not to leave any footprints or other signs of his visit. The building was constructed partly of stone with a modern wooden extension providing the space for the public rooms with their large doors opening onto the patio. He concluded that as long as these weren't armoured, it wouldn't be difficult to breach them. Even if they were, one or two of Stanley's specials would probably do the trick. His survey completed, he stealthily crawled back to the relative safety of the wood and rested a while, delighted by the absence of guard-dogs.

Careless Anthony, careless, he thought.

From his vantage point, he counted three other men in the room with Anthony. Two of them, much taller than the other, paced up and down, almost in time as if they were twins. The third stood motionless by the glass, carrying an AK47 automatic. Mater felt a sense of relief that he hadn't attacked. The Makarov would have been little match for the AK.

No, he concluded, *We'll return soon but then the firepower will be in our favour.*

He wound his way back down the hill, sliding occasionally on the damp undergrowth. Reaching the fence, he worked along it until he found the stick still secure in the netting. Climbing back over required the same technique but avoided having to negotiate the overhang. Instead, he briefly gripped the top wire and then dropped down, parachute rolling as he landed. He put his shoes back on and then searched for the Makarov. The glint of its barrel caught his eye, and he picked it up, wiping earth from the grip before returning it to his pocket. It was already past midnight, and he realised he had probably missed the last bus. He would have to trot to the airport and quickly find a tram or taxi to carry him back to the city otherwise the two o'clock deadline would pass. Then the others would abandon the flat. He knew it wasn't far, but it occurred to him that Anthony could also take advantage of the airport's proximity. He just hoped that whatever had spooked the men in the house didn't cause them to flee the nest.

At the airport, Mater impatiently joined a queue of tired people waiting for taxis. No-one took much interest in the rather dishevelled sweaty man in a torn coat smeared in mud and without luggage. But, when it came to Mater's turn, the taxi driver insisted on payment up front before agreeing to drive him to his destination. Mater feigned being a little under the influence and offered an inappropriately large denomination Koruna note. The driver responded angrily, grumbling that he had no change but his demeanour changed immediately when Mater casually and drunkenly suggested he keep it all. Once underway, Mater pretended to fall asleep only waking when the taxi reached Jeremkova Street. He requested the taxi to stop and on opening the door, dramatically almost fell out. The driver called after him in Czech, revved his engine and departed at speed. Mater straightened himself up and walked briskly to the flat, the exercise inhibiting the cold that tried to invade his clothes. It was one fifty two in the morning.

Arriving home, he saw light seeping through the curtains. He rang the doorbell in the agreed code and waved his arms to keep warm while he waited for someone to let him in. When he heard footsteps inside approach, he took out the Makarov and held it ready in case an unwelcome guest opened the door. His anxiety was unfounded as Pete appeared from behind it, expressed obvious relief, and welcomed him in. In the living area, Mater saw Hefty sitting in an armchair also looking concerned.

'I know it's late but I'll make some coffee and then we'll debrief while memories are still fresh,' he announced.

'You OK Hefty?' he asked.

Hefty grunted while Pete cleared the table ready for the discussion. With mugs of steaming coffee in front of them, and Pete poised with pen and paper, Mater called the meeting to order.

'OK, I'm delighted we are all back safe and sound. Well done. I suggest we describe our adventures in turn. You first Hefty. Looks like you want to get something off your chest.'

Hefty got up, walked across the room and returned with his coat. He handed it to Mater, pointing to the small hole punched through the right pocket; scorched and frayed. Mater examined it briefly.

'Shouldn't keep lighted cigars in your pocket Hefty,' he joked. 'Tell us what happened.'

Hefty relayed the evening's events describing how the target house no longer existed and his encounter with the young Neo-Nazis on the tram and then in the road.

Mater listened without interruption until a despondent Hefty had gloomily finished before picking up his now cold coffee and giving his reaction. 'Well, sounds as if it was a bit too exciting, doesn't it? The little shit, if he survives, won't be growing a beard any time soon. But we have to hope that he or his friends don't agitate the whole DS organisation. That could be inconvenient.'

'Understatement and a half,' interjected Pete.

'Sorry, boss,' added Hefty, looking downhearted. 'I haven't fucked up the entire show, have I?'

Mater shook his head. 'You had no choice. I think you were being generous in simply trying to wound him. He was fortunate it wasn't me holding the gun.' He turned to Pete. 'Any better luck?'

In a similar manner to Hefty, Pete described in detail his journey to the café, his observation of the house opposite and then his brief closer look at the property. At the end of his resumé, he handed Mater the pile of mail he had removed from the overflowing mailbox.

'I doubt the address has been used for a considerable time,' concluded Pete.

Mater nodded in agreement while turning over, examining carefully and then opening each item of post. Although everything was written in Czech, it was clear that many were utility bills; their red print suggested payment was long overdue. Mater selected a few items of potential interest, folded them and slipped them into his pocket.

'Pete,' queried Mater, 'You mentioned that you were anxious not to spend too much time roaming around the house, even though you believed it was unoccupied. What unnerved you?'

'Bugger,' answered Pete, 'I forgot to mention the CCTV. I'm sure it was active, and if so, I didn't know when or whether an alarm would be triggered somewhere. I decided I wasn't going to hang around long enough to find out.'

Mater's expression changed from simple curiosity in Pete's description to one of deep concern. His brow furrowed, and he sat for a few moments without speaking. Pete and Hefty watched him closely and waited in silence. They had learnt to recognise when he had something significant to say.

'Bugger is right,' announced Mater finally. 'The CCTV quite possibly alerted our targets.' He relayed his evening's work in detail, focusing on the argument he had partly overhead and the gist he gathered from it.

'The problem we now face is that our enemy may opt to flee or pre-emptively try to locate us and attack. We can assume that, as we have been untroubled so far, there have been no leaks from the ISS or from our embassy. But if they have extensive connections in the local criminal underworld, it won't be long before they find us. I'm afraid it leaves only one option.'

Pete and Hefty knew exactly what Mater was going to recommend, but they didn't interrupt allowing the boss to justify his plan.

'Men, we have a definite sighting of our main target at the only obviously active location. Unfortunately, we know little about the building and even less about how many armed individuals live there. Who knows how well trained they are or willing they may be to lay down their lives for the foreigner in their midst, who is quite possibly their paymaster? But we cannot wait for their chances to improve. In fact, the longer we do, I believe the greater the danger. Unless either of you have a better idea, we move on the farmhouse tonight and whatever the outcome, leave the country immediately after. I'll contact the embassy to arrange our urgent extraction. If we can, let's get a couple of hours sleep and then we'll load the hire van with everything we need before daylight comes. After that some more rest. Then I'll brief you on my plan for the attack.'

The three retired to bed but although shattered none were likely to sleep, knowing too well the coming night might be their last. Mater lay on his bed, refusing to let his eyelids droop, revising again and again the layout of the farmhouse, noting the locations of its potential weaknesses and places for covering fire. It wasn't going to be easy. He was relying on two men with no recent active service, but this was the hand he held and he had to play it the best way he could. He set the alarm on his mobile phone for 04.30. They would have just over an hour to sort out the kit and discreetly transfer it to the hired vehicle.

Chapter 34

Just before his alarm buzzed, Mater switched on the light then climbed from the warmth of his bed. In the adjacent bathroom, he stood facing the mirror fixed above the sink and splashed cold water repeatedly over his face stimulating the blood flow in his cheeks and brain. He scrutinised the image framed before him. 'You look awful,' he said to his reflection, 'When this is over, I'm forcing you to take a proper break. I might even convince you to find another job but first we have to fight to win. And we will win, rest assured, old man, we will win.'

He picked up a towel and rubbed the loose skin of his cheeks and neck. He padded out to the living area and tapped firmly on Pete's and then Hefty's bedroom door.

'Rise and shine soldiers. Tonight we're going to kick ass.'

As Pete and Hefty dressed and made more coffee, Mater slipped out of the flat to retrieve the hire van and parked it in front of the garage. Within an hour, the tools of Mater's trade had been stowed in the VW T5 and the vehicle returned to its original parking place.

Mater walked back, checking carefully no-one followed him. He noted the morning rush was shortly to begin. Commuters appeared in the street, wiping the light frost from their windscreens or hurrying to the nearest tram and bus stops.

At the flat, Mater suggested the men got more rest. He would sleep after he had contacted the embassy. He took out his phone and dialled the number provided on the cover of the Office file. It was a while before the night duty officer answered. Mater suspected he had been asleep as the weary voice asked him to repeat his codeword: night-time Prague rarely generated much excitement. Mater was sure he detected a yawn.

'I don't care, it's nearly six in the morning, put me through to the military attaché now,' he urged.

A few moments later, another voice, more awake although clearly agitated, spoke to Mater asking him to explain the need for the early call. Mater apologised then placed his request for an aircraft to be on standby to fly him and his team from Prague, if necessary, during the next twenty-four hours. He also gave details of the vehicle that was going to need to have its contents removed and be repatriated clean to the hire depot. He asked for the driver who had met them at the airport to return that evening and simply drive the diplomatic van around the city for an hour or two before returning to the embassy. Finally, could someone lay their hands on a pair of serious bolt croppers and the driver deliver them when he came? The attaché didn't think it would be a problem and repeated back Mater's demands. Mater thanked him, apologised again and ended the call.

Suddenly, Mater felt exhausted. Dawn had broken and his preparatory work was almost done. The final tasks could wait a few hours. He sat down in an armchair, facing the large living area windows obscured by drab curtains, placed the Makarov beside him and despite his best efforts fell fast asleep. In his dreams, he saw Anthony standing over the bodies of his friends, grinning from ear to ear, goading him. Mater took aim with his submachine gun but each time he pulled the trigger Anthony laughed at him. The repeated explosions emerging from the weapon's muzzle simply discharged smoke and flame but no lead. He was shooting blanks and his adversary roared at his failure.

The banging finally penetrated Mater's subconscious, and he jumped from the chair, clutching his weapon. A thin band of sunlight pierced the room, penetrating the darkness through a small gap between the curtains. The noise outside took on a metallic timbre and Mater relaxed, recognising the sound of dustbins being emptied in the street. He looked at his watch. Nearly four o'clock. Better get the others up and finish their preparations. Once again, he knocked on the doors of his men, rousing them. He boiled the kettle ready to make a hot drink. They might be temporarily away from home but they could still enjoy the tradition of afternoon tea.

A few minutes later and Hefty and Pete emerged looking distinctly refreshed. Their years of sleeping rough had endowed them with the ability to sleep whenever and wherever. He poured the tea and invited them to join him for some refreshment and the briefing. Over the next two hours, the three men scoured the satellite images of the farmhouse and its environs. They memorised details from Mater's sketches of the site, photographs of the targets, rendezvous points and the timetable for the assault. Mater demanded that each man could identify every detail and recall the embassy emergency contact number should they need urgent assistance from the Foreign Office.

As dusk approached, Mater sat back in his chair satisfied that all the preparation that needed to be done had been done. Pete and Hefty noticed his demeanour had changed: Mater appeared to be calm, confident, almost serene. They found his stance reassuring, and confidence infectious. Mater went over to the kitchen area and began to cook. He chuckled as he sliced into an onion.

'Don't worry guys; I'm not making anything too special, simply a big bowl of pasta; carb loading. This won't be our last supper.' Pete and Hefty were pleased to hear it.

At half past eight, the three men loaded their personal bags into the diplomatic van and waited for the embassy driver to arrive. At precisely nine o'clock they observed, from the living room window, the familiar figure climb the external staircase and heard the doorbell. Mater checked using the spyhole he was alone before opening the door and inviting him in. He apologised for not being able to offer the man a drink but explained the flat had been completely 'cleaned'. There was no residual evidence of Mater's team's stay. The driver carried a large bag. He opened it and took out a pair of industrial bolt croppers.

'Busy night ahead, sir?' he asked as he handed over the tool.

'Expect so,' answered Mater, determined not to give away further information. 'You understand that you're not to drive the van straight back to the compound, but to roam randomly around the city for a couple of hours. And I would be grateful if you avoided the 19th district.'

'Perhaps acting as a decoy to lure away anyone interested in your activities there?' suggested the official.

'Who knows?' replied Mater, 'Let's just say your contribution is important to the mission. That should be enough, shouldn't it?' He patted the driver on the shoulder who knew he had probed too much.

'Of course sir. I'll do my best.'

Mater handed him the keys. The two men descended the flat's internal stairs. The driver jumped into the van and secured his seatbelt. He mouthed good luck to Mater who waved then pressed the remote control, opening the garage doors. The van's engine started, the vehicle drove out into the street and away. Mater closed the door again.

Time to go, he thought.

Chapter 35

Less than an hour later, if anyone had the curiosity to notice, a deep blue VW T5 could be seen driving along the quiet roads of Prague's District 19. Mater, in the driver's seat, never breaking the speed limit or jumping red lights, concentrated on reaching their destination safely. Pete, beside him, held a Glock 17 handgun ready but out of view. In the back, Hefty crouched amongst the mini arsenal, secured to the vehicle's floor. At 10.17pm, the van turned off the main highway into Tuchomericka. Mater drove a short distance before reversing into a space between mature trees, hiding it from the road and the track that led to the target. He switched off the engine and headlights. It was very dark, overcast with no moon. Pete gently opened his door and quietly went to the back to unlock the rear doors. Hefty, wearing night vision goggles climbed out and handed him a pair. The two men scanned the surrounding woods. They were alone. Hefty moved forwards and spoke to Mater.

'All quiet boss,' he said, handing Mater another set of NVGs.

Twelve minutes later, each man was fully tooled up. Helmets and gloves on but no body armour. Mater had decided they would need to move fast and the extra weight would definitely hinder three middle-aged men working their way up the hill. Pete and Hefty held their MP7s in their arms at the ready, Glock 17s holstered and rucksacks containing the PE4 explosive, grenades and detonators. Before picking up his own equipment, Mater climbed back into the van and released the handbrake, allowing it to roll into the lane, blocking it. Mater carried his own weapons and the hardware for cutting the fence. He wasn't sure Stanley's specials would be needed but he had tucked them into his backpack as well just in case. He slipped into the cover of the pines and signalled to the others to follow him. From now on, communication would be by hand gestures alone. With the goggles, it was easy to avoid fallen branches and roots and they made rapid progress. They soon reached the perimeter fence. Mater slid the rucksack off his shoulders and took out the bolt cutters. He listened carefully. Silence. The first cut of the fence caused the wire to spring apart with a loud ping which was immediately followed by the sound of dogs barking. Mater cursed quietly. Clearly the enemy had decided to increase their defences. He wondered what else had changed over the past twenty-four hours. The three men looked at each other, green light escaping from their NVGs casting a ghoulish glow onto their faces. They moved their heads, trying to work out how many guard-dogs there were, listening intently to hear if they were approaching. Pete and Hefty watched Mater, wondering whether he would continue with the attack. Mater delved into his bag and withdrew what seemed to be a small grenade. He handed it to Hefty and then returned to cutting the fence. As he nipped the last wire necessary to make a man sized opening, the dogs closed in. Mater quickly dragged the wire together again and temporarily secured it, leaving a tiny defect at the top. Two Alsatians appeared, growling, snarling and throwing themselves at the mesh. Hefty pulled the pin from the Stanley special and posted it through the gap. All three men sprinted away as grey smoke bellowed from the device. Within seconds, the barking stopped, and both dogs collapsed as the narcotic vapour overcame them. Mater waited for the agent to

377

disperse before returning and prising the wire apart once more. He drew his knife, climbed through the hole and approached the first animal readying himself to drive the blade through its chest. A hand grabbed his arm, and he swung around to see Hefty holding a roll of duct tape. Hefty forced Mater's knife down and then knelt next to the unconscious animals. Using the strong sticky tape, he bound their jaws and legs. Mater wavered between anger and amusement.

'You big softy, Hefty', he whispered. They were now committed to return the same way if Hefty was going to release the hounds. He sheathed his knife.

In the farmhouse, the dogs had caused only brief alarm as they often barked when they detected an animal or bird amongst the trees, rapidly falling silent again as the frightened creature fled. Mater and team moved slowly and carefully towards their target. At the edge of the wood Pete found a suitable hiding place from where he could give covering fire as the others continued on to the house. The French doors were closed and curtains behind them drawn, denying Mater the opportunity of finding out how many defendants they faced. The blare of a television seeped from the building. He hoped the occupants were engrossed in it or had gone to bed, maximising his chances of surprise. To the side of the patio doors, Hefty laid down his rucksack, took out a preformed PE4 charge and quietly moulded it to the glass. He gingerly inserted a detonator then connected it to the electronic firing system. Once happy it was securely fixed, he indicated to Mater for them to withdraw. Hefty lay on the ground holding the firing unit while Mater knelt at the other side of the doorway clutching two grenades, both pins removed. Mater nodded to Hefty who pressed the fire button. In an instant, the garden and its surroundings were illuminated by a dazzling flash accompanied by a deafening noise. Shards of glass showered the lawn and shredded the thin curtains as the toughened glazing disintegrated. Mater threw his grenades through the breach and during the brief delay before the devices exploded, picked up his MP7. As further debris flew from the house accompanied by bellows of smoke, Mater and Hefty launched themselves into the building. The destruction caused by the explosives was extensive. Inside, Mater and Hefty swung their heads rapidly from side to side, using their NVGs in the now pitch black room to search amongst the debris for any threats. On a sofa, pushed across the room by the initial blast, sat a body lacerated and motionless, mouth and eyes open, clothing partly stripped and bloodied. Hefty discharged a short burst into the torso. The corpse twitched as the rounds penetrated but made no other movement or sound. Mater held up his hand to stop Hefty and listened. Footsteps above. He beckoned to Hefty to follow. The two men ran into the connecting hallway and towards the staircase at the far end. As they crossed the hall someone above fired an automatic, the bullets peppering the plasterwork behind them. Mater and Hefty dropped to the ground and rolled under the cover of the mezzanine. Mater lying on his back, emptied a full magazine through the ceiling, causing wood and plaster, and then water from a holed pipe, to rain down. Above them they heard shouting in Czech followed by the patter of at least two people running away along the first floor. The noise faded. Mater reloaded and then indicated to Hefty to provide covering fire as he swiftly moved to the stairwell. Above him to one side he saw light leach into the galleried landing. He lifted his NVGs and crept up the stairs keeping low, weapon ready. Hefty leant against the hall wall and swung his MP7 back and forth, covering the balcony. At the top Mater noticed a pool of blood staining the white carpet, with a trail leading towards the light coming from the end of a corridor. The landing's floor was punctured by Mater's bullets. He waved to Hefty to join him and then took out another grenade. With Hefty beside him, he pulled the pin and threw the device towards the light. There were brief shouts before the loud thud of the explosion muffled the human voices. The house reverted to total darkness and Mater lowered his NVGs again before they rushed down the corridor. Doors led off from both sides. At each one, Mater and Hefty paused briefly before shoving it open and checking inside. Finally, they reached the last door at the far end. As they stretched to push it, a burst of gunfire from within splintered the door's thin wooden panels, cutting Hefty's gloved hands and he dropped down in pain. Avoiding the line of fire, Mater reached around and fired back, blindly emptying his weapon directly through the door.

Outside, Pete watched gun-flashes illuminate a first-floor window. Then it opened, a figure climbed out and hung from the sill, hesitating to drop the few metres to the ground. Pete broke cover and ran towards the house pointing his MP7 at the man clinging to the ledge. As Pete approached, the man let go but before he hit the earth, a hail of copper capped lead thrust him against the wall and he slumped to the ground.

Mater, hearing the shooting outside, made the decision to leave Hefty nursing his wounds, break down the door and enter. He kicked hard at the shattered door, causing it to fall in off its hinges. Inside he spotted someone collapsed on the tiles, surrounded by fractured ceramic from the broken sink and bidet, gasping and clutching his abdomen, an AK47 lying to his side. Mater moved forward and booted the automatic away. Even with the limitations of the NVGs, Mater recognised the man from the Office file photos. He had no doubt. This was one of Liam's assassins. The man groaned. Mater looked down and saw him holding his guts in his hands, the wormlike form of his intestines slowly pulsating. Mater knelt down beside him.

'Where's Anthony?' he demanded. No response.

Mater tried again. 'Where's Antinin, you little shit?'

The man groaned again and then transiently fell unconscious.

Mater kicked him and tried a different tack. 'If you tell me where Anthony is I will get you help; there's no need to die.'

The man slowly shook his head.

'You won't say or you don't know?' Mater asked.

The injured man lay confused, no longer hearing Mater clearly. He moaned and shook his head again, blood flicking from his spattered blond hair. Mater pulled out the Makarov and held it to the man's forehead.

'Last chance.' He paused. 'Time's up. This is for Liam,' he said bluntly and squeezed the trigger.

The man's head shattered, splattering brains across the wall behind and his hands slumped to each side allowing the abdominal contents to slide out. Mater replaced his hand gun, stood up, picked up his MP7 and went back to help Hefty. Hefty looked at him directly, the ghoulish green of their respective NVGs reflecting off each other.

'Not sure that matches the spirit of the Geneva Convention, boss,' he said quietly, holding his own wounds firmly.

Mater didn't answer but tore his shirt into bandages for Hefty's sliced hands, binding them tightly, stemming the seepage of blood.

'You OK?' he asked, adding, 'Sorry, but I only look after the good guys.'

He picked up Hefty's weapon and the two men made their way back to the ground floor. In the living room, Mater returned to the body lying on the sofa. He bent down to examine the dead man's face and turned to Hefty.

'That's the other bastard,' he said, 'Retribution and fair justice for Liam.'

This time it was Hefty who didn't respond. Mater moved to the open doorway and waved to Pete who had retreated to his vantage point. Pete emerged from the shadows and padded across the lawn.

'Boss. I got one trying to escape from a first-floor window,' he announced, almost with pride, when he joined the others.

Mater felt a surge of hope. 'Well done, show me Pete.'

Pete led Mater and Hefty to the place below where the final battle had been fought. The body lay as it fell, face down, riddled with gunshots. Mater kicked it with his boot and when there was no response, reached down to roll it over.

'Bugger,' he said, 'It's not Anthony.'

Mater and Pete returned to the house to search for clues as to Anthony's whereabouts. Unknown to them, at the same time, a figure dressed in plain clothing hurried toward the main road past a dark blue VW van blocking the access track.

Hefty sat in silence on an old oak garden bench looking out over the lawn, keeping guard. His hands throbbed but his thoughts drifted elsewhere. In the darkness, he imagined he was back in London occupying a similar bench in one of the many parks scattered across the city. He could hear faraway traffic and the sound of aircraft climbing overhead. It all sounded so familiar yet so distant: a different life.

In Prague that same evening, a diplomatic van had roamed from district to district, its driver obeying his instructions to the letter. But as it turned off Ruska highway in District 4 and entered the narrow Bulharska Street, its driver failed to notice a large refuse lorry approaching from behind at speed. He had no time to react as the truck rammed him, crushing the vehicle against a concrete wall. The emergency services called to the scene were surprised by the extensive damage and the destruction caused by the subsequent fire. They assumed the van must have been travelling far too fast to make the corner. The driver hadn't had a chance. The remnants of the diplomatic plates eventually enabled the Czech authorities to notify the embassy of their loss. The DS celebrated, convinced they had achieved their revenge.

Hefty's thoughts were broken by Mater and Pete emerging from the house having completed their rapid fruitless search.

'Time to withdraw,' ordered Mater.

The three men disappeared back into the woods with all their equipment, pausing at the fence only to release, at Hefty's insistence, the dogs from their bindings. At the van, they packed away their kit and changed into clean clothes. Mater asked Pete to drive him into the centre of the city. Near to the famous Charles Bridge he pulled over. Mater shook Pete's hand and got out.

'Meet me here in twenty-four hours. If I don't appear, go to the embassy. They'll be expecting you. I'll catch up with you later. I have one more card to play.'

He opened the door and stepped out into the chilly Prague air.

Chapter 36

In the early morning, Mater sat in a bar directly opposite the Central Mosque, waiting and watching. He fingered a slip of paper, rolling it back and forth in his palm. In his other hand, he held a glass of local beer. It was delicious, but he only sipped, careful to make it last. He couldn't afford to enjoy the dark amber liquid in his usual way and risk weakening his powers of observation or diminishing his reaction times. If Anthony emerged, the chase would begin. It might prove to be Mater's final opportunity to catch him. The deaths of Anthony's foot soldiers meant he was likely to flee. If he reached another country safely, the authorities there might not be so willing to turn a blind eye to the British team's activities. Time ticked by. Mater pretended to read a Czech newspaper, conveniently left lying nearby, using the broadsheet to hide his face and deter other customers from striking up a conversation with him.

Mater finished his drink and returned to the bar to order a coffee. While the bartender loaded the espresso machine with more beans, he leant against the counter and continued to watch the world outside. Suddenly, Anthony appeared at the mosque's entrance. He stood alone and fleetingly looked both ways before briskly tripping down the steps to the street. Mater threw down a large denomination Karuna note and made for the exit. The barman looked up in surprise, holding the cappuccino in his hand. He was about to call after his customer but spied the money sitting there and resumed cleaning glasses, intermittently stopping to enjoy the coffee himself.

Mater crossed the street, checking as he went for the reassuring presence of the Makarov in his coat pocket. Anthony's destination seemed to be the main rail station. Mater would have to corner him before he got there otherwise he might escape by boarding an international train. Just before the station, Anthony halted, and checked behind. He scanned the column of pedestrians walking in his direction. One figure abruptly stopped to look in a shop window. He wasn't sure but could it be Mater? Then the man turned to face him and their eyes met. Anthony was certain now. He dashed over the busy road, causing a taxi to swerve and other vehicles to sound their horns and walked rapidly in the opposite direction, towards the Vltava River. Mater's passage across the same road was delayed by the stream of traffic but he did not lose sight of his quarry. On the other side, he quickened his pace but his acceleration was matched by the man he chased. Pursuer and pursued crossed the water at the Most Lejii, the distance between them barely decreasing.

Where are you going? thought Mater, concerned Anthony was leading him to a place where he could call in reinforcements and turn from being the hunted into the hunter.

Mater needn't have worried. Anthony was on his own, his support network blown apart, but hopeful he would lose Mater in the parts of Prague he knew best. At the far side of the bridge, Anthony turned left and hurried to the funicular railway that runs up Petrin Hill; a large wooded park criss-crossed with footpaths. Mater sprinted after him but was too late to catch the little carriage as it set off for the summit. He spotted a zig-zag path running alongside and followed it, chasing the train as it slowly clanked higher and higher. His chest heaved, and he wished he was twenty years younger. Fleetingly, he imagined he was back at the cottage in Kent, making his daily run up Burham hill. Then reality returned, and he pressed on, breathing deeply though measuring his pace. If only he had trained harder: he had to reserve some energy to continue the pursuit at the top. Anthony, the lone passenger, stepped out of the funicular and hearing Mater's footsteps closing, started jogging towards the Zrcadlove. He expected the ornate building containing the mirror maze to be busy with tourists. Once there, he could disappear. Mater caught a glimpse of his prey in the distance, following a track that weaved between tall old trees, just coming into leaf. He ran faster, the excitement of the chase distracted him from the burning in his thighs.

Anthony arrived at the entrance to the Zrcadlove and after glancing behind, dived inside. His luck had run out. There were no tourists. The drizzle had deterred other visitors from visiting the park. Mater, fifty metres back, saw him enter.

'Got you,' he gasped.

He slowed his pace, took out the Makarov and checked it. He walked swiftly to the door and with the weapon held in his hand but hidden in his coat pocket, he entered the maze. On another day, he would have enjoyed the confusion created by the multiple reflections. But, today he wasn't a sightseer, instead a killer determined to hunt down his adversary. He called out.

'Anthony, it's over. I've got you. You can't run anymore.'

From behind a pillar the face of Anthony, pale and tired, appeared in the gleaming mirrors.

'Mater, let's talk. I can explain.' He sounded confident, not at all frightened. To Mater, it was disconcerting. Mater took out the Makarov and pointed it at an Anthony, uncertain whether he was real or an illusion.

Yes, you need to. I won't hurt you. Not yet, anyway, he thought.

Anthony emerged from behind a pillar and stood a few paces from his adversary.

'Well done for tracking me down. Excellent tradecraft although if I had been braver you might not have found me.'

He held up his right hand and displayed his shortened middle finger.

Mater trained his gun on his former colleague. 'I assume you're unarmed, but keep both your hands where I can see them.'

'How did you work out where I was hiding, Phil?'

Mater reached into his pocket and took out the little slip of paper. 'Your mosque's prayer times for Ramadan sent to your bolthole in Kondanska Street. I guessed you wouldn't miss your evening prayers. You should have been more careful to empty your mailbox.'

Anthony chortled. 'They taught you too well. So what's the final score? I got four of yours and I assume you got four of mine. I suppose it's a draw although maybe I have an extra card to play, a winning ace.'

He chuckled again but Mater was not laughing; he wanted answers.

'Anthony, you need to explain why you decided to try to destroy me and my unit. What caused you to change from being one of Control's trusted deputies to the treacherous murderer of my operatives?'

Anthony didn't answer, but posed his own questions instead. 'How did you know it was me? What made you connect Antinal and Anthony?'

Mater fixing his eyes on Anthony's, responded with a question of his own. 'Why did I choose Mater as my nom de guerre?'

'Search me,' answered Anthony flippantly, 'Mater, Mutti, Mummy, who cares? Perhaps you considered yourself to be the mother of all those bastards I arranged to be killed.'

Mater shook his head but continued to stare, the Makarov steady in his hand. 'Did you know or even have an inkling as to my wife's maiden name?'

This time Anthony shook his head.

'Let me tell you. It was Mehta. A common enough surname in Indian society but my Ananya was anything but common. She was unique: intelligent, beautiful, kind, and resourceful. And always determined to improve relations between her native India and Pakistan. That's why we stayed in Islamabad for so long. Her work demanded she lived in the country which proclaimed hatred of her own. She never tired of trying to promote peace. She was also a wonderful mother until she was murdered.'

Mater noticed Anthony's expression change. A strange smile, almost a leer appeared, his lips curling upwards. He butted in.

'I think it's time I played that card.'

He purposefully paused sensing the tension rising between him and his adversary.

'I was responsible for the planting of the booby-trap that killed your wife,' he announced pompously.

Mater reeled, every muscle supporting his heavy frame, struggling to keep him upright. He felt sick, fought to focus, to concentrate. He fought the urge to end Anthony's life there and then.

'You were what! You did... Say that again, you bastard!'

'I planned the bomb.'

Anthony emphasised the word 'bomb', twisting the emotional knife inside Mater's spinning head.

'You fucking cunt,' snarled Mater, barely able to contain his rage or his urge to destroy the man standing in front of him.

Mater swallowed hard, telling his trigger finger to freeze. He fought to keep the gun's muzzle steady and directed at Anthony's chest.

'Tell me why? What was it that drove you to kill my Ananya and our two innocent young children? For fuck's sake, they were only six and four years old. What did they do wrong? How could you do that?'

Mater paused. He needed know everything, even if it might not be the whole truth, before he dispatched the traitor with a bullet to his head. His family had been destroyed twenty-one years ago to the day. He could wait a little while for Anthony to answer. But he couldn't face the future without knowing what really happened. Tears formed in his eyes, blurring his vision and he let them collect and then fall, not blinking.

Finally, Anthony spoke coldly. 'The device was meant for you, not for your family. I was expecting you to leave later that night. It had been arranged for someone to invite Ananya and the children to another event, separating them from you. For some reason she and the kids left the function early, used your car and so the bomb took them, not you.'

Mater recalled every moment of that appalling fateful day. The ambassador had invited everyone to his birthday celebration. A real family affair. Mater had been working at the embassy during the morning, having driven himself from their home in the suburbs. Ananya and the children arrived by taxi just before lunch was served in the garden. It had been a lovely occasion but there were few other youngsters present and the kids grew restless. They disrupted, as children are apt to do, the lengthy after-lunch speech delivered by the ambassador's wife in praise of her husband. Ananya had whispered to Mater that she would take the little ones home, leaving him to enjoy the free-flowing champagne. He had given her the car keys and kissed her tenderly on the cheek before doing the same to each child. He never saw them again. The vehicle travelled less than a hundred metres before the blast destroyed it, instantly killing all three occupants. The embassy's windows shook but held. Mater and members of the embassy's security team had run out into the street while the ambassador and his wife were hurried into a safe room. As the pall of smoke dispersed, Mater had recognised the tangled wreck in the middle of the road. It lay at the edge of the crater made by the device that had been fixed underneath the car's chassis. He knew straightaway nobody had survived and fell to the ground, banging his fists on the hot tarmac until they were bruised and bleeding. It was the first time he asked why and he carried on asking the same question for nearly three decades. And now the perpetrator stood in front of him.

'But why? What did I do to make you want to kill me?' he asked in desperation.

Anthony stared at Mater and answered without hesitation, his voice cold and precise. 'You disrespected the prophet. You insulted Islam. Don't you remember that little vacuous speech you gave a couple of months earlier during the security briefing with the ambassador?'

Mater tipped his head to one side. 'Vaguely, we had frequent joint meetings. Remind me, what did I say?'

Anthony trembled with anger. 'You told everyone that all those devoted to the Islamic faith would not rest until every non-believer was destroyed. Your only solution; to quench the fire before it grew out of hand. You declared war on me and mine.'

Mater looked at him incredulously. 'How long have you been a Muslim?'

'All my life. This battle between my beliefs and yours has persisted for centuries. I am just another warrior, blessed to be able to take part in this ongoing conflict. It was my whole reason for joining the Office. My raison d'être.'

Mater's hands trembled uncontrollably. 'You misheard and misjudged me. I've never said 'ALL', never! Your fight with me has been based on a simple misinterpretation, a single short word, although I believed and still believe a few, like you, are intent on jihad. Just as there exists fanatical devotees of all religions. But explain, if you failed to kill me with the bomb, you had many opportunities to finish the job later, so, why didn't you?'

Anthony smirked. 'To make you suffer. I knew your family meant everything to you and you would never forget them. I hoped that each moment of every day you would remember them and wonder why.'

Mater knew he was right. He had suffered almost constantly. When the anguish became too much, he would remove the plastic briefcase from its hiding place, open it, and once again, putting the birth certificates and passports to one side, finger the tatty photographs and stroke the two frayed soft toys; tears streaming down his face as he gazed at the pictures of his beautiful wife and children. Only a few simple photos from long ago but when he saw them, he could feel his loved ones, warm and close, as if they had never left him. He would never let go.

'You bastard, you fucking bastard.'

Mater struggled to refrain from pulling the trigger.

'So, if I was your problem, what made you decide to kill Mick, Tiny, Liam and Charlotte and why now?'

Anthony sighed. 'Ah, two reasons, Philip. The first, your unit was simply too successful. After the Iraq war, almost every mission you embarked upon involved soldiers loyal to my cause and you killed so many; always without remorse. The other; I'm getting old, retirement looms and the opportunity to access information about you and your team will soon disappear. It was time to finish the job. I must admit I took immense pleasure in watching each of your friends die, particularly Mick. You were right about the coke can. Made in Russia. Very effective in flattening even the strongest. He came to with the plastic bag already in place, sealed around the neck. You should have seen the panic in his eyes as he fought to breathe his last.' A leer grew on Anthony's face.

Mater ignored Anthony's sadistic grin and pointed the Makarov directly at his head, suddenly feeling calm and clinical.

'Anthony. You're sick, psychotic, a fanatic and a lunatic.'

Anthony, hands still raised, simply shrugged his shoulders.

'I accept I'm fanatical. I believe in certain things, you others. You kill. I kill. It's all about ideas and I have no doubt about mine. They have real value; are the true and proper path. You hold a different point of view, live an alternative life but fundamentally we're really the same, our past, present and futures separate yet intertwined. Yin and Yan.'

Mater had heard enough philosophy and plenty of lies and falsehoods. He forced his mind back to the task in hand.

'Who inside the Office gave you the information needed to track us down?' he demanded.

Anthony slowly lowered one hand and held his index finger against his sealed lips. Mater waved his weapon, indicating his prisoner should raise his hands again, though he understood by Anthony's response that he wouldn't give up his source, if ever there was one.

Suddenly from behind, Mater thought he heard other visitors enter the maze complex. He couldn't be certain the footsteps didn't belong to back-up for Anthony. It was time to finish their conversation.

'I don't believe you will be going to heaven, Anthony,' Mater announced softly.

Anthony laughed and then snarled, 'Go on, shoot me because I do.'

In the hall of mirrors infinite Anthonys faced the same number of pistols. Mater squeezed the trigger. The weapon jammed. He glanced at it and tried to release the blockage but was too slow. Anthony, as skilled as his adversary, grabbed his opportunity and immediately backed away, passing between pillars and mirrors. Mater raised the Makarov again, just in time to see a thousand Anthonys disappear. He lowered his gun.

'You'll not be going to heaven today, I'm not granting you your wish,' he snarled.

As the footsteps grew louder, he hid behind a pillar and watched. The multiple images of a young happy family, laughing and shouting at the giant mirrors, flashed by. As he watched, Mater desperately suppressed feelings of jealously, loneliness and envy that had replaced the fury of a few moments ago.

Chapter 37

The next day a dark blue hire van passed through the security gates at the British Embassy. Mater, Pete and Hefty removed their personal belongings from the rear of the vehicle and climbed from the subterranean garage to the grand hall of the ambassador's residence.

The baroque stone and wrought iron staircase wound in a gentle curve to the first floor. An official accompanied them up the stairs.

'Please follow me. There's a gentleman from London to see you.'

He opened the heavy oak door to the main reception room and ushered the men inside. Control was standing by the elaborate marble fireplace, talking to the Ambassador, each holding a tumbler containing an amber liquid.

'Ah, Phil, do come in. The ambassador tells me that the Czechs are delighted with our efforts or should I say yours.'

Mater, Pete and Hefty left their bags by the entrance and walked across the vast Persian rug that covered the ancient parquet. Control shook each man's hand vigorously and introduced the ambassador.

'My team,' he said proudly, 'Anonymous but effective.'

He turned to Mater. 'I believe you caught them all. The Czechs say they enjoyed watching you deal with every one of the bastards.'

Mater hesitated. 'All but one, sir. The kingpin escaped but I'm confident the threat to the Office has been contained. If I may, sir, I'll brief you in detail, in private, at a later date.'

'Well,' said the ambassador, grinning, 'It sounds as if you all deserve a celebratory drink. Whisky all round?'

'Something soft, if possible please,' requested Pete.

'And me too,' added Hefty.

The ambassador looked surprised but remained diplomatic. 'Of course, gentlemen. Her Majesty's Government will toast you with whatever is your choice of poison and non-alcoholic drinks are generally pretty toxic in my view.'

He laughed at his own joke. Control chuckled politely while the others kept their silence. Control spoke next. 'Your flight to London has been scheduled for tomorrow morning. I will arrange for all the kit to be returned to Stanley. Until then, you can rest here at the Embassy. Your work is done. Mater, I'm planning to visit our mutual friend in Yorkshire soon. If, it's acceptable to you, I could debrief you there.'

The ambassador picked up the receiver on the internal telephone lying on a nearby occasional table and asked for some cordials to be delivered. The toast would wait until each man had a full glass.

Epilogue

One week later, Mater and Control sat alone in the lounge of Langley Hall; the Office chief anticipating a full report from Mater so that he could advise the minister of yet another service success. It would help him secure more resource and anyway, he was intrigued to discover how Mater's little experiment had worked out.

Mater gave a detailed account of recent events. Control listened attentively, his elbows rested on the arms of his chair, fingers crossed in front of his face, using the index finger of his right hand to pull at the lax skin of his cheek. He didn't interrupt, patiently saving his questions until Mater had finished speaking.

Mater noted that the boss was delighted that the men who had been directly involved in the murder of his staff had been eliminated. And there was the added bonus that British-Czech relations had been enhanced. But Control had been unable to hide his disappointment that Mater failed to either arrest or kill Anthony. Ideally, he would have liked to have had the opportunity to interrogate him. It might have helped him understand where the weaknesses within the service lay. To Control, Mater's explanation that his weapon had jammed at the worst possible time seemed unlikely; almost too coincidental. It planted in the chief's mind the first seeds of doubt about Mater's ability and more importantly loyalty. He kept his thoughts to himself but realised he would have to organise the surveillance of both a known traitor and also one of his most trusted lieutenants. Once back at the Office, he would order Simon to lead a team to do both tasks. When Mater finished, Control handed over the small plastic briefcase.

'I didn't open it,' he said.

Mater nodded and thanked him.

'Enjoy a well-deserved break, Phil and keep the rest of the cash. You'll need a holiday and money to find somewhere to live. When you're ready, get in touch and I'll see what I can do to employ you and your men. Remember we are one happy substitute family.'

Control's last comment stuck in his mind: 'substitute'. The word needled. Perhaps he had looked inside the case after all. And it could be he knew more about Anthony than he would ever reveal. The incident in Islamabad was long ago but widely remembered within the service. It appeared to Mater that as soon as one question was answered another arose to take its place.

Control departed after dinner and, ignoring the rules on drink driving, drove his wife's Mercedes back to London. Mater retired to bed in good time but found sleep difficult. Control was right, he needed a break.

The next morning Mater sat eating breakfast with the Major, enjoying one of his excellent fry-ups.

'I'm most grateful for everything you've done,' he said, resting his knife and fork on the empty plate. 'Without your help, I'm not certain we could have succeeded.'

'So, you did win then. Your boss suggested the biggest fish got away.'

Mater thought for a moment. 'He's right when the result is viewed from our perspective, but the main target didn't get what he wanted. Although there's no guarantee he won't cause us more problems, there is every chance he will just lie low. He knows that even if we can't catch him, he will be watched to the day he dies.' Mater finished his coffee. 'I'll leave as soon as I've packed and take up your offer to drive me to the railway station.' He reached down and patted the dogs that had decided to encircle his feet. 'I'll miss you,' he said, looking down at their sorrowful eyes.

'I'll miss you too,' said the Major, assuming Mater was speaking to him. 'It's been good to be part of the action again, even if these days I can only play a minor role. Don't forget this old soldier if you ever need me again or simply somewhere discrete to stay.'

Less than an hour later, the Major's wife's battered car could be seen entering the city of Harrogate. The driver sported a neat moustache and flat cap. In the passenger seat sat a middle-aged man with thin grey hair and dark sunglasses. A casual observer might think they were just friends out for the day or maybe even an older gay couple simply on a shopping excursion. No-one would guess their real roles or identities. As the Nissan passed the Stray, Mater asked the Major to pull over.

'If it's OK with you, I'll walk to the station from here. I could do with the exercise before I sit on the train for the next few hours.'

The Major stopped the car. Mater climbed out and went to the rear of the vehicle, opened the boot and lifted out his bag. He walked around to the driver's side and tapped on the window. The Major wound it down.

'Thank you again,' he said, 'Oh, and I nearly forgot...'

He reached down and unzipped his holdall. He looked to check no-one was watching before handing over the Makarov. 'Very useful it was too.'

The Major beamed, his moustache twitching. He took the weapon and quickly hid it in the glove compartment.

'Never know when it might be needed again,' he said. 'Have a safe journey Mr. Randall.'

Mater watched the little car splutter into life and slowly drive away. He turned and walked into the park. He had time to spare and the fresh air would do him good. The cherry blossom was now in full bloom and to Mater, the gentle breeze blowing petal confetti heralded the onset of spring and a new beginning. He strolled towards the bandstand where on a nearby bench two scruffy characters appeared to be engaged in conversation. As Mater drew near, he recognised them both. One man's face was almost covered by facial hair while the other was a familiar man with a Scottish accent. He walked over to them. Both stopped talking and looked at him.

'Ah, the wanderer returns,' said the one with the beard, 'I hope she hasn't kicked you out, my friend.'

Mater smiled, recalling his excuse for occupying the bench.

'No, unfortunately she left or should I say was taken from me by someone, but I'll survive.'

'What a bastard,' commented the man.

'Never a truer word spoken,' responded Mater.

He turned to Jock who eyed him without showing any sign of recognition.

'A friend of yours?' Mater asked the bearded man.

'Becoming so. We rub along fine. Arrived here a little while ago. It's a big park. There's room enough for us both.'

Mater reached into his bag and took out an envelope. He opened it and withdrew a thick wad of bank notes. He divided it in three, keeping a third and gave the rest, in equal share, to the others.

'Have a drink on me,' he said.

The men gazed quizzically at the cash in their hands and then Mater, their faces showing surprise and delight. Then Jock spoke for the first time.

'Why?' he asked blankly.

Mater ignored the question and smiled again.

'Look after yourself John McLaren.'

Jock raised his eyebrows and without hesitation stuffed the money in his pocket. Mater picked up his bag and walked away, not once looking back.

Fortiter et celeriter

To the reader: Thank you for buying this book. For every book sold, a donation is made to the charity 'Shelter', established in December 1966 to help the homeless.

12738417R00217

Printed in Great Britain
by Amazon